# SAKS & VIOLINS

This Large Print Book carries the
Seal of Approval of N.A.V.H.

# A BED-AND-BREAKFAST MYSTERY

# Saks & Violins

# Mary Daheim

**THORNDIKE PRESS**

*An imprint of Thomson Gale, a part of The Thomson Corporation*

THOMSON

GALE

Detroit • New York • San Francisco • New Haven, Conn. • Waterville, Maine • London

**THOMSON**

**GALE** ™

**LIBRARY OF CONGRESS CATALOGING-IN-PUBLICATION DATA**

Daheim, Mary.
  Saks & violins : a bed-and-breakfast mystery / by Mary Daheim.
    p. cm. — (Thorndike Press large print mystery)
  ISBN 0-7862-9096-X (lg. print : alk. paper) 1. Flynn, Judith McMonigle (Fictitious character) — Fiction. 2. Women detectives — Northwest, Pacific — Fiction. 3. Bed and breakfast accommodations — Fiction. 4. Large type books. 5. Northwest, Pacific — Fiction. I. Title.
  PS3554.A264S25 2006b
  813'.54—dc22                         2006026997

U.S. Hardcover:
ISBN 13: 978-0-7862-9096-3
ISBN 10: 0-7862-9096-X

Published in 2006 by arrangement with William Morrow, an imprint of HarperCollins Publishers.

Printed in the United States of America on permanent paper
10 9 8 7 6 5 4 3 2 1

# SAKS & VIOLINS

# CHAPTER ONE

Judith McMonigle Flynn gnashed her teeth, slammed the front door so hard that the screen rattled, and decided to call the police. She had gotten as far as the kitchen when her husband, Joe, sauntered in from the pantry.

"What's wrong?" he inquired, noting his wife's grim look.

"Rudi," Judith snapped. "Rudi and his violin. I can't stand it another minute. And neither can the B&B guests. I'd like to strangle your first wife for renting her house to that awful man."

"Come on," Joe said, trying to sound reasonable. "You were elated when Vivian decided to stay year-round in Florida. Face it, you've never really liked having her live so close to us in the cul-de-sac."

Judith admitted that was true. The situation had always been awkward, though in fairness, Vivian Flynn hadn't turned out to be as big a pain as Judith had feared. For one thing, Vivian — or "Herself" as Judith had nicknamed her — spent at least half of the year in a condo on Florida's Gulf coast. When she was in residence on Heraldsgate Hill, Vivian was usually too busy drinking her way through the day to pester her ex-husband and his second wife. Herself was a creature of the night, and whatever she did after hours seldom disturbed Judith and Joe or the guests at Hillside Manor B&B.

But Rudolf Wittener had brought a new element into the cozy cul-de-sac of agreeable neighbors. "I'm talking about her choice of a tenant," Judith declared. "You know many of our guests complain about Rudi practicing his damned violin or playing his own recordings at all hours. The last straw was during that hot spell in August when he rehearsed outside — in the nude. That poor woman from Vermont fainted."

"No wonder," Joe remarked, his green eyes mischievous. "She'd probably never seen her husband in the nude. *I* might faint if I saw that guy naked. He's so skinny that she could have shipped him here from Vermont in a mailing tube."

Judith tried not to smile. "I'm serious. Talking to Rudi didn't do any good. We both tried that. He knows you're a retired

8

policeman — that doesn't bother him. Some of the other neighbors have complained, too, including Carl and Arlene Rankers. I even spoke to his wife or girlfriend or whatever she is. Zip. He just keeps sawing away."

"I thought the girl was his daughter," Joe said, taking a gingersnap out of the sheep-shaped cookie jar on the kitchen table.

Judith shook her head. "Definitely not. At least she doesn't call him 'Daddy.' She uses his first name. Hers is Taryn, I think. She gives music lessons in the basement, but luckily you can't hear that."

Joe poured himself a mug of coffee. "If it's true that he's taken on a job as assistant concertmaster with the symphony, the season's under way. Didn't they already have their big gala about a week ago? He'll be playing or at rehearsals most of the time. Besides, we're into fall. The weather's changing. Doors and windows will be closed. I'll bet you fifty bucks we won't be hearing much of Rudi for a while."

"You'd better be right," Judith said. "I'd bet a lot more than fifty that we've lost several potential return visitors in the two and a half months since Rudi moved in."

Munching on the gingersnap, Joe

shrugged. "You've got to admit, he plays well."

Judith shot Joe a dirty look. "Yes. But even if he doesn't actually practice more than an hour or so a day, he plays those tapes or whatever over and over again, and they're way too loud. I'd like to kill him."

The gold flecks that had danced in Joe's eyes — magic eyes, Judith called them — faded. "Don't say things like that."

Judith grimaced. "No. No, I shouldn't."

"You do have a history when it comes to dead people," he said, and though he tried to keep his voice light, his expression was somber.

"I know." Judith put a hand on his arm. "I swear to you, I don't want history ever repeating itself."

Joe tried not to look dubious.

"I'm calling from our new slum," said the muted voice at the other end of the line.

Judith frowned. It *sounded* like Cousin Renie, but the words didn't quite fit. "Yes?" Judith replied in a noncommittal tone.

"Bill and I have to sell the house."

It was definitely Renie. *"What?"* Judith practically shouted.

Renie sighed loudly. "How else can I pay off those bills from the San Francisco trip?

10

When Cruz Cruises went belly-up after the homicide investigation last March, I not only lost their graphic-design account, but I never got reimbursed for my — our — expenses."

Judith thought back to the long — very long — weekend she had spent with Renie in San Francisco. They were supposed to go on a cruise to the Cook Islands, but on the night of their departure, murder had intervened. The trip was eventually canceled — and so was the cruise line, which had more problems than a dead owner.

"Surely," Judith said wryly, "you're not including all those clothes and shoe bills you ran up at Saks Fifth Avenue and Neiman Marcus. I assume they weren't business expenses."

"Well . . ." Renie paused. "They are. I've tried to deduct my clothes from our income tax, but the IRS is so unreasonable. Don't they realize that I can't meet clients in the old crap I wear around the house?"

That, Judith had to admit, was true. Renie's at-home wardrobe consisted of ratty T-shirts, baggy sweatshirts, and tattered pants. She looked — as Renie and Bill's children insisted — like a bum. "You spent a grand on shoes alone at Neiman Marcus," Judith pointed out. "And I know you must have shelled out five times that much at Saks. You even bought me clothes — which I've finally paid you back for."

"Yes, yes," Renie said impatiently, "but there are other considerations. Like food and clothing and The Children."

Judith hung her head. She really didn't want to hear any more complaints about the three married Jones children and their spouses. They all lived in distant locales, but were constantly short of funds. Tom, Anne, and Tony Jones had decent jobs, but none of them made big salaries. Anne's husband was still studying to be a doctor; Tom's wife was involved in Catholic charities in Guam; Tony's spouse had turned her law degree into a virtual charity, too, devoting her practice to pro bono work with Native Americans in New Mexico. All of the in-laws' parents had sufficient money to help — but they weren't saps like Renie. Despite Bill's solid, sensible advice, Renie had always spoiled their children. And now she was paying the price — usually a big one.

"What about your other clients?" Judith asked. "Aren't you busy? Bill still gets consulting fees for his psychology patients, doesn't he?"

"Yes," Renie replied, sounding defensive.

"Although he's cut his client list back. He *is* retired, after all."

"And?"

"And what?"

"You. Aren't you working on a couple of brochures right now?"

"They're not bringing in big bucks," Renie said. "I'll have them done by Wednesday. That's the trouble with billing by the hour. I try fairly hard to avoid exaggerating the time I actually spend on a project. Frankly, I could have blown these two pieces out of my ear."

Which meant, Judith figured, that Renie's CAJones Graphic Design would submit a bill for about three times the real amount that her cousin had spent working. But the job would be done well. Renie had talent, if not ethics, going for her.

"It's September," Judith pointed out. "Doesn't your business always pick up after everybody comes back from summer vacation?"

"Usually." Renie sounded glum. "The economy's still in the dumps around here. Didn't you say the B&B wasn't getting as many reservations lately?"

"Well . . ." Judith glanced at the calendar she kept on the bulletin board by the sink. "There's always a lull after Labor Day. But it's true — October isn't filling up the way it usually does, and this week and next, I have more vacancies than I'd like."

"You told me Joe was cutting back on his private investigations," Renie said. "That can't help."

"He, too, is officially retired," Judith responded with a frown. "Let's face it, coz. We're not getting any younger. Joe won't take clients who require long surveillance stints. He refuses to stay up all night sitting in the car waiting for adulterers to make whoopee or watching insurance scam artists do the tango from dark till dawn."

"I don't blame him." Renie sighed again. "I have to finish my cardboard sign, 'Will Design for Table Scraps.' "

Judith wished her cousin luck. Hanging up, she scrutinized the calendar more closely. Only two of the six guest rooms were taken for the night, only one for Tuesday and Wednesday, and three for Thursday. The weekend looked better. All but one of the rooms had been reserved for Friday and Saturday. There might be late-comers, of course. Occasionally, visitors would stop by at the last minute, hoping to find accommodations available.

The phone rang again. Judith figured it was Renie, calling back to complain some more. But the caller ID displayed an unfamiliar area code. Judith answered in her best professional voice.

"Are you reputable?" the cultured female voice inquired.

"I beg your pardon?" Judith said, surprised.

"Your establishment was mentioned by someone in your neighborhood who has never actually stayed at Hillside Manor," the woman replied frostily. "We're seeking a convenient location for our visit, but we also require utter respectability."

"I'm Judith Flynn, the owner," Judith said. "I assure you, I run a first-class B&B. It's a large older home in a quiet neighborhood on a cul-de-sac. We're located less than ten minutes from downtown and no more than five to the civic center, where the opera house and several other attractions are located."

"I know," the woman said. "I'm calling to see if you have two rooms for Wednesday and Thursday of this week. I must have assurances that your inn is above reproach."

"You can check us through the state B&B association," Judith responded, straining to sound polite. "The phone number is . . ." She paused as Gertrude hustled through the back door in her wheelchair.

"Hey, Toots," Judith's mother shouted in her raspy voice, "who swiped my dirty moving picture?"

Frantically, Judith motioned for Gertrude to shut up.

"What was that?" the woman at the other end of the line demanded.

"Nothing!" Judith said quickly. "That is, one of my employees asked who *wiped* the . . . picture."

"I thought she said *moving* picture," the woman said incisively.

"Yes . . . uh . . . the picture had been moved. So we could wipe it. Because it was dirty."

"And a bunch of baloney," Gertrude put in, wheeling around the kitchen. "I should sue."

"Baloney?" the woman on the phone said in a puzzled tone.

Judith moved out of the kitchen as quickly as she could, despite her artificial hip. "She's looking for baloney. For one of our guests named Sue. I'll make a reservation for you if you give me your name."

There was a long silence at the other end of the phone. To Judith's horror, Gertrude and the motorized wheelchair were coming from the dining room into the living room. Again moving fast, Judith went outside via

16

the French doors and latched them behind her.

"Yes?" she said in an encouraging voice.

"Very well," the woman finally replied. "The last name is Kluger. I'll spell that for you."

There were no writing supplies on the back porch. As Gertrude pounded on the French doors and shook her fist, Judith committed the name to memory.

"I'm Andrea," the woman continued, "and my husband's name is Dolph. We also need a second room for my daughter, Suzanne. Her last name is Farrow."

"She's an adult?" Judith inquired. "We don't accept guests under eighteen."

"Suzanne just turned thirty," Andrea Kluger informed Judith in a stilted voice. "I wouldn't dream of bringing small children to a B&B. You have no pool."

Through the small glass panes, Judith saw Gertrude clutching her chest, throwing back her head, and then falling forward. Either she was faking a heart attack — or she wasn't. A sense of panic overcame Judith.

"Yes, fine," Judith said in a rush. "We'll see you . . . Wednesday?"

"Don't you want my credit-card information?" Andrea asked.

Gertrude was slumped forward in the

wheelchair.

"I'll get it after you arrive," Judith said, reaching out to unlatch the door. "Thank you. Good-bye."

Clicking off, she practically fell back into the living room. "Mother!" Judith cried. "Are you okay?"

Gertrude didn't move. Judith couldn't bend down very far for fear of dislocating her artificial hip. But she could take the old lady's pulse. Anxiously, Judith lifted her mother's limp, gnarled right hand. Every two years, Judith took a Red Cross refresher course so she could handle emergencies with guests. She knew how to take a pulse.

But she couldn't find one in her mother's wrist. Judith froze. Maybe she hadn't felt in the right place. Her own hands were trembling. Gertrude was very old and very frail. It would hardly be surprising if . . .

In a daze, Judith looked around for the phone. She'd dropped it on her way into the living room. The receiver had bounced under the baby grand piano. There was no way she could reach it without getting down on the floor. Joe wasn't home. He'd gone to the hardware store on top of Heraldsgate Hill.

*Phyliss.* Judith's cleaning woman was upstairs, working in the guest rooms. Reluctantly leaving her mother in the wheelchair, Judith went across the long living room and into the entry hall, shouting at Phyliss from the bottom of the stairs.

But Phyliss didn't respond. Judith, who was accustomed to all sorts of crises, suddenly felt helpless. It was one thing to discover the body of a stranger or even someone she knew only slightly. Somehow, she had managed to stay calm and efficient when her first husband, Dan McMonigle, had died. He had eaten and drunk himself into a massive four-hundred-plus pounds and been ill for some time. It was different now. This was her mother, who seemed invincible.

Then she remembered her cell phone. It was in her purse, in the kitchen. She had started to move out of the entry hall when she heard those wonderful words:

"Hey, Dumbbell! Where are you?"

"Mother!" Judith cried, hurrying back into the living room.

Gertrude was sitting up, though she looked pale and shaken. Her faded eyes stared at her daughter. "Is this where I'm supposed to say, 'Where am I? What happened?' "

Judith tried to smile. "Yes. What *did* happen?"

"Darned if I know," Gertrude said, shaking her head. "I just came over queer all of a sudden." Her wrinkled face was etched with worry. "Do you think I had a stroke?"

"Can you move your hands and feet?" Judith asked.

"Can I ever?" Gertrude snapped. "Would I be in this stupid contraption if I could walk?" She slapped both hands on the wheelchair's arms. "I'm lucky I can still play cards."

"Well," said Judith, "your hands seem okay, and your face looks fine, except you're a bit off-color."

"So's that dopey movie," Gertrude declared. "No wonder I passed out. In *Gritty Gertie,* I act like a tramp. That's not me. The movie's too suggestive."

The film that had been based on Gertrude's life had undergone many script changes, and although it had ended up showing the trials and tribulations of a member of the so-called Greatest Generation, there was far more fiction than fact in the story line. When *Gritty Gertie* had been released in July, Gertrude had refused to see it in the theater. Judith, Joe, Renie, and Bill had gone instead. They were prepared for the changes, but still dismayed. Joe couldn't understand why they hadn't kept to the original concept of an ordinary twentieth-century woman surviving history's tragedies and triumphs. Judith worried that her mother's reputation had been tarnished. Bill, who was a knowledgeable movie buff, had critiqued the production in his usual no-frills manner by stating that "it was a piece of crap." Renie had complained because she didn't get extra butter on her popcorn.

Finally, the producers had sent an early release of the DVD version over the weekend. Gertrude had watched it Sunday night and pitched a fit. In fact, she wouldn't even see it through its lugubrious two-and-a-half-hour length.

"That's it!" she'd cried when the movie version of Gertie had started to undress in front of her gangster lover after a Charleston contest in the Roaring Twenties. "Nobody sees me in my underwear! Or less!"

Recalling how distressed her mother had been over the film's final cut, Judith tried to calm the old lady — and herself. "You've been upset," she said to Gertrude as Sweetums crept into the living room through the open French doors. "You should see a doctor."

"Phooey," Gertrude said. "I had a little

spell, that's all. I swooned. So what? When's supper?"

"It's only three o'clock," Judith replied as Sweetums prowled around the wheelchair, rubbing his big orange-and-white furry body against Gertrude's legs.

"Hunh." Gertrude, whose color was returning to normal, looked disappointed. "I thought I was out for a lot longer than that."

"You should probably drink some juice and have a little snack," Judith said as Phyliss Rackley entered the living room. "I'm going to make an appointment with the doctor."

"How'd you know?" Phyliss asked, her white sausage curls practically standing on end. "I've been feeling poorly all day."

Phyliss frequently felt "poorly." "What is it today?" Judith asked in a weary voice.

"My spleen," Phyliss replied, watching Sweetums with a wary eye. "So that's where that horrid cat is. He was trying to suck my breath."

"Nonsense," Judith snapped. "That's a myth. Cats don't try to suck the breath out of humans."

Phyliss was eyeing Sweetums with distrust. "That's no ordinary cat. That cat is Satan's spawn."

It was an old employer-and-employee

argument. Between Phyliss's hypochondria and religious fanaticism, there were times when Judith wondered how she'd managed to put up with the cleaning woman all these years. Except, of course, that Phyliss was very good at her job.

"Why," Judith demanded, "do you think Sweetums was . . . trying to do what you said he was doing?"

Gertrude shot Phyliss a sidelong glance. "Nut," she muttered. "Didn't I always say as much?"

Phyliss looked chagrined. "It was my spleen," she said, dancing a bit as Sweetums sniffed her orthopedic shoes. "There were only two guest rooms to prepare today, so I thought I'd lie down for just a minute. I felt unbalanced."

"You are," Gertrude said.

Phyliss glared at Gertrude; Judith glared at Phyliss.

"Is that why you didn't come downstairs when I called you?" Judith asked sharply. "You were taking a nap?"

"I was resting my eyes," Phyliss replied, still trying to sidestep the cat's inquisitive nose. "Or trying to. That's when that . . ." She glanced at Sweetums, who had finally sat next to her feet and was gazing up with as innocent an expression as his type of feline could manage . . . "That *creature* jumped up on the bed and began to go for my poor face!"

"He was just curious," Judith declared. "That's the way cats are. You don't," she added meaningfully, "usually lie down on the job."

"True enough," Phyliss mumbled. "But my spleen . . ."

Judith waved a hand. "Never mind. I have things to do. So do you, Phyliss. Come on, Mother, let's go into the kitchen."

But first, Judith remembered to ask Phyliss to retrieve the phone from under the piano. "We all have our health issues," she reminded the cleaning woman in a more kindly voice.

Phyliss seemed placated, but watched Sweetums to make sure the cat didn't follow her.

Gertrude's doctor didn't have an opening until Thursday, but a nurse practitioner could see the old lady the following morning at ten. Judith accepted the compromise. She was putting the last of the gingersnaps on a plate for her mother when the front doorbell chimed.

"Drat," Judith murmured. "Who can that be?" Family and friends always came in the back way. It was too early for guests to arrive. Check-in time was 4 P.M.

Judith recognized her new neighbor immediately. But she wasn't absolutely certain of the visitor's name. "Hi," Judith said in a friendly voice. "What can I do for you?"

A slight smile played around the young woman's finely chiseled mouth. "I'm Taryn Moss from the house we rented —"

"Yes," Judith interrupted, beaming. "You give piano lessons, right?"

Stepping over the threshold, Taryn nodded. "In the basement. Where it's quiet."

Judith felt that was Taryn's way of apologizing for Rudi Wittener's disturbances. "I imagine you play very well yourself," she said, closing the front door. "Won't you come into the parlor?"

Taryn shook her head, which was crowned with a jumble of black curls. "I can't stay. I have a pupil at four, so I must prepare. But I needed to ask a favor. I understand — that is, the other Mrs. Flynn told me — that besides running your B&B, you have a catering business."

"Not anymore," Judith replied. "I gave that up years ago. We enlarged the B&B, so I had to focus all my attention on our guests."

"Oh." Taryn's thin, attractive face fell. Judith figured her for midtwenties, at least fifteen years younger than Rudi Wittener. "That's a shame. I was hoping you could bail me out."

"I could recommend someone," Judith offered.

Taryn looked pained. "It's only a small group, less than a dozen, if that. But our place is really small."

Judith knew the house well. *Too* well, and not just because of Vivian Flynn's off-and-on residency. An older couple had lived there for years, and the wife had been brutally killed. The property had gone up for sale, but even though the sellers had given full disclosure of what had happened on the premises, Herself had been undaunted. Murder was a minor obstacle in the first Mrs. Flynn's journey to alcoholic oblivion.

"The thing is," Taryn went on before Judith could make any other suggestions, "three of the guests plan on staying at your B&B. In fact, Mrs. Kluger may have already contacted you."

"Oh!" In the anxiety over Gertrude's "spell," Judith had forgotten about the Kluger reservation. "Yes, she called just a short time ago."

Taryn nodded. "Rudi told her about Hillside Manor. You see, Dolph Kluger is

Rudi's mentor. He's coming to visit us."

Taryn didn't look very excited at the prospect. "How nice," Judith said in a noncommittal tone.

"Mrs. Kluger's daughter by her first husband is also coming," Taryn continued, still without enthusiasm. "What I thought was that if we could have the little party at your B&B . . ." Leaving the sentence unfinished, she shrugged.

Judith wanted to keep peace in the cul-de-sac. It was crucial for her business, and also important to the rest of the longtime neighbors. "How about this?" she said. "You can give the party here, but supply your own food and beverages."

Taryn's face brightened. "That's wonderful. We'll pay for using your place."

"A minimal fee," Judith said. "Just to cover . . . any breakage or spillage." She smiled in her friendliest manner. "A hundred dollars?"

"That's fine," Taryn replied, also smiling. "Wednesday evening, around six?"

Judith considered. "I don't know how many other guests will be staying here. Six to seven is the usual social hour. Could we make it for seven so we don't disrupt the regular schedule?"

Taryn nodded. "Okay. We'll probably all

go out to dinner afterward. Should we provide glasses and plates and such?"

"No," Judith answered. "I have plenty of serving items. You can use the oven or the microwave to warm up any hot appetizers."

"That's so nice of you," Taryn declared, looking genuinely pleased. "I've been dreading this."

Judith was puzzled. "You mean, asking me to host the party?"

Taryn shook her head. "Not that so much as . . . oh, it'll be fine."

"Of course it will," Judith assured her. "I'll do my best to make sure everybody has a good time."

Judith would keep her word to make the proper preparations. But a good time was far from the way she'd later describe the event.

# CHAPTER TWO

Nurse Practitioner Davis could find nothing seriously wrong with Gertrude. Her vital signs were good — for a woman of her age. Various blood tests were taken, with results due in a few days. It might, the nurse practitioner suggested, be that Gertrude needed new glasses. It had been over two years since her trifocal prescription had been changed. Judith couldn't get an appointment with the ophthalmologist for another three weeks.

"I can see fine," Gertrude declared on the way home. "Look out for that deer!"

Judith was driving down the city's main north-south avenue that led to the bridge over the ship canal. "That's not a deer. It's a motorcycle."

"With antlers?"

"The rider doesn't have antlers," Judith replied.

"Then he must have horns on his head,"

Gertrude said stubbornly. "I always figured that was the case with people who ride motorcycles."

"Actually," Judith said as she drew closer to the cyclist, "it's a cop. I better slow down."

The cop kept going, past the turnoff to Heraldsgate Hill at the far end of the bridge. As Judith drove up the hill, she asked her mother if she'd mind waiting in the car at Falstaff's Grocery.

"I have to get a couple of items for dinner," Judith said. "I forgot there was a sale on whole-bodied fryers."

"Have they got whole-bodied people?" Gertrude asked. "I could use a new one. My original's falling apart."

"The nurse practitioner said you were in remarkably good health for your age," Judith reminded her mother. "It'll take less than five minutes."

Inside the store, Judith bought two of the chickens — one for that evening and the other to put in the freezer. She also picked up some fresh broccoli. Three minutes later, she was headed for the checkout stand. Renie was already there, her cart piled high.

"I thought you were broke, coz," Judith said, gazing at the multitude of items, which included Kobe beef steaks, New Zealand lamb chops, French cheeses, and three cans of Alaskan smoked salmon.

"I am," Renie replied, "but Bill and I still have to eat. The dog-food aisle didn't look that tempting."

"Neither do you," Judith remarked, taking in her cousin's droopy red T-shirt with its Arkansas Razorbacks hog logo, stained black sweatpants, and shoes that looked like they'd slogged through a pigsty.

"Thanks," Renie snapped. "I was about to say that you certainly look better since you gained a few pounds. But I won't tell you now."

"Thanks anyway." Judith and Renie were the closest of cousins, and could say just about anything to each other without creating permanent hard feelings. Each had been an only child, and their families had lived two blocks apart. All her life, Judith had fought a weight problem, but in the past couple of years she'd dieted strenuously because less meat on her bones was easier on her hip. She'd gone too far, however, getting run-down and looking gaunt. Finally taking Renie's advice to add a little weight, she'd also acquired a new hair color, a golden-streaked brown to cover the prematurely white hair that had made her look much older than she really was.

Renie pushed her cart up to the counter. "I've spent all day trying to track down new clients," she said to Judith as the checker began to scan her items. "I'm coming up empty."

"The B&B isn't doing much better," Judith admitted. "A few more reservations have trickled in, but I've been reduced to earning a hundred bucks by letting Rudi's girlfriend hold a party tomorrow night for some of the guests who're staying with us."

"You should've charged three times that much," Renie declared, getting out her checkbook.

"They have to provide the food and drink," Judith replied. "I didn't feel I should ask for more. It's a neighborly peacekeeping gesture."

Renie stopped in the act of rummaging for a pen at the bottom of her huge handbag. "Hey — didn't I hear that the symphony was going to start a big fund-raising drive? That usually requires promotional materials. Some of the other cultural groups in town are trying to raise money. They've all had attendance problems in the past few years because of the dot-com slump. I should call my old pal Melissa."

Melissa Bargroom was the classical-music critic for the local newspaper. "What are you talking about?" Judith asked.

Renie had gone back to rummaging. The checker indicated a pen on the counter. Renie shook her head. "No, thanks. I'm an artist by trade. I can only use my own pens." She kept digging. "Melissa would know if the symphony needed any design work. I assume Rudi will be at your party, too. Maybe some other symphony people will show up. I could put a flea in their ear. Damn! Where *is* that pen?"

"Rudi's new to the symphony, and the gathering is very small," Judith said. "Why don't you get Melissa to mention your name? She knows all those people."

"I should," Renie agreed. "Still . . . oops!" She dropped her handbag, spilling its contents all over the floor. Lipsticks, gum, breath mints, nail files, keys, bankbooks, Kleenex, eyeliner, hairbrush, cell phone, dental floss, compact, mascara wand, pillbox, several coins, two pens, a pair of champagne-colored underpants, and what looked like a wilted stalk of leafy rhubarb rolled around the aisle.

Judith couldn't bend over to help Renie retrieve her belongings. "Underpants? Dare I ask?"

"Hey," Renie replied without so much as a blush, "at our age, you never know."

33

Judith shrugged. "So what's that thing that looks like rhubarb?" she asked, ignoring the mutters of customers who had queued up behind the cousins.

"Rhubarb," Renie replied, scrambling around on the floor.

"You hate rhubarb," Judith said.

"I know." Renie finally gathered everything together and dumped all of it except one of the pens back in her handbag. She saw the checker eyeing her with curiosity. "I didn't shoplift the rhubarb. I got it out of a neighbor's garden a while ago."

"Of course you didn't shoplift, Mrs. Jones." The checker, who was thirtyish and whose name tag read *Alana* smiled faintly. She seemed accustomed to Renie's peculiar antics. "Our produce is always *fresh,*" Alana added as some of the customers in line began moving to other registers.

"Right." Renie scowled at the total on the register's digital readout. "Sheesh. A hundred and twenty bucks. I hope I still have that much in our account. Oh, well." She finished writing the check and handed it over to Alana.

"So why are you carrying rhubarb in your purse?" Judith asked as the courtesy clerk bagged Renie's items.

"I forgot it was there," Renie admitted.

"Everything falls to the bottom in this satchel. I was going to do a brochure for a coop grocery, but they went bust before I could finish it. Can I come tomorrow night?"

"To the party?" Judith shrugged. "I can't see the point, but go ahead. I won't have much to do, so we can sit in the kitchen and visit."

"I'd rather schmooze," Renie said. "Who knows? Maybe somebody from the symphony board will be there."

"I doubt it," Judith responded, paying cash for her few items. "Oh, shoot!" she cried. "I left Mother in the car. She must be wondering why I've taken so long."

"Tell her it was my fault," Renie said, following the courtesy clerk to her Camry. "I lost my underpants."

"She'll believe it," Judith replied with a sigh. "By the way, they told Mother at the clinic that she's fine."

"No surprise there," Renie muttered. "So's my mom. It sounds like they were the life of the party on that cruise they took last spring. It must have rejuvenated them."

Judith nodded. "Between your mother's social skills and my mother's cardplaying, they had a wonderful trip."

"That's more than we had," Renie responded, thanking the courtesy clerk and closing the Camry's trunk lid. "We never got out of port in San Francisco."

"Don't remind me," Judith said.

Gertrude had rolled down the window and was barking at a poodle in the car that was parked in the next stall.

"Now what?" Renie asked before getting into the Camry.

Judith shook her head. "Never mind. Mother's having a dog-fight."

Renie merely shook her head and got into her car. Gertrude was still barking at the poodle that, of course, was barking right back.

"Mother," Judith said as she slid into the driver's seat, "stop. It's only a dog. He's getting tired of waiting all alone."

"So was I," snapped Gertrude. "Who do you think started it?"

"I should have guessed," Judith murmured, reversing out of the diagonal parking space. "You shouldn't exert yourself. You might have another spell."

The old lady snorted. But for all of their daughters' bravado, both Gertrude and Aunt Deb were very old and quite frail. Like her sister-in-law, Deborah Grover was also confined to a wheelchair. Judith cast a fond sidelong glance in her mother's direction.

Gertrude was still feisty and her tongue might be sharp, but her heart was . . . well, sometimes it *was* hard, but at least it was still beating.

The rest of the day and the following morning were routine. Besides Mr. and Mrs. Kluger and Suzanne Farrow, Judith had four other guests — newlyweds from Green Bay, and a middle-aged couple from Japan who had indicated that they didn't speak English very well. Judith was accustomed to foreign visitors, especially from the Pacific Rim, and had instructions printed in several languages. Over the years, her guest list had become increasingly global.

Phyliss was doing laundry, Gertrude was playing bridge at Aunt Deb's apartment with their old cronies from a Catholic charity they'd belonged to for fifty-odd years, and Joe had taken on a case involving a title search for some waterfront property south of the city. He was at the county office, doing research to ferret out the various aliases one of the alleged owners had used. Mike had called from the ranger station up at the pass to say all was well. Just before school started, he and Kristin had taken their two boys to Disneyland. They'd had a wonderful time, and Judith wished that she and Joe could have gone along to see the excitement in their grandsons' eyes. But August had been busy at the B&B. Fortunately.

The front doorbell interrupted Judith in the middle of filling wonton wrappers with shrimp. Maybe, she thought, going through the dining room and entry hall, it was Taryn Moss with party preparations.

But although a woman stood on the porch, it wasn't Taryn. Instead, it was a redhead in her forties, porcelain skin etched with fine lines and wide-set gray eyes. She looked delicate, almost wispy, but her manner indicated that there was steel somewhere in those fine bones.

"I'm sorry to intrude," she said in a soft, yet compelling voice, "but I'm Elsa Wittener. I'll be attending the party here tonight, and I wanted to check everything out beforehand. Do you mind if I come in?"

Judith noticed that an older-model blue Honda was parked at the curb. She wondered if it belonged to her visitor. "Please," Judith said, stepping aside. "I'll show you the living room. It's quite large."

Elsa stood just beyond the open pocket doors that separated the living room from the entry hall. Her gray eyes took in every detail — including the oak buffet, the armoire that held the TV, the matching sofas, the bay window, the fireplace, the plate rail, and the bookcases.

"I see you have a piano," she remarked. "How nice. Do you play?"

Judith shook her head. "Not very well. My cousin and I took lessons when we were kids, but neither of us had any talent. The piano is for guests."

Elsa nodded. "May I try it?"

"Of course."

The women walked to the other end of the room. As usual, Judith had a jigsaw puzzle set up on a card table near the piano. The work in progress was the old Paris Opera house at night.

"You must like music," Elsa remarked, glancing at the half-finished puzzle.

"Oh, yes," Judith replied, "but I'm not very knowledgeable. My cousin is quite an opera buff, though."

Elsa remained standing, but began to play. To Judith's surprise, she sounded almost professional.

"That's lovely," Judith said when Elsa finished the brief recital. "What was that?"

"Part of a Bach piano concerto," Elsa replied. "This instrument has a decent sound, but you might consider having it tuned."

Judith grimaced. "It's been a while."

Elsa nodded as she started to walk away from the piano. "I can tell. Where should we set up the drinks and food? On that buffet?"

"Yes, that's how I usually do it."

"You have all the necessary serving pieces, of course," Elsa said. "Will they be set out?"

Judith was growing a little vexed. The newcomer acted as if Judith was a novice at playing hostess, not to mention tone-deaf. "Certainly. I'll put everything you'll need on the dining-room table since we won't be using it for dinner this evening. But I need the buffet from six to seven for my other guests' social hour." Judith started out of the living room. "The dining room is in here," she said over her shoulder. "The kitchen is just beyond it. I already told Taryn she could use the oven and microwave if she wanted to."

"She forgot to mention that," Elsa said in a disapproving tone. "Taryn isn't very organized and details are beyond her. That's why I wanted to make sure everything is in order."

Judith pointed to Grandma and Grandpa Grover's oak dining-room table, which was decorated with a crimson chrysanthemum centerpiece. "That's where I'll put everything."

Elsa, however, was gazing at the break-front. "You have some nice pieces in here," she remarked.

"They're heirlooms," Judith said as they strolled back into the living room.

Elsa paused to study the Flynns' CDs and tapes. "Very eclectic," she remarked.

"True," Judith said. "We've collected all sorts of music over the years, going back to vinyl and even beyond. My parents and grandparents, my son, my first husband — we all had different tastes."

"So I noticed." Elsa regarded a heavy-metal group's tape with disdain.

"Mike — my son — didn't take all of his recordings with him when he moved," Judith said, feeling she needed an explanation. "I hate to throw them away." Indeed, she hated to throw anything away. All of her family's possessions symbolized fond memories. *And why,* Judith thought to herself, *do I feel I have to defend myself to you, Elsa Wittener?*

"By the way," Judith said before the next sheathed criticism could flow from Elsa's lips, "are you Rudolf Wittener's sister?"

Elsa smiled slightly, but her gray eyes were as cold as snow clouds. "No. I'm his ex-wife."

"Oh." Judith was taken aback. "I didn't

mean to pry. I was just trying to sort out the party guest list in my mind."

"You needn't bother." Elsa's smile remained in place as she examined a blue Wedgwood plate on the oak rail above the buffet. "Is that an heirloom as well?"

"Yes," Judith replied. "Most of the plates are. All but one of the Hummels are mine or my mother's. We both have a fondness for them."

Elsa glanced at a figurine that depicted two children looking up at a roadside shrine. "Charming," she commented. But the word lacked conviction. "I must go. Thank you."

Judith followed Elsa to the door, but the other woman said nothing more except for a perfunctory good-bye. Judith peered through the window in the door. The Honda remained parked at the curb, but Elsa was walking along the cul-de-sac, headed toward Rudi's home, the second house from the corner.

Judith gazed back at the Honda. She thought there was someone sitting in the passenger seat, but she couldn't be sure. Nothing moved. Perhaps it was a coat or jacket that had been slung over the back of the seat. With a shrug, she returned to her wonton wrappers.

The Japanese couple, whose last name was Kasaki, arrived punctually at four o'clock. Their English was better than they had indicated. Judith was able to learn that they were on a West Coast tour that would include Las Vegas. The Kasakis were very excited at the prospect of seeing the Strip — while, Judith figured, probably losing a lot of yen in the process.

The honeymooners, aptly named Bliss, showed up at Hillside Manor fifteen minutes later. They were African-American, biochemists, and big Green Bay Packer fans. Joe, who got home just as they arrived, took over the greeting duties and admitted a soft spot for the Packers ever since they'd beaten Dallas in a championship game on a frozen field in 1966.

Just before five, Judith received a call from a woman who said that she and her husband had been stranded at the airport. "Our flight was canceled," she explained in a fretful voice. "We can't leave until late tomorrow morning, and all the hotels near the airport are full of conventioneers. My husband and I stayed with you four years ago. Hillside Manor was so pleasant. By any chance do you have a vacancy?"

"I do," Judith replied, trying to place the couple whose last name was Theobald.

"Come right ahead. You'll make it just in time for the social hour."

Mrs. Theobald expressed her gratitude and hung up. Five minutes later, the Kluger party arrived.

Andrea Kluger was a slender woman probably closer to sixty than fifty with ash-blond hair, deep blue eyes, and perfect makeup. Her husband, Dolph, was perhaps nearing seventy, but a large, bald man whose vigor hadn't been dimmed by age. Mrs. Kluger's daughter, Suzanne, had her mother's coloring, though her frame was much leaner. She wore no cosmetics, but glowed with health. Still, Suzanne struck Judith as somewhat withdrawn.

"We had to wait forever for our luggage," Andrea said in annoyance. "The conveyor belt broke. Travel these days is so difficult."

"Only six minutes," Dolph said with the trace of a European accent. He glanced fondly at his wife. "Andrea doesn't like waiting."

Andrea had the grace to look faintly embarrassed. "Admittedly, patience has never been one of my virtues. But I mustn't bore you, Mrs. Flynn." She gazed around the entry hall. "Yes, this looks quite nice. We don't usually stay in bed-and-breakfast establishments."

Judging from the designer luggage, Andrea Kluger was accustomed to traveling first-class.

"But so close to dear Rudi," Dolph said in his hearty manner. "That was the priority." He handed Judith his cashmere overcoat. "I don't need this in your balmy autumn weather. It was chilly when we left New York. I shall go see Rudi immediately. Which way?"

Before Judith could show him Rudi's house, Andrea put a hand on her husband's arm. "Really, darling, must you? We'll be seeing him in less than two hours. You should rest. It was a long flight."

"I rested on the flight," Dolph responded. "You expect me to race up and down the aisle? Do push-ups in the tiny restroom? Come, come, I must go. We have only a limited time here, and Rudi has rehearsal tomorrow with performances in the evening."

"As you like." Andrea had the air of a woman who was used to losing arguments with her husband. Or, Judith thought, at least over small matters. "Don't stay too long," she cautioned. "Rudi and his . . . friends have to get ready for the party. Suzanne and I will go up to our rooms." She turned to Judith. "Keys, please."

Judith fumbled with the keys to Rooms Three and Four. Fortunately, neither the Blisses nor the Kasakis had wanted to pay the higher rate for Room Three, which was the largest and therefore the most expensive. She'd been able to give it to Dolph and Andrea. The room, however, shared a bathroom with Room Four, which was where Judith had booked Suzanne.

"A moment, please," Judith said to Andrea. "I must show Mr. Kluger where Mr. Wittener lives."

Dolph's long strides beat Judith to the door. "Pay no attention to my lovely wife," he said in a low voice. "She fusses. She sometimes fumes. But she means well. She is a good woman — the best."

"I'm sure she is," Judith said, though she wasn't convinced. "Your stepdaughter is very quiet."

"Usually," Dolph said as Judith opened the door. "Suzanne's a freak."

Judith looked surprised. "A freak?"

Dolph nodded. He was obviously anxious to be on his way, barely able to contain his energy. "A physical-fitness freak. So much exercise! It can't be good for you. Now where is my dear Rudi?"

Judith pointed out the Wittener house. "So modest," Dolph murmured, hurrying down the porch steps.

Judith refrained from saying that with increasing property values on Heraldsgate Hill, even an ordinary bungalow such as Vivian's could fetch two grand a month. But if Dolph lived in New York City, he was probably accustomed to even higher prices.

Andrea and Suzanne were still waiting. Judith glanced at the six pieces of luggage. She'd be lucky if she could carry one at a time.

Suzanne apparently noticed Judith's hesitation. "Let me," she said. Effortlessly, she stowed a suitcase under each arm and picked up two more. "Mother, you can take the carry-on and the fold-over."

"I'll get the fold-over," Judith said quickly. "I'm sorry, but I have an artificial hip."

"No problem." Suzanne was already mounting the stairs with ease.

Andrea picked up the carry-on along with Dolph's overcoat, which Judith had hung on the hat rack. She followed the women a little breathlessly. The fold-over was heavier than she'd expected.

"Room Three?" Andrea asked when they reached the second floor.

Judith nodded. "Room Four is yours, Ms. Farrow."

Suzanne placed one of the smaller suitcases outside of Room Four.

"My daughter travels light," Andrea remarked with apparent amusement.

Judith opened the door to Room Three. Andrea stopped on the threshold, studying the space. "Yes, this is quite nice," she said after a long pause. "It will do."

"I'm glad," Judith replied. "We remodeled a few years back."

"You have good taste," Andrea declared. "I particularly like your wallpaper. It's very William Morris."

"It is a William Morris design," Judith said proudly. "All of the wallpapers are inspired by him except for two from Clarence House."

"Excellent." Andrea nodded approval. "I'm afraid I've always associated B&Bs with gluts of chintz and stuffed animals on the bed."

Judith was very pleased. She hadn't seemed to get a very good grade from Elsa Wittener, but her stock had risen with Andrea Kluger. "I went for elegance," Judith said, "rather than cutesy. And quality. These wallpapers cost more, but they last forever. Refurbishing rooms means losing income while the work is under way."

"Very sound." Andrea nodded again. "My first husband would have approved. Blake carried on the family tradition of quality over quantity in the manufacture of musical instruments. His ancestors were Italian, originally Farranzelli, but his great-grandfather changed it when the immigration officials at Ellis Island couldn't spell it properly. Thus, my husband became a Farrow. Blake Farrow the third, to be exact."

"Is he still in the business?" Judith asked.

Andrea shook her head. "No. His younger brother runs it now. Blake was killed a few years ago in a fox-hunting accident in New Jersey. He was only forty-nine."

"I'm sorry," Judith said. "My first husband died at the same age."

"An accident?" Andrea inquired.

*A train wreck,* Judith thought to herself. That had been Dan McMonigle, a self-created accident waiting to happen. "No. He was ill." The idea of Dan riding to the hounds was so preposterous that Judith had to turn away. The closest he'd ever have come to that kind of sport was betting on the dog races. And losing.

Andrea had entered the room. Suzanne stacked the suitcases against the wall while Judith hung the fold-over on the closet door. After pointing out the shared bathroom and other amenities, she accompanied Suzanne to Room Four.

"I didn't ask what your stepfather actually does for a living," Judith said as Suzanne immediately opened both windows to let in the autumn air.

"He guides and advises musicians," Suzanne said. "He used to teach, too."

"I see," Judith said, watching Suzanne pull her blond hair away from her face and tie it up in a ponytail.

"I'm going to work out," Suzanne said.

"Good for you," Judith responded. "Enjoy your stay."

Suzanne didn't reply.

As soon as she turned onto the first landing of the stairs, she saw Dolph Kluger stomping toward her. He was red in the face and perspiring.

"Are you all right?" Judith inquired.

"Yes. No." The big man edged past Judith and kept going.

It appeared to Judith that Dolph's visit with "dear Rudi" hadn't gotten off to a good start.

But she didn't know that the worst was yet to come.

# CHAPTER THREE

Renie arrived at five minutes to seven, just as the Kasakis, the Blisses, and the Theobalds were preparing to leave for their individual evening activities.

"I made shrimp dump for dinner," Renie said. "That way, I knew Bill wouldn't linger at the dinner table. He loathes it."

"How could he not?" Judith murmured. "Joe barbecued ribs. The weather's supposed to get colder over the weekend. This may be one of the last times we can use the outdoor grill."

"Good," Renie said. "I love the fall. The leaves are turning." Renie's head was turning, too, in the direction of the living room. "I see your other guests are heading out. Where are the partygoers?"

"They gather at seven," Judith replied. "Everything's set up."

"What about the ones staying here?" Renie devoured the lone crab wonton that had been left on the serving tray for the social hour.

"They haven't come down yet," Judith replied. "I heard Suzanne Farrow thumping, though."

"Thumping?"

"She's been working out. Suzanne is very fit, if somewhat uncommunicative. She may be the strong, silent type."

"Not musical, then," Renie remarked.

"No." Judith stared out through the window over the sink. "For some reason this group makes me uneasy."

"A foreboding?" Renie inquired, taking a Pepsi out of the fridge.

"Oh — not really. I suppose it's because Rudi has been so annoying and now he's going to be under our roof. Maybe I just feel awkward."

"Understandable. But you can avoid him. Where's Joe?"

"He went to Gutbusters to get a couple of things," Judith replied.

Renie laughed. "Nobody gets 'a couple of things' at Gutbusters. You know it's all about volume discounts. Joe'll need a truck to bring everything home. That's why I hardly ever go there. I end up with enough shampoo and soda crackers to last until doomsday. The last time I was there I found a real bargain on bat bait and got six packages."

"We don't have bats around here," Judith pointed out.

"I know," Renie said with a sigh.

"He's buying Mother's Uncle Tom's fiber cereal. Gutbusters is one of the few places around here where you can get it," Judith explained. "Mother eats it to keep regular."

"So does my mom," Renie said between sips of Pepsi. "I found a store across the lake that carries it and bought a bunch of boxes. I was meeting a client over there. In the days when I had clients," she added with a wistful expression.

Judith jumped at the sound of the doorbell. "Here comes somebody. It's straight up seven o'clock. Maybe it's Taryn. Or Elsa."

"Who's Elsa?" Renie asked as Judith exited the kitchen.

"The first Mrs. Wittener," Judith said over her shoulder.

But the caller was neither of the women Judith expected. Instead, a young man with long brown hair and rimless glasses stood on the front porch carrying a big carton. Judith opened the door.

"Hi," he said in greeting. "I'm Fritz Wittener, Rudi's son. I've got a bunch of party stuff."

Judith introduced herself. "You can put the box on the buffet in the living room," she said. "How soon are the others coming?"

Fritz shrugged his narrow shoulders. "Whenever. Pa doesn't like to be rushed, and Ma's still organizing."

"Organizing?" Judith repeated.

Fritz nodded. "That's Ma's thing. She organizes."

Before Judith could inquire further, Renie wandered into the living room. "Do you live nearby?" Renie asked after Judith introduced her.

He nodded in an offhand manner while removing a chafing dish, a covered tray, and several liquor bottles from the carton. "Got ice?"

"Yes," Judith answered. "I keep plenty on hand."

Fritz nodded again as he placed the various liquor bottles on the buffet. "Got any beer? I don't drink this other stuff. I guess Ma considers beer lower-class. It wasn't on the list."

"Yes," Judith repeated. "I've got Miller light, a couple of microbrews, and I think there's some Red Stripe. I'll check."

"No rush." He placed two boxes of crackers on the buffet. "Where's the cheese plate?" He spoke to himself as he unwrapped the tray. "That's vegetables and dip. Maybe Olive's bringing the cheese."

Judith shot him a curious look. "Olive?"

"Olive is Pa's assistant," Fritz replied. "She lives in an apartment around here someplace."

The doorbell sounded again. Renie, who had been standing halfway into the living room, volunteered to admit the newcomer. Judith heard Taryn's tense voice. "Are you the maid?" she asked Renie.

"I was," Renie replied, "but I quit. Mrs. Flynn wouldn't feed me."

Judith had gone into the entry hall. "This is Serena Jones, my cousin," Judith explained. "Taryn Moss, our neighbor."

Taryn smiled fleetingly at Renie. Carrying two grocery bags, she moved quickly into the living room. She was dressed with casual elegance, an ecru peasant blouse and dark green velvet pants. Her only jewelry was a pair of gold studs in her perfect ears. "You've done a good job, Fritz," she said. "Thanks."

"Sure," Fritz said, lounging on the sofa. "Are Pa and Ma still alive?"

"Of course!" Taryn's laugh was hollow.

"You know perfectly well that despite the divorce they're on good terms."

Fritz looked at Taryn over the top of his glasses. "Right. They're tight. It's great." The words didn't carry much conviction.

Judith had a feeling that Taryn's assertion had been made for her — and for Renie's — benefit. "We'll be in the kitchen if you need us," she said, giving Renie a nudge.

They were halfway through the entry hall when Suzanne Farrow came down the stairs. She was dressed very simply, in black silk slacks and a matching tailored blouse. Nodding at the cousins, she proceeded into the living room.

"Hello, you two," she said to Fritz and Taryn.

Judith heard the pair reply in monosyllables. Suzanne spoke again, more sharply. "Well, Fritz? How about a kiss?"

"Ahhh . . ." The young man sounded ill at ease. A pause ensued.

"Thank you," Suzanne said. Silence followed.

"Not a very cheerful bunch so far," Renie remarked when the cousins were back in the kitchen. "It's a good thing you're not responsible for them having fun."

"Fun," Judith repeated. "It's not a concept I'm associating with them so far. Don't you sense a certain lack of congeniality?"

"As opposed to animosity, hatred, and hostility?"

"Yes. Or maybe I'm imagining things," she said, hearing someone else at the front door. Before she could get to the dining room, Taryn admitted the newcomer.

"You forgot the caviar and the eggs and the bread for toast points," Elsa said in an accusing voice.

"Oh!" Taryn exclaimed. "Let me take them into the —"

"Never mind," Elsa snapped. "I'll do it myself."

She breezed into the kitchen, nodding curtly at Judith and Renie. "I need a toaster," she announced.

"What's a toaster?" Renie asked, a puzzled look on her face.

"Excuse me?" Elsa retorted.

Judith was already standing by the toaster. "It's right here. It holds four slices." She glanced at Renie. "This is my cousin Serena —"

"I'll need all four." Elsa ignored Renie, her keen eyes fixed on the toaster. "I'll wait until the others arrive. What else did Taryn forget?"

Judith realized Elsa wasn't addressing anybody except herself. "How many people are coming?" she asked.

"What?" Elsa turned sharply. "Eight. Didn't Taryn inform you?"

"She told me it would be a small gathering," Judith replied, feeling a need to defend Taryn.

"She's very imprecise," Elsa said, and left the kitchen just as Dolph and Andrea Kluger came downstairs.

"Eight, huh?" Renie looked disgusted. "So no symphony bigwigs. Rudi's my only hope of making a connection, and he's a newcomer. Drat. Opportunity doesn't knock."

Judith was ticking off the number of guests in her head. The Klugers, plus Suzanne; Rudi and Taryn; Elsa and Fritz; Olive the Assistant. Perfectly ordinary people, really. So why, she wondered, did she feel on edge?

Faintly, she overheard Elsa greet the Klugers. Or at least she heard Dolph's booming voice, exclaiming with delight. Andrea and Elsa's words couldn't be heard from the kitchen. Indeed, Elsa scarcely spoke at all before the trio went into the living room.

Renie ogled the caviar on the counter. "Tell me about Dolph."

"Dolph is Rudi's mentor," Judith replied. "I assume he was his teacher and has guided

Rudi in his career."

"Rudi's not exactly a star on the concert circuit," Renie pointed out. "I mean, you have to be talented to play in a major symphony orchestra, but that's a far cry from being a concert soloist."

Judith shrugged. "You know more about that than I do."

Renie looked thoughtful. "Sometimes it depends on the personality, not the talent. Real stars have to be willing to get up in public, all alone on the stage, and take great risks. Self-confidence — ego, if you will — is as important as raw ability. Rudi might be able to play like Paganini, but that doesn't mean he was ever driven to become a concert violinist. It's safer to get lost in a crowd. If you screw up, it doesn't show as much. The audience may not notice and the critics won't savage you."

"I never thought of it that way," Judith admitted. "My only encounter with a world-famous music star was when that unfortunate tenor stayed here."

Renie's expression was noncommittal. "Yes." It was clear that she didn't want to upset her cousin by recalling the circumstances of the tenor's onstage demise.

A flustered Taryn entered the kitchen. "Elsa says I must make the toast for the caviar." She espied the toaster. "Where's the bread?"

Judith indicated a Falstaff's grocery bag that Elsa had left on the counter. "In there?"

"Oh!" Taryn smiled uncertainly. "Of course. The hard-boiled egg garnish is here, too." With nervous fingers, she opened the packaging on the loaf of bread and removed four slices. "Elsa's so efficient. And organized. I suppose it comes from working in that bookstore."

"Elsa works in a bookstore?" Judith asked.

"Yes," Taryn replied, putting the bread into the toaster slots. "She worked at one of the big chains for years in New York, but just switched jobs. She and Fritz moved to Heraldsgate Hill this summer. Elsa got lucky. There was an opening at the bookstore on top of the hill."

"I haven't been in there for a while," Judith confessed. "I'm an ex-librarian. I tend to borrow, not buy, books."

"Shame on you," Renie admonished. "It's a nice store. I bought a book for one of our kids up there a week or so ago. They had it shipped to Guam. But I didn't see Elsa. At least I don't remember her."

"It might have been her day off," Taryn said, preparing the caviar and eggs. The four pieces of bread popped up. "No butter,

60

right? Oops!" She dropped a toast slice on the floor.

"Don't worry," Judith soothed. "The floor's clean. Nobody will know the difference." All the same, she was glad this wasn't an official guest. Judith didn't want her clientele to think she regularly scooped their food off of the floor, no matter how assiduously Phyliss cleaned it.

Taryn assembled the caviar plate and took it into the living room. Judith shook her head. "She's always struck me as fairly composed. Taryn's been the voice of reason in our battles over Rudi's violin playing. But Elsa seems to have an unsettling effect on her."

"No wonder," Renie remarked. "Ex-wives can make current girlfriends nervous. Elsa would unsettle me if I had to be around her much." She gazed inquiringly at Judith, who was rearranging the spice rack. "Frankly, you look a little unsettled yourself."

"Me?" Judith stopped herself from putting a hand to her mouth. She'd been a nail-biter as a child, and every so often the old habit tried to reassert itself. "Well — a little. That is, there's something volatile about this situation. Or awkward, at least. Maybe it's just because I've had those run-ins with Rudi."

"That's probably what's bothering you. You should make a brief appearance to show him you don't hold a grudge."

Resolutely, Judith put both hands behind her back. "I'll do that when they're ready to leave."

Renie stretched and yawned. "I should go home. I can't make any headway with this crew."

Judith glanced at the schoolhouse clock. Its clicking metal hands informed her it was seven thirty-five. "You're going to abandon me?" she said in a tone of reproach.

Renie shrugged. "Why do you have to hang around the kitchen? Aren't they self-sufficient with Elsa in charge?"

"I still feel responsible," Judith said. "Ordinarily, I'd spend the evening in the family quarters because the guests are usually out and about. But this is different. Besides, I want to make sure I get paid. Taryn hasn't given me a check yet."

"Ah, yes. Getting paid. I barely remember how that feels."

"We could bring Mother in and play three-handed pinochle," Judith suggested.

"No thanks," Renie replied. "She'll want to play for a quarter and I can't afford it. She always wins."

Renie, however, made no immediate move

to leave. In the silence that fell between the cousins, the clock ticked on. *Tick-tock, tick-tock.* Judith's apprehension was moving up the scale as the clock ticked and clicked the night away. "I don't hear any heated exchanges, so they must be getting along," she pointed out. "They seem quite civilized."

"The only one I can hear is Dolph," Renie said. "An occasional bellow or hearty laugh."

"Maybe they plan on going out to dinner," Judith said, cleaning up toast crumbs. She felt a need to keep busy. *Tick-tock, tick-tock.* For some reason, the old clock seemed unusually loud. "I didn't see Olive come in, did you?" she asked her cousin.

"No," Renie replied, still not moving from the table. "Dammit, coz, now you've got me on edge."

"I think I'll take a peek." Judith moved quietly out of the kitchen, through the dining room, and into the entry hall. To excuse her presence, she paused to check the guest registration. Holding the leather-bound book in her hands, she glanced into the living room.

Rudi and Dolph were chatting by the buffet. Their conversation seemed intimate, as if they were the only two people in the room. Rudi wasn't as tall or as broad as his mentor, but he was broad-shouldered and his eyes were blue, the color of a mountain lake.

Suzanne and Fritz were on the window seat, though they didn't seem to be conversing. In fact, Fritz was edging away from Suzanne. He reached the far corner, pressing up against a throw pillow. Suzanne frowned as she took a sip from her wineglass.

Elsa was on one of the sofas, cradling a large snifter and talking earnestly to a plump, gray-haired woman Judith assumed was Olive the Assistant. Olive sat stiffly, her face expressionless. She looked as if her thoughts were miles away until Elsa poked her in the shoulder.

"Well?" she said, her sharp voice carrying into the entry hall as she pointed to a nineteenth-century German plate on the oak rail above the fireplace. "Is that real or a reproduction?"

Olive glanced upward. The plate, featuring painted tulips, had belonged to one of Judith's great-aunts. The assistant murmured her reply, which Judith couldn't hear.

Elsa looked annoyed. "You ought to know. You're the expert."

Olive nibbled on some cheese and didn't respond.

Judith's gaze shifted to Taryn, who was

moving nervously around the room, apparently making sure that the guests had ample food and drink. None of the visitors seemed to notice Judith. She replaced the guest registry and returned to the kitchen.

"No high hilarity," she reported to Renie, "but no apparent animosity, either."

Taryn reappeared a moment later. "Fritz would like a beer. I'm sorry, I didn't bring any. He told me you had some Red Stripe."

"Sure," Judith said. "I'll get it from the fridge."

"Thank you." Taryn moistened her lips. "I feel so stupid. I keep forgetting that Fritz is over legal drinking age, and I didn't think to ask —"

"Really," Judith interrupted, handing Taryn the bottle of Red Stripe, "it's fine. Don't even consider putting it on your bill."

"Are you sure?"

Judith nodded. Taryn thanked her again and left the kitchen.

"I thought," Judith said after her guest had gone, "she might pony up the check at that point."

"You know where to find her," Renie said, finishing her Pepsi and finally getting up from the chair.

"You're really going?" Judith asked, looking disappointed.

"I might as well, coz. Contrary to your furrowed brow, it doesn't seem like anything odd is going to happen. Besides," Renie went on, collecting her purse, "I parked in your driveway. When Joe comes home with his crates and barrels from Gutbusters, he'll want to pull in closer to the house. I'd better get out of the way."

"I suppose you're right." Judith started walking with Renie down the narrow hallway that led to the back door. "I'm sorry the party was a bust as far as you're concerned."

"Frankly, it sounds like a bust for the partygoers," Renie said. "I've never heard any group having less fun." She stopped in midstep, almost forcing Judith to collide with her. "Until now. What was that?"

Judith felt a tingling along her spine. "A thud — or a clunk?"

The cousins remained in the hallway, mouths shut, ears alert. At first, they heard only the ticking clock. Then a woman's cry and a man's shout came from the direction of the living room. Judith and Renie whirled around, hurrying to the source of the commotion.

Everyone — except Suzanne, who was leaning against the armoire — was crowded between the matching sofas in front of the fireplace.

"Call a doctor!" Dolph shouted.

"What's wrong?" Judith asked, moving closer to the group.

"It's Elsa," Rudi said, staring downward. "She passed out."

"A doctor!" Dolph cried. "We must have a doctor!"

Despite a sense that her worst fears had been justified, Judith spoke calmly. "Please — everyone should move away."

Bewildered, the others seemed to recognize the authority in Judith's voice. Slowly, they obeyed except for Fritz, who refused to leave his mother's side. Elsa was awkwardly lying half on and half off the sofa, her fall caught by the coffee table's edge. Judith's worst fear almost overcame her. But she had to be sure. Cautiously, she moved toward the unconscious woman and took hold of her wrist.

"There's a pulse," Judith said. *Thank God,* she thought.

Renie was near the cherrywood table where the telephone was stationed. "I'll call 911," she said.

"Yes," Judith agreed. "She may have merely fainted, but we don't want to take chances."

"A doctor!" Dolph repeated, very red in the face as he was pushed toward an easy chair by Andrea. "We must have a doctor!"

"The medics are very capable," Judith declared.

"He means," Andrea said, "for himself. It may be his heart."

"The medics can handle that, too," Judith responded.

"Brandy," Dolph said, his voice now hoarse.

"Yes, of course," Andrea replied. "Dolph's cure-all," she murmured in an aside to Olive the Assistant, who had planted her plump little body by the buffet.

Rudi and Fritz were moving Elsa back onto the sofa. Her breathing seemed almost normal and her eyelids fluttered. Judith saw Renie hang up the phone.

"Still alive, huh?" Renie whispered as Judith joined her. "That's a nice change."

"It sure is," Judith said in relief. "Nerves, maybe. She couldn't have had that much to drink in such a short time."

"Not unless she had a head start," Renie remarked.

The cousins exchanged glances as they heard the approaching sirens. The fire station was only about a quarter of a mile away. Judith knew the drill all too well —

the firefighters, the medics, maybe an aid car or ambulance. But at least this time, the summons had been put in for a person who was still alive. On other occasions, there had been no need for medical assistance.

Judith refused to dwell on those morbid memories. Elsa was coming to, looking dazed, but apparently in satisfactory condition.

"Rudi . . . what happened?" she asked in a befuddled voice.

"You passed out," her ex-husband replied, his expression grim. "I warned you not to come."

"Don't be ridiculous," Elsa retorted, sounding less confused. "I can handle the situation after all these years."

"Ma," Fritz put in, "don't try to be so freaking brave."

The sirens had grown very loud. "I'd better go to the door," Judith murmured to Renie.

Passing the buffet, Judith noticed that the liquor bottles provided by the guests all bore expensive labels: Booker's Noe bourbon, Précis vodka, Oban scotch. Andrea was pouring brandy from a bottle Judith didn't recognize. The quick glimpse at the words on the bottle looked like it was a Spanish product. During her first marriage, Judith had learned most of the regular name brands from her second job tending bar at the Meat & Mingle. The clientele there would have been just as happy drinking Old Swamp Scum out of a cardboard box.

The firefighters had pulled up first; the medic van was right behind them. Judith stepped outside. "This way," she said in a weary voice as the emergency personnel began to enter the house. "A guest passed out. She's in the living room."

Renie went out onto the porch, too. "Drat. The fire engine's blocking my car. I can't leave now."

"They shouldn't be here too long." Judith looked out into the dusk of the cul-de-sac. "Here comes another one. Oh!" She grimaced. "It's Joe! What will he think?"

"What he always thinks," Renie replied. "You've got another body."

"Maybe I can waylay him," Judith said as Joe's red MG circled the cul-de-sac, seeking a parking place. "I'll tell him they're here for Mother."

"That'll cheer him up," Renie said.

"Don't be mean." Anxiously, Judith watched Joe back into Rankerses' driveway next door. By chance, none of the Rankers offspring were visiting, thus allowing room for the MG. Joe erupted from the driver's seat of his classic sports car and hurried toward the porch.

"What the hell's going on now?" he demanded in a voice unlike his customary mellow manner.

"Nothing," Judith assured him. "Just a fainting spell. Rudi's ex passed out. She's fine. Honest."

Joe looked unconvinced. "So why aren't you inside, tending to your guest?"

"Because she's not an official guest," Judith said. "You know — I just rented the space. Besides, it's nothing serious. Maybe it's a virus. These days, they have all kinds of odd symptoms. She already came to." Aware that she was babbling, she shut up.

Joe scowled at his wife and gestured behind him. "How long do I have to leave the car parked over there?"

"Oh . . ." Judith shrugged. "Not long. Here's Carl and Arlene now."

The Rankers were fairly galloping along the sidewalk. "Yoohoo!" Arlene cried. "Is someone dead? Do I know whoever it is?"

Arlene was famous for keeping track of everybody who lived — or died — on Heraldsgate Hill. Her command post at the kitchen window — or the dining room or the bedrooms or the bathroom — was legendary. Before Judith could respond,

71

some of the other neighbors had come outside, too. She saw the Steins and the Porters approaching.

"Nothing to see here!" Joe shouted in his best policeman's voice.

"Nonsense!" Arlene shot back. "I can see plenty. A fire engine, a medic van, flashing lights, and an open front door. Has there been another murder?" she asked in a hopeful voice.

Everyone had gathered on the sidewalk just below the porch steps. Judith scanned their familiar faces, illuminated at intervals by the emergency vehicles' flashing lights. She'd certainly put her neighbors through some perilous moments in the past few years. They were all such decent people. She owed them an explanation.

"It's nothing, really," she insisted as Ted and Jeanne Ericson came out of their house that sat between the Flynns' and Rudi's rental. "A fainting spell. Taryn Moss asked to use Hillside Manor for a small party. One of the guests passed out."

"Rudi?" Gabe Porter said, looking as if he wished it might be so.

"His former wife, actually," Judith clarified. "Elsa Wittener."

"Damn!" Gabe punched his right fist into his left hand. "I was hoping he'd fallen on

72

top of his violin and smashed it!"

"Oh, I wish!" cried Naomi Stein. "We should be so lucky!"

"Aaargh!" Jeanne Ericson groaned. "You don't have to live next door to him. Sometimes he practices until two in the morning."

"Drums," Gabe murmured. "I've got my old drums stored someplace. I've wanted to get them and pound away under Rudi's window."

"I gave your drums to the Salvation Army years ago," Rochelle Porter said. "Gabe honey, for a black man, you got no rhythm."

Gabe shot his wife a look of displeasure. "I did, in my day."

"Then I missed that day," Rochelle retorted.

"Former wife?" It was Arlene who spoke, sniffing at the evening air as if she could smell scandal. "I didn't know Rudi had one around here." She turned to Carl. "Did you know and not tell me?" she demanded in an accusing tone.

"Of course not," Carl replied with a beleaguered expression on his craggy face. "Why would I deliberately annoy you? I can do that without trying. *Sweetheart*," he added with a mischievous grin.

"Is Wittener Jewish?" Naomi asked. "I

thought he might be. I was afraid he'd join our temple, and then I'd have to stop complaining."

"Can't you tell?" Arlene inquired of Naomi.

"By looking?" Naomi frowned. "Not really. It was his name, more than his looks."

"Honestly!" Arlene exclaimed. "Doesn't anybody know *anything?*"

The firefighters were trooping out of the house. Judith didn't recognize any of them. "You're the owner?" the senior member of the company asked Judith, who saw that his ID tag read *Conley.*

"Yes. That's my husband." She pointed to Joe, who was talking to Carl and Hamish Stein.

The firefighter nodded. "Okay. Ms. Wittener seems all right, but her husband and her son insisted she see a doctor."

"Ex-husband," Judith corrected.

The firefighter shrugged. "Whichever. This is a B&B, right?"

"Yes, but —"

"I've heard about this place," he interrupted with a smirk that was only partially hidden by a bristling rust-colored mustache. "I'm new to this company. See you around."

*I hope not,* Judith thought. But she smiled.

"Well?" Arlene was on the porch, next to Judith.

"Rudi and Fritz are taking Elsa to the hospital as a precaution."

"Fritz? Who's Fritz?"

"Rudi and Elsa's son."

"How old?"

"Twenty, twenty-one?"

"What does he do?"

"I don't know, Arlene," Judith said, growing impatient. "I only met him tonight. Elsa Wittener works at the bookstore."

"Ah!" Arlene seemed pleased with that nugget of knowledge. "What can I do to help?"

The offer was sincere. Arlene was as good-hearted as she was inquisitive. "Nothing, really," Judith said as the fire engine pulled out. Joe walked over to the MG. Renie waved good-bye and headed for the Camry. "I'm hoping they'll all leave now. The party ought to be over."

"I'll help you clean up," Arlene insisted. "Serena has deserted you."

"She has to move her car so Joe can park somewhere other than in your driveway," Judith explained.

"So let me help."

"Fine." Judith knew that although the gesture was real, Arlene also wanted a close-up look at the partygoers. The two women went inside just as the medics came out of the living room.

"Mrs. Flynn?" one of them said.

"Yes?" Judith saw that his name tag identified him as *H. R. Santos.* He looked vaguely familiar.

"Mr. Wittener is going to drive Ms. Wittener to Bayview Hospital," Santos said. "She seems fine, but it'll reassure everybody. We don't need an ambulance."

"That's good," Judith said. "What about Mr. Kluger?"

Santos made a face. "There's nothing wrong with him. He claims to have heart trouble, but his wife told us he's never had an actual attack. I told him to go for a nice walk. He can use the exercise."

"Good idea," Judith remarked. "He's on the hefty side."

Entering the living room, Judith saw Rudi and Fritz helping Elsa get to her feet. She looked pale, but none the worse for her fainting spell. Dolph and Andrea Kluger apparently had gone to their room. Suzanne Farrow was nowhere in sight, either. Perhaps she had also retired upstairs. Obviously, any dinner plans had been canceled.

Taryn was standing by the buffet, nervously tapping one of the liquor bottles with her short fingernails. "I feel worthless," she declared.

"We all do," Judith said. "Anyway, the crisis is over."

Taryn darted Judith a sharp glance. "Is it?"

Judith didn't have a chance to respond. Olive the Assistant was coming toward her.

"I'm getting the wraps," she said in a husky voice, and introduced herself to Judith and Arlene. "I'm Olive Oglethorpe," she said with a tight little smile. Olive held out a soft, plump hand. "How do you do?"

"We do whatever we can," Arlene responded, looking closely at the other woman. "Don't you live around here? I've seen you somewhere."

Olive nodded. "I live nearby, in the Empress Apartments."

"Aha!" Arlene exclaimed as Renie burst through the front door. "I've seen you at Falstaff's and Holliday's Drug Store and Moonbeam's. Only recently, though." The last words were a virtual question.

"I moved here when Rudi did," Olive replied, clearly anxious to continue on her mission. "Excuse me, if you will."

Renie had hurried past Arlene, Olive, and Judith. "Forgot my purse!" she called over her shoulder. "See you later."

Judith and Arlene stood by as the Witt-
ers prepared to leave. Elsa, however, was
protesting.

"This is a waste of time," she declared. "I
feel fine, except for an upset stomach. It
must have been the caviar that Taryn
bought. It wasn't Russian, it was American."

"Please, Elsa," Rudi said, "let us put our
minds at ease. You know how distractions
upset me."

"I certainly do," Elsa snapped. "At least
any distractions I've ever caused. Some,"
she went on with a sharp glance at Taryn,
"seem to have a far more pleasant effect."

"Elsa, please . . ." Rudi's dark, angular
face seemed genuinely distressed. "Becalm
yourself. You know I still care about you."

Fritz shook his head. "Jeez."

Olive helped them with their jackets and
sweaters. Judith heard Renie bang the back
door behind her.

"Good luck," Judith said as the others
started out the door.

"Interesting," Arlene murmured. "So
much hate. So much love."

Judith was used to Arlene's contradictions.
In this case, however, her neighbor might
not be off the mark. "A complicated situation, maybe," she remarked.

And immediately felt embarrassed. Taryn

was standing just a few feet away, still at the buffet. "What should I do with all this liquor?" she asked in a bewildered voice.

"Who paid for it?" Judith asked.

"Elsa, I think," Taryn replied.

Judith suggested that they cap the open bottles and put them in the box that Fritz had brought. "We'll tidy up and bring everything over later," she went on. "You look worn out, Taryn. Why don't you go home and rest?"

Taryn ran an unsteady finger over her left eyebrow. "Maybe I will. I've got an awful headache. Elsa . . . well, I shouldn't say it, but Elsa always gets me flustered."

"I understand," Judith said with a kindly smile. "Go home, rest."

Taryn did as she was told. Judith and Arlene began the cleanup process. It took them less than fifteen minutes. Meanwhile, Judith heard Joe coming in and out, going back and forth to the basement. Predictably, he'd bought great quantities of items at Gutbusters.

"As long as I'm here," Arlene said when she and Judith had finished, "I should go see your dear mother. We haven't had a visit in almost a week."

"Oh, would you?" Judith gave her neighbor a hug. "You're such a comfort. And

Mother thinks the world of you and Carl. You can tell her what happened here this evening. That is, if she noticed. Sometimes she has the TV on so loud that she can't hear it thunder."

Arlene always enjoyed being the first with the local news. Indeed, Judith called her neighbor's grapevine ABS — for Arlene's Broadcasting System. "I'd be delighted," Arlene said, heading for the back door.

A moment later, Judith heard someone in the entry hall. She went out to see who was there. Dolph Kluger was putting on his tan raincoat.

"I'm taking the medical people's advice," he announced. "I'm going for a walk. It's a very pleasant evening. You must have marvelous views from this part of the hill."

"We do," Judith agreed. "Just one block up, there's a park with a panoramic view of downtown, the bay, and — when it's light out — the mountains over on the peninsula."

"Very well." He left the coat unfastened. "I shall see for myself."

Judith retreated to the kitchen. Suddenly she was very tired. Joe still hadn't reappeared. She sat down at the table and considered making a cup of tea. It seemed like too much effort. So she simply sat there, nursing her aching hip and listening to the schoolhouse clock.

*Tick-tock, tick-tock.*

*Ticking your life away,* she thought suddenly, and shivered. *The sound of doom.*

She was being fanciful. Shaking herself, she got up. There was no corpse, no mystery, nothing to fear.

So why was she still anxious?

# CHAPTER FOUR

Judith's anxiety temporarily turned into outrage. She took one look at the Gutbusters bill Joe had handed her and blew a gasket. "Four hundred and eighty-seven dollars? For what?"

"Your mother's cereal," Joe replied reasonably. "I had to buy a carton. Two cartons, actually, since it'll save a trip later."

"Even Mother can't live that long," Judith replied. "What else?" She scrutinized the items on the invoice. "Ninety-six rolls of toilet paper. That's okay — we'll use that. Forty-eight rolls of paper towels. That's a bit much — Phyliss and I use rags for minor cleanups. But thirty pounds of butter? Twenty-four fryer chickens? Eighteen slabs of bacon?"

"I put it all in the freezer," Joe said, taking a microbrew out of the fridge. "You'll use it all eventually."

"We don't have room in the freezer," Judith declared.

"We do now," Joe said. "I took out that haunch of venison. You're never going to cook it."

The venison had been the gift of a guest who had spent the night after a hunting trip the previous November. "You're right," Judith admitted. "Where'd you put it?"

"In the garbage, where else?"

Judith grimaced. "The garbage won't be collected for almost a week. That venison is going to smell awful by next Tuesday."

Joe frowned. "Maybe we'll have a cold snap. It'll refreeze."

"It was sixty-two degrees today," Judith said. "You know we almost never have frost until at least the end of October."

"Hmm." Joe sipped the microbrew out of the bottle. "I'll figure something out. So the party was a dud, huh?"

"I'm afraid so," Judith replied. "I didn't even manage to mend fences with Rudi. Now that I think about it, I never even talked to him. Of course I didn't want to be intrusive."

"Not your fault," Joe said, glancing at his watch. "It's almost nine. I'm going to go upstairs and watch TV. Want to come?"

"I might as well," Judith said. "I'm beat."

Joe went out of the kitchen to the back

stairs. Judith stayed behind to prepare the morning coffee. She'd just set the timer when Andrea Kluger entered the kitchen.

"Dolph's not back yet," she said. "I'm getting worried. Is this neighborhood safe?"

"Yes," Judith replied. She'd lost track of time. "How long has he been gone?"

"Half an hour at least," Andrea said, her face now devoid of makeup and looking rather pale. "He's not much for walking. I thought he'd only be out for fifteen minutes or so."

"Well . . . it's a nice evening, and I told him he might go up to the park, where he could get a lovely view of the city," Judith said. "In fact, it's a popular spot any time of day or night. You can see all the downtown lights and buildings and the ferryboats coming and going. They have benches there. He may be sitting and enjoying the sights."

"A park?" Andrea looked even more concerned. "Parks can be dangerous. That is, in New York, the wrong sort of people sometimes show up at parks. It's better than it used to be, but still . . ."

"I understand," Judith said, nodding. "We have our own drug dealers and vagrants and homeless persons. Frankly, the main problem with Heraldsgate Hill parks is teenage parties. Now that summer's over and school's back in session, they usually occur on weekends. We have police patrols, of course." She didn't add that the hill had only one car assigned to the area on a regular basis.

"I was wondering if Suzanne should go look for him," Andrea said. "The problem is, we wouldn't know where to search."

The schoolhouse clock showed that it was nine-thirty. The phone rang. Judith excused herself and grabbed the receiver from the counter.

"Judith?" said the voice at the other end. "This is Miko Swanson."

Miko was a Japanese-born widow who lived in the corner house next to Rudi Wittener. Judith realized that she was the only neighbor in the cul-de-sac who hadn't come outside when the emergency vehicles converged at Hillside Manor. Miko was elderly, but still spry.

"Are you all right?" Judith asked.

"Yes, yes, I am fine," Miko replied, though she didn't sound quite like her usual composed self. "But I'm very worried."

"About what? The fire engine and medics who were here earlier?"

"No, no. It's the man on the sidewalk."

Judith's grip tightened on the receiver. She turned away from Andrea and moved toward the hallway. "What man?" she asked softly.

"I think he fell," Miko said. "But he's not getting up. Could you or Mr. Flynn come?"

"Of course. We'll be right there. Maybe you should call 911."

There was a pause at the other end. "I don't want to cause a fuss," Miko finally said. "So often, older ladies make a nuisance of themselves. I wouldn't want them to think I'm an alarmist."

"This is different," Judith asserted. "This isn't *you* with an imaginary problem."

"That's so. But I'll wait until you get here."

Judith hung up. "I have to help an elderly neighbor," she said to Andrea, though she didn't look her guest in the eye. "I shouldn't be gone long. The front door is unlocked until ten. Did Dolph take his key?"

"I'm not sure. If he's not back by then . . ." Andrea raised her hands in a helpless gesture.

Judith was in the hallway, putting on her jacket. "I'm sure he will be," she said, keeping the anxiety out of her voice. "Why don't you and Suzanne have a drink?"

"No. I'll just watch by the window in the front door."

"Okay." Judith considered getting Joe, but

didn't want to waste time. She took her cell phone out of her purse and left the house.

Except for the streetlamps, the cul-de-sac was dark. Judith walked as fast as her artificial hip would permit, keeping to the curving sidewalk. As she turned the corner she saw Miko Swanson's diminutive figure on her front porch. Judith also saw what looked like a big heap of clothing on the pavement.

She froze.

"Judith?" Miko called softly.

"Yes." The word came out on a gulp.

"Is he all right?" Miko asked in a worried voice.

Judith gathered her courage. "I'm not sure," she admitted, stepping closer.

As she had feared — almost expected — it was Dolph Kluger, his big body in the big raincoat sprawled across the sidewalk. He wasn't moving; he didn't seem to be breathing. Judith wished she had a flashlight.

Cautiously bending down, she studied Dolph's profile. He looked as if he were in severe distress — or had been. With trembling fingers, she felt for a pulse. *The second time in one evening,* she thought, a record even for Judith.

This time, the result was far more distressing. She could find no sign of life, no flicker of pulse, no tick-tock from the heart. This clock had stopped. Judith said a silent prayer for the dead man.

Straightening, she fumbled for the cell phone in her jacket and called 911. She had to look up at Miko's porch to make sure of the address. The old lady was starting down the stairs. Judith waved for her to go back.

"I'm afraid he's . . . dead," Judith said after she clicked the cell off. "You'd better go back inside."

But Miko stayed on the second step. "Who is it? Not one of our neighbors, I hope!"

"No," Judith replied. "He's . . . a guest at my B&B."

"Oh." Mrs. Swanson didn't seem surprised. "That's a shame."

A car passed on the through street, but the driver didn't slow down, apparently not noticing anything other than two neighbors chatting. The large maple tree in the parking strip helped conceal the women — and Judith thought with a pang, the latest corpse.

"He — Mr. Kluger — mentioned some kind of heart trouble," Judith said. "Would you mind calling Mr. Wittener? He knows this poor man."

"The violinist?" Mrs. Swanson shuddered,

seemingly more disturbed by Rudi's music making than the sight of a dead body on her sidewalk. "Oh, my. I'm afraid I'm not very friendly with Mr. Wittener."

Sirens could be heard in the distance. Again. Judith sighed. "Maybe Rudi or Taryn will come outside when they hear the emergency personnel arrive."

Mrs. Swanson gestured at Dolph's body. "Were they here earlier for this man?"

"Uh . . . no. One of the other guests had a fainting spell. It wasn't serious. In fact," Judith went on, "it was Mr. Wittener's former wife. The group had a little party at my —"

She stopped speaking as Suzanne Farrow came racing around the corner. "What's going on? Mom heard more sirens. Is it Dolph?" She saw the body and answered her own question. "Oh my God!"

Andrea Kluger had emerged from the cul-de-sac. "Suzanne?"

Suzanne turned quickly to her mother. "Stop! Don't look!"

"Nonsense!" Andrea snapped, pushing past her daughter. Then she saw Dolph, too, and screamed.

Suzanne was strong, but not strong enough to stop her mother from rushing to Dolph's crumpled form. "Dolph!" she shrieked. "Dolph! Say something!"

Judith put a light hand on Andrea's shoulder. "I'm afraid he can't," she said. "I'm so sorry, Mrs. Kluger."

The emergency vehicles were pulling up — the fire engine stopping across the street, the medics finding space at the curb in front of Mrs. Swanson's house, the ambulance parking at the cul-de-sac entrance.

Andrea didn't look up. She kept shaking Dolph and calling his name. Suzanne stood on the sidewalk, holding her head in one hand and clutching at her Nike warm-up jacket with the other.

Judith saw Medic Santos approaching with his kit. "I don't think you can help this one," she murmured.

Santos gave her a solemn look before he and his partner bent over the body. One of the firefighters gently tugged at Andrea. "Ma'am?" he said. "Please, could you move away?"

Andrea refused to budge. Suzanne came to her mother's side, begging her to get up.

"Dolph!" Andrea wailed. "Dolph!"

"Ma'am!" the firefighter shouted at the bereaved woman. "Please!" His face was illuminated by the flashing lights. Judith recognized him by his rust-colored mustache. It was Conley, the battalion chief who had spoken to her at the B&B. "You must come away now," Conley ordered. "They have to do their job."

At last, Suzanne was able to pry her mother loose. "Let's go back inside. It feels damp out here. That silk robe won't keep you warm."

"I'll never be warm again!" Andrea cried, leaning against her daughter. "Two husbands dead! I'm a jinx!"

"Two?" Conley looked at Judith. His expression was puckish as he lowered his voice. "You got the other one in your B&B?"

"That's not funny," Judith retorted just as Joe appeared. "Mrs. Kluger was widowed before she married this one," she added, moving away from the firefighter.

"What've we got?" Joe asked in his most professional manner.

Somehow, he must have conveyed his status as a law enforcement officer. Conley seemed to snap to attention. "Deceased male, sixty-five, seventy, possible heart attack. You're the other half of the B&B . . . sir?"

Joe shot Judith a wary glance. "I'm Joe Flynn, retired police detective. Yes, I live at Hillside Manor with my wife. You were here earlier, right?"

Conley nodded. "I'm afraid you ran out of luck with this one . . . sir."

"So it seems." Joe rubbed the back of his head as he gazed down at Dolph. "I don't believe I met this particular guest." He gave Judith a baleful glance. "You'll have to interrogate Mrs. Flynn for details."

Judith thought Joe looked as if he wished Conley would turn the fire hoses on her. She turned away, ignoring the other neighbors who had come not just from the cul-de-sac, but the houses that lined the east-west thoroughfare. She had no desire to answer questions from anybody at the moment, including the emergency personnel.

Instead, she approached Andrea and Suzanne, who were still standing at the corner. "How can I help?" she inquired.

Andrea kept her head down. It was Suzanne who answered. "Mom wants to know what's going to happen. Wherever they take my stepfather, she wants to go along."

Judith winced. "Probably," she said quietly, "to the morgue. It would be easier if you formally identified your stepfather now. The morgue isn't a very pleasant place. Further arrangements can be made from Hillside Manor when . . . you're both ready."

Andrea's head jerked up. "I'm going with Dolph."

Suzanne looked at Judith. "You can't change her mind. I never can," she added in a pitiful whisper.

Judith frowned. Andrea Kluger was used to having her own way. That had been apparent from the first phone call to Hillside Manor. "She'd better change," Judith said, speaking as if Andrea wasn't there. Which, in a sense, she wasn't. Judith realized that the Widow Kluger was still with Dolph. "I should tell Rudi and Taryn what's happened."

Judith moved down the cul-de-sac without looking back. She'd glimpsed a patrol car — *the* patrol car — approaching from the south face of Heraldsgate Hill. The last thing she wanted to do was talk to the cops. Judith would let Joe handle his former colleagues.

The Wittener doorbell chimed, grating further on Judith's nerves. As renters, Rudi and Taryn apparently hadn't had the nerve to change the bell's sound, which was Herself's version of "How Dry I Am."

After a few moments, Taryn appeared at the door. She was still wearing the ecru peasant blouse she'd had on for the cocktail party. "Oh, hello," Taryn said in a whisper. "Is something happening in the street?"

"I'm afraid so," Judith replied. "May I come in?"

Taryn made a face. "Ah . . . no. Rudi's

gone to bed. He has a rehearsal tomorrow. I don't dare disturb him. I hope those sirens didn't wake him up. He's only been in bed for half an hour. It often takes a while for him to settle down."

Judith felt awkward, but she had no choice except to blurt out the facts. "Mr. Kluger has died."

"Oh!" Taryn cried, and swiftly put a hand over her mouth. "How?" The question was again a whisper.

"I don't know," Judith answered, making sure she kept her voice down. "Maybe it was a heart attack. You will let Rudi know, won't you?"

"I —" Taryn stopped, her hands rubbing up and down her hips. "Not tonight. He'd be so upset. He worshiped Dolph. Oh, dear! And to think he was here less than half an hour ago!"

"Here?" Judith's gesture took in the house.

"Yes. He stopped by about nine, or a little after." Taryn paused. "Rudi didn't go to the hospital with Elsa and Fritz after all. Elsa told Rudi it wasn't necessary — they were making too much of a fuss over her." Taryn paused again, frowning. "Now that I remember, when Dolph was here, I didn't think he seemed like himself. At the time I supposed it was because he was upset about Elsa."

"He was fond of Elsa?"

Taryn was starting to back away. "They'd known each other for years, when Rudi and Elsa were together. In fact, Elsa was Dolph's pupil at one time. I must go." She closed the door quietly but firmly.

Judith descended the three steps from the porch, gazing out into the street. The medics were packing up, preparing to leave. So were the firefighters, although Arlene seemed to have conered Conley. Judith hurried toward the B&B, noticing Carl standing on his porch.

"One of yours?" he called out.

Judith paused. "Yes. A Mr. Kluger."

Carl merely nodded. Unlike his wife, he wasn't one to pry.

Judith felt like a jinx. That's what Andrea had called herself. *She's not the only one,* Judith thought, going inside. *She doesn't know the half of it.*

The Kasakis entered the house just after Judith had hung her jacket in the hallway. She went out to meet them, expecting a deluge of questions. But they smiled cheerfully, informed her they'd had a wonderful dinner with a fine view of the bay, and wished her good night. Maybe, Judith thought gratefully, the Japanese didn't pry, either.

Joe returned five minutes later. "Hey," he said, looking sheepish, "sorry I was a jerk." He kissed her temple. "I always expect the worst."

Judith was too tired to wrangle. "Forget it," she replied, leaning against him. "Frankly, I don't blame you. For some reason, I was on edge all evening. But at least Dolph wasn't murdered."

"That's right," Joe said, nuzzling her neck. "The medics thought it was a heart attack. They ought to know. Let's go to bed."

Judith hesitated. "I feel as if I should stay up until Mrs. Kluger and her daughter get back."

"They're together, they'll be fine. You look beat."

"I am," Judith admitted, then ran her finger along Joe's jawline. "But not *too* beat."

Joe grinned, the gold flecks dancing in his eyes. "I'm glad to hear it."

Arm in arm, they headed for the back stairs.

Thursday morning was cloudy, though the weather forecast promised that the sun would break through by midday. The

Theobalds, who had to catch a late-morning flight, came down for breakfast at eight o'clock. The Kasakis arrived a few minutes later, but apparently the Blisses were sleeping in. Around nine-thirty, Judith heard Suzanne thumping in her room, no doubt determined to keep to her exercise routine no matter what tragedy befell the family.

Judith was waving off the Theobalds when Joe came into the entry hall and kissed her cheek. "I'm off," he said.

"Off? To where?" He was dressed in his oldest clothes, a flannel shirt and faded jeans that were just a trifle snug around the midsection.

"I'm not doing real work today, remember?" Joe replied. "Bill needs some help with the plumbing under their kitchen sink. You know he's not exactly a handyman."

"True." Renie's husband was brilliant when it came to intellect, but just looking at a wrench gave him an anxiety attack. On the other hand, Joe wasn't much of a repairman, either. "Why didn't Bill call Carl? Carl's good at that sort of thing."

Joe scowled. "And I'm not?"

"Well . . . you're not very patient when things don't go right."

"Hey," he said, heading out the back way, "Bill and I work as a team. We'll be fine."

If, Judith thought, Joe and Bill were a team, the score could end up Sink 48, Husbands 6. With season-ending injuries. But she smiled and wished him luck.

Suzanne entered the dining room just as the Kasakis finished breakfast. "Coffee and a bran muffin for me," she said. "Yogurt, if you have it."

Judith had yogurt in a half-dozen varieties, but only blueberry muffins. She apologized.

Suzanne shrugged. "I guess I'll have to make do. By the way, I called the morgue this morning. They say we'll have to have an autopsy. I don't like that."

"I don't blame you," Judith replied. "Does your mother know?"

"Yes." Suzanne bit her lip. "She's all for it. She insists Dolph never had any heart problems. He *thought* he did, but the doctors never confirmed it. Frankly, my stepfather was something of a hypochondriac."

"He seemed like a man who enjoyed life," Judith remarked, realizing that Suzanne seemed very loquacious this morning. Maybe Dolph had somehow kept her tongue-tied.

"Very much," Suzanne replied, studying the varieties of yogurt Judith kept in the refrigerator. "I'll have the blackberry, please.

Yes," she continued, "Dolph had a great appetite for life. That's probably what brought on the heart attack. Often there's no warning. I own a health club, and I coaxed him to exercise there, but he wouldn't do it. He insisted the only muscle he needed to exercise was his brain."

To Judith's surprise, Suzanne sat down at the kitchen table instead of in the dining room. "Wouldn't you be more comfortable out there?" Judith inquired, pointing to the swinging half doors that led to the guests' eating area.

Suzanne shook her head. "I'm fine right here. I was raised with too much formality. Even breakfast was served in the family dining room. I have my own place now. I can eat on the floor if I want to."

"You were brought up in New York?" Judith asked, pouring coffee for Suzanne and for herself.

"No," Suzanne replied. "Not in the city, I mean. Our home was in Great Neck on Long Island. A brick Tudor with eighteen rooms for the three of us. Even as a kid, I thought it was wasteful. Why did we need that much space? In China, twenty people squeeze into boxes smaller than one of our garages. It doesn't seem right."

"Is that where your mother and stepfather

still live?" Judith asked, sitting down across from her guest.

"Not anymore," Suzanne said. "Mom sold the house after Dad was killed. I was in high school by then, but I boarded. She moved into a Manhattan co-op, but she never liked it. The fact is, Mom didn't like living alone. When she married Dolph, they bought a brownstone not far from Central Park. It's nice, two stories, but I prefer my little place in the Village. My health club's only two blocks away."

"Very convenient," Judith noted. "How long were your mother and Dolph married?"

"Almost ten years," Suzanne replied, scrutinizing the blueberry muffin Judith had put on a plate. "Is this low-fat?"

"Frankly, no," Judith admitted. "My theory is that most guests want to indulge themselves when they're away from home."

"I suppose that's generally true."

"However," Judith explained, noting the slight hint of disapproval in Suzanne's voice, "I always ask guests to inform me of allergies or other dietary considerations. My first husband developed diabetes, in fact."

"Did he have a problem keeping his weight down?" Suzanne asked.

Judith felt like saying no and dropping the

subject. Dan had no problem because he never tried. He'd just kept getting bigger and bigger and bigger until . . .

She was rescued by the arrival of the Blisses in the dining room. They were holding hands and looking very content. She hadn't mentioned Dolph's passing to the Kasakis or to the Theobalds, so she wouldn't inform the Blisses, either. None of them had been present during the two emergency runs. Informing the other guests would put a damper on their visits. If nobody asked, Judith wouldn't tell.

Although the Theobalds had checked out, the Blisses and the Kasakis were staying another night. Judith had one new reservation booked for Thursday, two middle-aged women from Kansas City. The weekend had filled up, which presented a problem if Andrea and Suzanne decided to stay an extra night. Judith had to play a waiting game. It wouldn't be the first time. Juggling last-minute arrivals and departures was part of her job description.

By the time Judith had taken care of the Blisses, Suzanne had finished her breakfast and announced that she was going for a run. After warning her to be careful in case the pavement was damp, Judith took the cordless phone down the hallway from the kitchen and sat on the back stairs, where she couldn't be heard. It was early to call Renie — not yet ten — but she figured her cousin would be up and semiconscious if Bill and Joe were working in the kitchen.

A drowsy voice answered, saying something that might have been interpreted as hello.

"Coz?" Judith said.

"Huh?"

"Are you awake?"

There was a long pause. "No," Renie finally said. "I'm up, but I'm not awake."

"Did Joe tell you what happened after you left last night?"

"Joe? Is he here?"

"Are you still in bed?"

"No." Another pause. "I got up about ten minutes ago. All I saw in the kitchen was two butts under the sink. One scrawny, the other rotund. I assumed they were our husbands, but I didn't think to ask."

"Where are you now?"

"In the bedroom," Renie replied, beginning to sound almost normal. "I can't wash my hair. They've turned the water off."

"Dolph Kluger died last night."

"No!"

"It was a heart attack, they think." Judith explained how Dolph had gone for a walk

102

and never come back.

"That's terrible," Renie declared. "Poor Dolph. Poor you. But at least he wasn't . . . well . . . you know."

"Right. But they're going to do an autopsy anyway," Judith added.

"That's probably wise," Renie remarked. "Oh, drat! There's somebody on my other line. Let me check my caller ID." A moment of silence followed. Judith waited. "I'm not answering," her cousin said. "It's an area code I don't recognize, and it's probably Saks Fifth Avenue or one of my other creditors. Double damn."

"Did you call Melissa Bargroom?"

"Not yet. Melissa's so quick-witted that I have to be a hundred percent alert when I talk to her," Renie explained. "This call is business, not our usual madcap repartee or gaggle of gouging gossip."

"Gosh," Judith said, "the madcap part sounds like fun."

"It is," Renie replied a bit grimly, "but not now. I'm in a hole. Broke. Queer Street."

Judith heard a noise in the dining room. "I'm sorry you have to go to debtors' prison, coz, but I think someone here needs me."

Andrea Kluger was standing by the breakfront, staring at the various pieces of Grover family china and glass. Her back was turned to Judith, but apparently she'd heard her hostess's approach. "Just coffee, please. With milk."

"Right away," Judith said, retracing her steps through the swinging doors.

As Judith poured the coffee, Phyliss appeared from the back stairs. "So you had another guest go to meet Jesus," the cleaning woman said.

Judith made a shushing gesture. She hadn't told Phyliss about Dolph's demise. "How'd you find out?" Judith whispered, steering Phyliss back into the hallway.

Phyliss looked indignant. "I'm not one to snoop, but I heard that young woman from Room Four on the phone in the hall upstairs. She was calling a funeral parlor."

"It's a shame," Judith said. "The widow's in the dining room."

Phyliss's shrubby gray eyebrows wiggled up and down. "Room Three?"

"Yes. The younger one is the dead man's stepdaughter."

"You think they'd like me to recite Scripture to uplift them?"

"I don't know if they're religious," Judith said, still whispering.

"Then I could save them," Phyliss asserted. "I've saved quite a few folks in my time. I just keep at it until they see the light, and the next thing you know, they're saying, 'God help me!' Then off they go, practically at a run, ready for heaven."

*Or a stiff drink,* Judith thought. But she simply nodded. "I'm sure you make an impression, Phyliss. I'd better get back to Mrs. Kluger."

"Let me know if she needs me," Phyliss called.

Judith apologized for the delay in delivering the coffee. "My cleaning woman had some questions," she told Andrea.

"Housekeepers can be a treasure — or a problem," Andrea said, sitting down at the table. "Do you mind if I smoke?"

Ordinarily, Hillside Manor's guest areas were smoke-free. But Gertrude persisted in lighting up whenever and wherever she damned well felt like it. Judith could hardly refuse, especially under the circumstances. "Let me get you an ashtray," she said. "There's one in the minibar by the window."

"I never smoke in front of Suzanne," Andrea declared. "She's so opposed to it. But she won't finish her run for at least half an hour."

Judith placed a black Wedgwood ashtray next to Andrea's coffee mug. "How are you feeling?"

"Numb." Andrea's gaze traveled beyond Judith. "Dolph was such a presence. You've no idea how much he influenced and inspired some of today's finest musicians. At least three of them are world-renowned. The memorial service will no doubt be huge. The problem is scheduling. So many artists are scattered — they're involved in tours or concerts. I'm wondering about holding the service at Carnegie Hall."

"I had no idea your husband was so prominent," Judith said, slipping into Grandpa Grover's captain's chair.

"He worked behind the scenes," Andrea said. "Dolph was all about his protégés. Oh, he had an ego. A temper, too. No patience with undisciplined students. But what an ear!" She smiled wistfully. "And such an ability to bring out the best in his protégés."

"What all did he teach?"

"Violin," Andrea said proudly. "Cello and piano at one time. In later years, he focused exclusively on the violin. He understood all instruments — and the human beings who played them."

"So Rudi was one of those lucky pupils," Judith noted. "Have you spoken with him today?"

"No." Andrea took a sip of coffee and a puff of her cigarette. "Rudi has rehearsal.

There's a symphony performance tonight. Dolph and I planned to attend. Now . . ." She shook her head.

"Yes," Judith said in a sympathetic tone. "That would be difficult . . . I mean, for you."

The doorbell rang. Judith excused herself. All she could see through the door's window was a mound of flowers.

"Yes?" she said, opening the door.

Olive Oglethorpe raised her head above the lavish bouquet. "Mr. Wittener sent these to Mrs. Kluger. I picked them up at Robin Hood Florists as soon as they opened this morning."

"How nice," Judith said. "Won't you come in? Mrs. Kluger is having coffee in the dining room."

"I think not," Olive replied. "I have work to do. Thank you all the same." She handed the flowers to Judith.

"Wait," Judith called as Olive turned away. "Please. How is Elsa this morning? Is she out of the hospital?"

Olive barely glanced over her shoulder. "I wouldn't know."

"I thought Rudi might have mentioned her condition," Judith said.

"Why should he?" As she stood looking up from the top porch step, Olive seemed to find the comment puzzling.

"Elsa is his former wife and he's the father of their son, Fritz," Judith said. "Divorced or not, they seem to be on good terms."

Olive turned away, gazing at the porch swing. "I don't always believe everything I see. Or hear."

"I don't either," Judith declared, wondering if Olive was to be believed.

"Very wise," Olive said, looking again at Judith. "I must go."

Judith watched Rudi's assistant trot off in a brisk manner. Olive's abrupt attitude was puzzling. But perhaps Olive didn't know Andrea very well. In any event, life in the musical world seemed to go on, with or without Dolph Kluger.

"Rudi sent these," Judith said, placing the bouquet on the dining-room table. "Should I put them in your room?"

"Well . . ." Andrea seemed disconcerted. "No. Why don't you leave them here? We can't take the arrangement with us."

Judith carried the bouquet to the makeshift bar. It was very lavish and very fragrant: pink daylilies, red roses, purple gladioli, yellow spider chrysanthemums, green bells of Ireland, and white iris were set among lush ferns and baby's breath. There was no card.

Andrea was lighting a second cigarette. "I'll have more coffee, please," she said in a lackluster voice.

The phone rang. Judith excused herself again. It was Renie, practically screaming in her ear. "I'm wild!" she yelled. "Bill and Joe went to the plumber's to get a new pipe, and when Bill tried to charge it to our debit card, he got rejected!"

"You said you were broke," Judith reminded her cousin.

"Not *that* broke," Renie snapped. "We have money in our checking account. Or so I thought. But the bank says we don't. I already called them. My damned credit cards are gone!"

"What?"

"You heard me," Renie growled. "Somebody stole all my credit cards. They're no good, they're all maxed out — except for the debit card."

"That's awful," Judith said in commiseration. "How could that have happened?"

"What do you mean?" Renie said in an angry voice. "It must have been someone at your house last night who rifled my purse. I haven't been anywhere else. What kind of crooks are you hosting these days?"

"None," Judith said firmly. "Not this time anyway."

But Judith was wrong.
Dead wrong.

# CHAPTER FIVE

At three o'clock that afternoon, the medical examiner informed the police that Dolph Kluger had been poisoned. Thirty minutes later, Detective Levi Morgenstern called Hillside Manor and asked to speak to Andrea Kluger.

Judith didn't recognize Morgenstern's name, nor did he tell her why he was calling. She knew, of course, that he wasn't the bearer of good news.

Suzanne Farrow happened to be in the living room, browsing through the bookcases. When Judith said that Andrea was wanted on the phone, Suzanne shook her head emphatically. "Mom's taking a nap," she responded. "I'll handle this."

The young woman looked stricken as she listened to Detective Morgenstern. "That's impossible," she said. "There must be a mistake."

Judith was standing by the bay window.

She caught Suzanne's eye and knew at once that Dolph Kluger hadn't died of natural causes.

By the time the call was finished, Suzanne had slumped onto the window seat. "Thank you," the young woman finally said before hanging up and handing the phone back to Judith.

"I don't know how to tell Mom," Suzanne said after she'd relayed Morgensterns' message. "She'll . . . well, I don't know what she'll do."

Judith didn't know what to do, either. In fact, she started to laugh. And laugh and laugh.

Suzanne was stunned. "Mrs. Flynn! Why are you laughing? This is terrible!"

Exerting every ounce of self-control, Judith managed to stop laughing. "I'm sorry," she said. "It's such a . . . shock. Tell me again about the poison traces. Did they say what kind?"

Suzanne still eyed her hostess curiously. "They called it 'preliminary findings,' " she clarified, dry-eyed, but trembling slightly. "I can't remember exactly. He mentioned potassium and calcium and oxalic acid and . . . something else. The police are coming."

"Of course." Judith sounded resigned.

"What did Dolph eat yesterday?" she inquired.

Suzanne stopped pacing. "They served something on the plane. I'm not sure what it was — I wouldn't dream of touching airline food."

"Did he eat anything else before he came here?"

"No," Suzanne said. "We came straight from the airport."

"But he stopped to see Rudi right after you all arrived," Judith noted. "And again after the party. Do you know if they fed him?"

Suzanne shook her head. "I doubt it."

Judith didn't speak for a few moments. She was dreading the arrival of the police, but even more, facing Joe. He'd come back from Renie and Bill's house around one o'clock. Since then, he'd been working in the yard doing fall cleanup.

"Excuse me," Judith finally said. "I have to talk to my husband."

She left Suzanne sitting on the window seat. Dealing with Andrea was a mother-daughter problem. Judith had her own domestic dilemma.

Outside, Joe was stuffing dead flower stalks and leaves into a plastic bag. Gertrude was sitting on the patio in her wheelchair, telling Joe what he was doing wrong.

"You didn't cut that fuchsia bush back enough, Dumbbell," she barked. "Those things have to be pruned to the ground. And leave the hollyhocks alone. They haven't finished reseeding."

"Why don't you recede?" Joe muttered, his ruddy face even redder.

Gertrude spotted her daughter coming down the porch steps. "Hey, goofy, tell Lunkhead here how to clip that camellia by the corner of the house. It's too leggy."

"Somebody's too mouthy," Joe retorted. He looked up at Judith. "What's wrong? You look funny."

"She always looks funny to me," Gertrude put in.

"Funny?" Judith burst out laughing.

"Crazy, too," Gertrude said. "What's so comical, goofy?"

Judith stopped laughing just long enough to blurt out the facts: "Dolph Kluger was poisoned."

Joe stared at his wife.

"What else is new?" Gertrude muttered, but her gaze was fixed on Sweetums, who was poised to catch a sparrow that had perched in Rankerses' huge laurel hedge. "Forget it, Fur Ball," she called to the cat. "You're too fat to fly."

Judith managed to assume a somber expression as she waited for the eruption from Joe. She could hardly blame him.

"That's rotten luck for Kluger," Joe said, wiping perspiration from his forehead with the back of his hand. "When are the cops coming?"

"Soon." Judith maintained her sobriety while studying her husband's impassive face. "Aren't you upset?"

Joe shrugged. "What's the point? It won't bring Kluger back." He turned to the hedge. The sparrow flew off just as Sweetums sprang from his crouch. "Would Carl mind if I trimmed those branches on our side?"

"I doubt it," Judith replied vaguely. Joe's reaction was odd. Usually, he pitched a five-star fit when she got involved in foul play.

Gertrude wheeled herself closer to Judith. "What's wrong, kiddo? You look like the pigs ate your little brother. If you ever had one."

Judith sighed. "One of our guests passed away last night."

"Passed away? Where to?" Gertrude made a face. "Why do people say somebody 'passed away'? They croak, they go sticks up, they kick the bucket. It's all the same, isn't it? Dead's dead."

Judith put a hand on her mother's shoulder. "Yes, you're right."

"Look at Lunkhead now," Gertrude said in disgust. "He's going at that hedge with hand clippers. Why doesn't he use pruning shears?"

"He's doing his best," Judith said. "Joe's not a real gardener."

"You're telling me?" Gertrude inched forward in her wheelchair. "If I could get out there, I'd —" She stopped, her wrinkled face crumpling.

Judith patted her mother. "I know. You were always terrific when it came to keeping up the yard. You taught me everything I know."

Gertrude sadly shook her head. "That was a long time ago."

"I can't do what I used to in the garden, either," Judith said. "Not with this artificial hip."

"I know," Gertrude echoed. And, like an echo, her voice was hollow.

Judith called her cousin before the police showed up. "I'm not really surprised," Renie admitted. "I didn't think your luck could hold. But why are you giggling?"

"I can't help it," Judith confessed. "It may be a form of hysteria. You know Grandma

Grover's saying — it's better to laugh than to cry."

"Yes," Renie said thoughtfully. "She also added that as far as we're concerned, it won't matter to us a hundred years from now. Go ahead, laugh your head off. You've got a right to do whatever you feel like doing. It sure beats falling apart. At least you have plumbing."

"I'm sorry Joe couldn't help Bill fix the sink," Judith said.

"The plumber's supposed to be here by six," Renie said. "It's a good thing they bill us instead of demanding money on the spot. I hate to bring this up, but are you certain you've no idea who robbed me?"

"I don't," Judith said. "Are you *sure* it couldn't have happened somewhere else?"

"I've retraced my steps. The only places I went yesterday before I came to your house were Venezia Gardens and Holliday's Drug Store."

"You had your credit cards then?"

"Well . . . yes," Renie replied slowly. "I ended up not buying anything because I was too poor. But I didn't leave my purse unattended."

Judith had to give Renie the benefit of a doubt. Through the parlor window, she could see an unmarked police car entering the cul-de-sac. As she rang off, a tall, lean man in his forties and a short, sturdy auburn-haired woman got out of the vehicle. They might be wearing civilian clothes, but they had "police" written all over them.

Judith went onto the porch to greet them just as Joe was coming down the walkway between Hillside Manor and the Rankerses' hedge. He reached the officers first. Apparently he didn't know them, either. He put out a hand and introduced himself.

"And this," he said, gesturing at the porch, "is my wife, Judith."

A squad car was coming into the cul-de-sac. Joe stayed on the sidewalk while Morgenstern and his partner climbed the front steps.

"Levi Morgenstern," the male detective said in a solemn voice. "This is Rosemary O'Grady."

Judith shook hands. "Please come into the front parlor," she said. "It's more private." It was also more discreet, since guests could be arriving at any moment.

"We'd like to see where the body was found," Morgenstern said. "The EMTs told us that the victim collapsed on a nearby sidewalk."

"Follow me." Judith started down the steps. Joe was talking to the uniforms. "Darnell! Mercedes!" Judith cried, recognizing the man and the woman. "You're back on Heraldsgate Hill."

"Oh, yes, Mrs. Flynn," Darnell replied with a tip of his cap. "We couldn't stay away. We asked for a transfer from across the ship canal. It's usually so quiet up here. Except for . . . uh . . ."

Judith waved a hand. "Never mind."

Joe beckoned to Judith. "Show everybody the way, my love."

*My love?* Joe never used that sort of endearment. In fact, he wasn't much for any kind of nicknames these days. It had taken her years to break him of the habit of calling her the much-despised "Jude-girl." But she nodded and started across the cul-de-sac.

Once again, Miko Swanson had come onto her front porch. Perhaps she'd seen the police cars and had anticipated a visit. Judith waved at the old lady.

"She's the one who first spotted Mr. Kluger," Judith explained.

"I'll talk to her," Rosemary volunteered, smiling brightly at Judith.

"She's elderly, but very sharp," Judith said, pointing to the approximate spot where Dolph Kluger had collapsed. "Is this right, Mrs. Swanson?" she called out.

Miko nodded. "Possibly a few inches closer to the parking strip. It was quite dark, of course."

Darnell and Mercedes went about their business, combing the area for evidence. Rosemary went up to the Swanson porch, taking notes. Levi Morgenstern fingered his long chin and looked thoughtful.

"Which direction was the victim facing?" he finally asked Judith.

"East," she replied. "As if he were returning to the B&B."

"From where?" the detective inquired.

"He was going for a walk," Judith said. "I suggested he go to the park. It appears that he didn't. It's steep, of course. And he stopped along the way to call at the house next door." She pointed to the Wittener residence. "That's why Mr. Kluger and his family came to town — to visit old friends who are renting that house."

Mercedes Berger looked up from the base of the maple tree. "Isn't that the house where . . . another incident occurred several years ago?"

Judith nodded. "Yes. But it was sold very soon after that. It's a rental now."

"We'll talk to them," Morgenstern said, and started to sneeze. "Excuse me." He got out a packet of tissues and blew his nose several times. "Allergies. Sorry."

Judith nodded. "I understand. I have them, too, especially in the spring."

"Mold," Morgenstern said. "And cats. I can't get near cats, especially the long-haired kind."

"Oh." Judith looked away.

Rosemary had finished her brief interview with Miko Swanson. "Is the widow ready for us?" Morgenstern asked, wiping his nose.

"I'm not sure," Judith admitted, waving farewell to Mrs. Swanson. "Mrs. Kluger was asleep when you phoned. Her daughter, Suzanne, is available."

"First things first," Morgenstern muttered, striding toward the B&B. "Hillside Manor," he said under his breath as he saw the small sign on the lawn. "Where have I heard that before?"

Rosemary had fallen into step with Judith. "You're FATSO, aren't you? I'm a huge fan."

Judith stared at the young woman. "You mean — that Web site for so-called amateur detectives?"

Rosemary nodded emphatically. "Oh, yes. You inspired me to become a detective."

"You're kidding," Judith said in disbelief.

"I'm not," Rosemary insisted in her chipper voice. "I found your site four years ago, after you solved that murder in the Alhambra Arms Apartments at the bottom of the hill. I was on patrol at the time and I decided if you could be a detective, anybody could be. And look at me now! This is my first homicide. I know you'll be able to help me solve it."

Judith was flabbergasted. The Internet site had been started by some admirers who'd learned of her skills in solving murder mysteries. Occasionally, she'd receive e-mail from a fan, but rarely did she look at the site itself. It was too embarrassing. Her official cyber name was FASTO for Female Amateur Sleuth Tracking Offenders, but had been corrupted into FATSO. Having counted calories all her life, it was not an appellation — or a reputation — that pleased her, despite her five-foot-nine height.

"Don't believe everything you read on the Internet," Judith whispered to Rosemary as they went inside. "I've just been lucky."

"You're awesome," Rosemary said. "Please call me Rosie. Don't worry, I won't call you FATSO."

"Thanks," Judith said in a faint voice before informing the detectives she'd go in search of Mrs. Kluger and Ms. Farrow.

Joe was still outside with Mercedes and Darnell. They were engaged in deep conversation. Judith couldn't tell what they were talking about, except that Joe apparently had said something funny. The uniforms were both laughing. It had better not be at her expense, Judith thought as she went upstairs.

Suzanne, looking concerned, was coming from her mother's room. "Mom needs something for her nerves," the young woman stated.

"Does she have a prescription that can be refilled through a local pharmacy?" Judith asked.

Suzanne frowned. "She did."

"But not anymore?"

"No." Suzanne wouldn't look at Judith.

"I don't know what to tell you," Judith said. "All I have are pain pills for my hip."

Suzanne's eyes slowly moved to Judith's face. "What kind?"

"Percocet," Judith answered.

Suzanne flexed her fingers. "Could she have two or three?"

Judith shook her head. "My doctor is very strict. I barely get enough to get me through a month, and I never take more than a half at one time. She's not in pain, is she?"

"Not physical pain," Suzanne replied.

"Percocet might make her sleepy, though. That would help."

"She should talk to the police first," Judith insisted. "They can come up here."

But Suzanne rejected the idea. "Mom's not up to that. Tomorrow, maybe."

Judith was normally compassionate to a fault. But this was literally a matter of life and death. Even the Andrea Klugers of this world shouldn't thwart the law. "Fine," she said quietly. "No interview, no Percocet. In that case, the detectives want to talk to you — now."

Suzanne paled. "I can't leave Mom alone. She's already lost one husband. Mom feels cursed." She took a sharp breath. "I can't be . . . I can't," she finished lamely, and clamped her mouth shut.

"Then they'll come upstairs and talk to you in your mother's room. Don't you want to know what happened to your stepfather?"

Suzanne sighed. "Of course I do. But *poison* . . . do you understand what that might imply?"

"I certainly do," Judith retorted, trying to stifle another laughing fit. Abruptly, she turned her back and clamped a hand over her mouth.

"Mrs. Flynn?" Suzanne sounded alarmed. "Are you crying?"

Controlling herself, she slowly turned back to Suzanne. "I'm overcome with emotion," she said. "Of course I understand. Whatever it implies may have happened while Mr. Kluger was a guest at my B&B. Come, Ms. Farrow. We're wasting time."

Suzanne paced back and forth in the open area of the hallway. "I'll be down in five minutes, okay? I have to call someone first. Where's the local phone book?"

"Right there next to the wicker settee," Judith replied. "There's the guest phone, too."

Suzanne paused before going across the hall to the settee. Judith went back downstairs.

Joe was settled in the parlor with the two detectives. Darnell and Mercedes had gone off to deliver the bad news to Rudi Wittener and Taryn Moss. Morgenstern had stopped sneezing, but started wheezing. He held an inhaler in one hand and tissues in the other.

"I've been giving them the background," Joe said, looking out the window next to the small stone fireplace. "Or what little I know about it. By the way, I think some guests are arriving. Shall I do the honors?"

"Would you?" Judith gave Joe a grateful look. "Thanks."

Morgenstern took several gasping breaths

from the inhaler and regarded Judith with watery red eyes. "You really don't have a cat?"

"Is that what my husband told you?"

Morgenstern nodded. "He said he didn't own a cat."

Judith shrugged. "That's true."

"Then you must have a serious mold problem here," the detective remarked in a snide tone.

"It's an old house," Judith said, "but it's been renovated recently. There's mold everywhere this time of year, especially on the leaves."

"That maple tree," Morgenstern said, more to himself than to the others. "That must be it."

"Rhododendrons, too," Judith noted. "We have several. I'm sorry you're miserable."

Rosemary offered her partner a sympathetic glance before turning to Judith. "Detective Morgenstern moved here from Phoenix three years ago. He didn't suffer nearly as much down there, but his wife is from this area. He made quite a sacrifice for her."

With his lean body and sunken cheeks, Morgenstern definitely had the air of a martyr. "It was the least I could do. My wife hated the heat in Arizona. We'd been there almost twenty years. The dry air helped my sinuses. My lungs, too." He sneezed again.

Judith wondered when they'd get down to business. "Perhaps you'd like to hear about the Klugers," she said.

"Oh, yes!" Rosemary leaned forward on the window seat by the small bay window. "Please tell us all about them."

As concisely as possible, Judith summed up the events prior to Dolph's death, starting with the phone call from Andrea. Morgenstern coughed, sneezed, and wheezed the entire time; Rosemary hung on Judith's every word, taking rapid-fire notes. Sponge-like, she seemed to soak up Judith's words as if they'd been coined by Shakespeare.

"Amazing recall!" Rosemary exclaimed when Judith had finished. "Awesome recap!"

Morgenstern looked less impressed. "You say the cocktail party was lifeless, Mrs. Flynn. You weren't actually in attendance, correct?"

"That's true," Judith responded, "except for the part where I mentioned that I looked in on them. And, of course, my cousin and I could have heard any high spirits or hilarity from the kitchen."

"Do you know," Morgenstern inquired, "the cause of Mrs. Wittener's faint?"

"I haven't heard anything official," Judith replied as a knock sounded on the parlor door, "but she was taken to Bayview's emergency room. Excuse me. That's probably Mr. Kluger's stepdaughter."

Suzanne, looking pugnacious, entered the room. "My mother is distraught," she declared, refusing the offer of a chair. "I've been trying to contact our doctor in New York City, but it's after-hours back there."

Judith hadn't sat down again. "Should I leave?" she asked the detectives.

Morgenstern started to speak, but ended up coughing instead. Rosemary vehemently shook her head. "No, that's not necessary." She winked. "This is informal, isn't it, Levi?"

Morgenstern attempted to nod while stifling a cough. "I understand," he finally said to Suzanne between sniffles, "that your stepfather was visiting a neighbor here, Rudolf Wittener. Mrs. Flynn informs us that" — he paused to blow his nose, a honking sound that would have made a goose preen — "that they've known each other for many years and were — as far as she could tell — very close."

"That's true," Suzanne replied stiffly. "My stepfather remained close to most of his former students and protégés. That is, as close as possible, given their careers in other countries, particularly in Europe."

Morgenstern nodded. "Was there a special reason for this trip?"

"It was the first of four visits along the West Coast," Suzanne answered, moving to the old tiles in front of the hearth. "We were going from here to California. One of Dolph's protégés is making his concert debut with the Berkeley Symphony, another is performing with the San Diego Orchestra, and a well-known violinist has a concert in Los Angeles. My stepfather usually made at least two trips a year to hear his people perform."

"Then this was a goodwill visit," Morgenstern said.

Suzanne glared at the detective. "Dolph didn't need to create goodwill. It already exists. Do you suggest otherwise?"

"Certainly not," Morgenstern said, taking a cough-drop container out of his jacket pocket. "I meant it only in a positive way." He slipped a lozenge into his mouth.

Judith heard the doorbell sound. "Excuse me," she said. "It may be some of my guests."

Mercedes and Darnell were at the door. Behind them were two other people Judith didn't recognize.

129

"Forensics," Darnell said with an apologetic expression. "We have to treat your house as a crime scene."

"But," Judith protested, "do we know if there's been a crime?"

"That's what we're trying to figure out," Darnell replied. "I mean, it's a suspicious death. You understand."

Judith did. All too well. While she might have encountered a few dead bodies elsewhere over the years, it had been some time since Hillside Manor had been involved in a homicide.

Mercedes gestured at the two young men whose uniforms identified them as law enforcement personnel. "This is Tommy Wang and Mitch Muggins," Mercedes said. "They're really nice guys."

Tommy was stocky, square-faced, and of Asian descent. Mitch was a skinny six-footer, some of whose ancestors had been African. They both looked too boyishly naive for their often grisly jobs.

Morgenstern emerged from the parlor, sucking on a cough drop.

"Hi," Judith said to the newcomers. "Welcome to the House of Horrors." She couldn't help herself. She began to laugh.

Morgenstern was so startled that he choked, coughed, and spewed out the cough drop. It flew across the entry hall — and struck Sweetums right between the eyes. The cat howled, growled, and raced off toward the dining room.

Morgenstern stared at the fleeing animal in horror. Judith couldn't control her hilarity. She wondered if she'd die laughing.

# CHAPTER SIX

"Cat!" Morgenstern cried.

"C-cat?" Judith stammered between fits of laughter.

"Mr. Flynn told me," Morgenstern said angrily, "you didn't own a —" He broke off, honking like a giddy goose.

"It isn't my husband's cat," Judith declared, finally pulling herself together. "It belongs to my mother. She doesn't actually live with us. Furthermore, people don't *own* cats. Cats own humans."

Morgenstern was beginning to recover from the latest attack, but his face was blotchy and there were hives on his hands. "Keep that animal away from me," he ordered, his voice hoarse. "Now let's take care of business." He turned to the forensics team. "Let's start with garbage."

Judith sighed. "This way," she said, leading the two young men into the kitchen. "There's some under the sink and the rest is outside. It hasn't been collected yet. Oh — by the way, the liquor bottles are still here, too. Someone was supposed to carry them over to the Wittener house, but that hasn't happened yet."

"Lucky for us," Mitch murmured. "We'll need the serving items, too, whether they've been washed or not."

Morgenstern hadn't joined them in the kitchen, but Rosemary appeared just as Tommy was removing one of the plastic bins from under the sink. The policewoman grimaced at Judith. "Is this going to upset your B&B plans? I mean, you'll have to get everybody out of here except for the guests who knew the vic."

Judith frowned slightly. "We don't know if Mr. Kluger was a victim, do we?"

Rosemary moved closer to Judith and lowered her voice. "That's the problem. Until we hear differently, we have to treat this as a suspicious death. Suicide can't be ruled out, but it sounds unlikely. Is it a big hassle to relocate the other guests?"

"Yes," Judith replied. "All but one of the other rooms is taken. That means finding vacancies for three other parties."

Rosemary seemed genuinely concerned. "Are they already here?"

Judith said she'd have to check the registration book. Rosemary followed her out into the entry hall. Sure enough, Joe had checked in the two women from Kansas City. "There's one more couple coming," she told Rosemary. "They're flying in from Philadelphia and won't arrive until around eight. If I can find another B&B for them, they can be paged at the airport. But that still leaves the two holdovers and the women who got here just a few minutes ago."

"Is it doable?" Rosemary inquired as the crime-scene team looked uneasily at their surroundings in the entry hall.

"Yes," Judith said after a pause. She hated to move the Blisses and the Kasakis, but she didn't have much choice. "I'll call my main resource."

Ingrid Heffelman, Judith's nemesis at the state B&B association answered the phone.

"What now, Flynn?" Ingrid demanded sarcastically. "Did you get another guest bumped off?"

"It didn't happen inside the house," Judith retorted.

Ingrid's sharp intake of breath could be heard over the line. "No! Even you couldn't have that happen again! Honestly, I'm beginning to think your license should be yanked. In fact, you seem to have a license to kill, just like James Bond."

"It's not my fault," Judith contended, her dander raised. "What am I supposed to do? Have my guests fill out a form stating that they have no homicidal intentions?"

"That's a thought," Ingrid snapped. "Or maybe they don't have them until after they've checked in to Hillside Manor. You're a ghoul, Flynn, the archangel of death in the netherworld of innkeepers."

"I don't need to hear this right now," Judith declared. "Can you help me or not?"

"Do I have a choice?" Ingrid snarled. "I can't have B&B clients sleeping on park benches or in Dumpsters. I'll get back to you. But I'm calling a meeting of the state board. You'll come up for review."

"Swell," Judith said, and hung up just as the doorbell rang again. A very pale Taryn Moss asked if she could come in and collect the leftover liquor from the previous evening. "Elsa will get it from us when she feels better."

"I'm afraid you can't take the bottles away," Judith said. "Since the cause of Dolph's death isn't official, anything he had to eat or drink last night must be checked by the police. By the way, did you serve him food or drink when he stopped at your house yesterday? He seemed . . . a little off when he came back."

"No." She shook her head vehemently. "He stayed just a few minutes both times. Dolph —" She broke off and twisted her hands together. "My dishes are here. There's one of Olive's, too — unless she picked it up earlier when she delivered Rudi's flowers."

"She didn't," Judith said.

"Oh, dear." Taryn's distress mounted. "Her serving dish is a family heirloom, dating back at least two hundred years. If anything happens to it, she'll have a fit."

"I'll see that Olive gets it. How is Elsa, by the way?" Judith asked.

Taryn looked bleak. "Shaken, but recovering."

Judith felt compelled to ask one more question. "And how is Rudi taking all this?"

"Rudi?" Taryn blinked several times. "He doesn't know. I mean, he knows that Dolph died, but . . ." She spread her hands in a helpless gesture. "Rudi can't be disturbed before a performance. He's upset about Dolph, of course. He worshiped his mentor. But Rudi has to put that aside until after the concert tonight. He's so disciplined. Personal matters are out of the question when he's performing publicly."

"Amazing," Judith said, trying to look

136

suitably impressed. "His son isn't musical, is he?"

"What?" Taryn seemed startled.

"Fritz. I don't recall hearing anything about him being involved with music," Judith explained.

"Oh." Taryn looked relieved. "No. He likes music, but only in the way that his peer group likes it."

Judith smiled kindly. "You're not so far out of that peer group yourself."

Taryn blushed. "The age difference between Rudi and me isn't so large. I'm twenty-eight. What's ten years, more or less?" She shrugged. "With Fritz, it's like having a younger brother. Elsa is supermom. She dotes on Fritz, and vice versa. It's better for me to back off. Family relationships can get complicated." Taryn made a nervous gesture with one hand. "Especially this family," she murmured.

"We all think our own family — or our spouse's family — is a little . . . different," Judith said. "It can be difficult." She didn't want to mention that the worst difficulty was the woman who owned the Wittener rental. *I should be grateful to Rudi and Taryn,* Judith thought. *At least their presence translates as Herself's absence.* "Excuse me," she said hastily. "The phone's ringing."

"Oh! I'm going." Taryn hurried from the porch and all but ran across the cul-de-sac.

Ingrid had found two vacancies so far, for the Blisses and the Kasakis. Both were fine establishments in the heart of the city, and, Ingrid added acidly, no one had ever been murdered at either of them.

After hanging up, Judith realized that she hadn't seen Joe since he'd been outside talking to Mercedes and Darnell. Maybe he was still working in the yard. Clouds had formed in the afternoon, but the air was pleasant and the sun wouldn't set for at least another hour.

Tommy and Mitch had finished bagging the kitchen garbage. "We'll have to do the rest of the rooms and the Dumpsters," Mitch said. "Is anybody upstairs?"

"The victim's widow is asleep in Room Three," Judith replied. "Room Six is occupied. I'll give you my master key for the other rooms. Oh — my cleaning woman is doing laundry in the basement. There's a wastebasket there, but it contains mostly dryer lint and fabric softeners."

"Got it," Mitch said.

Judith pointed the pair toward the back stairs. Phyliss came up from the basement just as Mitch and Tommy were going down the hall.

"Have you been saved?" she asked, juggling a full laundry hamper.

"Pardon?" Tommy said.

Judith spoke up before Phyliss could continue. "They're police. Don't start evangelizing. They might arrest you for interfering with justice."

"Hunh." Phyliss eyed the young men warily. "What about freedom of religion?"

"Not now, Phyliss," Judith warned as the forensics team headed upstairs.

"What's that all about?" the cleaning woman demanded, setting the hamper down on the kitchen floor.

"Mr. Kluger's death," Judith explained. "Apparently, he was poisoned."

"Aha!" Phyliss's eyes lit up. "Lucifer's on the loose around here again! I tell you, this is a godless place. You let too many sinners stay in this house."

Judith opened her mouth to argue, but stopped before a word came out. The cleaning woman might be a bigoted religious fanatic, but she was beginning to wonder if Phyliss wasn't right. Hillside Manor seemed to attract more than its share of sinners, especially the kind who broke the commandment "Thou shalt not kill."

Judith returned to the parlor just as the interview with Suzanne Farrow ended. Morgenstern's parting shot was a stern admonition to have Mrs. Kluger available by eight-thirty the next morning. A grim-looking Suzanne left the room without so much as a glance at Judith.

"Not very helpful," Rosemary declared. "Ms. Farrow claims everybody adored her stepfather."

"That's a bit odd," Judith said, remaining near the door in case some of her guests returned from their activities. "Dolph Kluger was a man who could make — or break — aspiring musicians. People like that always have enemies. Rivals, too."

Rosemary nodded vigorously. "Exactly. You are marvelous."

"No," Judith said, "I'm not. It's only logical. Apparently he was a very influential man in the music world. He must have offended numerous people over the years. The problem is, we don't know if any of the disaffected were at the party."

Morgenstern, who had been using his inhaler, cleared his throat. "Frankly, I wouldn't think the party attendees included that type. We're going to talk to the former

Mrs. Wittener and her son after we interview Taryn Moss. Rudi Wittener won't be available until tonight's concert is over."

Darnell Hicks tapped on the doorframe. "Excuse me," he said, looking apologetic. "We just had a robbery report phoned in."

Morgenstern coughed twice before responding. "If you're done here, go ahead." He scowled at Darnell, who remained standing in the doorway. "Well? What's keeping you?" the detective demanded. "The thief may still be on the premises or in the neighborhood. Why aren't you going to the robbery site?"

Darnell looked pained. "I'm already there," he said. "The theft took place at Hillside Manor. A Mrs. Serena Jones made the call."

Judith wanted to strangle Renie. Granted, credit-card theft was a serious crime. But it wasn't murder, and Judith still had doubts about her cousin's insistence that the robbery had taken place at the B&B. Renie was inclined to get rattled under certain circumstances. In recent weeks, she'd left her car keys at the bank, forgotten to retrieve her expensive sunglasses from Goliath's Bagels, and pulled out from Falstaff's parking lot with her handbag on the Camry's roof.

"That's my cousin Renie," Judith informed Darnell. "You remember her. She *thinks* someone got into her purse while she was here last night. Frankly, I can't imagine any of the guests doing it."

"But," Darnell pointed out, "one of them may have killed Kluger."

Judith sighed. "You know perfectly well that homicide and unarmed robbery are very different types of crimes."

"That's right," Rosemary chimed in. "What about your other guests? The ones who weren't associated with the Kluger party?"

Judith shook her head. "They weren't around when my cousin was here, and she left before they returned. In fact, Mrs. Jones spent all of her time in the kitchen with —" Judith stopped. "Actually, she went outside for a few minutes when the emergency vehicles showed up for Elsa." *And then forgot her purse and had to come back.* "Damn," she said under her breath.

Rosemary heard her. "What?"

The phone rang, sparing Judith an answer. Ingrid had found two more vacancies, all located fairly close to downtown.

"Thank you," Judith said in genuine gratitude. "Am I still up for court-martial?"

"You bet," Ingrid said. "Just as soon as I

can get everybody together."

Resignedly, Judith went upstairs to inform the women from Kansas City that they would have to move.

"But we're unpacked," the taller of the two said. "We were going to rest and come down for the social hour."

"It's been canceled," Judith admitted. "I'm terribly sorry. We have an unforeseeable crisis here. Really, you'll be much more comfortable at the Bee's Nest. I'll pay your cab fare. It's not far."

Neither woman was appeased. "We won't be back," the shorter woman snapped. "You came highly recommended. I can't think why."

Judith apologized again, but the departing guests remained annoyed. Next on her unpleasant to-do list was a call to the airport, requesting that the couple from Philadelphia be paged when their flight arrived. After she hung up, the Kasakis came through the front door.

They accepted the move with only mild displeasure. Luckily, they didn't demand an explanation other than Judith's glib, if vague, mention of illness. Renie might have had her checking account tapped out for a few hundred bucks, but Judith had already lost at least six hundred dollars for a single

143

night. There'd be more money down the drain if the crime scene wasn't cleared by Friday. She was booked through the weekend, and that didn't count the Kluger rooms, which should have been vacated by then.

When she got back to the parlor, Morgenstern was on his way out. "We're done here," he said, scratching at his hands, "except for the forensics team. That'll take a while. My partner is outside with them now, seeing what they found in the Dumpsters."

"Fine," Judith said tersely. "Good luck."

Dutifully, she followed the detective to the front door. The Blisses were ascending the porch stairs. Just as she moved to greet them, Judith heard a scream. Morgenstern froze on the sidewalk, the Blisses paused in midstep, and Judith swerved in the direction of the cry. A moment later, Rosemary came charging around the corner of the house.

"They've found another body!" she shouted. She stopped in the middle of the sidewalk, gagging.

"No!" Judith was stunned. It was impossible.

She saw Mitch and Tommy hurrying up behind Rosemary. "Not human," Tommy called out. "It's an animal."

"Rookies," Morgenstern breathed. "They can't tell an ox from a human."

"It's not an ox," Judith asserted. "It's a deer."

Rosemary stopped in her tracks next to the flower bed by the porch. "A deer? You mean — like Bambi?"

"No," Judith said. "Not at all like Bambi. A vicious deer, a bunny killer, a deer that *sucks the breath*."

Rosemary clapped her hands to her face. "You mean — like cats are supposed to do with babies?"

Wheezing a bit, Morgenstern stepped between the two women. "Enough. Mrs. Flynn, do you have a hunting license?"

"I didn't shoot the deer," Judith replied staunchly. "My husband isn't a hunter, either." She explained about the guest who had left the venison meat in the freezer.

Morgenstern's reddened eyes narrowed at Judith. "I see."

Judith wasn't sure that he did, but she kept her mouth shut. The Blisses, she noted, were looking horrified.

"But *another* body?" they both echoed, clinging to each other.

Judith tried to assume a kindly expression. "You heard my explanation. It's venison by any other name."

"But what about the other . . ." the not-so-blissful Bliss bride started to say before Judith held up a hand.

"Unfortunately, one of our guests — an older man — died last night." Judith took each of the Blisses by the hand and led them onto the porch. "He was quite famous in the music world, and since this is a commercial establishment, there has to be an investigation. I'm terribly sorry, but you're going to have to stay at another B&B tonight. I've already made the arrangements. Let's go inside so I can give you the information."

The Blisses were no longer clinging to each other. Instead, they were glaring at Judith — and then at each other. "You picked this place," Mrs. Bliss said to her groom. "I told you I'd do it."

"It was recommended," Mr. Bliss said in a defensive tone, "by one of your idiot friends at the university . . ."

The bickering Blisses took their argument inside the house. Judith let them go. She could sort out the details when they'd calmed down. Going back down the steps, she saw Mitch approaching the lead detective. He was holding an evidence bag in his gloved hands.

"We found this in the Dumpster, sir," he said.

Morgenstern frowned at the bag, which appeared to contain some kind of greenery. "What is it?"

Tommy reached inside his jacket and took out a piece of paper. "We got the tox report just before we got here. The poison was a combination of oxalic acid, potassium, calcium oxalates, and anthraquinone glycosides. The combination comes from rhubarb leaves. That's what we found in the Dumpster."

Morgenstern turned to Judith. "Did you cook with rhubarb in the last few days?"

*Rhubarb,* Judith thought. Why did it ring a bell? "No," she replied. "I never do. Anyway, it's past its prime around here by early September."

"Do you grow it?" Morgenstern asked.

Judith shook her head. "No." *Rhubarb.* Something was tickling her brain. "Our neighbors do." The Porters, the Ericsons, and the Dooleys were always trying to foist off their extra rhubarb on the other neighbors. Like zucchini squash, the crops flourished in local gardens.

"Did your guests use rhubarb for their party food?"

*Rhubarb.* The stalky stuff was driving her

crazy. "Not that I know of," Judith said, "though most of the food was brought in already made."

Mitch gestured toward the crime-lab vehicle parked at the curb. "We've collected the dirty plates and dishes along with the liquor bottles and whatever else we could find that may've been connected to the party," he informed his superior.

"Good." Morgenstern sneezed once. He turned back to Judith. "Have you washed any of the glasses or dishes from last night?"

It was a question Judith had been dreading. "Yes. I washed my own serving items — glasses, serving dishes, silverware. I have to run the dishwasher at least twice a day for my B&B."

"Too bad," Morgenstern murmured before signaling to Rosemary. "Let's go."

*Rhubarb.* Judith watched the detectives cross the cul-de-sac to the Wittener house.

Rhubarb. Judith remembered.

Renie had carried a stalk of rhubarb in her purse.

# CHAPTER SEVEN

"What," Judith demanded on the phone, "did you do with that rhubarb you were carrying around in your handbag?"

"I tossed it," Renie replied. "Why do you ask?"

"Where? When?"

"Ohhh . . . yesterday." Renie paused. "At your house, actually. I was looking for a stick of gum and I noticed I still had the damned rhubarb in my purse, so I chucked it in your garbage under the sink."

"It had leaves on it, right?"

"Right. That was the whole point for my artwork," Renie said impatiently. "I wanted to render the entire plant. Why do you care? Why aren't you dusting for prints to see who stole my credit cards?"

"Because that's what Darnell and Mercedes are doing right now," Judith retorted, glancing from the entry hall into the living room, where the officers were working. "You never had your purse anywhere but the kitchen, did you?"

"No," Renie replied. "They're wasting their time if they're going around the rest of the house. What's with the rhubarb?"

"It seems that rhubarb leaves were used to poison Dolph Kluger," Judith explained.

"Really?" Renie sounded surprised. "They couldn't have been from *my* rhubarb. Aren't the leaves the only poisonous part?"

"That's right," Judith said. "I remember that from when Dan went through his composting phase. We actually grew rhubarb in those days. We grew a lot of vegetables because we couldn't afford to buy real food."

"I know the feeling." Renie sighed.

"Anyway, Dan wouldn't compost the rhubarb because of the leaves. He thought the poison might get in the soil and cause problems for the next crop of his worm-eaten radishes and bug-riddled beets."

"That's it!" Renie said suddenly. "I had my credit cards at your house."

"How do you know?"

"Because," Renie explained, "I found the gum inside my wallet, between the credit-card compartment and my checkbook. The sticks get loose in my purse sometimes."

"Wild animals could get loose in your

purse," Judith pointed out.

Renie didn't argue. "Did you tell them *I* had rhubarb?"

"No," Judith replied. "I opted for discretion at this point, not wanting to see you hauled off in handcuffs as a murder suspect. Besides, I couldn't get a good look at the rhubarb through the evidence bag to tell if all the leaves were still attached. I'm hanging up now," she said wearily. "I have to finish evicting the Blisses. I'll let you know what's happening with your stupid robbery report."

"It's not stupid," Renie insisted.

"It is compared to murder," Judith countered.

"At least Kluger doesn't have to worry about debt," Renie huffed.

"You're crass," Judith said. "Good-bye, coz."

Carrying their luggage, the Blisses were descending the stairs when Judith set the phone down on the dining-room table. To her dismay, they both still looked angry.

"Where is this new dump?" Mrs. Bliss asked.

Judith gave them the address and the directions. "I'll pay your cab —"

"We already called a car service," Mr. Bliss interrupted. "The cabdrivers in this town are madmen. You can deduct the transportation expense from our AmEx bill. It costs fifty dollars plus a ten-dollar tip."

His bride started for the front door. "We'll wait outside. And we won't be back."

The Blisses made their exit.

Judith dragged herself upstairs to make sure the honeymooners hadn't left anything behind in their haste to leave Hillside Manor. Reaching the second floor, she noticed that the residential section of the phone book was lying on the floor. Cautiously, she bent down to pick it up. It was open to the *W*s — the *WH*s through *WI*s. But no Wittener, E. or R., was listed. The directory had been published before Elsa or Rudi moved to town.

But Judith was certain that Suzanne had tried to find the number for one — or both — of them. She wondered why.

Judith held her head, which had begun to ache while she was talking on the phone to Renie. She was in the kitchen taking two Excedrin when Joe breezed in through the back door.

"How's it going?" he asked in a chipper voice.

Judith wasn't feeling nearly as cheerful. "Where've you been?" she demanded. "You

152

completely disappeared after Mercedes and Darnell showed up."

Joe wore his most ingenuous look. "In the toolshed, playing gin rummy with your mother."

*"What?"*

He shrugged. "I decided to keep a low profile. And I kept Sweetums away from Morgenstern."

Joe's sacrifice struck Judith as enormous. She set the empty water glass down and hugged Joe. "I can't believe you were so thoughtful!"

"Thanks." There was a touch of sarcasm in Joe's voice.

Judith pulled away to look into her husband's face. He seemed serious, yet there was something in his green eyes that she couldn't quite gauge. "I didn't mean that you aren't thoughtful as a rule," she explained, hoping the Excedrin would take hold quickly and dispel the pounding headache. "I meant that you usually avoid Mother. And Sweetums, for that matter. Not to mention that you haven't seemed terribly upset over another suspicious death involving the B&B."

"People change," Joe said, his expression remaining the same.

The answer was too glib. It wasn't like Joe.

None of it was like her husband, who usually pitched a five-star fit when Judith got into one of her murderous messes. She didn't really blame him. As a homicide detective, he knew better than anyone the inherent dangers in tracking down killers. Worse yet, Judith was admittedly a rank amateur. She had risked her life — and occasionally Renie's — in her attempts to seek justice. But she couldn't help it. Nobody should get away with murder.

Judith shrugged. "Yes, people sometimes change. I'm sorry. I'm sort of frazzled."

"No wonder." He looked past Judith to Darnell and Mercedes, who were entering the kitchen. "Still here?" he asked.

"We're checking out the robbery report," Darnell said.

Joe turned to Judith. "What robbery?"

Judith grimaced. "Renie insists that somebody stole her credit cards while she was here last night."

Joe looked skeptical. "Your cousin has too much imagination. Is that why Bill couldn't use his debit card at the plumber's?"

"Yes. Fortunately — or not — their other credit cards were already maxed out."

"Bill was really mad," Joe remarked. He returned his attention to the officers. "I don't suppose you've had any luck."

Mercedes shook her head. "Plenty of fingerprints everywhere. We told Mrs. Jones not to touch her purse or wallet until we got to their house, just in case we might find something. As you know, the best way to nail credit-card perps is through the purchases, especially if the stores have surveillance cameras."

Joe agreed. "Keep on it."

Darnell and Mercedes seemed to take Joe's words as dismissal. "Right," Darnell said, with a tip of his cap to Judith. "We'll turn the case over to the regulars, though. We're still on patrol."

Mercedes nodded in agreement with her partner. "We'll keep a special eye on your place, of course."

"Of course," Judith said faintly, trying to smile.

"Good cops," Joe noted after the duo had left. He glanced up at the schoolhouse clock, which showed that it was nearly six. "Where are all the guests?"

"All two of them?" Judith said bitterly. "Morgenstern made me evict everybody except Mrs. Kluger and her daughter. This is costing us a bundle."

Joe shrugged. "It can't be helped." He took a beer out of the fridge. "By the way, your mother wants to know when you're bringing her supper out to the toolshed. She says you're late."

"Oh, good grief!" Judith tugged at the strands of her highlighted hair. "She refuses to stop insisting that her so-called supper has to be served at five o'clock. How many years have I tried to tell her that I can't always make it on time and prepare for the guests' social hour?"

"She's set in her ways," Joe said calmly.

"Then you make dinner," Judith retorted. "Now that you're so chummy with Mother, she'll probably like it instead of griping about what I cook."

"Will do," Joe said agreeably. "How about beef Stroganoff with rice and fresh green beans?"

"Fine," Judith replied. "The last time I made Stroganoff, Mother asked if that's what the Bolsheviks used to kill the czar and his family."

Joe chuckled, took a sip of beer, and opened the fridge. Judith started out of the kitchen.

"I'm going to get some fresh air," she announced. "Maybe it'll help my headache."

"No social hour?" Joe asked as he selected a package of frozen sirloin out of the freezer compartment.

"Our mother-daughter guests can socialize with themselves," Judith responded. "Assuming, of course, that Mrs. Kluger is awake."

The first thing Judith noticed was that the detectives' unmarked police car was gone. Taking a deep breath of the mild autumn air, she walked around the cul-de-sac to the Wittener house. She rang the annoying "How Dry I Am" bell three times before there was any response.

Taryn Moss opened the door just enough to reveal that she was wearing a short cotton robe. "Sorry," she apologized. Her face gleamed as if she'd just scrubbed it. "I'm running behind schedule to get ready for the concert. Those detectives interrupted me."

"I wanted to apologize about the dishes and other things that the police took," Judith said, inching her way to the threshold. "I'm afraid there's nothing I could do about it."

Taryn gave a shake of her head. "Never mind. The only irreplaceable one is Olive's." The words were rushed in an edgy manner. "Excuse me," she said, backing away, "but I have to get ready. Thanks for stopping by."

Taryn shut the door.

Judith walked back to the sidewalk. Before she could take more than a couple of steps,

Miko Swanson called out from over her back fence. Judith turned around and headed toward the corner lot, away from Hillside Manor.

"How are you?" Mrs. Swanson asked in her gentle, faintly accented voice. "You have so many troubles."

Judith leaned against the fence. "I'm tired," she admitted.

The older woman nodded and set down the clippers she'd been using to deadhead her chrysanthemum plants. "I'm quitting for the day. It's getting dark. The police are gone, I see. Is it true that they think Mr. Kluger was poisoned on purpose?"

"That seems to be the case," Judith said with a frown.

Mrs. Swanson shook her head. "Such wickedness. Still . . ." Her dark eyes gazed off into the gathering twilight. Perhaps she was thinking of the murder that had occurred next door to her. "Was Mr. Kluger a nice man?" she asked after a long pause.

"He seemed to be," Judith said. "I didn't get to know him."

"No, of course you wouldn't." Mrs. Swanson sighed. "It's so hard to know people — even when you have been acquainted for many years. Their minds and hearts remain a mystery." She offered Judith an ironic little smile.

Judith glanced at the Wittener house. "I'm curious. Do Rudi and Taryn have many visitors other than Taryn's piano students?"

Mrs. Swanson smiled mischievously. "Judith, do you think I'm one of those old ladies who sit at the window spying on the neighbors?"

"Actually, no," Judith said. "Arlene may not be old, though she keeps an eye on everybody. That's not all bad. But her view of the Wittener and Ericson houses is partially obscured by their hedge. You work in the garden quite a bit. It still looks lovely, by the way. You must occasionally see or hear some of what goes on."

Mrs. Swanson grimaced. "I hear too much as far as that violin music is concerned. In truth, I've often been forced to neglect my flowers this summer because I couldn't bear to listen to Mr. Wittener practicing. Oh, he plays very well, but when he repeats passages over and over . . ." She held up her hands, which were covered with green gardening gloves.

"We could hear it, too," Judith said. "So could the guests."

"Such dedication is good, I suppose," Mrs. Swanson remarked, "but it is difficult to maintain a social life. That's why very few people come to call."

"I wondered," Judith said. "The party at the B&B was small. I gather Rudi and Taryn hadn't made many friends since moving here."

Mrs. Swanson nodded. "True. In the months since they moved in, I've seen only the plump little lady who seems to work for Mr. Wittener and the young man. His son, I believe."

"Not Mrs. Wittener? That is, the ex-wife?"

Mrs. Swanson was slow to answer. "Once or twice, maybe. She has beautiful red hair, does she not?"

"Yes. It seems she and Rudi are on amicable terms." Judith looked sheepish. "That's what I've been wondering about."

"People divorce for different reasons," Mrs. Swanson said. "Often, the reasons are very silly. And then there are those who remain married despite great unhappiness between them." Her eyes strayed to the Wittener house. "You understand."

Judith did. The wife who had been murdered there years earlier was disliked by almost everyone. She had been a thoroughly unpleasant woman who had made her family — and the neighbors — miserable.

"I thought," Mrs. Swanson went on, "that

it was an unhappy house. But Mrs. Flynn — the other Mrs. Flynn — has endured no tragedy."

"Not while she lived here." As far as Judith was concerned, Vivian Flynn's tragedy had been marrying Joe. Over the years, the union had wreaked havoc with several lives — including Judith's.

Mrs. Swanson knew the history. She said nothing, but regarded Judith with sympathy. After a moment, she turned away, picking up a few dead leaves and stuffing them into a yard waste–recycling bin. She shook her head. "Oh my, this one's full."

Judith looked at the bin. "Let me roll that out to the curb for you."

Mrs. Swanson nodded. "How kind. Will it bother your hip?"

Judith had come around to get the green plastic bin. She tested its weight before she answered. "No, it's very light."

"Thank you, Judith," Mrs. Swanson said, removing her gardening gloves. "I'm going in now. The damp night air bothers my arthritis."

The bin could be wheeled with just one hand. Waving good-bye to Mrs. Swanson, Judith proceeded down the sidewalk and around the corner to the front of the house, where she positioned the bin on the parking strip near the curb.

Jeanne Ericson was arriving home from work as Judith walked back down the sidewalk. She and Ted were childless, though whether out of choice or because of a natural flaw, Judith didn't know. Arlene had asked Jeanne several times, but always got a noncommittal answer.

"Bad luck, Judith," Jeanne said, juggling her purse, laptop, and briefcase. "Ted and I feel so sorry for you having that guest die. I understand he had a wife and daughter."

"A stepdaughter," Judith corrected.

Jeanne shrugged. "Often, that's just as sad. Was it a heart attack?"

Judith realized that the Ericsons had been gone all day, and thus they hadn't been aware of the police presence. "Actually," she admitted, "he was poisoned."

"No!" Jeanne set her belongings on top of her dark blue Saab. "You mean, on purpose?"

"Possibly," Judith said. "At least that's the way the police are pursuing it."

Jeanne brushed her long blond hair away from her face and shook her head. "That's so awful. For you, too. You've had your share of problems over the years with guests."

*An understatement,* Judith thought, but typically cautious coming from a lawyer.

"The detectives may contact you," she warned. "That is, I assume they'll want to talk to all the neighbors to see if they know or have heard anything at the Wittener house, especially since you live next door to Rudi and Taryn."

Jeanne looked puzzled. "Rudi and Taryn? What have they got to do with it?"

Judith explained about the connection between Rudi and Dolph.

"I see," Jeanne said thoughtfully. "So it was Rudi's ex who passed out last night? I thought I recognized her."

"You've seen her around?"

"A couple of times," Jeanne replied. "That red hair of hers is hard to miss. What kind of poison was it? Old-fashioned arsenic or something more exotic?"

Judith's expression was wry. "Common garden-variety rhubarb."

"No kidding!" She looked dismayed. "The leaves, of course."

Judith nodded. "They're very toxic."

"I know," Jeanne said, frowning at the sidewalk. "Ted and I used to grow it. Remember, we usually brought some over to you and to Mrs. Swanson. But we always took the leaves off first."

"Yes," Judith said, watching Jeanne as she continued to stare at the ground. "I make a pie or a cobbler from your rhubarb. In fact, I didn't get any from you this year — just from the Porters and the Dooleys."

Jeanne finally looked up at Judith. "That's because we didn't have enough to give away." Her face was troubled. "The droughts the past couple of summers have been so hard on gardens with all the need for water conservation. We lost several shrubs and I'm not sure about that young beech tree. It looks sick to me."

Involuntarily, Judith swerved to look at the tall wood-and-steel-mesh fence that enclosed the Ericsons' yard. Ted was an architect who had bought the property shortly after he and Jeanne were married. A two-story Prairie Craftsman house in the same style as Hillside Manor had stood on the site, but had been ill treated by previous owners. Ted had leveled the old house and designed a modern structure, with stark angles and planes. Judith had never thought the architecture suited the cul-de-sac, but she'd grown used to it over the years.

"When the Goodriches lived next door," Jeanne went on, referring to the original owners of the rental, "Mr. Goodrich was always so generous with his fruit and vegetables. But the violinist and his . . . whatever . . . don't seem interested in yard work."

"No," Judith said absently, "they don't."

Jeanne shivered. "They seem a bit odd. Of course being odd doesn't mean they're . . . bad," she said.

"Of course not," Judith agreed.

But she wondered.

# CHAPTER EIGHT

Suzanne requested a bowl of soup for her mother. "Homemade, if you have it," the young woman specified. "Chicken with noodles and perhaps a bit of carrot."

Judith occasionally made soup, but only in the winter months. "I'm sorry," she apologized. "I have only canned."

Suzanne looked disconcerted. "She hates prepared foods. Is there somewhere I can buy freshly made soup?"

"Yes," Judith said. "Falstaff's Grocery makes their own soup. So do a couple of other stores at the bottom of the hill."

Suzanne looked at her watch. "I finally talked to my mother's doctor in New York. He was phoning in a prescription to Holliday's Drug Store. It'll be ready around seven. Is Falstaff's near there?"

"Just a block away. Would you like me to drive you?"

"I'd rather walk — or run," Suzanne

replied. "It's almost six-thirty. I'll leave now."

Judith gave Suzanne directions. "What about you?" she asked. "We're having beef Stroganoff. There should be enough for your dinner."

"I'd rather pick up something at this Falstaff place," Suzanne answered. "I prefer all natural, organic foods. Besides, I eat very little meat and avoid beef entirely."

Accustomed to the varied diets of guests, Judith nodded. "I understand. How is your mother feeling this evening?"

"Slightly improved," Suzanne replied, beginning a series of stretching exercises in the middle of the living room. "She's starting to plan the memorial service. We hope to ship Dolph's body to New York by Saturday at the latest. There'll be cremation, with his ashes scattered over the hills of Eisenach, where he and Bach were both born."

Just watching Suzanne's lithe body go through its routine made Judith's hip ache. "That's what he wanted?" she inquired.

"According to Mom," Suzanne said as she finished and stood up straight. "Bach was Dolph's favorite composer."

"What about the memorial at Carnegie Hall?"

Suzanne adjusted her sweats. "Mom's

working on that. It's tricky, with the music season in full swing." She headed for the entry hall.

The door closed as Joe informed her that dinner was ready. He'd already taken Gertrude's portion to the toolshed.

"How's your sleuthing?" Joe asked after they'd sat down.

"I'm not really sleuthing," Judith replied. "I haven't much to go on. I don't know these people. Maybe I should just stay out of it."

Joe looked noncommittal. "Your choice. Morgenstern is capable, I understand. His partner's a rookie, so she has no track record. Still, she seems earnest."

Joe's laissez-faire attitude was beginning to drive Judith crazy. "How would you conduct this investigation?"

Joe speared a mushroom slice with his fork. "I always started with the spouse. He or she's the most likely suspect. Even if the killer is somebody else, the spouse probably has a pretty good idea who did it. As you know, that can get tricky, because often the spouse is protecting another family member — a child, a brother, a sister — or, of course, a lover. Suzanne's a stepdaughter, right?"

Judith nodded. "Mrs. Kluger's first husband died in a hunting accident."

Joe chewed thoughtfully. "Mistaken for a moose?"

"No," Judith said. "He was foxhunting in New Jersey."

"Interesting." Joe bit into a chunk of tender beef.

"A man can hardly be mistaken for a fox," Judith pointed out.

"But he might have been a big bad wolf," Joe said. "Hunt-club accidents don't involve guns."

Judith savored the rice and sour-cream sauce. The meal was delicious. Her headache had abated and her appetite was better than she'd expected. "I haven't heard what kind of accident it was," she allowed. "A fall from his horse, maybe."

"The Klugers had no children together?" Joe asked.

"Not that I know of," Judith replied.

"Ex-wives," Joe said, before forking in a couple of crisp green beans.

"Elsa Wittener?"

"Well . . . no," Joe said after a pause. "Kluger. Was this marriage to Andrea — that's her name, right? — his first?"

"I don't know," Judith admitted. "But unless he remained a bachelor until his sixties, there must be a former marriage or two.

Possibly children as well. Maybe I could check him out on the Internet."

Joe looked bemused. "Why not ask? That's your usual MO."

Judith shot Joe a curious glance. "Why are you being so helpful?"

Joe's expression was innocent. "I'm only taking an interest. Of course," he went on, though his tone didn't change, "if you resent my suggestions, I'll stop."

"Oh, no!" Judith asserted. "I'm grateful. Really. It's just not like you. I mentioned that earlier. It feels . . . strange."

Joe shrugged. "I guess I'm mellowing in my old age. Anyway, tomorrow I'll have to meet with the attorneys about that title search. I won't be around much. More Stroganoff?"

"No, thanks," Judith said. "It's terrific, but it's also rich. I'm still watching my weight."

"You're looking good," Joe said, dishing up a second helping of rice and sauce for himself. "Those ten pounds you put back on suit you."

Judith couldn't help but smile. The truth was, she'd gained closer to fifteen, but now she'd hit a plateau and intended to stay there. The only bad part was that Joe had been eating more to encourage her. She figured he'd passed by his own plateau nearly twenty pounds ago. Judith hoped he'd become more weight-conscious. The plateau could grow into a mountain, as it had with Dan.

"I like your hair, too," Joe said, "especially now that you're getting it cut a little shorter."

Judith smiled. It had taken years of prodding from Renie before she'd had the nerve to do anything about her prematurely gray hair. Her husband's compliments made it impossible for her to nag him about his own weight, so she kept quiet.

Renie called after dinner. "I just got off the phone with Melissa Bargroom," she said. "We're having lunch tomorrow. Her treat, since I'm poor. But she did give me a rundown on Dolph just off the top of her head. He's quite famous."

"Great," Judith broke in. "Does that mean she's going to spread the story of his death all over the newspaper?"

"No. Melissa is a sympathetic person," Renie explained. "This is a tricky story, which the city desk is playing down. Dolph's not a local, no matter how distinguished he may be in international music circles. If Melissa pushed this thing, she'd have to mention the Rudi connection. Our symphony conductor and the board members wouldn't like that any more than Rudi would, and Melissa has to keep close ties to them. Nothing other than a brief account of Dolph's demise will appear in the newspaper — much less on TV — unless an arrest is made."

"Whew!" Judith relaxed slightly. "I really don't need reporters on the lawn. I've been there and done that, and it wasn't much fun."

"Right. Anyway," Renie continued, "Dolph's former pupils and protégés include a half dozen of the top violinists and at least one piano virtuoso whose names you know. Dolph was born in Germany, but fled with his parents shortly before World War Two. He had some musical talent, but not enough to make a name for himself, so after the war he returned to Germany. That's when he began to teach, and was very successful from the get-go. Along about 1970, he began to commute between Munich and New York. He settled in Manhattan after marrying Andrea. He is, according to Melinda and quoting from an obituary she once wrote about a notorious madam, 'loved by all.' "

"Speaking of love," Judith said, "had he

been married before he hooked up with Andrea?"

"Yes, first to a fairly well-known opera singer. The second wife was a patron of the arts whose first husband was a Hungarian nobleman and whose third husband — after Dolph — was a wealthy Greek shipping magnate. Both are high profile and neither had kids by Dolph. Thus I assume they're not involved with the current group of suspects. That's all I got since Melissa had to hang up in a hurry. Her daughter had just put Melissa's BMW sports car in reverse instead of forward and crashed into a Japanese cherry tree. I'll find out more tomorrow."

"Good," Judith said. "I'm getting nowhere fast. Maybe I should go buy a book."

"They're open until eight," Renie said. "In fact, I want to return a book — for cash. The pages were misnumbered, but I didn't discover that until I got to the next-to-the-last chapter."

"Well . . . okay," Judith agreed. "I'll see you at the bookstore in five minutes."

Heraldsgate Hill Books was tucked into a small but charming building on the avenue. The owners were a married couple who had started the business fifteen years ago.

Gretchen and Tyler Bergosian were middle-aged ex-Californians who had decided to escape the frantic pace of Los Angeles. When Judith arrived, Gretchen was behind the counter, ringing up a customer who had purchased two of the current bestsellers.

Judith lingered in the children's-book section, which was tucked into a cozy corner. She probably should patronize the bookstore more frequently, but as a former librarian, she was loyal to her local public library, where she could not only check out books for free, but catch up on news of her former colleagues.

"Coz!" Renie nipped out from behind atlases and almanacs. "Are you hiding? It's ten to eight. Sleuth now, or forever hold your clues."

"Gretchen's busy," Judith whispered. "I don't see anybody else working in the store. They must have left for the day."

"Gretchen's going to do the same," Renie said. "She'll lock up and leave us to spend the night in the store."

"Well," Judith noted, "we won't lack for reading material."

Renie gave Judith a small shove and grabbed the first book at hand. "Get up there. Buy this atlas."

Judith looked at the cover. "An atlas of

Antarctica? No thanks." She handed the book back to Renie.

"How about a Thomas Guide to streets and roads?" Renie suggested, reshelving the atlas and taking down another volume.

"North and South Dakota? Come on, coz, get real. I could use a new local guide. They're helpful for guests."

As Renie flipped through the shelf, Judith noticed that her cousin's sweatshirt was on in reverse. The Seafarers' logo for the local baseball team was printed on the back.

"You put your sweatshirt on the wrong way," Judith remarked.

"So what?" Renie reached into the pocket of her baggy pants. "Look at this message from the so-called inspector. Usually, they thank you for your business."

Judith took the fortune-cookie-size slip of paper from Renie. *Dear Cheap American Customer: I have NOT personally examined any details of this inferior garment. What do you expect when I am making two dollars (USA) a day to work in rat-infested Asian sweat factory? I hope this item gives you a rash.*

"Goodness," she gasped.

"I'm wearing it the right way," Renie insisted. "The logo's on backward, not the shirt." She pulled another volume off the shelf. "Here's one for the state, revised last year. Will that do?"

"No," Judith said. "I want the city guide."

But Renie couldn't find one. The cousins trooped up to the counter just as Gretchen Bergosian was going to the front door, apparently to lock up.

Gretchen gave a start. "I didn't realize anyone was still here," she said, smiling at the cousins. "How are you, Serena?"

Renie held out the biography that she'd been reading. "I'm fine, but Ben Franklin's out of order. The book skips from page two hundred eighty to three hundred twenty. Something's amiss."

Gretchen grimaced. "That occasionally happens with publishers. I'm so sorry. I'll find you another copy."

"Actually," Renie said, "I'd prefer a cash refund. I know how the book ends. Ben dies and ends up on a hundred-dollar bill."

Gretchen, however, shook her head. "You know our policy, Serena. We don't give cash refunds, we exchange or give a store credit."

Renie looked thoughtful. "Okay." She tapped the portrait of Franklin on the cover. "I'll exchange this picture of Ben for one on a hundred-dollar bill."

The bookstore owner looked as if she didn't know whether or not Renie was serious. "But," she began tentatively, "it cost only twenty . . ."

Renie waved a hand. "Yeah, yeah, I know what it cost. Never mind. Give me the store credit. I can put it toward buying a guide to poorhouses in the area."

Gretchen still seemed somewhat bewildered. "Poor houses? Do you mean for renovation or . . . *poorhouses?*"

Judith intervened. "My cousin is joking." She ignored Renie, who emitted a growling sound. "I haven't been in the store for a while, I'm sorry to say. I also must apologize for coming at closing time."

Gretchen smiled faintly. "You own the B&B just off Heraldsgate Avenue, don't you? I saw you a year or two ago at a library tea."

"Yes," Judith said, putting out her hand. "We weren't formally introduced. The last time I was in the store, I believe your husband waited on me."

"That's very likely," Gretchen said. "How can I help you?"

"I'd like a book on poisons," Judith blurted.

"Why, yes," Gretchen replied. "We have two in stock. They're both textbooks. *Casarett and Doull's Toxicology* and another titled *Poisoning and Drug Overdose.*"

"The first one sounds good," Judith said.

"I'll get it," Gretchen volunteered. After going to the door to hang up the "Closed" sign, she headed into the shop's nether region.

"I couldn't *not* buy something," Judith murmured.

"You've got poison on the brain," Renie said quietly.

Gretchen returned with a sizable tome. "We only carry one copy at a time," she explained. "That'll be ninety-nine dollars plus tax."

"Ninety-nine dollars?" Judith gasped. "Wait! How much is the other one?"

Gretchen reflected. "That runs about fifty."

"You don't have anything less expensive?" Judith inquired.

"These are texts," Gretchen said patiently. "We sometimes carry a writers' guide to poisons, which comes in paperback and is part of a series. It sells for under twenty, I believe. We have one copy."

She disappeared again. Judith grimaced. "I suppose twenty bucks isn't too big an investment for information."

"In movies, private eyes slip stool pigeons a twenty all the time," Renie said.

Gretchen returned, looking puzzled. "I

can't find the book. Let me check something." She went behind the counter to her computer. "We definitely had a copy a week or two ago, but I don't see any record of it being sold. That's odd. It must have been an oversight. I can order one for you, though."

"Um . . . sure," Judith said. "That'd be great."

Gretchen again turned to her computer and began typing. "They have copies in the warehouse. The book should be here Monday or Tuesday at the latest. I'll call you."

Judith smiled warmly. "Thanks so much. By the way, how's Elsa Wittener feeling today?"

Gretchen clapped a hand to her smooth, pink cheek. "That's right! She had that fainting spell at your B&B! I didn't put two and two together. Elsa's feeling much better, but she took the day off."

Judith nodded sympathetically. "I felt so badly about what happened to her. Did she give you any idea of what was wrong?"

"Stress, I gather," Gretchen replied, shutting down the computer.

"Stress?" Judith echoed.

"Life's stressful," Gretchen said without inflection.

Judith nodded. "I understand. I've been a

single mother raising a son. Fritz is what? Twenty or so? I remember what Mike was like then. It was a difficult time," she added, not stretching the truth too far.

"Fritz is twenty-one," Gretchen said. "He's a good kid, really, but he hasn't figured out what he wants to do with his life. Ty and I have an only son, too, so we remember how hard it was for Wally to find his niche. But once he did, he settled right down. That's why we moved up here. Wally took a job with Microsweet."

"That's wonderful," Judith enthused, watching Renie stroll off among the history shelves. "We're lucky that our son and his family live fairly close, too. He's a forest ranger, about an hour away up at the pass. Of course it's nice for Elsa to have Fritz living with her. I understand they haven't been on Heraldsgate Hill very long."

"They moved here this summer," Gretchen replied, tidying up the counter.

"I suppose," Judith mused, "Fritz wanted to be close to his father."

"I'm not sure it wasn't a coincidence," Gretchen said, glancing at her watch and frowning. "Elsa told me that Fritz had wanted to come west for a long time." She gave Judith a weary little smile.

Judith took the hint. "We mustn't keep

you." She called out to Renie, who popped around from the end of a row of books. "Let's go, coz."

Thanking Gretchen once more, the cousins departed. "Moonbeam's?" Renie asked.

Judith gestured at the small café next to the bookstore. "Let's go in here. We won't have to drive four blocks and repark our cars."

Little Havana had a Cuban theme, but there wasn't a picture of Fidel Castro — or a cigar — in sight. Judith and Renie sat at a rough-hewn window table near a poster showing the music museum, which depicted a careworn Moorish facade.

"They feature Café La Llave espresso," Renie noted. "I don't need a caffeine jolt this late at night."

Judith scanned the one-page menu. "Here's a Café Aroma Decaffeinated. That's more like it."

Renie went up to the counter and placed their order. When she came back to the table, Judith was looking glum. "I didn't get much for twenty bucks," she complained to Renie.

"Elsa?" Renie shrugged. "Gretchen was being discreet."

"I suppose there was one salient fact," Judith remarked.

"The sales-record oversight?"

As so often happened, the cousins seemed to be on the same wavelength. "Yes. Was the poison book stolen — or bought? And by whom?"

"They don't have security devices like some of the bigger stores," Renie pointed out. "Nothing beeps, buzzes, or goes *boom* if you walk out the door with something you haven't paid for."

"We can't jump to conclusions, though," Judith asserted, looking out the window onto the veranda that led to the sidewalk. Several people were enjoying their beverages outdoors. A border collie lay sprawled at one woman's feet. "Anyone could have shoplifted that book."

Their coffees arrived, steaming hot in big yellow mugs. "Why," Renie said, putting both hands around the mug to feel its warmth, "do I think you don't believe that?"

"Experience," Judith said. "God knows I've had plenty of that." She leaned back in the chair. "Good grief! Here comes the odd couple — Suzanne and Fritz. Don't look."

Renie stiffened like a sculpture. "Okay," she said, without moving her lips. "Are they coming in here?"

"Yes. No. They're stopping to pet the dog." Judith paused. "Rats! I think Suzanne saw us through the window. They've turned around. They're going back down the street."

"What's that all about?" Renie murmured.

"That's what I'd like to know," said Judith.

Friday morning got off to a rough start. Judith knew she should have called Ingrid at the B&B office sooner, but she'd put it off, hoping that she could avoid relocating the weekend guests. But at precisely 8 A.M., she called her nemesis, Ingrid Heffelman.

"Crime scene, huh?" Ingrid said, relishing the words. "Of course. What about bubonic plague or weapons of mass destruction? You want your guests moved? Try H-bombs! Ha ha!"

"Ingrid . . ."

"Okay, okay. I'm fed up with your corpses and crises. Your guests would be better off staying at The Bates Motel."

"Just find them substitute inns," Judith said, weary of Ingrid's barbs. "Let me give you their names and cell-phone numbers, if they have them."

An hour later Morgenstern and O'Grady showed up on Hillside Manor's doorstep. Judith had made sure that Sweetums was hidden away in the toolshed with Gertrude.

Neither Suzanne nor Andrea had yet made an appearance, however. Indeed, Judith hadn't seen Suzanne after spotting her with Fritz outside of Little Havana.

"Cops again," Phyliss announced after going to the front door. "No uniforms. Can't the city afford costumes for these people?"

"You know my husband never wore a uniform when he was on the force," Judith reminded the cleaning woman.

"Too cheap for him, too, huh?"

Judith merely shook her head and went into the entry hall, where the detectives were waiting.

"Where's Mrs. Kluger?" Morgenstern demanded without preamble.

Judith explained that the widow hadn't yet come downstairs.

"Then," the detective said, beckoning to Rosemary, "we'll have to go to her."

The duo climbed the stairs. Judith offered no protest. The detectives were simply performing their duty.

Moving up to the first landing, she couldn't see what was happening on the second floor, but she should be able to hear some of the conversation. Indeed, the sound of knocking reverberated down the staircase. Morgenstern was calling out to Andrea Kluger.

Suzanne responded. "She's still asleep," Judith heard the young woman say. "Please leave her alone."

"Ms. Farrow," Morgenstern said in a reasonable tone, "if your stepfather was poisoned intentionally, aren't you and your mother anxious to discover who did it?"

Suzanne's reply was inaudible.

"Then," Morgenstern went on, "we must proceed with our investigation."

The phone rang. Reluctantly, Judith descended the three steps from the landing to the credenza, where she'd left the receiver. Phyliss came into the entry hall just before Judith clicked on the phone.

"Keyhole?" the cleaning woman inquired, cupping a hand behind her ear and gesturing up toward the second floor.

Judith realized what Phyliss meant. "Do what you have to," she said before answering the call.

"Coz!" Renie's voice came through loud and clear, especially since it was not yet nine-thirty in the morning. "The fraud cops traced the debit charge! They just left."

"You were up to greet them?" Judith asked as Phyliss went through the dining room to do her snooping via the back stairs.

"No, but Bill was, and he woke me because I had to verify that it wasn't my signature on the charge slip."

"Only one charge?" Judith asked. "Where?"

"Barnaby's at the bottom of the hill," Renie replied, referring to a large drugstore. "They're open twenty-four hours a day, and this charge was made yesterday morning at seven-fifteen."

"For what?"

"Vitamins, over-the-counter sleep medications, toiletries, and pain patches," Renie recounted, "totaling two hundred and twenty-four dollars and eighty cents. We had about two-fifty in checking, so that wiped us out as far as plumbing parts were concerned."

"Did they catch whoever used the card on their security camera?"

"They only have them in the pharmacy area," Renie said. "The clerk who waited on the perp was at the end of her shift and dead tired. She didn't ask for ID. She vaguely recalls that it was a woman. They were fairly busy with customers on their way to work."

"Is it a clerk you know?"

"One who works the night shift?" Renie said, aghast. "Are you kidding? The only employees I know are there from eleven until two. That's when I run errands."

"I know," Judith agreed, aware of her

cousin's routine. "Surely this clerk must remember if the woman was old or young, black or white, tall or short."

"You'd think so," Renie said, sounding irritated. "But you know how it is — most people don't pay attention. Heck, let's face it — I don't always study the clerks who wait on me at places where I shop. We're all too wrapped up in ourselves."

Judith knew this was true, though she herself was an exception, always taking a personal interest even in the most casual exchange. "If we narrow the possibilities to the women who were here night before last," she said, "that leaves Taryn, Andrea, Suzanne, and possibly even Elsa, depending on when she was released from the hospital's emergency room. Oh — and Olive Oglethorpe. I really should talk to her. She lives up the hill a block or so."

Renie paused before speaking. "Can you limit the actual theft to a woman?"

Judith was on the landing again, trying to hear what was going on upstairs. All was silent. "What do you mean?" she asked her cousin.

"The purchaser may not have been the thief," Renie pointed out. "One of the men could have taken my credit cards. Some of the accounts are in Bill's name, too. Of course everything but the debit card was maxed out, and therefore useless."

"You're saying that Fritz could have handed the card over to Elsa or Rudi did the same with Taryn or even Dolph, since he was still alive and drinking when the emergency people came for Elsa."

"I'd say Elsa's out of it as the thief," Renie said. "I didn't leave my purse unattended while she was still going in and out of the kitchen. It was only after she passed out that there would've been an opportunity for her to pinch my stuff."

"But why?" Judith mused. "Why would anyone in this bunch steal your cards in the first place? They don't seem the type."

"Crazy, maybe," Renie said, "like kleptomaniacs. They steal things they don't need or want."

"But this one actually used your debit card," Judith pointed out as she saw Phyliss coming back through the entry hall shaking her head. "Hey, coz, I have to go. I'll call you back later."

Phyliss looked aggrieved. "Nobody in the hall. Couldn't make out a word listening at the keyholes. Just mumbles, coughs, sneezes, and a wheeze or two."

"Hunh. Quiet as a church," Judith remarked.

"Not *our* church," Phyliss declared. "We make a joyful noise unto the Lord. You wouldn't believe all the hallelujahs, amens, and praises. They'd knock your socks off."

"I imagine that's so," Judith murmured. "Well, at least Mrs. Kluger isn't hysterical. You could have heard that."

"I'm usually not one to pry, you know," Phyliss asserted with a self-righteous look. "But this is different. I haven't seen hide nor hair of that Kluger woman in two days. She might as well be dead, too."

Judith gaped at Phyllis. The remark might be glib, but given Hillside Manor's history, it could also be true.

# CHAPTER NINE

"Don't say we could have another dead body!" Judith cried. "That's not the least bit funny!"

"Funny?" Phyliss sniffed in disdain. "I wasn't being funny. Around here, you never know. All sorts of queer, ungodly doings. Take that crazy fiddler, for instance."

"At least we haven't had to listen to him practice the last few days," Judith pointed out.

"I don't mean that," Phyliss said darkly. "I mean yesterday morning right after I got here."

"Yesterday?" Judith stared at the cleaning woman. "What are you talking about?"

"Finding him in the living room," Phyliss said. "You were out with your heathen mother in the toolshed. That fiddler was in the living room, he walked right in just because the front door was unlocked. Talk about nerve!"

"What was Rudi doing?"

Phyliss smirked. "He *said* he was looking for a bracelet. I suppose his tart of a girl-friend lost it. Living in sin! She's lost more than a bracelet, if you ask me."

"Exactly where was he?"

"By the buffet," Phyliss said. "He must have just come in. He jumped about two feet when he saw me."

"What did he do then?"

Phyliss shrugged. "He snooped around on the floor and under the furniture. I watched him like a hawk." Phyliss looked very pleased with herself. "Finally, he left. No bracelet. Served him right. It probably fell off outside in the bushes when his strumpet was doing Jezebel's Dance of the Seven Veils."

"I thought that was Salome," Judith remarked.

Phyliss clapped a hand to her cheek. "You're right! It was Salome! I thought you Catholics never read the Bible."

"We don't," Judith said with a straight face, "but years ago I saw the movie with Rita Hayworth." She frowned at the cleaning woman. "You should've told me about Rudi sooner."

"I got busy," Phyliss declared. "What else am I around here except busy? Since when did you complain about me not working?"

"Never," Judith admitted. "You're a hard worker. I'm always pleased with what you do for us. But there's a murder investigation going on here. The police might regard Rudi Wittener's behavior as suspicious." *As do I,* she thought.

"I didn't know that then," Phyliss said with a sulky expression. "I'd just got here. I hadn't seen you yet."

Judith smiled wanly. "That's okay, Phyliss. I realize that you're used to all sorts of people coming and going around this house."

But, Judith wondered, was Andrea Kluger alive? Phyliss armed herself with the vacuum cleaner and headed for the living room. Judith went upstairs, where Rosemary was coming out of Room Three.

"Mrs. Kluger is difficult," the rookie detective announced.

Judith sighed in relief. "Then she's . . . okay?"

"Define *okay,*" Rosemary said, going over to sit on the love seat next to the stair rail, where she consulted her thick notebook. "She acts groggy, but I suppose that's because we woke her up."

Judith straightened the magazines in the rack next to the love seat. "Does she have any idea who might have poisoned her husband?"

Rosemary brushed at her tan flannel slacks. "No." She brushed some more. "Is this cat hair?" she asked, examining bits of yellow fur.

"Well . . . as I explained, Mother's cat wanders in when the doors are open during the summer."

Rosemary dimpled. "Not too often, I hope. Detective Morgenstern will have a fit. Not to mention another allergy attack."

"Will Mrs. Kluger and her daughter be allowed to return to New York with the body?" Judith asked.

Rosemary shrugged. "Not my call. What do you think?"

Judith leaned her hand on the love seat's wicker back. "I have no idea. I'm not really a detective."

Rosemary laughed. "Hey — you're the greatest! Oh, I know that in the media the police are often credited with solving cases you've gotten involved with, but word gets out. Certain people *know.*"

"Which certain people?" Judith inquired.

"Oh . . ." Rosemary feigned innocence. "Let's say veterans who've known you for years. Maybe not in so many words, of course. Longtime cops tend to keep their own counsel." She winked at Judith.

*Woody,* Judith thought. Woodrow Wilson Price had been Joe's partner for years. He was the soul of discretion, but also a man of integrity. If pressed, he might hint at Judith's role in some of the homicide cases. She decided to drop the subject.

"I assume," Judith said, getting back to the point, "that as long as Andrea and her daughter aren't suspects, they'd be allowed to leave."

"True," Rosemary allowed. "But Morgenstern's a stickler, and so's our new chief. This is a high-profile case. Have you seen the news?"

"I haven't had time," Judith admitted. "I would imagine the reports from headquarters are very limited."

Rosemary nodded. "You got it. 'Music Bigwig Dies of Apparent Heart Failure; Police Investigating' — or something like that."

"Yes," Judith said thoughtfully, "that's the way I figured it'd be handled at the outset. Did they . . . ah . . . mention where Mr. Kluger died?"

"It was very vague," Rosemary replied. "I think they said he'd been out for a walk while visiting friends on Heraldsgate Hill."

"That's vague enough." Judith turned as

Morgenstern exited Room Three.

"I've advised Mrs. Kluger to remain in the city for another day or two," the detective announced. "Frankly, she's in no shape to travel."

Judith frowned. "I understood she'd been making arrangements for her husband's memorial service."

Morgenstern shrugged. "She may have been, but not this morning. I gather she's been taking sedatives."

"Yes," Judith said. "Her daughter picked up a prescription last night at the local pharmacy on top of the hill. Would Mrs. Kluger be more comfortable staying at a hotel?"

"Ask Ms. Farrow," Morgenstern said, wiping his nose.

"I will," Judith said, wishing she could free up the B&B for more paying guests. It was the weekend, after all. "By the way — I should mention that Rudi Wittener sneaked into the house yesterday morning."

"What?" Morgenstern stared at Judith over the top of his handkerchief. "Did you say he *sneaked* in? Just like that cat?"

"Yes, just like . . . the cat. The front door was unlocked. It usually is during the day," Judith explained. "I assume you were able to interview Rudi last night after the symphony concert."

Morgenstern nodded and put the handkerchief back in his pocket. "He seemed quite upset, not particularly helpful."

Judith nodded once. "He was able to perform, I gather."

"Yes," Morgenstern said. "Wittener claimed that his mentor had inspired him from above. Or some such nonsense." The detective snapped his fingers at Rosemary. "Come, we should check to see what the robbery unit has found out about that damnable bow."

"Bow?" Judith echoed. "What kind of bow?"

"Violin bow," Morgenstern replied as Rosemary got to her feet. "It belonged to Wittener. He says it's some sort of musical treasure. We'll be in touch." He started down the stairs.

"Wait!" Judith called, following Rosemary, who was behind Morgenstern. "When did this happen?"

"Yesterday," Morgenstern said, without turning around. "Or so Wittener thinks. It might have been the previous night." He had reached the bottom of the stairs. "The man is very imprecise about time. It seems unimportant to him. Musical temperament, I suppose."

Rosemary lingered as her partner went out the front door. "Do you think," she whispered to Judith, "that this missing violin bow could have something to do with the murder?"

"I've no idea," Judith admitted. "It's the first I've heard of it."

"I could use some help," Rosemary murmured, hurrying to catch up with Morgenstern. *"Please."*

Judith watched the unmarked car drive away. It was a damp autumn morning, with dew heavy on the grass and rain clouds hovering over the hill. In the doorway, she took a deep breath, savoring the fresh, earthy air. The cul-de-sac looked so serene, so quiet. It was hard to believe that a man had died a violent death on the very edge of Judith's little world.

But that was reality. As Renie would put it, Judith had a tendency to stick her head in the sand about certain matters. Not, however, when it came to somebody getting away with murder.

Her reverie was interrupted by Suzanne Farrow. "Mrs. Flynn?" the young woman called. "Who sent that bouquet in the dining room?"

"Olive delivered it for Rudi to give to your mother," Judith said, closing the door and looking up at Suzanne on the staircase.

"Oh." Suzanne seemed disappointed. "Has anyone called for me?"

"No," Judith replied as Suzanne slowly reached the lower landing. "Were you expecting someone?"

Suzanne shook her head. "Not exactly."

"I thought," Judith said, "you might be looking for Fritz."

Suzanne carefully stepped down into the entry hall. "Never mind," she said, avoiding Judith's gaze. "I have a request. I'd like to send for Mom's maid. She's also a nurse." The young woman looked again at Judith. "Since Mom and Dolph were going to be traveling, Estelle was given two weeks' vacation. She's visiting relatives in Oregon, so she could be up here in a matter of hours."

*A paying guest,* Judith thought. "Of course. She can stay in Room One, catty-corner from your mother."

Suzanne nodded. "I'll call her right away." The young woman started back up the stairs.

She'd reached the halfway point when the doorbell rang, barely audible over the sound of the vacuum cleaner in the adjoining room. Suzanne turned. "Not the police again, I hope."

The bell rang again before Judith could

respond. "I don't know," she called back to Suzanne.

But the bearded man at the door wasn't anyone Judith recognized. "May I help you?" she said, hoping it wasn't one of the guests who had been turned away.

"No," he shot back, barging past her and looking up at Suzanne. "But she can!" he shouted, pointing a finger up the staircase. "She can tell me who murdered my father!"

Suzanne whirled around so fast that she would have fallen down the stairs if her quick reactions hadn't allowed her to grab the newel post. "Gregory! Why couldn't you stay away?"

Gregory was standing at the bottom of the stairs, flapping his arms like a lame bird trying to take off. To Judith, he actually looked a little like a bird, with his sharp nose, small eyes, long dark hair, and matching beard.

"You know I couldn't! Now talk to me!"

"I've nothing to say to you!" Regaining her balance, Suzanne fled up the stairs.

Gregory followed, but tripped over his long black raincoat. Trudging up behind the fallen man, Judith leaned down. "Are you okay?" she asked.

"No!" He had a rather high, piercing voice. His long, lean fingers clutched at the carpet runner as if he were trying to claw it to shreds. "Leave me alone!"

Judith stood on the second step below him. "If you don't get up, I'll call the police," she said.

Gregory stopped clawing the carpet. Indeed, he didn't move at all for several seconds. "Very well," he finally said.

Judith cautiously backed down the stairs while Gregory struggled to get to his feet. "I can't," he groaned. "My ankle may be broken."

Phyliss had vacuumed her way into the entry hall. Seeing Judith — and the legs of the man on the staircase — she froze. "What now?" she asked, switching off the vacuum. "Is that Mr. Flynn or another corpse?"

"Neither," Judith replied, fit to be tied. "It's a visitor. He hurt his ankle."

"Shall I pray over him?" Phyliss inquired.

"No," Judith replied. "Help me get him sitting up."

"I can help *and* pray," Phyliss responded, folding her hands and casting her eyes up to the ceiling. "Dear Lord of all, hear my prayer; You know I care. Never let my cry rankle; help fix this man's busted ankle. Amen."

"Fine," Judith said, wearily going back up the stairs.

Gregory didn't resist as the two women carefully moved him into an upright position. But he moaned and groaned, apparently in pain.

"Can you put any weight on your ankle?" Judith asked.

Slowly, Gregory flexed his right leg before attempting to touch the nearest step. "Aaargh!" he cried. "No, no! It hurts too much!"

Judith couldn't bear the thought of another emergency vehicle arriving at Hillside Manor. If necessary, she'd drive the injured man to the clinic of his choice.

"Let's get you onto the sofa," she said. "We can help you scoot down the stairs. I'll hold up your leg so you don't damage it further."

Gregory appeared reluctant, but after a long moment's hesitation, he nodded once. Phyliss, who was sinewy by nature and strong for her age, grasped the man by the shoulders. Judith cradled his right leg at the calf. She noticed that he wore slightly rumpled dark slacks, black socks, and black loafers. The socks were thin enough that Judith could see there was indeed a slight swelling of the ankle.

*Bump, bump, bump* went Gregory, one stair at a time. When the trio reached the main floor, Judith suggested that he lean on her and Phyliss. "Hop, if you can," she said. Although he seemed slim, she didn't want his weight on her artificial hip.

Gregory hopped, again resembling a lame bird. Judith guessed him to be in his thirties. There was no gray in his beard or long hair, and his face was virtually unlined. If he was Dolph Kluger's son, he didn't look at all like his late father.

One of the side chairs was closer than the sofa. "Here," Gregory moaned. "I can't go on."

Judith didn't argue. "Fine," she said, helping Phyliss ease the man into the chair. "Let me get a footstool."

While Judith dragged the needlepoint-covered footstool from across the room, Phyliss examined Gregory's ankle. "Not much that I can see, mister," she declared. "As usual, my prayers got answered. The Lord works in mysterious ways, but sometimes He's pretty fast. A turn, a twist, a sprain, maybe. I've tended to many an injury in my day. Our church-choir members are always falling off their risers. Too much enthusiasm in their praises. Sometimes they get carried away — literally."

"It is swollen, though," Judith pointed out as she gingerly propped up the foot. "You should probably stay off of it for a while."

"Brandy," Gregory said. "I should like some brandy. My father always drinks it when he's distraught."

"Strong spirits!" Phyliss exclaimed. "Don't you know that alcohol is Satan's brew?"

Judith didn't need a temperance lesson from the cleaning woman. "Phyliss, would you mind making sure Room One's ready for a guest?"

"What guest?" Phyliss gestured at Gregory. "This one?"

"No," Judith replied. "Mrs. Kluger's maid is supposed to arrive later today. And check Room Two." It was possible that Gregory would have to stay on. Given the apparent animosity between him and Suzanne, it would be better to keep them as far apart as possible.

Looking disgruntled, Phyliss made her exit. Judith excused herself to go into the dining room and fetch brandy from the makeshift bar in the antique washstand.

"You're Gregory Kluger?" she asked, returning with a snifter containing an inch of Courvoisier.

He accepted the drink but avoided the question. "My poor father. Do you know who killed him?"

"I don't," Judith replied, feeling confused.

"Please accept my condolences. I didn't realize that Mr. Kluger had a son."

Gregory raised his eyes to the ceiling. "I'm not surprised."

Judith was searching for a tactful way to elicit more information. "Did you just arrive in town?"

Gregory's dark eyes narrowed over the snifter's brim. "Certainly not. I live here. I've lived in this city for two years."

Judith perched on the nearby sofa arm. "Where do you work?"

"At the University," Gregory replied after taking a small sip of brandy. "I'm in music."

"How interesting," Judith remarked, her friendliest manner in place.

Gregory shrugged.

"May I get you something besides the brandy?" she asked.

Gregory shook his head. "Not now. Later, perhaps. Are you going to call a doctor?"

Judith stared at her uninvited guest. "Do you know any who make house calls?"

"I thought you might," Gregory said. "Running an inn, and all."

"We could use one," Judith murmured. "If you really think," she said in her normal voice, "the ankle may be broken, I can take you to an emergency room. I assume you have medical coverage."

"Yes," Gregory replied after another sip of brandy. "I'd rather not go, though."

"Why not?"

Gregory scowled. "I don't like doctors. Or nurses."

"But if it's broken, it won't mend by itself," Judith argued.

"Yes, it will." Gregory finished the brandy and handed Judith the empty snifter. "I feel better. Do you have any scrambled eggs?"

"All my eggs are unscrambled," Judith replied, growing vexed. "I buy them in the shells."

The irony seemed lost on Gregory. "Oh? Yes, of course."

"I can scramble the eggs," Judith volunteered reluctantly.

Gregory, who had been staring off into space, looked at Judith. "Could you? That would be wonderful."

She rose from the sofa's arm, holding the empty snifter. "Do you want toast? Or bacon?"

"Yes. I haven't eaten this morning. I've been too upset." Gregory managed an ingenuous expression. "You see, I was supposed to meet my father yesterday for lunch. I didn't hear from him, and found out only last night what had happened. I don't pay attention to the news media. It's too dreary."

Judith headed for the kitchen. In the entry hall, she noticed a small leather address book on the floor. Gregory must have dropped it while he was being carted downstairs. In an age of electronic data keeping, she was mildly amused to see that a thirty-something man would keep his information in a handwritten format.

There were gold-embossed initials on the well-worn cover: *GJR.* Maybe the address book didn't belong to Gregory. The initials should end in a *K* for Kluger.

Defying her conscience, Judith tucked the address book into the pocket of her navy slacks. She was getting eggs out of the fridge when Suzanne tiptoed into the kitchen from the back stairs hall.

"Is he gone?" she whispered.

"Gregory? No. He may have sprained his ankle."

"He's a fake!" Suzanne asserted, still whispering. "He's not Dolph's son. He's crazy."

Judith set the egg carton on the counter. "What's his real name?"

"Gregory Radinksy," Suzanne replied, her voice hushed but angry. "He was Dolph's student years ago. He has a mania about Dolph being his father. You must get him out of the house. He could be dangerous."

Having seen the initial *R* on the address book, Judith was inclined to believe Suzanne. "I'll see what I can do," she said. "At the moment, he doesn't seem to be able to walk."

"Call a taxi," Suzanne retorted. "Get rid of him before Mom finds out he's here."

Judith was reluctant to make promises. Gregory Radinsky might be an impostor, he could even be crazy — but he was also a potential source of information.

"I'm going to make him something to eat first," Judith told Suzanne. "I offered, and I'll carry through."

Suzanne looked disgusted. "You're a sucker. He'll con you. That's what he does."

Judith didn't respond. Suzanne stalked back down the hallway.

While the eggs were cooking and the toast was toasting, Judith took the address book out of her pocket and thumbed through the pages. She didn't recognize any of the names — until she got to *M* in the middle. Taryn Moss's address and phone number were listed. Judith kept going. Sure enough, under *W* she found Rudi Wittener's information. Just to make sure, she went back to the *K* section. There were no Klugers.

But there was a connection of some kind

between Gregory and two of the other suspects. Judith intended to find out what it was. Maybe she was crazy, too.

But she wasn't stupid. Nor did she see that the incapacitated man posed any danger.

On the other hand, Judith did have a tendency to stick her head in the sand — and put her life on the line.

# CHAPTER TEN

Gregory was staring into space when Judith brought him his food. "By the way," she said casually, handing over the address book, "you dropped this in your fall."

"Oh — thanks." Gregory put the book in the pocket of his raincoat.

"Does your ankle hurt?" Judith inquired.

"Yes," he replied, poking at the eggs with a fork.

"Would you like some aspirin or Tylenol?"

"No, thank you. I don't use pills. They dull the senses." He tasted a small bite of eggs.

Judith sat down again on the sofa arm. "So tell me about you and your father. I barely got to meet him."

"A genius," Gregory said, eating another tiny bite of egg. "He had the ear. He knew talent. He was amazing. Oh, he could be a martinet, even a slave driver. And he had a temper. Once, he set fire to all my music books."

"But you must have talent, too," Judith said, watching Gregory nibble on the toast.

"Some." Gregory shrugged. "Enough to teach."

"Was it difficult to have your father as a teacher?"

Gregory frowned slightly. "Well . . ." he began just as Phyliss stomped into the living room.

"Your mother's corset stay got stuck in the dryer again," the cleaning woman announced. "I'm trying to fish it out, but until then the laundry's stalled."

"No problem," Judith said. "We won't have as much washing to do today with the empty rooms."

"I'll fix it eventually," Phyliss declared. "The Lord will provide." With a disdainful glance at Gregory, she marched away.

Judith was silent for a few moments, thinking and surreptitiously watching Gregory pick at his food. He acted as if she weren't in the room, eyes fixed on his plate and humming a vaguely recognizable tune. Maybe he *was* crazy. She didn't know what to do with the uninvited visitor. Suzanne's advice might be wise. But Judith preferred to keep Gregory under wraps, at least until the police had interviewed him.

She excused herself and went back into the kitchen, where she called the cell-phone number Morgenstern had given her.

"You say he claims to be Kluger's son?" the detective said, sounding wary.

Judith insisted that was what he'd told her, contrary to Suzanne's denial.

"We're at the opera house," Morgenstern said, "trying to track down Rudi Wittener. He wasn't at home this morning. Supposedly, he's around here somewhere. Keep this Radinsky fellow at your B&B. We'll be there shortly."

Judith's next call was to Renie. "Can you babysit?" she asked.

"What?" Renie was nonplussed. "Are the grandkids in town?"

Judith explained about Gregory. "I can't ask Phyliss to watch him, and Joe's working. Gregory doesn't think he can walk on his ankle, so he shouldn't try to escape. I get the feeling he wants to stick around anyway. But just in case . . ."

"What's your rush?" Renie asked. "Where are you going?"

"To see Olive Oglethorpe. She should be a good source of information."

"Why can't I visit Olive? I haven't had much practice babysitting," Renie said in a

vexed voice. "Our children haven't repro-
duced."

"You can't visit Olive because you don't
fib as well as I do," Judith said. "I have a
ruse to call on her."

"Oh, phooey," said Renie. "Okay, I'll be
over as soon as I can find a rope to tie
Gregory to his chair."

Judith's gratitude was genuine. "Thanks,
coz. I'm at loose ends. I don't have any real
guests, only suspects, and I'm getting
confused rather than making any progress
in trying to figure out if I'm sheltering a
killer. You know — just the usual."

"I know how it is to not have any customers — as in clients," Renie retorted. "It's
like . . . broke. See you."

Gregory was still toying with his meal
when Judith returned to the living room.
"Maybe," she suggested, "you should take a
nap. You seem worn out."

"You'd be worn out, too, if your father
had died suddenly," Gregory responded.

"Mine did, actually," Judith said. "But that
was years ago, and I've recovered." *As much
as you ever can,* she thought. Donald Grover
had died of an enlarged heart when Judith
was a teenager. "If you can manage, you
could hop over to this sofa."

"I'm not done eating," Gregory replied.

212

"You've barely started," Judith noted, her patience strained. "Would you like your plate warmed up?"

"It's fine." Gregory forked a morsel of egg.

Judith left him to his meal and went into the kitchen to find Olive Oglethorpe's address in the phone book. Rudi's assistant was listed under O. G. Oglethorpe. Writing the address on a Post-it note, Judith was about to take a look at the clothes dryer when Renie came through the back door carrying a cattle prod.

"What did you do?" Judith asked her cousin. "Fly over here? And what's with the cattle prod?"

"You know I hate to fly," Renie said, opening one of the cupboards where the pots and pans were kept. "I left as soon as I hung up. Traffic on the avenue isn't bad this time of day." She stuffed her purse into a Dutch oven. "There. Now maybe it'll be safe from your resident thieves. Where's the prisoner?"

"Hold it," Judith said. "I asked about the cattle prod."

Renie looked down at the two-foot-long weapon with the red handle. "It belongs to Bill. He used to take it on his walks."

Judith vaguely recalled when Bill had threatened to buy one after a neighbor had been mugged years ago. "Does he still use it?"

Renie shook her head. "Bingo died."

"Bingo?"

"The yappy Pekingese in the next block that used to drive Bill nuts," Renie said.

"I thought Bill bought it to ward off muggers."

"Well . . . I guess he did, originally," Renie said with a slight frown. "Bingo not only yapped like a demon, but he bit Bill a couple of times. Bill actually likes dogs, but Bingo was a nasty piece of work." She brandished the cattle prod. "It runs on C batteries. I might need it to defend myself against your latest goofball. Want to see how it works?"

"No, I do not," Judith declared. "I doubt you'll need it." She gestured toward the living room. "Gregory's in there. Morgenstern and Company may show up while you're here, but I shouldn't be gone long. Since you're standing by the cupboard, hand me one of those kettles."

Renie opened the cupboard again. "What size?"

"It doesn't matter," Judith said. "It's part of my ruse to see Olive."

Renie removed an orange-and-blue Belgian cookware one-quart kettle. "Take this one. It looks about fifty years old."

"It is," Judith said. "It's Mother's. Thanks."

"Are you going to introduce me?" Renie asked.

"Come on." Judith led the way back into the living room.

Gregory was still pecking away at his food like a newborn bird. "Gregory, this is my cousin, Serena. She's taking over the B&B while I run an errand."

Gregory warily eyed Renie. Renie eyed Gregory warily. "You look like Frederica," he said.

Resting the cattle prod at the end of the vacant sofa, Renie ran a hand through her short chestnut hair. She obviously hadn't had time to tame her thick, out-of-control coiffure that morning. The beat-up blue jeans and the baggy "Property of County Prison" sweatshirt didn't help her appearance, either. "That's funny," Renie remarked. "My husband told me I looked like hell this morning. I assume Frederica is an improvement."

"I doubt it," Gregory murmured.

As Renie sat down in one of the other side chairs, Judith took her leave. The initial encounter between cousin and guest had gotten off to a shaky start, but Judith figured that Renie could handle the peculiar young man. Especially if he couldn't walk very well.

On the other hand, Judith couldn't walk so well herself, especially uphill. She drove to the Empress Apartments, even though it was just a little over a block away as the crow flies. But not being a crow, Judith had to exit the cul-de-sac, reach Heraldsgate Avenue, climb a long block, turn left, and find a parking space near the stately old brick building that faced a viewpoint over the city and the bay.

The four-story building was an historical landmark, with expanses of green lawn and tasteful landscaping. Judith walked a quarter of a block to the entrance, which was set back from the street. The directory on the call box listed O. G. Oglethorpe as occupying apartment 312. Judith pressed the button.

A husky, echoing voice asked who was ringing.

Judith identified herself. "I'd like to return your kettle."

"My kettle?" There was a pause. "I didn't have a kettle. I had a very old family platter. Where is it?"

"That's odd. Someone told me the kettle belonged to you." Judith turned away from

216

the intercom but continued speaking. "The police took your cherished platter."

"Valise? Cherries?" Olive said in a puzzled voice. "I had no valise — and there were no cherries."

Judith moved farther away. "I can always give it to Morgenstern."

"Organ's what? Please speak up."

"I am," Judith mumbled. "I guess I'll try *Rudi*." She all but belted the violinist's name into the intercom.

"Just a moment," Olive said in exasperation. "I'll come down."

Judith stood in the arched doorway admiring the early autumn plantings of mums, asters, and winter pansies. She gazed beyond her immediate surroundings toward the viewpoint park with its striking steel square-and-circle sculpture. The downtown area and the bay were partially obscured by a thin morning fog. Judith glimpsed a super-ferry playing peekaboo through the mist as it sailed into port.

"Mrs. Flynn?" Olive stood with the door half-open. "What about Mr. Wittener?"

"Oh." Judith feigned surprise. "May I step inside the lobby? It's rather damp out here."

"You may not," Olive declared, her stout little body planted like a tree stump. "Again — what about Mr. Wittener?"

217

Judith removed the kettle from the Falstaff's bag in which she'd been carrying it. "Does this belong to him or to Taryn?"

"I wouldn't know," Olive replied. "I've never seen it before." She started to close the door.

Judith put her foot in the way. "I can't ask Mr. Wittener. He's with the police." *Probably,* she thought. *If they could find him at the opera house.*

Olive's round face registered surprise. "He is?"

"Of course." Judith's expression was noncommittal even as she tried to nudge the door open another inch or two. "Surely you've also been questioned."

"Briefly," Olive replied, resisting Judith's efforts with the door. "It struck me as a mere formality."

After one more useless push, Judith shrugged. "I'm sure Rudi must have had a good motive."

Olive stiffened and stared at Judith. "Motive? What are you talking about?"

"To kill Mr. Kluger." She shrugged again. "It's obvious, isn't it? Rudi Wittener is the only person who really knew Dolph Kluger. Who else would poison him?"

Olive's face turned very pink; she was practically snorting through her porcine nostrils. "That's not so! How dare you? What about Kluger's wife and that step-daughter?"

Judith forced a dismissive laugh. "They'd travel three thousand miles to kill a man they lived with? Oh, come, come, Ms. Oglethorpe. That's very far-fetched."

Olive's face grew so red and her eyes glittered so brightly that Judith wondered if she was apoplectic. "Mr. Wittener would never harm anyone, let alone his mentor. I told the police as much!" She rubbed her hands up and down her gray tweed skirt as if she were erasing any sins on Rudi's soul. "You're nothing but a common gossip! Go away!"

Judith shrugged a third time. "Okay. What happened to Mr. Wittener's violin bow, by the way?"

The query caught Olive off guard. "I don't know. It's very disturbing." She stopped rubbing her skirt and wrung her hands instead.

"Yes," Judith remarked casually. "I understand it's very valuable."

"It certainly is." Olive gulped, licked her lips, and held her hands tightly together. "It belonged to Fritz Kreisler. It's a gold-and-tortoise Tourte bow. François Tourte invented the modern bow, and only a few of them are in existence today."

"My," Judith said, "that's quite a treasure."

"Kreisler was Rudi's idol," Olive said, her color starting to return to normal. "I must go now. Good-bye." She wedged herself against the door and gave it a hard shove. Judith had no choice but to move out of the way. She wasn't about to dislocate her artificial hip at the entrance of a landmark building in her own neighborhood.

But, she thought as she made her way back to the sidewalk, the wrong approach had been taken with Olive. Judith was angry for not using a different, more cunning tactic. Maybe she was out of practice.

She was still berating herself when she returned home and came into the living room. Gregory was now seated on the sofa with his foot propped up on a pillow on the coffee table. Renie was kneeling by the hearth tiles, which were covered with a dusting of ashes. The cattle prod rested next to the fireplace tools.

"So," she was saying to Gregory as she traced her finger in the ash, "I see the small dark-haired woman. She has great power over you."

"Yes, yes," Gregory said eagerly. "That's true. Only not so small. Or so dark."

"Yes," Renie said slowly, "I see that now.

She's . . . obscured by . . . a . . . cloud."

Judith stood stock-still by the buffet, baffled by her cousin's behavior.

"A cloud!" Gregory exclaimed after a pause. "Of course! She was a fan of Pink Floyd!"

"She was?" Renie said. "I mean, yes, she was. Definitely. I can tell that now. That was many years ago. Thirty or so."

Judith edged into the room as Gregory clasped his hands over his heart. "It wasn't all classical music with her. She had eclectic tastes, a very catholic ear."

"Right," Renie said, catching Judith out of the corner of her eye. "Oh, dang — the spell's broken."

Smiling briefly at Gregory, Judith walked to the matching sofa that faced the other side of the coffee table. "Well, coz, I see that the two of you are getting along quite well, even if you have made an ash of yourself. Your jeans are filthy."

Renie stood up and brushed at the faded denim. "I was utilizing my psychic gift of reading fireplace ashes," she explained, looking askance. "Gregory is impressed."

"Really." Judith knew that Renie had no psychic gift for ashes or anything else. Her cousin had once had a dream that a long shot named Louie's Hooey would win the feature at the local racetrack that day and insisted that they each place a fifty-dollar bet. Louie's Hooey had broken down in the far turn and had to be carted away in a pickup truck. "But your inspiration has fled?" Judith inquired.

Renie leaned against the mantel, one hand casually retrieving the cattle prod. "Your entrance ruined my focus." She looked very serious.

"Sorry," Judith apologized, before gazing at Gregory. She noticed that his empty plate sat on the coffee table. "How's your ankle?"

Gregory grimaced. "Painful."

Judith pointed to the plate. "Did you enjoy your meal?"

"No," he answered with a quick glance at Renie. "But *she* did."

Renie reached down and whisked the plate off of the coffee table. "Food shouldn't go to waste," she said. "If you want more, ring room service. We're going to the kitchen and clean up."

"But," Gregory said in a whiny voice, "what about my future?"

"It's uncertain," Renie replied, moving away. "I'll have to wait for the muse to descend again."

"You can't abandon me now!" Gregory cried. "What about your magic wand?"

For an instant, Renie looked blank. "Oh. Yes." She examined the cattle prod. "Its batteries are running out. So's my time. Later, okay?"

Gregory sank back on the sofa, pouting.

Judith followed her cousin into the kitchen. "What was that all about?" she whispered.

Renie scraped the plate into the garbage. "My new moneymaking career," she replied. "I'm going to read ashes for profit. I got the idea last night watching Bill try to start one of his commercial fire logs."

"That's the nuttiest idea I ever heard of," Judith declared.

"No, it isn't," Renie retorted. "Remember when we were kids and Grandpa and Grandma Grover used to tell us to look at the sparks on the back of the fireplace bricks and find faces or objects in them?"

"Vaguely."

"It's the same idea," Renie said. "When I set Gregory's plate down on the coffee table, I knocked some magazines on the hearth. A bunch of ashes flew out of the grate. I decided to see if I could actually pull it off. Besides," she added slyly, "it was a way of getting some information out of your latest goofy guest."

Judith grabbed Renie's arm. "Like what?"

"Ohhh . . ." Renie cocked her head and gazed around the kitchen's high ceiling. "Things. Stuff. Inheritance."

"Inheritance?" Judith hissed. "As in, who gets Dolph's money?"

"Mm-mmm." Renie fluttered her eyelashes at the ceiling.

Judith shook her cousin. "Talk to me. What did Gregory tell you?"

"It'll cost you," Renie said softly. "I don't study ashes for free."

Judith jerked at her cousin's arm. "Coz . . ."

Abruptly, Renie pulled free. "Watch it! You want to dislocate my good shoulder?"

Judith was contrite. "Sorry. Neither of us needs more surgery."

"You got that right," Renie responded. The hip and shoulder operations they had endured on the same day a few years earlier were never far from their minds. "Gregory insists he's Dolph's son. I'll admit he's a little fuzzy around the edges. There's a woman involved, but I'm not sure who she is except that her name may be Frederica."

"The Pink Floyd fan?"

"I guess." Renie went to the cupboard, got out a mug, and poured herself some coffee. "Gregory mentioned something about inheriting."

"As in money?"

Renie frowned. "Good point. As I said, the guy's ambiguous. It's like talking to cotton candy. No substance."

Judith nodded. "I don't know what to do with Gregory. The police are supposed to come by and interrogate him."

The doorbell chimed the instant Judith finished speaking. "Maybe that's the cops now."

The cousins both looked at each other and laughed.

"A common occurrence for us," Renie noted. "I'll stay out here. I don't want to become known as Rhubarb Renie, the Pitiless Poisoner."

Judith went to the door. A fair-haired middle-aged woman she'd never seen before stood on the porch with a suitcase on wheels. "Is this Hillside Manor?" she asked.

Judith saw a tan car parked at the curb. "Yes. I'm the owner, Judith Flynn. You are . . . ?"

"Estelle Pearson, Mrs. Kluger's maid."

Judith smiled as she stepped aside to let the woman pass. "I heard you were coming. You got here sooner than I expected."

"I was already on the road when I called Miss Suzanne," Estelle replied, wheeling her suitcase into the entry hall.

Judith couldn't quite figure out the woman's age. She had one of those bland, unlined faces that could have put her anywhere between forty and sixty. The fair hair was frizzy, held in place with a blue barrette. Estelle wasn't quite as tall as Judith, but her figure was more buxom. She looked extremely capable.

"Where is she?" Estelle asked.

"Both Mrs. Kluger and Ms. Farrow are upstairs," Judith said. "If you'll sign the guest registry first, I'll show you the way. A room has been prepared for you."

"Excellent." Estelle accepted a pen from Judith and inscribed her name in the guest registry, along with the same New York City address the Klugers had given.

"You must have known Mr. Kluger quite well," Judith remarked while Estelle was writing.

"Certainly." The maid scrutinized what she had written in small but precise letters. "I've been with Mrs. Kluger for almost twenty years."

"Then you must feel Mr. Kluger's loss keenly," Judith remarked.

Estelle bent down to grasp the handle of her suitcase. "The music world mourns him," she said without inflection. "Shall we go upstairs?"

"His son is here," Judith said. "Would you like to say hello?"

The maid gazed at Judith with cool blue eyes. "I beg your pardon?"

"Gregory," Judith said. "Mr. Kluger's son."

"Nonsense," Estelle retorted. "Please. I must see Mrs. Kluger."

"Fine." Judith led the way to Room Three. "Your room is just across the hall," she explained, pointing to Room One. "Ms. Farrow is in Room Four, next to her mother."

Estelle deposited her suitcase in the hallway before knocking on her mistress's door. "Madam," she called, "it's me, Estelle."

Suzanne opened the door to Andrea's room. "You're prompt," she said. "Come in."

Judith watched Estelle enter. Without so much as a glance at Judith, Suzanne shut the door.

"I'm getting paranoid," Judith said to Renie when she returned to the kitchen. "I could call this an open-and-shut case. Every time somebody opens a door, they shut it in my face."

"That's not like your usual luck with suspects," Renie noted, eyeing the cookie jar with longing.

"Go ahead," Judith urged. "I haven't baked all week. If there are any gingersnaps left, they're probably stale."

"I'll pass," Renie said. "I'm meeting Melissa Bargroom for lunch, remember?"

"You already ate Gregory's breakfast," Judith pointed out. "Your appetite never ceases to amaze me."

"Nor me," Renie agreed, checking the schoolhouse clock. "In fact, I should make my eggs-it — excuse the pun. It's after eleven, and I have to change clothes so that I don't look like Frederica — or hell."

"Estelle the Maid acts as if she knows nothing about Gregory," Judith said as Renie retrieved her purse from the cupboard.

Phyliss came through the hall from the basement stairs. "Aaargh!" she cried, spotting Renie. "Lucifer's companion!"

"Hi, Phyliss," Renie said, purse in hand. "Saved any souls today?"

Phyliss assumed a prim expression. "I cured that freak in the living room. His ankle isn't broken, just sprained."

"Good for you," Renie said. "How are you with male hair loss? Bill's getting kind of bald."

"Don't mock me," Phyliss warned. "You blaspheme."

"Frequently," Renie retorted. "See you." She left.

Phyliss made some sort of sign with her fingers. "To ward off the Evil Eye," she murmured. "Your pagan cousin makes my undies crawl."

"She's not a pagan," Judith asserted. "She's a Catholic, like me."

"Same thing," Phyliss said with a sniff. "All those idols. Statues with crowns. Priests with big funny-shaped hats. I saw one the other day on TV carrying a gold stick. What do they do with those things? Beat up on Protestants?"

"That was probably a crosier," Judith explained. "Bishops have them to symbolize their office as pastoral shepherds."

"Hunh. Lambs to the slaughter, if you ask me. I fixed the dryer. How's that for an answer to a prayer?"

"That's the kind of prayer I understand," Judith murmured.

"By the way," Phyliss said with a warning voice, "you'd better get that husband of yours to repair the basement window by the driveway. The rains are coming, and it won't shut."

Judith stared at Phyliss. "What window?" There were three small windows above the washer and dryer. Judith hadn't opened any of them since the first heavy rain fell just after the Labor Day weekend.

"The one on the right as you face the washer," Phyliss replied.

"I'll do that right now," Judith said. "But stay on this floor. The police may be arriving any moment. And check on Gregory. Make sure he's still sitting on the sofa."

"Don't trust him, huh?"

"I'm beginning not to trust anybody connected with this Kluger clan," Judith said grimly.

Unlike the back stairs and the main staircase, the basement steps weren't carpeted. Judith used them as seldom as possible, always fearing a fall, which could dislocate her hip. Indeed, her last trip to the basement had taken place when she'd closed the windows almost three weeks earlier. She would have asked Joe to do it for her, but it had also been time to get out her autumn decorations, including the gold, red, and brown wreath she hung on the front door. Judith knew that her husband would never be able to find what she wanted and might bring her a leprechaun or a St. Valentine's Day cupid. Men, even professional detectives, weren't very good at finding everyday objects — like their shoes, even though they could be wearing them at the time.

The windows facing the back and front yards were shut tight. So were the two that looked out toward the Rankerses' hedge. But next to the driveway, the window on the right was open. Like the others, it was a simple affair locked by a latch that slid into place. The only problem was that although Judith was tall, it was still a stretch to reach. She stood on tiptoe, straining to get at the latch. As she peered more closely, she noticed that the casement looked marred. There were a few splinters on the sill. It appeared as if someone had forced the window open, damaging the wood.

Judith managed to put the latch back in place, but was chary of touching anything else. Had someone tried to break into the basement? It was possible. The screen was easily removed from the outside. There was just enough space for a reasonably slim person to squeeze through the opening.

But why? When?

And who?

# CHAPTER ELEVEN

Judith realized she could be wrong. If she hadn't quite managed to latch the window securely in the first place, the wind might have blown it open. Sweetums could have done it.

But those splinters indicated human effort. She studied the basement with the eye of an inventory taker. The only value of the stored items was sentimental, especially the Christmas decorations that included a few surviving ornaments from Grandpa and Grandma Grover's tree. There were Joe's tools, of course, but he owned nothing expensive. The fishing tackle appeared untouched. So did the boxes that Mike had left behind, promising to move them out when he had more room. Judith knew that meant the boxes and cartons would grow roots before they ever left the basement.

The cartons that held old clothes were still there, along with the stack of empty gift boxes, the ironing board, the outmoded phonograph, and various other discards that Judith had never had the heart to toss out or give away. Nothing looked different or seemed to be missing.

Yet Judith was uneasy as she went back upstairs. Could someone have broken into the house the night of Dolph's murder? Could that same someone have come into the kitchen and taken Renie's credit cards? It didn't make much sense.

Judith was still mulling when she heard Phyliss admit Rosemary O'Grady.

"Where's your partner?" Judith asked as she met Rosemary in the entry hall.

"He had a doctor's appointment at eleven-thirty," Rosemary replied. "His allergies are really terrible. His doctor has a new kind of medication he wants Levi to try."

"I hope it works," Judith said. "Come into the living room and meet Gregory."

Rosemary held back. "Kluger's son?" she whispered.

"Allegedly," Judith said.

Gregory was still on the sofa, thumbing through one of the magazines Judith put on the coffee table for the guests' perusal. He didn't look up when the two women entered the room.

"Pears," he said, staring at a photo of fruit

in a copy of *Gourmet* magazine. "I'd like a pear. Separation foods — that's the secret."

Judith ignored the remark. "Gregory, this is Rosemary O'Grady. She's a police detective, assigned to the investigation of Mr. Kluger's death. She'd like to ask you some questions."

"We both would," Rosemary said in her perky voice. "Won't you join me, Mrs. Flynn?"

"Ah . . ." Judith saw that Gregory was vehemently shaking his head.

"I've already answered her questions," Gregory said, finally looking up. "I've nothing more to say." He leaned forward as Rosemary sat down on the opposite sofa. The magazine slid off his lap and onto the floor.

Rosemary's expression was apologetic when she spoke to Judith. "I'm afraid you'll have to leave the room, Mrs. Flynn." The detective turned just enough so that Gregory couldn't see her wink.

"Of course," Judith agreed.

She went as far as the entry hall, plastering herself against the wall that concealed the pocket doors Judith rarely used.

"May I see some ID, please?" Rosemary requested.

"I lost it." The statement was flat, as if it

had come from a robot.

"You have no ID?" Rosemary said, slightly incredulous.

"None."

"When did you lose it?"

"Yesterday. Or the day before. Maybe earlier."

"Do you drive a car?"

"No."

"Do you have a driver's license?"

"No."

The chipper note in Rosemary's voice was fading. "Do you have a Social Security number?"

"Yes."

"What is it?"

"I don't remember. I'm not good at numbers."

"What's your name?"

"Gregory . . . Kluger."

"What's your address?"

Gregory rattled off the name and number of an apartment house near the University.

"How did you get to Hillside Manor?"

"I took a bus. The bus stops a block and a half away, on Heraldsgate Avenue."

"Do you work?"

"Yes."

"Where?"

"At the University." Gregory's voice was

showing signs of impatience. "I'm in music."

Judith heard Rosemary sigh. "Why did you come here?"

"To find out what happened to my father, Dolph Kluger. Isn't that why you're here, too?"

"Yes." Rosemary cleared her throat. "My partner and I are assigned to the case. When did you last see your . . . Mr. Kluger?"

There was a pause, apparently while Gregory calculated. "About a year ago. He had a layover on his way to Hong Kong."

"When did you last speak to him?"

"Ah . . . what's today? Friday? It must have been Monday. Or . . . Sunday. He called to tell me his plans. That's when we arranged to have lunch."

Judith shifted her weight, trying to take the strain off of her artificial hip. She thought Gregory was speaking more freely, even exhibiting some animation.

"How did . . . your father sound?" the detective asked.

"Sound? You mean . . . his manner?"

"Yes."

"Like he always does. Jovial. Enthusiastic. Eager to see and hear his protégés."

There was another pause. When Rosemary finally spoke, her tone was faintly harsh. "He had no enemies?"

236

"Enemies?" Gregory sounded shocked. "Of course not. Naturally there are rivalries and jealousies in the music world. But enemies? No."

"The fact remains," Rosemary said, "someone wanted to kill him. I'm sure you want to learn who did it. If you don't know of any professional enemies, what about his personal life?"

"What about it?"

"Is Andrea Kluger your mother?"

"Andrea?" Gregory's reaction struck Judith as incredulous. "Of course not."

"Then who is your mother?"

"She's dead. She died long ago." Gregory's voice had a catch in it. "Please. I don't wish to talk about it. Go away now. I'm tired and in pain. I want a pear."

Footsteps on the stairs caught Judith's attention. She saw two sturdy legs and sensible shoes beneath a gray woolen skirt. Estelle Pearson was descending in a purposeful manner.

"Madam would like some vanilla pudding," the maid announced upon reaching the main floor. "Tea to accompany it. Irish Breakfast is her favorite."

"I only have English Breakfast tea," Judith said. "I think I have some pudding, though."

"Only English? That won't do." Estelle

looked at Judith as if she might not be quite civilized.

"There's a Trader Tim's four blocks from here," Judith said. "They carry a variety of teas."

"But you don't?"

Judith's response was cut short by Rosemary's appearance in the entry hall. "He's being difficult," she said with a grim expression.

"No kidding," Judith murmured.

Estelle glanced curiously at both Judith and Rosemary. "Who's difficult?"

Rosemary hesitated.

Judith didn't. "Dolph's son, Gregory. He's in the living room."

Estelle rocked slightly on her heels and blinked several times. "Dolph's *son?*" she finally said. "Ridiculous!" She folded her arms across her sizable bust. "Give me the directions to this Trader Tim's. I'll go get the tea. And the pudding. I know what she likes."

Rosemary intervened. "Excuse me. Who are you?"

The maid identified herself. "I arrived only a short while ago," she added. "I know nothing about what's happened except what Madam and her daughter have told me." She turned to Judith. "Where is this shop?"

Judith picked up a neighborhood map she kept by the guest registry. "We're here. Go to Heraldsgate Avenue and up the hill until you reach —"

"Pears," called a pitiful voice from the living room. "Pears, please."

Judith quickly finished the brief directions. "And would you mind getting some fresh pears? I'll give you the money."

"Of course you will," Estelle said.

Going into the kitchen to get her wallet, Judith shook her head and muttered to herself. "Difficult is right. They're all difficult. Or crazy. Now they've got me talking to myself."

When she returned to the entry hall a few moments later, Rosemary apparently had been quizzing a taciturn Estelle.

"I told you," the maid insisted, "I know nothing." Ungraciously, she accepted a twenty-dollar bill from Judith and left the house without another word.

Rosemary seemed irritated. "I'm beginning to think I don't have your knack for interviewing people. I couldn't even get this Estelle person to take a look at Gregory."

Judith sighed. "I'm not doing much better. I swear, just about everybody connected to this investigation is impossible to deal with. They're beyond snooty. They're ut-

239

terly self-absorbed. They're —" She stopped, and frowned. "They're afraid."

Rosemary's eyes widened. "Are you serious?"

"Yes." Judith had been backpedaling slowly into the dining room, out of earshot from Gregory or anyone else that might come into the entry hall. "From the start, they've all been . . . well, on the defensive. It's hard to describe, but I've dealt with enough different personalities to understand why people behave the way they do." She made a face. "I don't mean to sound pompous."

"No, no," Rosemary said vehemently. "You're not. I admire your people skills. Don't quit now."

Judith shrugged. "The only person involved who didn't act uptight or edgy is Dolph. Oh — and Fritz Wittener seemed normal, at least for a young man his age."

"We interviewed Fritz, as well as his mother, Elsa," Rosemary said. "She was very closemouthed, but he was okay, except for the usual reticence of his peer group." She smiled diffidently. "I should know. I'm not much older than Fritz. Guys don't talk much about feelings."

"They still don't when they get older," Judith noted. "By the way, this may sound crazy, but I have to tell you about our basement window. Let's go downstairs."

Rosemary carefully studied the marred windowsill. "You have no idea how long the window had been open?" she asked.

"No. If it wasn't latched properly — and I'll admit, it's hard for me to reach — the wind or the cat or even the house settling could have jarred it open. You know how it is around here — buildings — not just old ones — occasionally shift because of all the earthquakes."

"I can check for prints," Rosemary said. "Did you look outside?"

"I haven't had a chance," Judith admitted.

The two women went back up the stairs and outside. There was a strip of grass and a narrow flower bed between the driveway and the house. Most of Judith's rosebushes were planted in that area, along with some ground cover and several wallflowers that had sprung up from seed. The topsoil was damp from the occasional drizzle during the past week. Judith couldn't see any footprints, however.

"My husband's been doing yard cleanup," she said, "but he hasn't pruned the roses." She pointed to a deep red Abraham Lincoln bush that was still blooming. "It's too soon. We shouldn't have frost until November."

Rosemary was studying the distance between the window and the grass. "This flower bed's about three feet across, maybe a little more. A full-grown adult could lie on the ground between the grass and the house without leaving footprints. Once he — or she — had forced the latch, the person could scoot between the rosebushes. In fact, it'd be safer that way under any conditions. They'd avoid the thorns."

"True," Judith allowed, scanning the dirt for any sort of clue. "In a book or on TV, something would be left behind. A button, a thread, a hair — some item the crime lab could use. Unfortunately, I don't see anything suspicious."

Rosemary murmured agreement.

Judith paced along the driveway. "Nothing appears to have been stolen or even disturbed. Except, of course, my cousin's credit cards."

Rosemary nodded as they headed back inside. "It's too bad the store clerk couldn't identify the person who used Mrs. Jones's debit card. There's been no report of anyone attempting to use the other credit cards," she added, following Judith up the porch steps.

Judith opened the screen door. "My cousin told me they were maxed out."

"That doesn't mean someone didn't try to charge on them," Rosemary said. "The problem is, we wouldn't know unless the merchant became suspicious."

"Or knew Renie personally," Judith murmured as they entered the kitchen. "What's your next move?"

Rosemary glanced at her watch. "I'm supposed to meet Levi at Moonbeam's around one. I'd like to have him talk to Gregory. Maybe he'll have better luck."

"Dubious," Judith remarked. "So I'm in charge of this lame duck?"

"You can handle him," Rosemary said, heading out of the kitchen. "Let's hope Levi got some new allergy medicine. He's totally miserable."

Accompanying Rosemary to the front door, Judith heard voices in the living room.

"You got no spunk," Gertrude was saying. "What's this crazy diet you're on? I've never dieted in my life and look at me."

"I am looking at you," Gregory replied. "You're very old and very crippled."

"Up yours, young fella," Gertrude snapped. "Forget the crippled part. I'm getting around better right now than you are. And how do you think I got to be this old? By eating a bunch of sludge?"

"It's not sludge," Gregory said heatedly.

"You don't understand how Trennkost works."

"Bunk," said Gertrude.

Rosemary was looking at Judith in a curious manner. "Who is that?" she whispered.

"My mother. It's past her lunchtime. She must have come in the house looking for me. She can drive her motorized wheelchair up the back-porch ramp. We couldn't see her from the side of the house."

"Very convenient for your mother," Rosemary said in an indifferent tone. "I'm going now."

"Okay," Judith said, sensing a change in Rosemary's attitude, but unsure of the reason. "You don't need to hear Mother arguing with my latest intrusion."

Gertrude had positioned her wheelchair between the sofa and the coffee table. She turned her head when she heard Judith come in.

"Well, dopey," the old lady said to her daughter, "are you trying to starve me? Do you know what time it is, or have you forgotten where the big hand goes and the little one follows?"

"Actually," Gregory put in, "it's the other way . . ."

Gertrude waved him into silence. "Shut your yap. I'm talking to my idiot child here.

I don't need another nitwit barging in. What do you think this is? A Dumbbell Convention?"

Judith interrupted. "I'll fix your lunch right now, Mother. Tuna?"

"Put some pickle relish in it," Gertrude ordered. "And don't spare the mayonnaise. Butter, white bread, lettuce . . ."

"I know, Mother," Judith said grimly. "I've been making your tuna sandwiches for almost fifteen years."

"No wonder they taste so stale," Gertrude rasped. "You're still feeding me those old ones. Don't forget the chips and dill pickle. Get going." The old lady turned back to Gregory. "So what's this bo-diddly thing all about? I know what a diddly bow is — my papa had a guitar he made out of a cigar box."

Judith stopped before she got to the entry hall.

"I didn't say diddly," Gregory asserted.

"You sure didn't," Gertrude snapped. "You don't say much. You're kind of screwy, aren't you?"

Moving back into the living room, Judith gazed at her mother. "I never knew Grandpa Hoffman was musical. Did he have talent?"

"Couldn't play for sour owl sweat," Gertrude declared. "Tin ear. He played the paper comb, too, until he swallowed the paper and darned near choked to death."

Gregory had turned pale. "Good Lord!"

"Which reminds me," Gertrude said to her daughter, "I need a Bozo horn."

"For what?" Judith asked, surprised at the request.

Gertrude tapped the side of her wheelchair. "To put on Cora here," she said, using the nickname she'd given her apparatus. "How else can I get your attention? By Western Union? Besides," she went on with a fiendish grin at Gregory, "maybe I could play a few tunes on it, like Beethover."

"Beethoven!" Gregory cried. "My God!" He put his hands over his face.

Gertrude chuckled. "Kind of dingy, isn't he? Wasn't there a singer way back called Bo Diddley?"

"Yes, Mother," Judith said. "He was a rock-and-roll pioneer." She leaned over the back of the sofa. "What kind of bow *are* you talking about?"

The young man, who was still visibly upset, turned his head slightly. "My inheritance," he said in a low voice. "The Tourte bow that was stolen from me by . . . someone."

"Would that 'someone' be Rudi Wittener?" Judith asked.

Whatever color was left in Gregory's face completely drained away. He began to tremble. "You know?" he whispered.

"Um . . . yes," Judith said, wondering whether or not she did. "You were to inherit this bow from your father?"

He nodded. "My father knew Fritz Kreisler, who gave him that bow. It's become a family heirloom."

Gertrude rammed the sofa with her wheelchair. "My lunch is becoming a family heirloom. *I'm* a family heirloom. Get hopping, kiddo."

Judith smiled at Gregory. "I'd like to hear more about this fascinating bow," she said. "I'll be back after I've taken care of Mother."

"That sounds like a threat," Gertrude said, propelling herself after Judith. " 'Course, around here, anything could happen."

Judith had just finished taking Gertrude and her lunch tray out to the toolshed when the phone rang. It was Renie.

"Lunch was great," she announced, "if short. Melissa had to get back for a phone interview with a tenor who's coming here to sing the role of Cavaradossi in *Tosca*. She ordered the Caesar with prawns. I had the salmon. And chowder. With their delicious

247

fries. Oh, I started with the crab wonton —
to die for. Yum."

"What about Dolph Kluger?" Judith
asked, impatient with Renie's plundering of
Benji's menu.

There was a pause. Judith wondered if Renie was still picking luncheon remains out
of her teeth.

"Believe it or not," Renie finally said, "he
was quite a womanizer — at least until he
married Andrea. So it's possible that Gregory really is Dolph's son. Melissa told me
she'd never heard of Gregory, but she'd
check him out through the University's
music department."

"That's it?"

"Except for dessert," Renie said. "We
skipped it."

"Bravo," Judith responded sarcastically.
"It's a good thing you don't have much of a
sweet tooth. By the way, when you talk to
Melissa again, ask her how much a rare
Tourte violin bow owned by Fritz Kreisler
would be worth. According to Gregory,
Dolph had one and gave it to Rudi — or
Rudi stole it, and now it's missing. But
Gregory was supposed to — and I quote —
'inherit' it."

"Really?" Renie sounded surprised.
"Oddly enough, we got off on that same

subject. Melissa knows a local big-time collector of musical instruments. Fascinating man. Anyway, she mentioned something about a Tourte bow and said it's a three-hundred-and-fifty-grand item."

"Wow!" Judith exclaimed. "That sounds incredible for just a bow! What's a violin like a Stradivarius worth?"

"Plenty. But we didn't get into specifics about violins. That's when we had to decide about dessert."

"That type of bow's certainly worth stealing," Judith said. "I doubt that Rudi would've stolen it from Dolph, though. It's more likely that Dolph gave it to him. Or sold it."

"Symphony violinists make good money," Renie pointed out, "but not the kind that would put them in a six-figure category for collecting."

"But now somebody's stolen the bow from Rudi," Judith reminded her cousin.

"Right. How do you fence a bow?"

"The same way you fence artwork?" Judith suggested. "Secretly, to wealthy collectors?"

"Yes, that makes sense. Hey — got to go, coz," Renie said. "I've got a call on the other line. I think it's Saks dunning me again. I'm going to tell them I'm legally dead." She rang off.

Judith was thoughtful as she placed the receiver on the kitchen counter. If a violin bow was worth stealing, was it also worth killing for? She'd been involved in homicide cases where people had died for less.

Anger suddenly overcame Judith. Money, love, greed, lust, revenge — nothing was worth killing for as far as she was concerned. As she stood in the kitchen with its homely smells of tuna fish and coffee, there was a killer on the loose, perhaps under her own roof. It wouldn't be the first time.

She ought to be used to it, Judith told herself and tried to relax.

That was when all hell broke out in the living room.

# CHAPTER TWELVE

Suzanne was screaming at Gregory. Gregory was screaming right back at her.

"Impostor! Stalker! Lunatic!" Suzanne shouted.

"Liar! Cheat! Leech!" Gregory countered.

Suzanne was looming over Gregory's seated figure. "You're a miserable, pathetic phony!"

"You're a spoiled, good-for-nothing bitch!" he shot back. "You're not even related to my father!"

"Neither are you!!" Suzanne saw Judith out of the corner of her eye. "Oh!" She straightened up and joined Judith in the entry hall. "Sorry." She hugged herself, perhaps, Judith thought, to keep from doing Gregory bodily harm. "Mrs. Flynn, my mother is terribly upset that you've allowed this . . . *person* to enter your establishment. She can't have him under the same roof. *Can't*, not *won't*."

Judith wasn't pleased with Gregory's presence, either, but she'd be damned if Andrea Kluger dictated her standards of hospitality. "Then," she said with a lift of her chin, "your mother should move to a hotel."

"That's impossible!" Suzanne cried. "She's in no condition to move! How dare you! I'll call my . . ."

The young woman's irate words were drowned out by the arrival of Phyliss with the polisher she used on the entry hall's inlaid wood floor.

Judith winced. Phyliss was also singing at the top of her lungs. "Soon and very soon, we are going to meet the King . . ."

"Please!" Suzanne screamed. "Make her stop!"

Pretending she couldn't hear, Judith cupped her ear. "Excuse me?"

"The noise!" Suzanne shouted, pointing to Phyliss, who looked quite manic. "It's deafening me!"

"I can't stop her," Judith shouted back. Under the circumstances, it was impossible to explain Phyliss's relationship with the floor polisher. The cleaning woman referred to it as "Moses" and took fiendish delight in driving all manner of creatures — including Sweetums — out of her path.

Indeed, she had stopped singing and was

shouting that she was parting the Red Sea. "Make way for Moses!" she bellowed, heading straight for Suzanne. "Move it, Moabites! The Pharaoh's in pursuit!"

"Run!" Judith cried, hurrying onto the front porch. Suzanne had no choice but to follow. "That's better," Judith declared, closing the door behind her. But before she could say anything further, she saw a disheveled man standing on the sidewalk. Strands of longish brown hair straggled down his forehead, there was a scratch on one cheek, and he held a hand over his right eye.

"Mr. Wittener?" Judith said in an uncertain voice.

"I've been attacked," he said, sounding hoarse. "Look at my hand!"

He held out the hand that wasn't concealing his eye. There were several scratches on the back, superficial, but bleeding slightly.

"Who did this?" Judith asked as he came up the porch steps.

"Rudi!" Suzanne rushed to his side. "You're a mess! Why, your clothes are torn, too!"

Judith noticed that Rudi's slacks had a slight rent near the left cuff and his striped cotton shirt had a couple of small holes near the breast pocket.

The sound of the floor polisher no longer

253

reverberated from inside the house. Phyliss must have finished the small entry-hall area.

"Come in, sit down," Judith urged Rudi. "In the parlor." With no idea how they might react to each other, she decided to keep Rudi and Gregory separated. Nor did she want to turn her living room into a hospital ward.

Phyliss had unplugged the floor polisher and was eyeing Rudi warily. "I can pray over him, too," she offered.

"Later," Judith responded. "Get some antibiotic Band-Aids, cotton, and alcohol from the first-aid kit next to the sink."

"I could baptize him in the sink," Phyliss said. "Just in case."

"Phyliss . . ." Judith shot the cleaning woman a threatening look.

Rudi allowed himself to be led into the parlor. Suzanne solicitously settled him into the cushioned window seat.

"Who did this to you?" she asked, examining his wounds.

Rudi removed his hand from his face. There was a superficial scratch just under the lower lid, but otherwise his eye appeared undamaged.

"It wasn't a who," Rudi said. "It was a what. A big, white-and-yellow *what*." He stared malevolently at Judith.

She didn't react. "How did it happen?" she inquired innocently.

"I was . . ." Rudi rubbed at his forehead. "I was looking for something outside. This animal ambushed me from the bushes."

Phyliss returned with the first-aid kit. "You're kind of snoopy, aren't you?" she said. "What was it you were looking for the other day? Some bangle?"

"Ah . . ." Rudi frowned. "Yes, a bracelet. That's what I was trying to find just now."

"In our yard?" Judith asked.

"Yes." Rudi eyed Phyliss warily. "Is she going to tend to me?"

"I will," Judith volunteered, taking the kit from the cleaning woman.

Suzanne snatched the kit from Judith's hands. "I'll do it." She glared at her hostess. "I've known Rudi for years. He trusts me." She gazed into the violinist's blue eyes. "Don't you, Rudi?"

"Of course. How could I not?" His expression had warmed.

Suzanne examined the wrapping on the Band-Aid. "Antibiotic?" she said to Rudi. "I don't think that's necessary. Warm soap and water will do better. Let me get some from the bathroom. There's one just off the entry hall." She sprinted out of the parlor.

"Suzanne prefers natural products," Rudi noted.

"Naturally," Judith said with a touch of sarcasm.

Rudi didn't respond. He was examining the minor scratches on his right hand. "My God," he gasped, "how can I play tonight?"

"You have a concert?" Judith asked as Phyliss, grumbling all the while, stomped out of the room.

"Yes, yes — very difficult," he said. "It's a sonata for three violins by Giovanni Battista Buonamente. I am — as you may know — the assistant concertmaster."

Judith tried to look impressed. "That must be very demanding."

"It is," Rudi replied, carefully placing his left hand over the injured right. "I not only must play the violin, but act as the representative between the conductor and the other players. It's a delicate balance."

"You came here from Philadelphia, didn't you?"

Rudi nodded. "The Philadelphia Orchestra is so world-renowned that I wanted to go someplace where I could be noticed."

He spoke without arrogance. "This city has a fine symphony, but not the long-established reputation. It suits me."

Suzanne returned with a damp washcloth

and questioning look at Judith. "What kind of soap is this?"

"Oatmeal, the same as upstairs," Judith replied.

"Herbal would be better," Suzanne asserted.

Judith was about to quibble, but she heard the front door open. "Excuse me. I'll leave you to your ministrations."

Estelle Pearson had come into the entry hall carrying a Trader Tim's shopping bag. "I have your pears," she said. "There was no change from your twenty-dollar bill. In fact, you owe me forty-six cents."

"I'll deduct it from your bill," Judith said.

Estelle gave Judith a disparaging look. "That would be Mrs. Kluger's bill. She covers all my expenses. I doubt that she'll be paying you for this tragic visit. She's not only lost her husband, but she's on the verge of losing her mind."

Judith felt like paraphrasing Oscar Wilde by noting that if Andrea had lost not one but two husbands, she must be very careless. Instead, she spoke calmly: "I'm very sorry. In fact, I feel remiss that I've seen so little of Mrs. Kluger since the tragedy. Might she not feel better if she came downstairs or went out in the garden? The weather is quite mild and the fresh air would do her good."

Estelle dismissed the suggestion with an abrupt gesture. "She's certainly not going to leave her room while this Gregory person is in the house. Besides, I'm here now. I know how to care for Mrs. Kluger."

It occurred to Judith that perhaps she should change her approach in dealing with this self-important crew. Egos were rampant, trumping good manners at every turn. After all, Judith reasoned, her compassionate nature was a strong factor in dealing with people. Maybe she should try harder to make allies, not enemies. She certainly wasn't getting anywhere thus far.

"Let me help you make the tea," Judith offered. "I have a special English teapot I use." *When I don't put a mug of hot water in the microwave and toss in a tea bag,* she thought.

"Very well," agreed the maid. "I'll need a bowl and spoon for the pudding."

"Of course." Judith led the way through the dining room. With luck she could find the tea cozy Aunt Ellen had made out of Uncle Win's old long johns and given to Judith as a Christmas present some years earlier. The teapot was Royal Doulton's Sherborne pattern with pink and purple flowers. Judith had bought it on her honeymoon in Canada with Dan McMonigle. She found the tea cozy at the bottom of the linen drawer. It was made of red-and-white fabric, the colors of the long underwear that Aunt Ellen's husband had worn during cold Nebraska winters. Fortunately, Uncle Win had converted from wool to thermal fabric a couple of decades ago.

"Please don't think me callous," Judith said while they waited for the teakettle to whistle, "but I can't turn away someone who's injured himself under my roof. I've tried to get Gregory to go to an emergency room, but he won't. I'll do my best to see that he doesn't pester Mrs. Kluger — or Suzanne."

Estelle had sat down at the kitchen table. "He's quite mad, you know."

"He must have some sort of mania about Mr. Kluger," Judith remarked.

"He does indeed."

"How did Gregory know Mr. Kluger?" Judith asked, getting out English bone-china teacups and saucers from the cupboard.

"I believe he may have been a student," Estelle replied. "Briefly. That was before Mrs. Kluger married Mr. Kluger."

"That was ten years ago, wasn't it?" Judith said.

Estelle nodded. "They celebrated their

tenth anniversary in August."

"So," Judith mused aloud, "from what Suzanne told me, Mrs. Kluger was a widow for almost another ten years."

"Seven," Estelle replied. "I joined her while she was married to Mr. Farrow."

"So sad," Judith remarked. "I've been widowed, too. My first husband was only forty-nine." She forced herself to sound wistful. "I was at work when Dan passed away. Was Mrs. Kluger with Mr. Farrow when he died?"

Estelle gave Judith a sharp glance. "You mean at the foxhunt?"

"Yes. That's where it happened, wasn't it?"

The maid nodded once. "Yes. Mrs. Farrow — I mean, Mrs. Kluger — was there. But she didn't see the accident, thank goodness."

"That's just as well," Judith said as the teakettle whistled.

Estelle shuddered. "He died instantly, of a broken neck." She narrowed her eyes at Judith. "Why do you ask?"

Judith shrugged. "It's one thing to sit at the bedside and hold your loved one's hand. I would have done that if I hadn't been working." *Working because Dan rarely did, and in the last few years couldn't.* "But to see your husband killed right in front of you —

it sounds so horrible."

"Yes." Estelle turned away. "Yes, it was."

Judith frowned. The comment struck her as curious. But she didn't want to press her luck. "The tea should be ready in just a minute. I'll get a bowl for the pudding."

Setting out a tray, Judith watched Estelle out of the corner of her eye. The other woman seemed calm — except for a tic in her left eye. Judith hadn't noticed that before. Had the subject of Blake Farrow's death caused a nervous reaction?

"Suzanne must have been devastated," she said, placing two napkins on the tray. "I understand she was a teenager when her father died. My son was about the same age when I lost my first husband. It was very difficult."

"Suzanne compensates," Estelle replied, standing up. "In her own way, that is."

"Coping mechanisms," Judith remarked. "They help us survive."

"Yes." Estelle accepted the tray, but didn't resume eye contact. Maybe it was the twitch that deterred her. "Thank you," she said simply, and left the kitchen.

Judith put all but one of the pears in a wooden fruit bowl Uncle Cliff had made years ago on his lathe. She set the leftover pear on a plate, picked up another napkin,

261

and went out into the living room.

Gregory was asleep on the sofa. Judith left the fruit on the coffee table and headed for the parlor. Suzanne was still with Rudi, offering him soothing words.

He wasn't appreciative. "It's bad enough that my precious bow has been stolen," he complained. "But to play tonight without it and with this maimed hand . . ." He shook his head. "I can't possibly manage."

"Yes, you can," Suzanne insisted. She was kneeling in front of Rudi. "The scratches are superficial. By this evening, they'll be healing. You have other bows. You can make beautiful music with any type. Aren't you the one who told me Isaac Stern didn't care about what kind of bow he used?"

"I'm not Isaac Stern," Rudi lamented.

Suzanne patted his arm. "You're not Fritz Kreisler, either. But you have enormous talent. Where do you think the bow is?"

Unnoticed by the absorbed couple at the window seat, Judith saw Rudi gesture in the direction of the living room. "That lunatic, Gregory. He knew about it. He coveted it."

"When did he steal it?" Suzanne sounded very earnest.

"Probably after the performance Thursday," Rudi said, his undamaged hand resting on Suzanne's shoulder. "Or even before.

I don't use it every time. It depends upon the selections. I didn't realize it was missing until . . . I've lost track of time. What a terrible week!"

"How true." Suzanne lowered her head. "What's to become of us?"

Rudi looked up and saw Judith. "Did you just come in?" he asked in an anxious tone.

"Yes," Judith fibbed. "Is there anything I can do?"

Embarrassed, Suzanne stood up. "We're grieving," she said.

"Of course." Judith's smile was sympathetic.

Rudi waved the hand that now sported a small adhesive bandage. "You can contact the police to see if they've found my violin bow . . . or the bracelet. I'm beginning to think it was stolen, too."

"Was it valuable?" Judith inquired, moving to the hearth.

"Fairly," he said. "It was a Trinity bracelet from Cartier, three kinds of gold linked together. It cost around five thousand dollars."

"Did Taryn lose the bracelet the night of the party?" Judith asked.

"Ah . . ." Rudi scowled. "It must have been lost that night."

Judith couldn't remember if she'd seen

Taryn wearing the bracelet. All she recalled were her clothes — the peasant blouse and velvet pants. "The police bagged a number of items as possible evidence," she explained. "Have you checked with them about the bracelet?"

Rudi and Suzanne exchanged swift glances. "No," Rudi said. "That is, how could a bracelet be evidence?"

Judith shrugged. "Taryn was in the kitchen. It might have fallen off and ended up in the garbage by mistake. All the trash receptacles were considered evidence because Mr. Kluger's death has been determined a poisoning."

Suzanne was shaking her head. "No one would poison him on purpose. It had to be an accident."

"Of course," Rudi agreed. "Elsa was lucky. Dolph wasn't." His expression was pained.

Judith sat down in one of the straight-backed chairs in front of the fireplace. "Excuse me. I don't understand. What do you mean about your former wife being lucky?"

Rudi gave Judith a curious look. "She didn't die."

"But," Judith said, "I thought she merely fainted."

Rudi shook his head. "They took some

tests at the hospital. The results came back only this morning, shortly before noon. She was poisoned, too."

Shocked, Judith leaned forward in the chair. "By rhubarb?"

"A distillation of rhubarb leaves," Rudi replied. "Apparently, she ate or drank a much smaller quantity. She's also younger."

Judith's mind was whirling inside her head. What if Dolph hadn't been the intended victim? Or even Elsa, for that matter? "Can you recall exactly what was served the other night?"

Rudi couldn't remember, except for a cheese he'd never tried before. "It was a French Gratte-Paille — a very sharp triple crème. Delicious." Rudi licked his lips.

Hopefully, Judith looked at Suzanne, who was now leaning against the fireplace mantel.

"There were several cheeses," Suzanne said, frowning in concentration. "Olive brought most of them, I believe. She had also made a spinach-and-cheese quiche. Taryn provided fresh vegetables and fruit. Three kinds of dip with crackers — Taryn again, I think. Elsa had a prawn-and-cocktail-sauce plate from a local deli, Cuban coffee, herb tea, and puff pastries with chicken and herbs in cream sauce."

"What about the liquor?" Judith asked.

Suzanne gazed at Rudi. "I'm not sure."

He started to shake his head, then stopped. "Elsa had Fritz make a trip to the liquor store and the local wine shop. She gave him a list."

"So," Judith pointed out, "I assume the police have found out about Elsa's lab results. What they'll want to know is what Elsa and Dolph ate or drank that was the same — and that nobody else had."

"My stepfather drank wine," Suzanne said. "He preferred a 1985 Fritz Haag Brauneberger Juffer-Sonnenuhr Riesling."

Judith had never heard of it, but with an age and a name like that, it had to be expensive. "And Elsa?" she inquired.

"I'm not sure what she drank that evening," Rudi said vaguely.

"Whatever happened to Yosemite Sam at two bucks a bottle?"

The question came from the doorway, where Renie stood with a bemused expression and a pear in her hand.

"Coz!" Judith exclaimed. "I didn't hear you come in."

"I thought I'd check on my patient," Renie said, entering the parlor and flopping down in the other straight-backed chair. "I had to go to the post office to collect our food stamps."

Judith assumed Renie was kidding, but Suzanne and Rudi both regarded her with something akin to disapproval.

"What patient?" Suzanne asked after an awkward pause.

Renie gestured toward the living room. "Gregory Whoozits in there. He's sleeping like a log. I guess he doesn't want this." She took a big bite out of the pear. "Wassuh?" she asked with her mouth full. She nodded at Rudi. "Yulukafle."

Judith was used to translating her cousin's words when Renie was eating. "Rudi looks awful because he was attacked by a big orange-and-white cat."

"Rewy?" Renie's expression was innocent while pear juice dripped onto her bosom.

"Come into the kitchen, coz," Judith said, getting up. "You need a napkin. Or a bib."

By the time Judith had explained the latest news, Renie had finished the pear and opened a Pepsi. A steady rain had started to fall. The schoolhouse clock showed that it was exactly three o'clock on this darkening autumn afternoon.

"It must have been something that both Dolph and Elsa ate," Judith reasoned. "Dolph had brandy after Elsa passed out."

"But what did they both eat that nobody

else did?" Renie asked, finally mopping herself up with a paper napkin.

"I sort of recall Elsa with a snifter," Judith said, taking a Diet 7-Up out of the fridge. "She may have had brandy, too. Rudi's vague about the food."

"Elsa knows what she ate and drank," Renie pointed out. "Maybe Andrea kept track of what her husband was eating. She seemed like the attentive-wife type. Why don't you ask her?"

"I haven't even seen her," Judith said in a frustrated tone. "She's been holed up in that bedroom ever since the morning after the murder."

"So go up there and let yourself in," Renie urged. "Want me to come with you?"

"I doubt that Estelle — the maid — will let us in."

Renie shrugged. "It's your B&B. Tell her it's a safety check."

Judith considered the idea. "Okay. What have I got to lose?"

The cousins took the back stairs. The second-floor hall was quiet. Estelle apparently had taken her luggage into Room One. Judith approached Room Three with a purposeful stride and knocked twice.

"Innkeeper," she said in a loud voice.

There was no immediate response. The

only sound was the rain, spattering against the tall window above the second landing of the main staircase. The day had grown gloomy, with dense gray clouds rolling in from the mountains. A thunderstorm might be in the offing.

As Judith raised her hand to knock again, the door opened a scant two inches. Estelle peered out with suspicious eyes. "What is it?" she asked in a low, impatient tone.

"It's the last Friday of the month," Judith said in a businesslike voice. "We always conduct our safety inspection at this time. City regulations," she added, compounding the fib.

"Not now," Estelle said. "Come back later. Madam's asleep. I'll inform you when she's awake."

Renie elbowed Judith aside. "Sorry. This can't wait. I'm the inspector. I go off the job at four, like any good city employee working an arduous six-hour day. Move it."

"Excuse me?" Estelle cried softly. "You can't barge in here!"

"Watch me." Renie kicked at the door, which flew open and hit Estelle in the upper arm.

Judith followed her cousin into the commodious bedroom. A huddled form lay in the king-size bed. Renie marched around, studying every nook and cranny. Judith stayed next to Estelle, who was fuming.

"Safety indeed!" the maid muttered. "What kind of safety do you provide, Mrs. Flynn? My employer's husband died here!"

"Not exactly," Judith whispered. "He collapsed on the sidewalk."

Renie went into the bathroom. Estelle scowled. "That woman doesn't seem like an inspector. She's wearing tattered clothes. She looks like a homeless person."

"We're far more casual out here on the West Coast," Judith said. "This city invented grunge."

"Nothing to be proud of," Estelle declared. "Poor Madam!" The maid's eyes were now fixed on the bed. "She's a complete wreck."

"I'd really like to talk to her," Judith said with concern. "I've been remiss."

"Madam mustn't be disturbed. Doctor's orders." Estelle glanced toward the bathroom door, which was closed. "What's that person doing in there?"

"Don't ask," Judith murmured.

The maid suddenly looked alarmed. "Have you been in my room?"

"Not yet," Judith answered.

"I'll go with you."

"No need."

"I insist."

Renie finally emerged from the bathroom. "All clear," she said.

"Estelle wants to join us when we inspect her room," Judith said.

"Sure," Renie agreed. "Where are you?"

The maid informed Renie that she was staying in Room One. "Let's do it," Renie said.

Judith started to follow the other two women out through the door. But her cousin stopped abruptly in the hallway. "Hold it," Renie said. "Mrs. Flynn, do me a favor. I left my pen in the bathroom. Would you get it for me?"

"Of course," Judith said.

"You didn't have a pen," Estelle said in an accusing tone.

"Don't get smart with me," Renie snapped, grabbing Estelle by the arm. "Come on, let's hit it. I haven't got all day. There's beer to be drunk and pretzels to eat and . . ."

Judith didn't hear the rest of Renie's spiel. She hurried back inside the room and went to the big bed. She could barely see Andrea's ash-blond hair above the blue comforter. The woman's breathing seemed rather shallow. Judith hesitated, then gently prodded Andrea.

There was no response. Judith called her name. Nothing, only the rain and the wind in the trees. Frowning, she gave the bed-clothes a good shake. No reaction. She could just make out part of Andrea's profile, from forehead to lips. Without makeup, she was very pale.

Judith heard Renie and Estelle talking in the hall. Apparently, they were finished with the so-called inspection of Room One. Judith hurried to open the door.

"You must have left your pen downstairs," Judith said. "I couldn't find it."

"Hunh," said Renie. "Oh, well. Let's move on." She started down the narrow pas-sageway that led to the smallest of the ac-commodations, Room Two.

"That bathroom between Andrea and Su-zanne's rooms has more drugs than Holli-day's pharmacy," Renie said when they were well out of earshot. "Over-the-counter as well as a clutch of prescription drugs issued by a New York doctor."

"Such as?"

"Mostly sleeping pills, antidepressants, and tranquilizers," Renie replied. "I can't remember all the names, but I know what they're for."

Judith nodded. "That explains it. Andrea is drugged to the eyeballs. I wonder why?"

"Because she really is a wreck?" Renie suggested.

"Possibly. But," Judith went on in a worried tone, "I wonder if it's in somebody's interest to keep her that way."

# CHAPTER THIRTEEN

The cousins waited to finish their discussion until they returned to the kitchen.

"The obvious suspect in drugging Andrea is Suzanne," Renie declared, retrieving her Pepsi from the table.

"Definitely," Judith agreed. "She's the one who picked up the prescription refills. Of course, her motives might be pure. Maybe Andrea really is an emotional wreck. I don't blame her."

"She was a wreck before Dolph was killed," Renie pointed out. "Otherwise, the pills wouldn't be refills, which they are. You can tell from the labels."

Renie's back was to the swinging doors that led to the dining room. Judith raised one finger to signal quiet and leaned slightly out of her chair. Suzanne entered the kitchen. "Can I help you, Suzanne?" she inquired.

"Rudi has left the B&B," Suzanne said.

Renie swiveled around. "Is this an announcement, like Elvis has left the building?"

"Of course not," Suzanne asserted. "I merely wanted to let you know. I'm going for a run. I expect that Gregory will also have left by the time I get back. It's not safe to let him stay here. Trust me." She turned away and headed for the front door.

"I don't trust her," Judith declared. "Supposedly, her mother has been making funeral arrangements. I don't know how, when she's virtually in a coma. And another thing — Suzanne says she owns a gym or a health club in Manhattan. Yet I've never once heard her mention anything specific about it. Most people who run a business talk about it. I find it odd, especially since her schedule has been changed. You'd think she'd bring up some problems that her absence might cause."

Renie smiled. "You really are a most suspicious person. Don't you think the gym can run itself? She probably has a reliable staff. Besides, she knew she'd be gone a week or two if she was completing the West Coast trip with Dolph and Andrea."

Judith rubbed the 7-Up can in her hands. "You're probably right. Did you find anything of interest in Estelle's room?"

"Only Estelle, who watched me like a spy from a bad movie," Renie replied. "That room has no bathroom, so I couldn't look at anything except electrical outlets and the furnace vent." She made a face. "I couldn't get into Suzanne's room because her door to the shared bathroom was locked. I guess I'm not much of an inspector — or a sleuth, for that —" Renie stopped. "Where did you say Estelle came from?"

"You mean before she got here? Oregon. Why?"

"I noticed the airline tag on her suitcase," Renie said with a sly smile. "There was only one, and it was marked from JFK to here — not to Portland."

"Was there a date?"

"Yes." Renie's smile widened. "The twenty-fourth, which means she got here the same day as the rest of the Kluger group."

"Maybe even the same flight," Judith remarked thoughtfully. "She arrived in a tan car, a rental. I wonder if we could find out where she picked it up. It's still parked outside."

"I'll look," Renie volunteered, getting up from her chair. "There's usually a sticker or something to indicate which rental agency the car comes from."

While Renie was outside, Judith went into the living room to check on Gregory.

He was gone.

She knocked on the bathroom door off the entry hall. There was no response. Cautiously, she opened the door, but the bathroom was vacant. She peeked into the parlor. No Gregory. She'd just started up the stairs when Renie came back into the house.

"Hertz," Renie said. "Let's call their airport office. Hey — what's wrong?"

"The odd bird has flown the coop," Judith replied, "unless he's upstairs."

"If he's upstairs, you'd have heard a rumpus," Renie pointed out. "Gregory must've waltzed out the front door. Or limped." She put a hand on Judith's arm. "Stay put. I'll save you a trip." Renie went upstairs while Judith waited on the first landing.

She didn't have to wait long. Renie came back down, shaking her head.

"All's quiet on the second floor," she reported. "But you might want to look outside."

"Why?"

"I happened to look out the big window above the second landing," Renie said, going back up to the first landing to peer through the smaller, leaded window. "Suzanne and Fritz are in the Rankerses' hedge."

Judith ascended the two steps to stand by Renie. "In it? Where?"

"I don't see them now," Renie replied. "They weren't actually *in* the hedge, but they were standing by it, head-to-head like a couple of conspirators."

Judith went back down to the entry hall and cautiously opened the front door. "Nothing," she said. "Let's check the back."

The cousins stopped to look out the kitchen window over the sink. No one was in sight. They went to the back door. There, by the patio, stood Suzanne and Fritz, engaged in deep conversation. Judith opened the door a scant inch.

"What if she doesn't?" Suzanne was saying.

"She won't," Fritz replied. "Anyway, it's —" He stopped, gazing up at the gray clouds. "It's crazy."

"No, it's not!" Suzanne stamped her foot. "She has no right to interfere! She's ruining everything!"

"Oh, come on, Suze," Fritz coaxed. "Chill. What's the rush?"

"I'm not twenty anymore," Suzanne said

impatiently. "I can't wait to have a life for-ever."

"You can wait for a while," Fritz insisted. "What's a few days or even weeks? Besides, I —"

The toolshed door opened. Gertrude rolled to the edge of the ramp in her wheel-chair. "Get off my patio!" she yelled. "You're scaring Saint Francis and the birds!"

Suzanne jumped; Fritz swerved around to look at the old lady.

"Sorry," the young man said. "I was just leaving."

"Good idea," Gertrude snapped. "Make that times two."

Fritz all but ran in the direction of the driveway. Suzanne took a step after him but stopped, rocking back and forth on her heels. She gave Gertrude a dirty look and hurried away in the opposite direction, ap-parently heading for the front of the house from the Rankerses' side.

Judith quietly closed the door. "What was that all about?"

Renie shook her head. "The plot thickens. Suzanne has something cooked up with Fritz. But what? And who is *she?*"

"Elsa? Andrea? Taryn?" Judith shrugged as the cousins returned to the kitchen. "Let's get back to Gregory and look in the phone book. He claimed he didn't have any ID when Rosemary O'Grady questioned him, but said he lived near the University. I'll look up the Hertz airport number, too."

Gregory was unlisted, under either Kluger or Radinsky. Judith dialed the University's music department. She got a recording, informing her that the office was closed for the weekend.

Renie nodded. "Classes don't start until Monday. The departments don't always keep regular hours between summer and fall quarters. I remember that from when Bill taught there."

"I suppose Gregory could really be a crackpot," Judith said as she found the number for the car-rental office. "Let's try this." She dialed and somehow managed to reach an actual person. "This is Estelle Pearson," Judith lied. "I can't find the paperwork for my rental. Can you tell me when I'm supposed to turn the car in?"

The pleasant female voice at the other end went off the line to check. "You left the return date open," she said a few moments later. "Since you rented the car Wednesday morning, when you bring it back you should be here before noon or we'll have to charge for an extra day."

"Thank you. You've been very helpful."

After relaying the information to Renie, Judith concluded that Estelle probably had taken the red-eye from New York. "I'm guessing she wasn't on the same flight as the Klugers."

"Are you guessing they didn't know she was coming directly here?"

Judith shrugged. "I don't know — and won't guess. But this news makes her a suspect."

"You're right," Renie agreed. "Estelle was in town before Dolph was poisoned. I wonder where she was holed up."

"The police should be informed about her," Judith said. "I'll get in touch with Rosemary."

"Go for it." Renie, however, decided she'd better head home. "It's time for Bill's nap. I have to tuck him in."

"No, you don't."

"You're right. I have to tuck Oscar in, though."

Judith shook her head. "No. I refuse to discuss your stuffed dwarf ape. *He's not real.*"

"Yes, he is." Renie looked very serious. "Actually, he doesn't take a nap when Bill does. His snoring disturbs Bill. Oscar just rests his eyes."

"His eyes are glass."

"So?"

"Never mind. Good-bye, coz."

Renie left.

Rosemary answered on the third ring. Judith passed on the information about Estelle's early arrival in the city.

"You mean," Rosemary said, "she lied about coming from Oregon?"

"Obviously," Judith said, then caught herself. "Now that I think about it, Estelle never mentioned coming from Oregon. It was Suzanne who told me she was visiting relatives there."

"Interesting," Rosemary commented. "Oh, Mrs. Flynn, you manage to elicit the most fascinating information! I don't know how you do it!"

"I talk to people. Often, they let interesting things slip out."

"Yes," Rosemary agreed. "The problem is, most people aren't really listening. I mean, we're trained as detectives to listen, but so much of what people say is irrelevant. It's not everybody who can sort the wheat from the chaff."

"I've had a lot of practice," Judith said modestly. "You'll interrogate her?"

"Yes. Levi and I will be at the B&B as soon as we finish our paperwork." Rosemary lowered her voice. "Did you hear about the results concerning Ms. Wittener?"

"As a matter of fact," Judith responded, "I did. I figured the hospital would get in touch with you."

"It wasn't the hospital," Rosemary said. "It was an anonymous tip."

"Really?" Judith was surprised, but realized that she shouldn't have been. "You have no idea who called?"

"No," Rosemary replied. "It came in this afternoon from a pay phone on Heraldsgate Hill near Key Largo Bank. Can you hazard a guess?"

"It had to be Elsa or Fritz or someone closely connected to them," Judith conjectured. "Or even Rudi Wittener or Taryn Moss."

"Can you find out?" Rosemary asked.

"I don't know," Judith said candidly. "By the way, Gregory left unannounced."

Rosemary sounded startled. "I thought he couldn't walk."

"Apparently he could," said Judith. "I can't locate an address or phone number for him. You might want to put somebody on that."

"This case is very confusing," Rosemary declared, sounding frustrated. "Is it always this way?"

"Well . . . they are when they're not readily

solved," Judith admitted. "That is, where family members and friends are involved instead of just a barroom brawl or a drive-by shooting, murder gets complicated. It becomes personal. Very few people have no secrets or resentments. Not to mention greed and jealousy and all the other human emotions that come into play when the victim is intentionally killed."

"I heard you've solved murders in less than forty-eight hours," Rosemary said. "Time's running short."

"It's not a contest or a track meet," Judith pointed out. "Goodness, Rosemary, I'm not a wizard."

The detective's laugh sounded forced. "I know, I know. It's just that you're so wise."

"It comes with age," Judith replied drily. Unused to being fawned over, she wished that Rosemary would stop treating her like an icon. It didn't feel right.

"We ran Gregory through the database under both last names," Rosemary said. "He has no criminal record under Kluger or Radinsky."

"An address would help," Judith noted. "Not to mention a place of employment, such as the University."

"Oh, yes, of course." Rosemary paused. "Would it be convenient for us to stop by to interview this Pearson woman in the next hour?"

Judith heard the beep that signaled a call on her other line. "Sure, come ahead. I must dash."

The caller was Renie. "Guess who I saw on the way home," she said.

"Mmm . . . Elvis?"

"Not exactly," Renie said. "It was Gregory. I got stuck behind a U-Haul making a left on Heraldsgate Avenue in the next block from your house. I saw him walking — limping, actually — into the Empress Apartments. Isn't that where Olive Oglethorpe lives?"

"You're right." The apartment building was large, with many tenants, but Judith dismissed the possibility of Gregory calling on anyone other than Olive. "Somehow, he must know Olive well enough that she'd let him in. I certainly didn't pass muster. What's the connection?"

"Olive's Rudi's assistant," Renie remarked. "Somewhere in time Gregory must have met her, which means — maybe — that Rudi and Gregory are better acquainted than we thought. How long has Olive worked for Rudi?"

"Years and years, I gather," Judith said. "Long before they moved from Philadelphia. Somehow I've got to talk to Olive or you do."

"Me? I don't have time," Renie said. "I have to watch Oscar watch Bill take a nap."

"I don't mean right now," Judith responded, noticing that the rain had dwindled to a drizzle. "Think of some way you can get to her."

"A holdup? Breaking and entering? Come on, coz — you're much better at subterfuge than I am. Besides, she's seen me at your house."

"She wouldn't remember," Judith argued. "You rushed past her when you forgot your purse. Olive was concentrating on getting everybody's belongings together. Besides, you could dress like a real person and comb your hair and even put on makeup. You could fool anybody who's seen you as yourself."

"Aaargh," groaned Renie.

"Coz . . ." Judith's tone was coaxing.

"Let me think about it," Renie begged. "Doesn't Olive spend most of her time at Rudi's house? He and Taryn would know who I am."

"You'd have to catch her at home, probably in the evening," Judith said. "Like tonight."

"No." Renie was adamant.

"Tomorrow? It's Saturday," Judith added. "Olive probably won't be working."

"Don't call me," Renie said. "I'll call you — *if* I decide to do it."

That was good enough for Judith. She had dangled the bait. Renie was usually a typical trout — and a good sport.

Joe arrived home at exactly five o'clock. "I finally finished that title search," he said, hanging his tan raincoat on a peg in the hallway off the kitchen. "The property belongs to a dog."

"You mean the person is . . . a dog?" Judith asked.

"No. The owner is a beagle in Blue Earth, Minnesota," Joe explained, going to the fridge. "At least that's where Trix was in 1974."

"Trix probably doesn't live there anymore," Judith said. "He probably doesn't live anywhere. What happens next?"

Joe took out a can of beer and shrugged. "Not my problem. I'll be damned if I know why people put animals in their wills. Are they nuts or is it just to spite their rightful heirs?"

"Both, maybe," Judith suggested. "Does this mean you can take a few days off?"

Joe nodded. "Bill and I were wondering if it's too late into September to go salmon fishing off the coast. We had good luck last year, but that was right after Labor Day. He's making some calls."

"According to Renie," Judith said, taking a package of prawns out of the freezer section, "Bill can't afford to leave the city limits."

Joe, who had sat down at the kitchen table, snickered. "Don't believe everything Renie tells you. She tends to exaggerate."

"True," Judith said as the phone rang. She picked up the receiver from the counter and answered. "It's for you," she said to Joe before lowering her voice to a whisper. "It sounds like Rudi Wittener."

Joe frowned as he took the phone from Judith. "Flynn here," he said, then frowned some more. "Right now? I just got in. Make it twenty minutes, okay?" He hung up.

"What's that all about?" Judith inquired as she put the prawns in the microwave and hit the defrost button.

"Wittener has a case for me," Joe said. "I'll hear him out, but I'd just as soon go fishing."

"It might tie in with the murder investigation," Judith pointed out.

"That's your turf," Joe said. "I'm keeping out of it. That's another reason I wish Wittener hadn't called." He took a sip of beer.

"How much do these violinists make?"

"Fairly good money," Judith replied over the hum of the microwave.

"I was wondering if he could afford to pay me," Joe said after he'd opened a bag of pretzels. "I thought musicians were poor."

"Not major symphony musicians," Judith said, "though I really don't know much about it. Renie might."

Munching on a pretzel, Joe glanced out the kitchen window. "The rain's stopped." He took another quaff of beer and sat very still. "It's damned quiet around here. It seems weird."

"It *is* weird," Judith agreed. "No guests rustling about, no rushing on my part to prepare for the social hour, no money coming in from the vacant rooms. I hate it."

Joe stood up. "Then maybe I should see if I can make some money." He looked outside again. The setting sun was trying to break through the cloud cover. Joe frowned.

Judith knew what he was thinking. If the weather cleared, she'd ask Joe to finish the yard cleanup on Saturday. Unless, of course, he decided to go fishing.

Dinner was scheduled for six that night, with Gertrude's portion ready ten minutes earlier. Joe still wasn't back when Judith went out to the toolshed.

"Your cleaning woman is crazy as a bed-bug," Gertrude declared.

"What now?" Judith asked, making room on her mother's crowded card-table for the dinner tray.

"She wrecked my Y. B. Stout girdle," Gertrude said. "Can't that woman run a washer machine? And I don't want that crackpot coming near me singing that stupid hymn 'How Firm a Foundation' ever again!"

"What happened to your girdle?"

"She put the stays in wrong," Gertrude complained, waving a hand in the direction of the girdle that was lying on top of the laundry pile. "That crackpot tore the material. I can't wear it anymore. How can I keep my girlish figure?"

Judith examined the foundation garment. Sure enough, it appeared as if Phyliss had haphazardly forced one of the stays into its slot and ripped the fabric. Recalling that a stay had gotten loose in the dryer, Judith apologized.

"Frankly," she went on, ignoring the disgusted look on Gertrude's face, "this is a very old girdle. You have at least two newer ones. I'll put this one in the St. Vincent de Paul bag."

"Why does Saint Vincent need a girdle?

Hasn't he been dead for about four hundred years?" Gertrude poked at the prawns. "I don't like fat shrimp. Why don't you buy the little ones? I remember when your father and I used to go for walks along the waterfront and we'd buy a white paper bag of little shrimp for ten cents."

"That was then and this is now," Judith retorted, stuffing the girdle under her arm. "Besides, you've had prawns before and enjoyed them."

"I did?" Gertrude was skeptical. "You're just saying that because I don't always remember things."

"It's true," Judith insisted. "You like rice and green salad, not to mention the lovely rolls I bought at Falstaff's."

Gertrude studied the roll. "It's got grass in it. Dit you drop it out in the yard?"

"That's not grass, it's rosemary," Judith replied.

"Rosemary who?" Gertrude made another face. "Isn't she a cop? What's wrong with Parker House rolls? Now *that's* a roll. Tasty. Soft. Yum." She smacked her lips.

"I'll buy some Parker House rolls next time," Judith said, "or make them myself. Sunday, maybe."

"I should live so long," Gertrude said with a sigh. "I'm lucky if I make it to tomorrow."

"You will," Judith assured her mother with a kiss on the cheek. "What was the last day you missed?"

"I miss your father," Gertrude blurted. "How can you miss somebody after forty years?"

That was a question Judith couldn't answer. She still missed her father, too.

Not feeling like tackling the uncarpeted basement stairs, Judith stuffed the old girdle into a duffel bag she kept in the pantry. Her timing was perfect: Joe had left, but Morgenstern and O'Grady had arrived.

"We're here to interview Estelle Pearson," Morgenstern said. "Where is she?"

"Upstairs, where all the suspects hang out these days," Judith replied. "Or some of them, at any rate."

Morgenstern, who seemed to have his allergies under control, trudged up to the second floor. Rosemary lingered in the entry hall.

"We checked with the airlines," she said, lowering her voice. "That is, I did. Levi's much better, of course, but he's taking it easy since he went to the doctor. I'm encouraging him to let me do the grunt work. I should, after all, since he's the senior partner." Rosemary paused briefly, sup-

292

pressing a small smile. "Anyway, Estelle Pearson definitely arrived here Wednesday morning. She rented a car at the airport, but we haven't found out where she's been staying. Nothing's turned up at the local motels and hotels."

"Try the B&Bs," Judith suggested in a grim voice. "Some of them may be able to accept customers."

"Yes." Rosemary looked away from Judith. "I'm really, really sorry about the inconvenience."

"But are you really, really solving this case?" Judith asked.

Rosemary seemed startled by the query and stared at Judith. "Well . . . I assume you're way ahead of me."

"Rosemary . . ." Judith began in a weary voice. "I'm stumped. There are so many other things going on, such as the missing violin bow, my cousin's stolen credit cards, somebody breaking into our basement — and liars galore. Andrea Kluger is in a drugged stupor, Gregory Whoever-He-Is may or may not be nuts, Olive Oglethorpe won't let me talk to her, and I haven't had a chance to speak with Elsa Wittener or her son, Fritz. Suzanne and Estelle are so protective of the family's privacy that it's impossible to get anything helpful out of

293

them. My resources seem exhausted, and so am I."

"Golly." Rosemary was taken aback by Judith's confession. "I was so hoping you'd be able to help me. This is my first homicide, and I want to make a good impression." She appeared close to tears.

Judith sighed. "I'm sorry I'm a disappointment. I've been lucky over the years. People usually talk to me, confide in me, seem to relax because . . . well, if nothing else, I'm sympathetic and a good listener. This isn't happening with this crew. They simply won't open up."

Rosemary nodded. "I understand. I think." But the young woman still looked unhappy.

Judith felt helpless, frustrated. She racked her brain for ideas. "Something's going on between Fritz and Suzanne. Also, Suzanne and Rudi. I don't know what it is in either case, but it could be important."

"Can you find out?" Rosemary asked.

Judith tried to hide her exasperation. "I thought you and your partner might do that."

"But you're so good at that sort of thing!" Rosemary asserted.

"Not this time around," Judith muttered. She studied the young detective's hangdog expression. "I have an idea."

Rosemary's face brightened. "Yes?"

"Get hold of someone in New Jersey," Judith said. "Find out how Andrea Kluger's first husband was killed in that foxhunt."

Rosemary looked puzzled. "Foxhunt?"

Judith nodded. "Mr. Farrow — Andrea's late husband — ran a company that made musical instruments. Is that a coincidence — or is it part of Dolph Kluger's murder?"

# CHAPTER FOURTEEN

Morgenstern and O'Grady came back downstairs twenty minutes later. Judith was in the kitchen, trying to keep dinner hot for Joe.

"Any luck?" she asked, coming out into the entry hall.

"Yes," Morgenstern replied. "Ms. Pearson informed us that she was never in Oregon. Her relatives live in this state, not in Oregon. Apparently, New Yorkers consider the Pacific Northwest as all one large and heavily forested entity."

"In other words," Judith said, "we're still a territory mapped only by Lewis and Clark?"

"That sounds like a fairly accurate appraisal," Morgenstern said drily. "We assume no subterfuge was intended."

"But," Judith noted, "Estelle was here before the murder occurred."

"True," the senior detective agreed. "She's

been with Mrs. Kluger for many years. Her father was the Farrow chauffeur."

"Born into service," Judith murmured. "It all sounds so class bound. I suppose that's because social distinctions in the West aren't so marked, at least up here in the Northwest Territory." She smiled at the detectives as they started for the door. "I'm glad your allergies have improved," she said to Morgenstern.

"It's a miracle," he declared. "My doctor prescribed a new drug. I've never had relief so quickly."

"Amazing," Judith remarked. "I'm glad for you."

Joe called to Judith from the kitchen. "Ah — your husband wants you," Morgenstern said. "We'll leave."

Rosemary gave Judith a warm smile. "Foxhunt," she whispered, making her exit.

"I came in the back way," Joe explained. "I didn't want to run into the cops. I saw their unmarked car. Did they arrest anybody?"

"No."

"Too bad," Joe said. "Let's eat."

Hurriedly, Judith served their dinner. "If it's dried up, don't blame me. What did Rudi want?"

"He asked me to find his violin bow," Joe

297

replied. "He doesn't think the cops are trying very hard. I told him the robbery unit was good, but I guess 'good' isn't good enough for Wittener. The damned thing's insured for over three hundred grand. I asked if it was made out of diamonds."

"At least it's insured," Judith said, pouring a small amount of drawn garlic butter on her prawns.

"That's not the point," Joe said. "It's the sentimental value."

"Yes. Apparently, it belonged to Fritz Kreisler. Did he mention a bracelet that Taryn lost?"

"No." Joe took a warm buttered slice of baguette out of the woven bread basket. "Is that missing, too?"

"Rudi says it is," Judith replied. "He's been looking for it around our place, so I assume she lost it the night of the party. By the way, I think somebody broke into our basement."

Joe paused with his fork halfway to his mouth. "No kidding? How come you didn't mention that earlier? I'm rarely shocked by crime, even when it occurs on my own private property."

Judith explained how she and Rosemary had examined the window above the washer and dryer.

Joe shook his head. "Just because the guests — or the visitors' guests — were already in the house or had access to it doesn't mean they'd want to be caught going into the basement. Though why the hell they'd want to go down there, I can't guess. I take it nothing's missing?"

"Not that I can tell," Judith replied.

Joe ate in silence for a few moments. "How many suspects besides your guests?"

"There's Gregory Whoozits and Estelle the maid, so we've got at least two outsiders," Judith said. "Frankly, I can't see Estelle wedging herself through that window. But where there's a will, there's a way." She ate another prawn before speaking again. "I gather you're going to take on Rudi's case?"

The gold flecks danced in Joe's green eyes. "He's offering ten percent of the bow's worth if I track it down."

"Wow!" Judith dropped her napkin. "That's at least thirty grand!"

"How can I refuse?"

"You can't," Judith said. "Let me tell you what I know about it."

For the next fifteen minutes while they cleared up from dinner, Judith related every morsel she could recall from Renie's information about the bow. She concluded by saying that Gregory had claimed it should belong to him as his "inheritance."

"Rudi didn't steal it," Joe pointed out, "unless he's trying an insurance fraud."

The phone rang. Renie's number appeared on the caller ID screen. "Hi, coz," Judith said. "Have you put on your disguise to visit Olive?"

"Something's off," Bill growled at the other end. "I hate the phone! Fix it! And where's my weird pop?"

Bill's words were for Renie, Judith gathered. She was aware that Bill Jones — along with his brother, Bub, an attorney — might be extremely smart men, but neither had ever mastered the telephone. She was also aware that Bill favored a certain brand of soda with names such as Quizzical Kiwi, Puckish Peach, Gargantuan Grape, and Fruit Is Stranger Than Friction.

"Your weird pop is that puce-colored stuff in the glass next to your left hand," Judith heard Renie say in a vexed voice. "Give me that phone."

"Puce?" said Bill, in a puzzled tone. "Did I buy the puce kind?"

"Hi," Renie said into the receiver. "Bill's trying to make a phone call. If you put Joe on the line and I hold the receiver for Bill, we might get some meaningful communication via this ultramodern invention of Alexander Graham Bell's. Here, Bill, stick this in your ear."

"Joe?" Bill barked.

"Just a minute," Judith said. "I'll get him."

Just as Judith handed the phone to Joe, Arlene breezed through the back door. "Yoo-hoo! It's me!"

"Hi, Arlene," Judith said, going down the narrow hallway to meet her neighbor. "Joe's on the phone. Let's go into the pantry. What's up?"

"As Teddy Roosevelt would say, 'Ask not what you can do for your neighbor, ask how you can get up San Juan Hill.' "

"Huh?" Judith couldn't hide her puzzlement.

"Well — that's not quite right," Arlene amended. "Heraldsgate Hill is what Teddy should've said. I just happened to be crawling through our hedge when I found this." She opened her hand to reveal a three-toned gold bracelet.

Judith stared. The elegant circles were entwined. It looked very much like the Trinity bracelet Rudi had described. "Dare I ask what you were doing in the hedge when it's almost dark?"

Arlene looked exasperated. "What do you think I was doing? How else can I get a view of the Wittener house except from the far

301

end of the hedge?" Her blue eyes brightened. "The Porters had lobster for dinner. Can you imagine the market price?"

"No," Judith admitted, wondering how Arlene had managed not only to keep surveillance on the Wittener house, but also to peek into the Porters' kitchen. "Of course Gabe does work for a produce company. Maybe he gets a deal from other vendors."

"Probably," Arlene said. "Like the Steins."

"The Steins?" Judith no longer heard Joe talking. Bill always kept his phone conversations brief. "Hamish doesn't work for a produce company."

"I know, I know," Arlene said impatiently. "But they're Jewish. Don't they get everything wholesale?"

"Not really," Judith said. "That's one of those ethnic clichés."

"Hmm." Arlene looked thoughtful. "I did have an Italian girlfriend who couldn't carry a tune. And I've known some Irishmen who weren't drunk all the time."

"Like Joe?" Judith said wryly.

Arlene nodded. "Yes, he's one of them. The nondrunks, I mean. As far as I can tell."

"Let me see that bracelet," Judith said.

Arlene handed it over. "It looks expensive. It's not yours, is it?"

"No," Judith replied, turning the handsome piece over in her hands. "It may belong to Taryn Moss."

"Oh, no," Arlene asserted. "There's an inscription. It's hard to read, but I could see it with my flashlight."

Judith backed up to get the benefit of the single bulb in the pantry. "You're right," she said, peering at the small, elegant letters. "It says, 'RW to SF' . . . and something else."

" 'Infirmity,' " said Arlene.

Judith looked even closer. "I *think* it's 'Eternally.' "

"Really?" Arlene's blue eyes narrowed as she looked over Judith's shoulder. "No, it's 'Infirmary.' "

Judith concentrated on the tiny letters. "It's 'Eternity,' " she finally decided. "It's called a Trinity ring."

"But not Taryn's," Arlene pointed out. "RW — for Rudi? Who's SF?"

Judith grimaced. "It may be Suzanne Farrow — Dolph Kluger's stepdaughter. I thought they were acting kind of chummy earlier today. I should've guessed. Come to think of it, I'm not sure he told me that the bracelet belonged to Taryn. I just inferred that."

"Rudi knew it was missing?"

"Yes. He's been looking all over the place for it, including in our yard and house."

Arlene shrugged. "He might have looked in the hedge. You'd be surprised at some of the things I find there."

"No, I wouldn't," Judith said, and meant it. The Rankerses' laurel hedge was enormous, a veritable fortification against the world. It seemed to grow almost as fast as bamboo. Any number of items had been lost in that hedge over the years, including one of Judith's guests.

Arlene frowned. "What was Suzanne doing in our hedge? Or do I want to know?"

"Maybe not," Judith replied, clutching the bracelet and starting out of the pantry. "Frankly, I can't imagine that — oops!" She tripped over the drawstring on the duffel bag and would have fallen if Arlene hadn't been there to steady her.

"Careful!" Arlene cried. "You'll hurt your poor hip!"

"I'm okay," Judith said sheepishly. "I should have taken that bag downstairs earlier. It's for Saint Vincent de Paul. When I don't feel like going all the way into the basement, I put discards in the pantry."

"They're having a drive Sunday for SOTS," Arlene said, referring to the parishioners of Our Lady, Star of the Sea, Catholic church. "Didn't you see it in the bulletin?"

"No," Judith admitted. "I missed it. I'll

have to get my other stuff out of the basement and take it up to church Sunday."

"Carl and I can haul it," Arlene volunteered. "We're borrowing one of our sons' trucks. We cleaned out the garage a couple of weeks ago. Let me take that bag now."

"Thanks," Judith said. "I'll try to remember to get the rest of it from downstairs."

"So," Arlene said as she picked up the duffel bag, "this Suzanne person has been doing the dipsy-doodle with Rudi? Goodness. How did I miss that?"

"Suzanne lives in New York," Judith said. "Whatever it is they have together is via long distance."

"Awkward," Arlene remarked. "But convenient."

"Huh?"

"So little opportunity to get on each other's nerves. You know — like living together. That's what makes things tricky."

"Yes," Judith said vaguely.

"Carl and I've always gotten along better when we're apart," Arlene pointed out. "Don't you find Joe less irritating when he's not around?"

"Well . . . I think I know what you mean," Judith allowed. "But I prefer having Joe with me."

"You haven't been married as long we

have," Arlene said, heading for the back door with the duffel bag trailing behind her. "Wait thirty more years." She slung the bag over her shoulder and suddenly looked anxious. "I must dash. Carl gets upset when I'm gone for more than fifteen minutes. He misses me so."

Arlene hurried out, leaving behind her customary crumbs of contradiction.

She'd also left the bracelet. Standing in the kitchen, Judith caressed its entwined circles as if it were a charm. Certainly it had given her an idea. Before she could act, Joe came in from the dining room.

"I've got to pack," he said, moving beyond his wife toward the back stairs.

Judith was stupefied. "Pack? What for?"

"The Kings are still in," he called over his shoulder. "Bill says it's hot right now out in the ocean and off the river bar. Everybody's limiting on salmon. We'll leave right away so we can get some sleep but still be there for first light."

"But —" Judith stopped as Joe disappeared up the stairwell.

"Great," she said to herself. Joe and Bill would probably be gone for the entire weekend. Rudi's treasured bow would remain in limbo — or be found by someone else. Judith could practically see thirty thousand dollars flying out the kitchen window.

It'd take Joe at least a half hour to get his gear together. With a heavy step, Judith went up to the second floor and down the hall to Room Four. Perhaps Suzanne was keeping to her own quarters. Whatever she was doing didn't seem to have included eating dinner.

Suzanne answered after the first knock. Apparently, she'd been exercising. She wore workout clothes and was perspiring.

"What is it?" she asked in a slightly breathless voice.

Judith held the bracelet in her palm. "Is this what Rudi was looking for?"

"Yes," Suzanne replied, reaching for the golden circles.

Judith snatched her hand away. "Good. I'll return it to Taryn right now."

"No!" Suzanne quickly composed herself. "I mean, I'll do it. Rudi's at the concert. Taryn's probably there, too. I'll slip it in their mailbox."

"That's a bad idea," Judith said. "There appears to be a thief on the loose around here. I'll keep the bracelet in our safe until I can give it to Taryn or Rudi."

Suzanne used the back of her hand to wipe the sweat from her brow. "I really think you should let me have it."

Briefly, Judith considered the physical advantage that the much younger, leaner — and far more physically fit — Suzanne had over her. If she tried to wrest the bracelet away from Judith, it would be no contest.

Which was exactly what Suzanne intended to do. Swiftly, she reached out and grabbed Judith's arm. "Don't meddle! Give me that!"

Judith clutched the bracelet as tightly as she could manage. She was still standing in the doorway. "Don't be silly," she said in a strained voice. "Don't you think this bracelet should be put where it —"

Suzanne viciously twisted Judith's arm. "Let go! I don't want trouble!"

Judith winced, but kept the bracelet clasped in her hand. Somehow, she also managed to keep her balance. But she knew Suzanne was bound to win the battle.

"Fish on!" Joe called as he emerged from the third-floor steps across the hall. "Whoa — what have we caught, my darling wife?"

Startled, Suzanne let go of Judith's arm. "Oh!" she exclaimed. "We were . . . ah . . ." Her face turned red. "It was a misunderstanding," she mumbled. "Sorry."

Joe, who was carrying an overnight bag, stood directly behind Judith. "Odd," he said in that deceptively mellow voice that had proved so effective with innumerable suspects and perps over the years, "since my wife rarely has misunderstandings with anyone. It's not her style."

"I said," Suzanne repeated, speaking more audibly, "I'm sorry. I'm under a terrible strain. Excuse me." She backed away, shutting the door on the Flynns.

"Damn," said Joe after the door was closed. "What's with her? Are you okay?"

Judith shook her tender arm. "Yes, I'm fine. But Suzanne isn't. She's got herself in a pickle."

"How so?"

"Come on downstairs," Judith said. "I take it you're ready to go."

"I've got to get my lucky salmon rod from the basement," Joe said as they went down the back stairs. "It's lighter and gives more play than the ones you get on the charter boat." He stopped before they reached the last step and put a hand on Judith's shoulder. "Is it safe to leave you with Ms. Muscle?"

"I think so," Judith said with an ironic smile. "Suzanne's right about one thing — she's definitely under a strain."

They'd reached the hallway to the kitchen. "Maybe Renie should stay with you while

Bill and I are gone."

"Renie's small," Judith said, then added, "but mean."

"That's what I'm saying," Joe asserted. "Bill and I are taking your Nissan, if that's okay. Your car has more room for the fish. Just take good care of my MG." He touched her cheek. "Why don't you have Renie come over tonight? I'd feel better if she were here."

"Maybe I would, too," Judith agreed. "I'll call her."

Joe headed for the basement. The safe was in the family quarters on the third floor. Judith didn't feel like walking that far, so she put the bracelet in the freezer between some pork chops and chicken parts.

Renie answered on the second ring. "Want to have a sleepover?" Judith asked.

Her cousin paused. "Can I bring Clarence?"

"No."

"You know I don't like leaving him alone," Renie responded. "Oscar's no help."

Judith wasn't in the mood for Renie's fantasies about the stuffed ape or the real Holland dwarf lop bunny. "When did you start sleeping with Clarence?"

"I've only done it once, when he was ailing," Renie replied. "He got lost during the night. We found him in one of Bill's slippers. Or what was left of it. Clarence wasn't as sick as we thought."

"Joe thinks I'm in danger," Judith said, not wanting to hear any more about Clarence, the only bunny she knew who had a complete wardrobe, including a tutu and resort wear.

"In danger?" Renie sounded mildly surprised. "Anybody specific?"

Lowering her voice, Judith related the incident with Suzanne.

"Okay," Renie finally agreed, "I'll come. But it won't be until around nine. Clarence always goes to bed at eight-thirty. Oscar usually stays up until ten, when Bill tucks him in for the —"

"Stop!" Judith commanded. "Just be here, okay?"

"Fine, sure," Renie said, irked. "By the way, I have an appointment tomorrow morning with Olive Oglethorpe."

Judith's tone changed immediately. "You do?"

"Yes. I'm selling her a retirement home."

"What?"

"You heard me."

"That's fraud. You don't own any retirement homes."

"Not true. Bill's retired. I'm selling her our house."

"But . . ." Judith was nonplussed. Renie might not be nearly as good a liar as she was, but when she told the occasional whopper, it was usually outrageous. This was no exception. "I don't get it."

"Never mind," Renie said. "The main thing is that I get to talk to her. What I say isn't as important as what she says to me. Right?"

"Right," Judith agreed. "Okay, I'll see you in an hour or so."

Joe came up from the basement just as Judith was hanging up. "I'm on my way," he said breezily, loaded down with fishing tackle, boots, rain gear, and his suitcase.

"I see you're really worried about me," Judith said, meeting him at the back door.

"Well . . ." Joe grimaced. "I mean . . . Renie's coming?"

"Yes," Judith conceded. "But I wasn't sure she would."

"She's a good kid — in her weird way." He kissed Judith's lips.

"See you sometime Monday. Make room in the freezer for the fish."

With a wry smile, Judith watched her husband head for the garage. She could have been endangered by terrorists, serial killers, suicide bombers, and gangs of every ethnic origin, but that wouldn't have stopped a fisherman spouse if the salmon were hitting off the coast. She sighed and closed the back door.

Judith remained on the main floor, not watching the TV set she'd turned on in the living room and not paying much attention to the latest issue of *Vanity Fair* she held on her lap. Her ears were attuned to any sounds from upstairs. But there were none. All was quiet. Far too quiet for a Friday night at Hillside Manor. She was used to the comings and goings of guests on a weekend — or those who chose to stay in and leave their everyday lives back home. The B&B was supposed to be a haven — but for the past few days it had seemed more like hell.

Renie arrived at eight-forty, carrying her big purse, an overnight case, and a garment bag.

"You look like you're moving in," Judith noted.

"I had to bring proper clothes for impersonating a retirement-home salesperson," Renie said. "Do I get Mike's old room or do I have to sleep with you? You talk and snore and even sing. It drives me nuts."

"You can have Mike's room," Judith replied.

Renie knelt on the arm of the sofa where

Judith had reseated herself. "You really are scared?"

"Well . . . let's say I'm uneasy," Judith temporized. "I don't want to go one-on-one with Suzanne again over that bracelet."

"You think it's hers and not Taryn's?"

Judith nodded. "But if Rudi and Suzanne are lovers, it must be a long-distance romance."

Before Renie could respond, the doorbell rang. Both cousins went to answer it. Elsa Wittener stood on the front porch, her red hair damp from the evening mist.

"May I come in?" she asked.

"Of course," Judith said. "You remember my cousin Serena?"

Elsa pursed her lips as she gazed at Renie. "I think so," she said.

"Don't worry about it," Renie assured her. "I'm eminently forgettable."

If Elsa thought Renie was being funny, she didn't react. "I owe you an apology," she said as Judith led the way back into the living room. "I caused an awkward scene for you the other night."

"That's hardly your fault," Judith said, indicating that Elsa should sit on the matching sofa. "You were ill. In fact," she added quietly, "I heard you ingested some kind of poison."

"Yes," Elsa said, perching on the edge of the sofa cushion. She seemed very tense. "Isn't that incredible? Apparently, it was the same type that was used to poison poor Dolph."

"Do you recall eating or drinking anything that Dolph had?" Judith asked in an empathetic tone.

"I'm not sure," Elsa replied, hands folded tightly on her knees. "Olive's quiche, perhaps. It was delicious, and I do remember telling Fritz to try it, but he told me that quiche was for the faint of heart. Or some such thing." She laughed in an unnatural manner. "These young men — they have to assert their masculinity."

"But," Judith put in, "you think Dolph may have eaten some?"

"Yes, it's possible," Elsa said slowly. "I saw Andrea preparing a plate for Dolph. I'm almost sure she had put a slice of quiche on it. But was that the source of the poison?"

Judith admitted she didn't know. "Frankly, I'm not sure there was any quiche left."

"There wasn't." Renie, who was sitting on the sofa's arm, looked sheepish. "I . . . um . . . polished it off while everybody else was outside with the emergency vehicles."

Elsa gasped and Judith stared.

"Coz!" Judith exclaimed. "But you weren't poisoned."

"I know." Renie turned doleful. "Are you sorry I wasn't?"

"Hardly." Judith tried not to smile. She didn't want Elsa to think she was taking the matter lightly. "But that eliminates the quiche. Or rather, you eliminated it."

Renie shrugged.

"There were other foods," Elsa pointed out, "but I suppose salads and fruit and such wouldn't be the type of thing people would poison."

"No," Judith said. "It'd have to be something where the rhubarb distillation would be undetectable. Did you drink brandy?"

"Cognac," Elsa said, but held up a finger. "Wait. Fritz refilled my snifter at one point. He may have poured from the brandy rather than the cognac bottle. They're so similar, and he's not familiar with hard liquor. He's strictly a beer drinker at his age. But I've thought and thought since the hospital lab results came back, and I cannot imagine why anyone would want to poison either of us. It must be an accident, and I was the lucky one. Or so Fritz tells me." She smiled fondly. "My son can be very protective of his mother. We're devoted to each other."

"That's lovely," Judith said. "Can I make

you a cup of tea?"

"No." The response from Elsa was abrupt, and she unclasped her hands in a flustered gesture. "I mean — that sounds so rude. I'm sure you're not going to poison me!"

"You never know," Renie murmured.

"Not funny, coz," Judith said with a sharp glance at her cousin.

"In fact," Elsa said, rising from the sofa, "I should be going." She looked toward the far end of the long living room. "Have you thought any more about having that piano tuned?"

"Honestly, I haven't had time," Judith admitted.

"No. Of course you haven't," Elsa said. "I understand." She walked to the piano. "It has such a lovely tone. I don't suppose you'd consider selling it?"

"I've never thought about it," Judith said. "I rarely play — and when I do, I'm not very good. But many of our guests enjoy taking a turn at it."

"I can see why." Elsa began fingering the keys, a bit tentatively at first, then with more intensity.

"Beethoven," Renie said. " 'Für Elise.' "

Elsa nodded as she continued to play. The cousins sat in silence for at least two minutes.

"Enough," Elsa said with a self-deprecating laugh. "I couldn't resist."

"You play very well," Renie said.

Elsa moved back into the middle of the room. "Not tonight. The damp bothers me." Her face was wistful. "Tell me if you ever decide to sell the piano. Mine's a spinet, and not nearly as fine an instrument."

"I tend to hold on to things," Judith said.

Elsa didn't seem to hear the comment. She was gazing up the stairwell. "How is Andrea? I've always thought her high-strung."

"She sleeps a lot," Judith said.

"Maybe I should look in on her," Elsa said in a doubtful voice.

"Go ahead," Judith urged. "She might like that."

Elsa kept staring upward but didn't move. "No," she finally said. "Tomorrow, perhaps. Good night."

Judith closed and locked the door behind her. "What was that all about?" she asked Renie.

"Darned if I know," Renie said. "Maybe she wants to steal your piano. There's a lot of that going around here lately."

"Too much," Judith responded, looking through the front door's peephole. "That's odd. Elsa's car — I assume that's her

Honda parked out front — is still there. She's going over to the Wittener house."

"So?"

"Suzanne says nobody's home. The place is dark." Judith paused. "Elsa's on the porch." Another pause. "She went inside."

"Did somebody let her in?"

Judith shook her head. "No. She must have a key."

"That's possible, I suppose," Renie said.

Judith kept watching. A light went on in the living room. "I don't get it. Elsa comes and goes in her ex-husband's house?"

"She might. They're not on hostile terms, are they?"

Judith finally moved away from the door. "Not that I know of. But I still wonder what she's up to. Whatever it is, I don't think it's good."

# CHAPTER FIFTEEN

"Joe hasn't taken down the porch swing," Judith said thoughtfully. "If I sat in it, I could see what Elsa's doing over at Rudi's house."

"How?" Renie demanded. "You've suddenly got X-ray vision?"

"I mean when she comes out," Judith explained. "If she's carrying something."

"Like a piano?"

"Never mind." Judith was impatient. "It can't hurt to watch, and she can't see me from behind the rhododendron and the camellia bushes if I sit at the far end of the swing."

Renie shrugged. "Go for it. But leave the door ajar so I can hear you scream if you're attacked."

Judith hadn't crossed the threshold before the phone rang. Renie had stayed in the living room and picked up the extension on the round cherrywood table.

"Define *here*," she said to the caller. "As in 'she's all here' or only partly?"

"Who is it?" Judith hissed from the entry hall.

Renie held out the receiver. "Your cop buddy, Rosemary O'Grady."

"Are you all right?" Rosemary asked Judith in a concerned voice. "Was that one of the suspects?"

"No," Judith replied, motioning for Renie to pick up the cordless phone in the kitchen. "It was my cousin, trying to be funny. She didn't manage it. What's going on?"

"You were absolutely brilliant to suggest checking into the foxhunt accident that killed Mr. Farrow," Rosemary enthused. "I have a cousin in Madison, New Jersey, who works for a string of newspapers. He covers local activist groups, including PETA — you know, for the protection of animals — so he keeps up with foxhunting because hunt-club members are always fighting with PETA about the foxes."

Judith remembered coming across People for the Ethical Treatment of Animals when she and Renie had been in San Francisco the previous March. "Are they involved in what happened to Mr. Farrow?"

"Oh, no," Rosemary replied. "That is, they were cleared of any culpability in his death.

An accident was ruled out, though stranger things have happened. The police finally ruled it a homicide."

Judith sat down in the side chair by the cherrywood table. She heard Renie's click on the other phone. "That's my cousin," she explained. "If she listens in I won't have to repeat all this."

"That's fine," Rosemary said in her chipper manner. "Two heads are better than one, especially when one is yours, Mrs. Flynn."

"Thanks," Renie put in. "My head still works fairly well. Usually."

"I'm sure it does!" Rosemary declared. "You're *family,* after all!"

"Tell us what happened," Judith urged, prepared to jot down a few notes on the tablet she kept by the phone base.

"It was October," Rosemary began, "which is the traditional time for foxhunts. According to the rules of this particular hunt club, competitors must ride in pairs or teams of three. But Blake Farrow never liked to ride with others. He was often disqualified, but never severely penalized because he was highly respected — and rich. Anyway, the master of the hunt and his partner — who happened to be Andrea Farrow, now Mrs. Kluger, of course —

322

started out, setting the pace. I guess that's what they do. Anyway, Blake and a companion whose name was Laurel Chandler rode off with all the others. Blake soon left Laurel behind. Somewhere along the course, Blake's horse was found without its rider. Shortly thereafter, Blake was found — without his head."

"Ugh," said Judith.

"Yes. He had been decapitated by a wire strung across that part of the course between two trees."

"Gruesome," Judith remarked.

"Very," Rosemary agreed. "Fortunately, Andrea was already back at the hunt club when she heard the awful news. But what's odd is that she and the master of the hunt had ridden through that same part of the course earlier without any incident. They weren't ever suspects, since the MFH was one of New York City's most upstanding citizens. He swore that Andrea never left his side, and no one questioned his word."

"Yet whoever put the wire there intended to harm Blake Farrow?"

"That's only an assumption," Rosemary replied. "Whoever it was must have known Farrow's habit of going ahead of the other riders."

Judith tried to ignore Renie, who was

standing by the buffet and making all sorts of querying gestures. "Was the case ever solved?"

"Not exactly," Rosemary said. "It was later discovered that someone at Farrow's musical-instrument company had been cooking the books. There were rumors of Mob ties, and it's possible that Farrow was killed by professionals. This was in Jersey, remember. The Mob still exists there."

"So I gather," Judith said. "Was the company financially sound at the time of Blake Farrow's death?"

"It was rocky," Rosemary replied, "but Farrow came from old money, so he left Andrea a rich widow. She sold the company to some German outfit."

"Who was playing games with the books?" Judith queried.

"Interestingly enough, the husband of the woman who was paired with Blake," Rosemary responded. "His name was Harry Chandler, an accountant. He was sent to prison, and died there in a fight with another inmate."

"Was he in the hunt party?"

"No. He didn't ride, and had an airtight alibi for that morning." Rosemary sounded disappointed. "It would've been perfect if he'd killed Blake Farrow. But there was no way to tie him to the murder."

"Did your cousin cover the story?" Judith inquired.

"No," Rosemary said. "Tommy — my cousin — was still in college at the time. He checked out the archives of the local papers including the chain he works for. The coverage was discreet, but Tommy also talked to a couple of veteran reporters who knew the background."

"That's quick work," Judith said. "Congratulations."

"I couldn't have done it if it hadn't been for you," Rosemary insisted. "Tommy was still at the office when I called him. Then, after he checked the archives, he went over to one of the local bars and questioned the old-time journalists who hang out there."

"You're working late tonight yourself," Judith noted. "Is Levi still on the job?"

"Oh — no," Rosemary said. "I made him go home. He's still worn out from his allergy attack."

"You've done great work," Judith declared. "Levi will be proud of you. I am, too."

"It's no big deal," Rosemary said modestly. "If you have any other brainstorms, be sure to let me know."

"Of course."

Renie had wandered into the living room

with the cordless phone. After both cousins hung up, Judith went to the front porch.

Elsa's car was gone and the lights were out in the Wittener house. Judith still felt in the dark.

"Why," Renie demanded, "are we watching the Food Channel? You think I don't already know how to make crepes?"

"You like food," Judith replied. "I like watching chefs. They have all kinds of interesting recipes and ideas."

"Do you ever make any of them?"

"Not really. Look, he's using a new kind of crepe pan."

"Why aren't you watching Sports Center or a war movie or the Führer like Bill always does at home?"

"Check out how high the heat is on that pan! I'd be afraid of scorching the crepes."

"Why do I suddenly miss John Wayne? Why do I want to see meaningless preseason NBA games? Why am I *here?*"

"That's a different kind of spatula. Wow — he can really flip those babies with that thing!"

"Tanks. Armor. Air-to-ground missiles. Bases loaded. Blocked shots. Dropped passes. Hockey pucks. Anything but this!"

"Unsalted butter — now there's a concept!"

"Ahem!" The sound came from Estelle Pearson, who stood in the living room by the buffet, arms folded across her chest.

"Oh!" Judith jumped. "What is it?"

"Miss Suzanne would like something to eat," Estelle said. "A crisp salad with a dressing that has no oil base."

"How about crepes?" Renie said. "Mrs. Flynn here is the world's greatest expert on crepes. Next to Chef Le Louche on TV, of course."

Judith immediately turned off the set. "I can use my own green goddess dressing," she offered. "I don't use oil. And what about Mrs. Kluger?" she inquired, rising from the sofa. "Has she eaten anything in the past few days? Have you?"

"I have my own health bars and beverages," Estelle replied. "Miss Suzanne is very insistent that we eat only healthy foods."

It occurred to Judith that Estelle's sturdy figure indicated that she was consuming more than bars and beverages. "Would Mrs. Kluger feel better if she came downstairs for a while? She's been cooped up in that room for an awfully long time."

"No." Estelle appeared unmoved by Judith's words.

"Okay." Judith sighed. "I'll prepare the salad. It'll take about twenty minutes. I'll bring it up when it's ready."

"Good." The maid turned on her heel and left the living room.

"Need help?" Renie asked.

"Sure." Judith headed for the kitchen with Renie following her.

"What can I do?" Renie inquired.

"Get out the romaine lettuce and anything else you can find for a salad," Judith replied. "Fortunately, I've got some green goddess dressing already made up."

"I see it," Renie said. "It's in a glass jar, right?"

"Yes. I wonder if Andrea would like some bread to —" Judith stopped and leaned against the counter. "I'm beginning to wonder about Suzanne and that gym or health club or whatever it is."

"What do you mean?" Renie had placed the salad-dressing jar on the counter by Judith and was gathering the greenery. "I thought we already discussed that."

Judith grimaced. "As Bill would say, 'Something's off.' "

"Oh? Want some weird pop?"

Judith shook her head. "What's weird is Suzanne. I'm still wondering if her business really exists."

"Did she ever give you a name?"

"No. But she said it was two blocks from her apartment in the Village."

Renie placed lettuce, tomato, cucumber, and scallions on the counter. "Do you have her address?"

"Yes," Judith said, taking a bowl out of the cupboard. "It's in the guest registry. Go get it — or take a Post-it note and copy it down."

While Renie was in the entry hall, Judith tossed the salad.

"Got it," Renie said, sticking the Post-it on the counter. "She lives on Christopher Street."

Judith looked at the address. "This means nothing to me," she admitted.

"Let's get a map," Renie said, sitting down at the computer.

"While you do that, I'll deliver the salad to Suzanne," Judith said.

Renie turned away from the keyboard. "Do you want me to watch your back?"

"No. If I need help, I'll yell."

At the top of the stairs, Judith hesitated. Was Suzanne in her own room or her mother's room? She decided to try Andrea's.

Estelle opened the door a bare three inches. "Yes?"

"The salad," Judith said, stating the obvious.

"Just leave it in the hall." Estelle closed the door.

"Damn!" Judith breathed. She'd tried to look inside, but could see only a huddled form in the bed. Andrea, she presumed. Suzanne was nowhere in sight.

"You're still alive," Renie said without looking away from the computer screen. "Any wounds?"

"No." Judith leaned on the kitchen counter. "Any luck?"

"I got the Greenwich Village map right away," Renie explained, "but I put in gyms and health clubs in the neighborhood and got zip. That doesn't mean there aren't any — some may not list on these sites — but it doesn't help much."

"Let's find a bar."

"Now? You want to leave the house unguarded?"

"I mean in the Greenwich Village neighborhood."

"Oh." Renie made several attempts, but found none listed on Christopher Street. "The best I can do is try one of the places in the adjoining blocks."

Judith glanced at the schoolhouse clock. "It's almost one in the morning. The bars should still be open, right? Let me call one."

Renie quickly printed out the page with the half-dozen listings. Judith dialed the first one.

"I'm trying to locate a gym or health club in the neighborhood," she said. "Could you tell me —"

"This ain't no gym, lady. This ain't no health club. Nutcase," the gruff voice said just before he hung up.

Her second attempt fared no better. "Get your eyes checked," the woman who answered snapped. "You called the wrong number."

Renie tapped the counter with her fingernails. "Give me that phone," she ordered. "You've lost your knack."

She dialed the third number. "Hey, buster, let me talk to Jack," she demanded of the youngish-sounding man who answered the phone. "Make it snappy."

Judith leaned over her cousin's shoulder, trying to hear what was going on at the other end of the line three thousand miles away. Faintly, she heard the name Jack being called out. A moment later, a drunken male voice spoke.

"Whaddaya want now, Vera?"

"Meet me at the gym," Renie said in an angry voice. "Now. I got trouble."

"What gym? There's no freakin' gym round here, you . . . Hey . . . Vera? You don't sound so good. Whass wrong?"

Renie clicked off. "No gym. You heard the Village idiot."

"How did you know somebody named Jack was in that bar?" Judith asked.

Renie shrugged. "There's always somebody named Jack in a New York bar."

"But does Jack know what he's talking about?"

"Hey — you're the one who doubted the existence of the place," Renie retorted. "You take it from here. What does the gym or no gym have to do with Kluger getting killed anyway?"

Judith tidied up from her salad making. "Maybe nothing. I just have a strange feeling about Suzanne. I think she's on a short leash, financially."

"Why?"

"Because," Judith said, "I'm guessing she stole your credit cards."

Renie had taken a Pepsi out of the fridge. *"What?"*

"I've thought that all along," Judith said, wiping down the counter. "Who else? According to the drugstore clerk at the bottom of the hill, it was a woman who bought all that stuff, including sleep aids and such.

Suzanne's an early riser. She runs. It'd be no problem for her to go down to the bottom of the counter-balance and get back up here in half an hour. Also," Judith added as she rinsed out the dishrag, "she went to Holliday's to get her mother's prescription renewal — but that's all she got. Yet you told me the bathroom cabinet was full of the kinds of things purchased on your credit — hey!"

Renie had run out of the kitchen, obviously heading for the second floor — and Suzanne. Judith started after her, but by the time she reached the entry hall, Renie had disappeared from the second landing.

"Coz!" Judith shouted. "Come back here!"

"Open this door, you thieving weasel!" Renie shouted.

Wearily, Judith trudged up the stairs, hoping to avert disaster.

Renie was pounding at the door of Room Four. "Come on out and give me my money, you chicken-livered crook!"

The door to Room Three opened. Estelle leaned out, making a sharp shushing sign. "Madam's sleeping! Please be quiet!"

"Be quiet yourself, you old bat," Renie snarled, waving one of her fists at the maid. "I want my money!"

"Coz," Judith said, trying to keep calm

and not think about how much her hip hurt from climbing the stairs, "cool it, will you?"

*"Cool it?"* Renie shot back. "What are you, some relic from the sixties, that era of no taste and no sense? I'm *not* cool, I'm hotter than a Dutch oven!" She turned back to the door and began pounding again.

"Miss Suzanne isn't in there," Estelle said in a low, angry voice. "She's in the bathroom."

"I don't care if she's in the army," Renie yelled. "Tell her to get her butt out here right now! I don't believe you! What's she doing — eating her salad in the bathtub? No oil but lots of suds?"

Estelle quietly but firmly shut the door.

Judith cautiously took Renie's arm. "Come on, Suzanne won't come out. Give it up. For my sake, if nothing else."

"No." Renie shook off Judith's hand.

"Coz . . ."

"No."

Judith shrugged. "Okay. Get me sued. Who cares?"

"She won't sue you," Renie argued. "My Suit is better than her Suit. I've got Bill's brother, Bub. Furthermore, he's free."

"To you, but not to me," Judith asserted. "I'm the one who'll get sued, and I'd never expect Bub to work for nothing." She winced and staggered. "Oh! My hip!"

Startled, Renie turned away from the door. "Are you okay?"

"I'm not sure," Judith said, reeling a bit.

Renie hurried to her cousin. "Let me help you. Sit on the settee."

"No. I need to lie down. I'm too tall for the settee. Oh!" She winced again.

"Did you dislocate?" Renie asked in an anxious voice.

"I don't know." Judith kept her eyes averted from Renie's worried face. "Help me get downstairs."

"Sure, come on, lean on me."

Slowly, the cousins started down the stairs. Judith put some of her weight on Renie.

"It's my fault," Renie said. "I made you run after me."

"Don't blame yourself," Judith insisted, reaching the first landing. "I don't think it's dislocated. I think I just twisted it. A twinge, really."

They stepped into the entry hall. Renie let go. "You're a fraud."

Judith did her best to look surprised. "What?"

"You heard me. You faked that just to get me away from Suzanne." Renie swore softly. "As usual, I swallowed your lie hook, line, and sinker. You'd think after all these years . . ." She shook her head in disbelief at her own gullibility.

"It's better this way," Judith reasoned. "Let's go back into the kitchen."

Renie followed Judith, but was still muttering self-recriminations.

"Drink your Pepsi," Judith said in a kindly tone. "It'll make you feel better."

Renie popped the top on the can she'd left on the counter and took a sip. "Thanks, I needed that. Okay, back to business. You conclude — with your irrefutable logic — that Suzanne has no money of her own because she has no income from a fitness business that doesn't exist because she had no start-up money because . . . ?"

Judith shrugged. "Because Andrea's a tightwad? Because she's a control freak? Because Suzanne wouldn't know how to run a business? Because New York City real estate prices are sky-high? Because Suzanne is in her thirties and hasn't found a career that suits her?" She sat down at the kitchen table. "There are tons of possibilities."

"Which turn Suzanne into a crook," Renie noted, leaning against the fridge. "How old was she when her father was killed?"

"Suzanne was in high school," Judith replied.

Renie considered the statement. "An only child. Like us. You'd think Dad would've set up a college trust fund by that time."

"We were only children," Judith pointed out. "Did we have trust funds?"

Renie shot her cousin a disparaging look. "Our parents had no funds, period. We were poor, remember? We still are."

"Okay, so maybe it was a college trust fund and Suzanne used it, but didn't do much with her education," Judith said. "She seems stunted to me."

"Her muscles aren't," Renie countered. "They're well developed."

Judith was tempted to bite her fingernails, but refrained. "Let's say that somewhere along the line, Rudi met Suzanne. The connection, of course, was Dolph, who'd married Andrea, Suzanne's mother. By that time, Suzanne was a grown woman — but Rudi was still married to Elsa. There was no way Andrea would approve of Suzanne's involvement with a musician who was a married man, no matter how talented he might be. Andrea puts her foot down, cuts off her daughter's money, and Rudi leaves New York for Philadelphia, where he takes up with Taryn Moss, and they move here this summer."

Renie put a hand to her head. "Jeez — I

can hardly follow this without a game program. Who's on first?"

"Wrong. What's on first, Who's on second," Judith retorted. "You know this cast of characters."

"I know the routine — I Don't Know's on third, right?"

"Never mind. Skip the Abbott and Costello act and let me finish." Judith poured herself a glass of water from the tap. "Rudi goes to Philadelphia, but he and Suzanne are still in love. They continue their romance via long distance." Seeing Renie's skeptical expression, she shook her head. "It happens, especially these days with the Internet."

Renie relented. "Okay. Not to mention that New York and Philadelphia are very close, and the two could have spent time together before Rudi moved here."

"Exactly."

"So how do I prove Suzanne swiped my credit cards?" Renie asked. "She's probably tossed them by now, having figured out they're no good. Whatever pittances we still have are in one of our other accounts at the Bank of Burma. I never carry around any information about our BABU money market fund."

"Then you can forget about it," Judith said. "For now."

"Hey — I'm still a victim!" Renie cried, pounding her fist on the refrigerator door.

"Don't dent the fairly new and very expensive fridge," Judith warned. "What's the point when you — and the cops — have no evidence?"

"I could get my money back? I could sue? I could afford food?"

"You're not starving," Judith pointed out, "skinny as you may seem. But credit-card and identity theft aren't capital crimes. I'm talking about murder."

Renie stared briefly at Judith. "Do you really think Suzanne's the guilty party?"

"She could be. Think about it," Judith said, getting up from the chair. "Dolph may have had great influence over Andrea. Maybe he stood in the way of Suzanne's checkbook and her romance with Rudi. After all," she went on, nudging Renie out of the path to the fridge, "love and money are big motives for murder. Suzanne may have had both."

# CHAPTER SIXTEEN

"Are they there yet? Are they there yet? Are they there yet?" Renie asked as the cousins headed for bed in the third-floor quarters.

"The husbands?" Judith made sure the door between the second floor and the stairs to the third floor was locked securely. "It's about a four-, four-and-a-half-hour drive to the ocean. Since midnight is upon us, I assume they're almost there. They should get a few hours of sleep before going on the charter boat."

The cousins climbed the short but steep narrow staircase to the small foyer. "Mike's old room is ready for you," Judith said, pointing to the door on her left. "Just ignore the toys and other stuff that he and Kristin leave behind when they visit with the boys."

"Okay." Renie hesitated. "What do you suppose your guests have been doing for the last couple of hours? I haven't heard a peep or a squeak out of them."

"I know," Judith agreed. "It's eerie. It's not normal, not even under these circumstances. I wish they'd leave or get arrested."

"The cops can't arrest all of them," Renie pointed out.

Judith looked bleak. "I know. But I wish they could. I've never had such a disagreeable bunch."

On that sour note, Judith and Renie retired for the night.

To Judith's surprise, Renie was up before ten. She came to the kitchen dressed in a matching dark green jacket and slacks that set off the lighter shade of green and the gold in her sweater. Her makeup had been applied and she had actually combed her hair. Even more remarkable was that she seemed alert — and pleasant.

"What time is your appointment with Olive?" Judith inquired, pouring Renie a mug of coffee.

"Ten-thirty," Renie replied. "I'll eat some cereal now. I never make a sales pitch on a full stomach."

"You've never made a sales pitch in your life," Judith said with a little laugh.

"You're nuts," Renie declared. "I've spent my career as a freelance graphic designer pitching myself and my talent."

"That's true," Judith allowed. "What kind of cereal do you want?"

"I'll get it," Renie said, opening the cupboard. "Did anybody come down for breakfast?"

"No," Judith replied, refilling her own mug. "I heard Suzanne go out to run about eight. She came back an hour later and went straight upstairs. She may be avoiding me after the awkward incident of last night. No Estelle — and, of course, no Andrea."

"Andrea must be starving to death," Renie said with a worried expression. "What has she had to eat since her husband got killed?"

"Soup and pudding," Judith said. "Of course Suzanne may have a suitcase full of health foods upstairs."

"I wish we knew a doctor," Renie murmured, pouring cornflakes into a bowl.

"We know plenty of doctors," Judith said.

"I mean one we could get to come in and examine Andrea."

"Suzanne probably wouldn't allow it," Judith responded.

"What if the police insisted?"

"That's an idea. Maybe I'll call Rosemary. Of course it *is* Saturday. She could be off duty. On the other hand, Joe used to work through the weekend on homicide cases.

And Rosemary seems like a go-getter."

"Give it a try," Renie said.

After Renie left for the Empress Apartments, Judith dialed the direct number Rosemary had handed out on her official card. The young detective answered on the second ring. Briefly, Judith made the proposal about bringing in a doctor.

"I'm genuinely concerned about Mrs. Kluger," she explained. "She appears to be in some sort of drugged stupor. I can't let that go on with a guest, suspect or not."

"That's a problem," Rosemary conceded. "But unless Mrs. Kluger or her doctor cooperates, I'll have to get a court order. That could be tricky, especially on a weekend."

"I understand," Judith said. "Have you learned anything new?"

"Levi is taking the weekend off to complete his recuperation," Rosemary explained. "I assured him I could handle any of the minor details that came along. I told our lieutenant that I really thought one of us should stay on board, given Mr. Kluger's prominence."

"So?" Judith said. "Has anything surfaced?"

"Mostly I've been doing background checks," Rosemary replied. "Rudi Wittener moved to Philadelphia seven years ago, not long after his divorce. That's where he met Taryn Moss, who was a private piano student working part-time at the Academy of Music. Elsa claims that moving here was Fritz's idea. He was bored with the East Coast, and wanted to come west. Anywhere from Canada to Mexico would do. I gather they chose this city so Fritz could be close to his father."

Judith reflected. "Granted, I've never spoken at length to Rudi since he arrived, but I didn't realize he had a son until the past few days. I'd never seen Fritz at the Wittener house until this week."

"Fritz seems fond of his father," Rosemary said, "in a way. At least he doesn't bad-mouth him."

"That wouldn't be a good idea in front of you and Levi," Judith noted.

"How do you mean?"

Judith paused. She wasn't sure what she meant. A fragment of conversation came back to her. "I happened to hear Taryn and Fritz talking about Rudi and Elsa before the party. It struck me that they were doing their best to make it look as if Fritz's parents still got along fairly well. Or at least Taryn was. Fritz was more . . . noncommittal. But," she went on, "Elsa mentioned that

344

Fritz is very protective of her."

"That'd be typical, I suppose," Rosemary remarked. "I have an aunt who's divorced. My cousin is about Fritz's age, and he acts like his mother's knight in shining armor."

Judith thought back to Mike's younger years. Whatever criticism she'd had of Dan McMonigle was never directed at him as a father. He had been a good parent, spending more time with Mike than Judith could. Of course Dan hadn't worked during most of those years, and Judith had two jobs to support the family. It was only fair that Dan had shouldered so much of the parental responsibilities. But fairness didn't always equate with reality. Dan, however, had taken his duties seriously. When he died, Mike was bereft. Later, Mike became more protective of Judith, especially if another man showed any interest in her. By the time Joe had reentered her life, Mike was grown and away from home. Otherwise, her son might have put up insurmountable barriers to the rekindled romance — and never discovered that Joe was his real father.

Rosemary had nothing more to add, but promised to keep Judith apprised of any new developments. The next hour seemed to drag. Judith realized she'd heard no thumping or any noise at all from the second floor. Apparently, Suzanne had confined her exercise to the earlier run.

The lack of communication with her guests was driving Judith nuts. It was so unlike Hillside Manor's usual routine. *Less work, more worry,* she thought as she stood at the bottom of the back stairs, wondering if she dared check on the second floor's strange trio.

"Yahoo!" Renie cried, thrusting open the back door and accidentally banging Judith in the rear end. "Ooops! Sorry, coz."

Judith rubbed her backside. "I'm glad you didn't knock me down, you idiot. Couldn't you see me through the window in the door?"

"I wasn't looking," Renie admitted, removing the green jacket and hanging it on a peg in the hallway. "Be nice to me, I'm full of important information." She gazed out into the kitchen. "Is it safe to talk?"

"Nobody's stirred a stump," Judith said. "That's what's bothering me. It's weird."

"Now I can eat a real breakfast," Renie announced, opening the fridge. "I'll make it myself." She began gathering eggs, bacon, and packaged hash brown potatoes. "Olive fell for my line like the salmon are going for Bill and Joe's bait. We hope."

Judith couldn't believe it. "You succeeded

with a bunch of hoo-haw where I failed? Incredible!"

Renie nodded as she put bacon in a skillet. "No problem. How do you think I bamboozled all those CEOs and other corporate big shots over the years? I can blah-blah with the best of them — including you."

"Great." Judith sat down at the kitchen table while Renie cooked. "So tell me what you learned."

"Olive has worked for Rudi about fifteen years," Renie began. "Before that, she was in the corporate world, at some big company in New Jersey. She wanted to quit the rat race, so she took early retirement. But Olive isn't one to stay idle." She stopped long enough to carefully flip her bacon. "When Rudi advertised for an assistant, she interviewed for the job because she told him she'd always been a music lover. He hired her, and the rest is history."

"That's it?" Judith asked, disappointed.

"Not quite." Renie looked smug. "I told her about our piano. Our *real* piano. I said it came with the retirement home."

The piano had been purchased by Aunt Deb when Judith and Renie were children. Aunt Deb and Uncle Cliff had thought their daughter should learn to play, but Renie

had absolutely no musical talent. By a fluke
— and the ignorance of a novice piano
salesman — Aunt Deb had managed to pay
a mere hundred and twenty-five dollars for
a solid rosewood English spinet circa 1830
that was a transitional instrument from the
harpsichord and didn't really sound like a
piano. Especially when Renie tried to play
it. But the bottom line was that the so-called
piano was worth thousands of dollars even
at the time of its sale some fifty years earlier.
The legacy of Aunt Deb's piano purchase
resided in the Jones household.

Renie put the hash browns into the skillet.
"Olive was intrigued, but mentioned that
the piano wasn't nearly as old as some of
her family heirlooms, including the serving
piece she brought to the party."

Judith rested her chin on her hands. "So?
That's not very helpful in solving our
mystery. Where did Olive live when she
worked for Rudi?"

"She moved from Somerville, New Jersey,
to Manhattan." Renie added the scrambled
eggs to the pan and placed two slices of
bread in the toaster. "And moved again to
Philadelphia and finally here."

Judith tapped her cheek. "A faithful body.
How old is she?"

"Sixty-one, come December."

"Thinking seriously about retirement?"

"Apparently. She can't wait to see the home," Renie exulted.

"Will she ever?"

"Of course not. Olive thinks it's in a new building at the bottom of the hill. I gave her the address of the basketball arena at the civic center. If she goes to look, she'll just think she's confused. Or I am."

Thoughtfully, Judith watched her cousin start to dish up. "Connections?"

"I asked," Renie replied. "References, nearest relatives, all the stuff you'd need to know if you were representing a real retirement home. Her parents have been dead for years, she's never married, and she had a sister who died quite some time ago. There was also a niece or a nephew, but I got the impression Olive hadn't kept in touch."

"Alone in the world," Judith murmured. "I always find that so sad. We're lucky to have come from a big family, even if neither of us had any brothers or sisters."

"True," Renie agreed, her plate now piled high. "What do I get to do next?"

Judith regarded her cousin with amusement. "You like playing Let's Pretend?"

"It keeps my mind off my debts," Renie said grimly. "It distracts me from wanting to throttle Suzanne."

Judith got up to pour herself more coffee. "Assuming it was Suzanne who stole your credit cards."

Renie had sat down and was stuffing her face. "Hooelz?"

"Who else? I don't know," Judith admitted. "It seems to me she has to be the culprit." She looked up at the high ceiling. "Why don't they come down? Why don't they eat? Why don't they *move?*"

"Want me to collect the salad stuff from last night?" Renie asked.

"No. No, no. You'll end up duking it out with one of them. But you're right," Judith said. "That makes a good excuse to go up there."

Renie had shoveled more eggs and hash browns into her mouth. "Gluck."

"I need some good luck," Judith asserted, heading down the hall.

She was almost at the top of the back stairs when she heard sobbing. Alarmed, Judith hurried down the hall, where she saw Suzanne sitting on the settee by the front stairs railing, crying her eyes out.

"Suzanne!" Judith exclaimed, her natural compassion coming to the fore. "What's wrong?"

"It's Mom!" she blurted through her tears. "She's dead!"

# CHAPTER SEVENTEEN

Judith was stunned. She stumbled against the table that held the guest telephone, magazines, and a half-dozen board games.

"Have you called a doctor?" Judith asked in a voice that cracked.

Suzanne, who had covered her face with her hands, shook her head.

Grabbing the phone, Judith dialed 911. *More emergency vehicles,* she thought with dread. Hillside Manor would be deleted from the state B&B association's list of recommended inns.

The female dispatcher sounded almost bored by Judith's call. "What have you got this time?" she inquired, apparently seeing the Flynn phone number and address pop up automatically on her screen. "Death? Dismemberment? Homicide? Sui—"

"Just send the damned medics!" Judith shouted angrily.

"I already have," the dispatcher said drily.

"I think they usually park about a block away from your house."

"Not funny," Judith muttered, turning away from Suzanne. "I ought to report you."

"Somebody ought to report *you,* honey," the voice retorted just before hanging up.

Judith sat down next to Suzanne. "What happened?" she asked the still-sobbing young woman.

But Suzanne seemed unable to speak other than a few incoherent words: "Sleeping . . . stopped . . . Estelle . . . pulse . . ."

"Where's Estelle?" Judith spoke more sharply than she'd intended.

Suzanne jumped. "There," she said in a hoarse voice, and pointed to her mother's room.

Judith got up, but before she could cross the hall, she heard Renie at the bottom of the stairs. "What's going on? Do I hear sirens?"

"Yes!" Judith shouted. "Let them in!"

She heard Renie swear, uttering some really bad words usually reserved for R-rated movies. Not that Judith blamed her cousin; she felt like saying a few of them herself.

Instead, she yanked open the door to Andrea's room. "The medics are here," she announced loudly.

Estelle, who had been standing with her

back to the window that looked out over the driveway, was impassive.

"Well?" Judith demanded, barely able to look at the still form in the bed. "Can you tell me what's going on?"

"No," Estelle said quietly but firmly.

Judith refused to be stonewalled. "This is my establishment. You are my guest. I'm responsible for you and for Ms. Farrow and Mrs. Kluger. I must insist that you tell me what's happened here. Is Mrs. Kluger actually dead?"

Estelle seemed to have turned to granite. "I won't say anything until I have a lawyer present."

Judith felt like tearing her hair. Or yanking out Estelle's. "All right," she said, taking a deep breath, "I quit." She stalked out of the room and planted herself in the middle of the hallway.

A moment later she heard heavy footsteps on the stairs. The usual EMT and firefighting crews — or as near as Judith could tell — arrived on the second floor with Renie bringing up the rear.

As soon as the medical personnel entered the guest room, one of the firefighters asked Estelle to move out into the hall. The maid started to protest but slowly edged away from the window. Judith glowered at her as she felt Renie's hand on her arm.

"What now?" she asked in a low, impatient tone.

Judith shot a quick glance at Suzanne, who had risen to her feet, but had her hands over her face. "Andrea's dead," she whispered. "I'm done, finished, kaput."

"Oh . . ." Renie let out another stream of obscenities, but at least she said them quietly. "What do you mean?" she demanded as Judith's last words sank in.

"I can't do this anymore." Judith's strong jawline was set. "I'm too old. This is the last straw. *I'll* buy your house as a retirement home."

Renie stared at her cousin. "You know it's not really for sale."

The firefighters, in their heavy equipment, crowded the area while the medics did what had to be done in the bedroom. Judith noticed that the battalion chief with the name tag *Conley* was among them. He, in turn, was looking at her.

"I had a feeling we'd meet again," he said, moving closer to Judith. "What kind of a place is this, really?"

"An abattoir," Renie snapped. "What do you think?"

Judith didn't speak, but folded her arms across her chest and looked straight ahead at the linen chests that ran from floor to ceiling in the hall.

Bemused, Conley stroked his thick mustache. "I was thinking of taking my almost ex-wife someplace around town for a farewell getaway weekend. I've obviously found the perfect spot."

One of the medics exited the bedroom. Judith didn't recognize the crew cut or the square, earnest face. Nor, she told herself, did she care. Josef Stalin could have shown up with a red cross on his chest and she wouldn't have given a damn.

"Who called this in?" he asked.

"I did." Judith refused to look directly at the medic.

"I'm afraid Mrs. Kluger is dead." The medic obviously despised giving bad news. "We'll need some information before we take her away."

"*You* need information!" Judith exploded. She pointed to Suzanne. "Ask *her*. Ask the maid hovering in the doorway. Don't ask me — I don't know a damned thing! And I don't want to find out!"

"Whoa!" Conley held up his hands. "Calm down. Don't take this personally."

"How else should I take it?" Judith demanded. "These people are plague carriers. Move them all out before I torch the place!"

Conley, whose demeanor had altered to pseudocompassionate, tipped his head to one side. "Hey, calm down. I thought you were an old hand at this."

"I quit," Judith repeated. "Quit, quit, *quit*."

"Police here," Rosemary announced from the stairwell. "I picked the 911 call off of the scanner on my way to get some lunch." She reached the second floor, her usually pert face suitably grim. "What have we got now?" she asked Judith.

"I quit."

Rosemary was startled. "You what?"

"You heard me," Judith snapped. "Talk to my cousin. Talk to anybody but *me*."

"But, Mrs. Flynn," Rosemary protested, "you can't —"

Renie intervened, putting out an arm between her cousin and the detective. "She can. She has. Don't pester her. I'll talk to you, if you need anything. Leave Judith alone. It may take my cousin a while to make up her mind, but once she does, don't try to change it."

The crew-cut medic had rejoined his partner in the bedroom. Rosemary asked Estelle and Suzanne to step aside. The maid glared at the detective, but grudgingly half carried the distraught Suzanne to Room Four. Judith turned her back on the others, gazing over the stair rail behind the wicker settee.

"How'd it happen?" Conley inquired of Renie.

"I've no idea," she replied. "Ask the maid."

"Hold on," he said. "By any chance is this the wife of the guy who keeled over on the sidewalk a few nights ago?"

"Yes," Renie said. "She's hardly left her room since."

"It looks like once she does leave, she won't be coming back," Conley remarked.

Judith tried to ignore the exchange. She caught the faint sound of footsteps downstairs.

"Yoo-hoo! Are you up there?" Arlene Rankers called.

Judith leaned over the banister. "Yes, Arlene. I'll be right down."

"I can be up faster than you can get down," Arlene asserted, climbing the stairs like a teenager. "Who's dead?"

Judith grimaced. "Don't ask me."

"Oh." Arlene was undaunted. If she had to quiz everybody in the house, she'd eventually get her answers. "Well?" she asked of Renie.

"Andrea Kluger," Renie said. "We don't know anything else."

Arlene made a face. "Oh, come, Serena —

357

you must know *something.* Everybody does." She turned to the battalion chief. "Conley, isn't it? You have to know. You're in uniform."

"Sorry, ma'am," Conley apologized. "I'm just here for the show."

"Maybe," Renie suggested as Judith started for the head of the stairs, "we should get out of the way, too. Wait for us, coz."

For the first time, Judith noticed that Arlene was holding something long and slim in her hand.

"What's that?" Judith asked, waiting on the top step.

Arlene ignored the question as she walked toward Room Three. "Just a peek. I hardly ever get to see the bodies."

Conley put out a long arm. "Hold it. You can't go in there."

Arlene gave the firefighter a pitying look. "Of course I can. Do you think I'm afraid of a corpse? You have no idea how many funerals I've put on at SOTS. I have a freezer full of funeral food. Mostly hearty casseroles, but some desserts, too."

Rosemary came out of the bedroom before Arlene could go any farther. "I'm calling the medical examiner," she announced. "This room is sealed off."

"But," Estelle objected, "you can't keep

Miss Suzanne from her mother's side."

"I'm afraid I can," Rosemary said gravely. "I've got two uniforms coming any minute to stand guard. Excuse me." She nudged Estelle and the still-distraught Suzanne out of the way.

But Estelle wasn't giving up easily. "Wait — are you implying there may be an autopsy?"

"It's possible," Rosemary said.

"That won't do," Estelle declared. "It's bad enough that there was one for poor Mr. Kluger, though I daresay that wouldn't have been permitted if Mrs. Kluger hadn't insisted that her husband had no history of heart trouble." The maid gave Suzanne a little shake. "You won't allow it, will you, Miss Suzanne?"

"Unf," said the overwrought young woman.

"You see?" Estelle's two chins both jutted, like an angry pug's.

Rosemary remained calm. "The matter may be out of the family's hands. There's been one homicide already. We must make sure that this death was natural."

"Of course it was," Estelle said sharply. "Madam died of grief."

"We'll see about that," Rosemary retorted. "Now please take Ms. Farrow away."

The maid shot Rosemary a dark look. "Very well," she said with obvious ill will. "Come, Miss Suzanne, we'll go into your room."

Rosemary stopped in midstep. "Don't bother trying to go through the adjoining bathroom. It's padlocked from the other side."

Estelle glared at the detective. "Really now!" But she and Suzanne went on their way to Room Four. "We must get legal counsel," she said to the grief-stricken young woman.

"I'm going downstairs," Judith announced, wondering why she'd lingered so long already.

"Me, too," Renie said. "I can't be of any help here."

"This isn't fair," Arlene declared, but she followed Renie, who was behind Judith. "Especially to your mother."

At the first landing, Judith glanced back at Arlene. "Mother's used to sirens around here. Besides, she doesn't always hear them."

"I don't mean that," Arlene said after they reached the entry hall. "I mean this." She brandished the long, fraying item that looked up close as if it were made of coarse gray hair.

"Good grief!" gasped Renie.

Arlene nodded. "Exactly. And such grief this corset stay must have caused your Aunt Gertrude. It's a wonder it didn't give her a rash!"

"That's not a corset stay," Renie said, her eyes huge. "That's part of a violin bow!"

"What?" Arlene held the item in front of her. "Oh." She stared at Judith. "Then what was it doing in your mother's old corset?"

Judith clapped a hand to her forehead. "I'm an idiot!" she cried. "How could I have been so blind?"

"I've no idea," Arlene said. "Why, your dear mother must have had to walk with her chin way up in the air. And how she breathed with this stiff thing I can't guess. You should sue the girdle maker. How could they make a garment like that? Third-world workmanship, I'd guess. Ecuador or El Salvador or one of those other 'dors' in South America. It's a good thing I sorted through the things I'm taking up to Saint Vincent de Paul at church tomorrow."

Renie made a dive at Arlene and snatched the bow out of her hand. "That thing is worthless, but the rest of it's priceless. Where is the wooden part? This horsehair gets replaced often."

"The dryer," Judith said in disbelief. "Phyliss!"

"Huh?" said Renie.

"What?" said Arlene.

Judith took a deep breath. "Phyliss complained the other day about one of Mother's corset stays getting stuck in the dryer. It must have been this part of the bow — which was ditched in the dryer by whoever stole the rest of it."

"Not in your mother's girdle, I hope," Arlene said.

Judith shook her head. "But the wooden part — the valuable section — could be somewhere else in the basement." She froze. "What am I saying? I don't care if there's an entire string section in the damned basement!"

"Let's go look." Renie started off, but she'd only got as far as the dining room when the uniformed officers arrived just as the emergency personnel were leaving.

"See you soon," Conley said with mock good cheer, saluting Judith.

She merely grimaced while the firefighters and EMTs tromped across the threshold.

Apparently the newcomers from the patrol unit were weekend replacements. Judith had never seen them before in her life.

"Mueller, is it?" Rosemary said to the

older of the two. "You go upstairs to Room Three and make sure nobody goes in. Syzmanski, I'll put you at the bottom of the stairs by the front door."

The uniforms nodded, giving Judith, Renie, and Arlene only the most fleeting of looks.

Rosemary gestured at the parlor door. "Let's go in there."

"You go," Judith said. "I think I'll bake a cake. Or something."

Renie grabbed Judith by the upper arms and propelled her toward the parlor. "Oh, no you don't, coz. Did I abandon you when you sank in the quicksand at the family cabin? Did I let you fall over that cliff along the creek when we were hiking with my dad? Have I ever let a homicidal perp kill you in cold blood if I could prevent it?"

"That's not fair!" Judith cried, but she didn't resist. Indeed, she couldn't. Renie was determined to shove her into the parlor.

Standing on the hearth, Rosemary smiled at Arlene. "You're Mrs. Rankers, aren't you?"

Arlene evinced surprise. "How did you know?"

Rosemary's smile tightened. "You call the police fairly often to report suspicious conduct, I believe."

"My husband is the block-watch captain," Arlene said in a self-righteous tone. "Of course we report suspicious activity. People we don't recognize. Pets not on leashes. Cars that look too shabby to be driven on Heraldsgate Hill. A surfeit of ugly bumper stickers."

Rosemary put up a hand. "Let's stay on track — please?" Her smile became brighter, if forced.

"About Mrs. Kluger . . ." Renie began.

Rosemary cleared her throat rather loudly. "Mrs. Kluger has died."

"Yes, yes," Arlene put in. "We already knew that." She glanced at Judith, who was sitting in the armchair next to her. "Didn't we?"

"Don't ask me any questions," Judith murmured.

"The cause of death is undetermined," Rosemary continued, "but it appears to be natural. That is, there was no sign of trauma."

"For Mrs. Kluger, maybe," said Arlene. "What about the rest of us? *I'm* certainly traumatized by all this."

Renie got up from the small bay-window seat where she'd been sitting. "I'm going to the basement. Excuse me." She went out through the near door, which led into the living room.

Rosemary's smile was nowhere in sight. Indeed, she looked perturbed. "What's Mrs. Jones up to?"

Judith felt compelled to answer. "We think we found part of the missing violin bow," she replied. "I believe it may have been hidden in my clothes dryer. My cousin has probably gone to look for the rest of it."

"Really?" Rosemary brightened. "Amazing! Honestly, Mrs. Flynn, you are absolutely marvelous!"

Judith bit her lip.

"She's right," Arlene declared. "You have a knack for solving murders. It's not fair for you to drop out." She looked at Rosemary. "Isn't that so, Ms. O'Grady?"

"Oh, definitely!" Rosemary enthused. "She's like a real detective."

Arlene nodded. "Just like Oliver Wendell Holmes, only with an artificial hip, instead of a deerstalker."

"I think you mean —" Rosemary started to say before Judith stood up.

"There's someone in the entry hall," she said. "I'll see who it is."

The newcomers, who had been let in by Officer Syzmanski, were Tommy Wang and Mitch Muggins from the crime-scene unit. Rosemary, who had followed Judith out of the parlor, greeted them.

"Just in case," she whispered to Judith. "Then we'll remove the body for the autopsy."

With deferential smiles for Judith, the two young men went up the stairs. Arlene was peering out from the parlor doorway.

"What about that bracelet?" she demanded.

Judith wished Arlene would keep her mouth shut. "You tell her," she said with a scowl.

Arlene did just that. "I don't know where Judith put it," she concluded.

Judith sighed. "The freezer. Try chicken parts and pork chops."

Rosemary traipsed after Arlene. Judith waited in the parlor, gazing out the front window and trying to concentrate on what else Joe needed to prune along the driveway. The rosebushes would have to wait until later in the fall. But her pink camellia could be cut back now.

Arlene and Rosemary returned. The detective was peering at the bracelet's inscription. She turned the ice-cold bauble in her hands. "Yes. It could refer to Mr. Wittener and Ms. Farrow. How interesting."

"I don't suppose," Arlene remarked, "this is a good time to ask Suzanne. There's always Rudi, though. Where *is* he?"

"What do you mean?" Rosemary inquired.

Arlene began ticking off neighbors on her fingers. "The Porters went to the state fair — it's the last weekend, and Gabe gets in free because his produce company supplies some of the food. The Steins are shopping for a new roof, though why they'd want to put it on this late in the year, I don't know. The Ericsons are staying at the ocean on a cheap motel rate because it's after Labor Day. Mrs. Swanson is at a luncheon with some other ladies, probably Queen Bess's tea shop because they like the little cakes there so much, especially with the cream-cheese frosting. I haven't seen Rudi or Taryn today, so I assume they're home. Why haven't all these emergency vehicles drawn their attention?"

Rosemary looked worried. "Let's hope they merely want to keep out of it," she said with the hint of a resentful glance for Judith. "I should've checked in with them." Her composure seemed to be eroding around the edges.

"I'll go over there right now," Arlene volunteered.

Rosemary started to protest, but stopped. "Be careful, Mrs. Rankers. This is a volatile situation."

Arlene left the parlor. At the front door, Judith could hear her interrogating Officer Syzmanski. His age, marital status, schooling, family connections — the works. It was Arlene at her best.

"She probably knows everything including his blood type," Judith said with a wry smile.

"This is quite an unusual neighborhood," Rosemary remarked. "It seems very close-knit."

"It is," Judith said. "That's why people like Rudi and Taryn don't fit in. They don't mix. And they cause problems."

*Like murder,* she thought. And wondered what Renie was doing in the basement.

And then, because she'd vowed to dissociate herself from the whole sordid business, wondered why she wondered.

# CHAPTER EIGHTEEN

"I suppose," Rosemary ventured, "you should give the bracelet back to Suzanne. It's not evidence in and of itself."

Judith sighed. She might be able to resign from solving the case, but she couldn't turn off her human emotions. "I feel sorry for Suzanne. She's lost both parents and a stepfather. Maybe I've been hard on her."

"How so?" Rosemary asked, glancing out the window, where rain had started to fall again.

Judith shrugged. "It doesn't matter." *I've got to keep my distance.* "I had some doubts about whether she really owns a gym or a fitness club in Greenwich Village." *Shut up. Forget Suzanne and the whole damned crew.* "But it doesn't matter." *Oh, yes it does.*

"There's no gym," Rosemary said. "Levi and I already looked into her background."

"Really." Judith poured herself a glass of water from the tap. "Does she work at all?"

"No. She occasionally volunteers, though. Youth groups, Special Olympics — that sort of thing."

"Hmm." Judith paused to sip from her glass. "Why would she make up a story about owning a gym?"

"You understand people better than I do, Mrs. Flynn," Rosemary said. "To make herself look good?"

"Possibly," Judith allowed, knowing she was falling into a trap but unable to save herself. "Or it's a fantasy she's had and never been able to do anything about. Did you and Levi look into her finances?"

"She appears to have an allowance," Rosemary replied. "It's automatically deposited into a checking account every month, and is always the same amount — three thousand dollars."

Judith considered the sum. "It's not a lot, especially for New York. But maybe she doesn't pay for her apartment in Greenwich Village."

"There is no Greenwich Village apartment," Rosemary said. "I'm afraid Suzanne gave you bogus information. She's always lived at home with her mother and stepfather."

"Well." Pity for Suzanne continued to swell. "She seems to have led a stagnant existence. It sounds so sad." Judith set her glass down on the counter. "Do you mean that the Greenwich Village address doesn't exist or that Suzanne lied about living there?"

"Oh, it's a real apartment address," Rosemary asserted. "It just doesn't belong to Suzanne. It's been occupied for the last five years by a couple named Seymour-Styles."

"Suzanne's certainly created a tissue of lies — or fantasies — for herself," Judith said as Renie appeared in the hallway, her expensive outfit covered in dust and cobwebs.

"Zip," Renie declared, going to the sink to wash her hands. "Zero, nada, no luck. It doesn't make sense."

"No bow?" Judith said. "That is, no back of the bow or whatever it's called?"

"*Stick* will do," Renie muttered. "I'm a mess."

Rosemary excused herself to go upstairs and check on the forensics team's progress.

"You might want to check on Suzanne, too," Judith called after the detective. She turned to Renie. "I can't help it. I feel sorry for Suzanne."

Renie brushed at some of the dust on her slacks. "The only-child syndrome bugging you, Ms. Quitter?"

371

Judith's black eyes snapped. "What do you mean?"

Renie plucked a long-dead spider off her sleeve and threw it in the sink. "You — and I — were only children like Suzanne. She appears to have had every material advantage — which we did not. But we had loving parents and a close-knit extended family. We were given a spiritual life. We had all the things that Suzanne may never have had. Not to mention that she lost her father at about the same age that you lost yours. You feel guilty, coz. If I weren't such a coldhearted little twerp, I'd feel guilty about Suzanne, too."

Judith didn't say anything at first. Renie was right. She *did* feel guilty. She often felt guilty, even about things she hadn't done. Judith was still blaming herself for Dan's early demise, despite knowing better. She had a logical mind. Why couldn't she reconcile reality with her emotions?

"Well?" Renie said.

"I haven't been very kind to Suzanne," Judith confessed.

"She isn't an easy person to be kind to," Renie pointed out. "It's that damned money and social status. On some level, people like us envy that sort. Remember when F. Scott Fitzgerald said, 'The rich are different,' and

Hemingway replied, 'Yes — they have more money.' It's true, that's all they do have. In this case, maybe Suzanne doesn't even have that, at least not of her own. Otherwise, she wouldn't steal my worthless credit cards."

"True." Judith drank more water. She hated it when Renie was right. Her cousin was too damned smug and got more opinionated with age. It was an aggravating combination.

"Okay. Mull," Renie said in a resigned voice. "What did I overhear when I came upstairs about that apartment not belonging to Suzanne?"

"It doesn't, never did, I guess," Judith said in a lackluster tone. "That's what's so sad. Suzanne has created these fantasies for herself — the gym, the apartment, the kind of independence you and I took for granted when we grew up. She's over thirty, and yet she's still a child. She has to pretend to make life bearable. Maybe on some level she even believes her own tall tales. Suzanne can't deal with reality."

"Reality can be rough," Renie remarked. "Shall I call the present tenants at the apartment Suzanne doesn't rent?"

Judith gave Renie a sour look. "No. I will. That's because I need to know for business purposes. Phony addresses are the bane of an innkeeper's life."

"Right." Renie kept a straight face as Judith picked up the receiver from the counter and dialed Manhattan directory assistance.

"Seymour hyphen Styles in Greenwich Village," she said when she reached an operator. "I think the 'Styles' part is with a *y*, but it could be an *i*." She waited, pen in hand. "Thanks." The phone began to ring at the other end. "Hello? Is this the Seymour-Styles residence?"

The Englishman's voice replied that indeed it was. "Who's calling, please?"

"This is Judith Flynn," she said. "I own a B&B, and I have some confusion in my guest records. Your address was given for one of our recent visitors, but it's not checking out. The last name is Farrow."

"I'm sorry," Seymour-Styles replied. "I don't know anyone named Farrow, certainly not in this building."

"I see." Judith paused. "Maybe it was a previous address. Could you tell me who lived in your apartment before you rented it?"

"I —" Seymour-Styles stopped. "Just a moment. My wife may recall. Daphne?"

Judith waited as she heard a muffled voice at the other end.

"Long shot," Renie said, more to herself

than to her cousin.

"Mrs. Flynn?" Seymour-Styles said into the receiver. "My wife informs me it was a musician by the name of Wittener. His first name escapes her, but she thinks he moved to Philadelphia."

"Thank you," Judith said. "You've been very helpful."

Disconnecting the phone, Judith gave Renie a bleak look as she relayed the information.

Renie shrugged. "You expected that, didn't you? I wonder if he lived there with Suzanne — or if that was wishful thinking on her part. She must have been there often enough to know the address."

"True," Judith said, gazing thoughtfully up at the ceiling. "I wonder if Suzanne has pulled herself together."

"Don't look at me," Renie replied. "I'm still trying to figure out why anyone would steal a priceless violin bow and then take it apart."

"To make it easier to conceal?" Judith suggested.

"Maybe," Renie allowed.

"I'll go upstairs and see if I can do anything for Suzanne," Judith said in a resigned voice. "I'll give her the bracelet. It might make her feel better. But," she added as she picked up the Eternity circles from the kitchen table, "I'm *not* going to sleuth."

"Okay." Renie was looking strangely benign.

Wearily climbing the back stairs, Judith considered her chances of being allowed to see Suzanne. Estelle was a tough obstacle to overcome. She had assumed the role of duenna, guardian angel — and possibly prison sentry. Only a fib would do, but Judith didn't have one in mind.

In the hallway, she saw Rosemary conferring with the forensics team. "Oh, hi, Mrs. Flynn," Rosemary called with forced cheer. "Tommy and Mitch are just leaving. I don't suppose you care what they found."

"No." Judith couldn't help it, but knew she sounded apologetic.

"Okay," Rosemary said. "It wasn't much, anyway. The body will be removed as soon as the ambulance arrives. It's on its way now."

"Good." She smiled faintly at the trio. "Thanks for your help, guys." An idea came to her. "Say — don't you need somebody to sign off on the release of the body?"

"Not really," Rosemary replied. "This is a law enforcement matter, given the possibility that Mrs. Kluger's death might be linked to her husband's. It's all part of the official investigation."

"Don't you want to be on the safe side?" Judith asked — and winked.

"Ah . . ." Rosemary's mouth curved into a pleasurable smile. "Yes, I see. Shall I ask Suzanne?"

"I'd ask Ms. Pearson, the maid," Judith suggested. "If not a relative, she's a longtime family employee."

"Good idea," Rosemary said, heading for Room Four. "I'll request that when she comes downstairs."

Judith had a feeling it might take a few minutes for the detective to deal with the maid. She excused herself to Tommy and Mitch before going into Room One.

Estelle's quarters looked almost as if she hadn't occupied the room. Her suitcase was open, but nothing had been put away. The bed was made — or never unmade if she hadn't slept in it. Perhaps Estelle had kept an all-night vigil at Mrs. Kluger's side.

Judith couldn't resist. The suitcase was already open, after all. With one eye on the doorknob to see if it moved, she began a careful search through the contents: cotton underwear, tailored skirts and blouses, thigh-high nylon stockings, basic toiletries, a flannel nightgown, Deer-foam slippers, a well-worn chenille bathrobe. There was nothing of interest in the main section or the side pockets.

Judith noticed a zippered compartment on the outside of the suitcase. She wrestled briefly with her conscience. Curiosity won in a landslide.

Inside, she found a large dog-eared manila envelope. The guards on the small brass clasp had been worn away long ago. Judith opened the flap. And paused. *Why am I doing this? I swore I wouldn't sleuth.*

But she couldn't help it.

The envelope contained several items, including Estelle's passport. Judith flipped through it quickly. The maid had been born in White Plains, New York; her current address was in Manhattan. During the past two years, she had visited the United Kingdom, France, Germany, Austria, and Italy. That made sense, if she'd accompanied Andrea Kluger when she went abroad with Dolph.

There was also a local city map, refolded to show the portion that included Heraldsgate Hill. Sure enough, an *X* had been marked for Hillside Manor. But a block and a half away, just off Heraldsgate Avenue, another address had been similarly noted. Judith knew at once what it was — the Empress Apartments. Why, she asked herself, would Estelle Pearson mark Olive Oglethorpe's residence? Had she stayed with Olive until arriving at the B&B? It seemed strange, since Olive worked for Rudi and Estelle was employed by Andrea.

Hurriedly, Judith flipped through the rest of the envelope's contents: the car-rental agreement made at the airport Wednesday morning; a return ticket to JFK, dated for the previous day; a notebook itemizing incidental expenses; and a checkbook.

Having gone this far down the road of privacy invasion, Judith couldn't put herself into reverse. She opened the checkbook with the name of the New York bank embossed in gold letters on the faux-leather cover. It was a money-market account with blank checks and a handwritten register showing Estelle's deposits and withdrawals. The current amount was three million seven hundred forty-six thousand dollars and sixteen cents. Withdrawals were infrequent and comparatively small. But regular deposits had been made on the second of each month and — at least for the past five months shown in the register — were in the amount of twenty thousand dollars.

"Maybe I should have been a maid instead of an innkeeper," Judith murmured to herself. "I probably work harder than Estelle."

Then it occurred to her that work might not describe what Estelle was doing. An uglier word came to mind — *blackmail.*

Hearing voices in the hall, Judith quickly put everything back in the envelope, slipped it into the outside pocket, and tugged the zipper closed. With any luck, Estelle would go straight downstairs. Room One was small, and the only place to hide was in the closet. Judith could never make it under the bed with her artificial hip.

"Some sleuth," she muttered to herself, listening at the door. "Why am I doing this?"

*Because you have to,* came the answer. *Because you're you, and you can't change at this stage of your life. You were brought up on fair play. You always seek justice. You can't quit now.*

Estelle's muffled, angry voice faded in the stairwell. Judith crept out into the empty hall. Apparently, Tommy and Mitch had departed. The only other person left — except for the dead Andrea — was Suzanne.

Judith knocked at Room Four. There was no response. A chill crawled up her spine. *Not another body.* But she was being irrational, she told herself. That would make Estelle — or somebody — a mass murderer.

Judith had gotten to the point where she suspected everybody and anybody.

"Suzanne?" she called, knocking again. Still there was no answer. With a heavy sigh, Judith opened the unlocked door.

Suzanne was sitting on the bed, her rigid back turned, her eyes fixed on the mirror over the old oak dresser that had belonged to Aunt Ellen before her marriage fifty years ago.

"Suzanne," Judith repeated, but this time more quietly. "What can I do for you? I feel absolutely terrible about what's happened."

Suzanne didn't speak. Judith wondered if she was in some kind of trance. Slowly, she approached the bed and stretched out her hand, brushing the young woman's arm. Suzanne felt feverish.

"I think you should see a doctor," Judith said. "You're on the verge of an emotional and physical collapse."

Suzanne didn't move. Indeed, she scarcely blinked.

Reaching into the pocket of her slacks, Judith removed the bracelet. "Here," she said softly. "You were right. This belongs to you. I'm sorry I hassled you."

Suzanne still didn't move, but her eyes shifted in the mirror image. She gasped as she saw the bracelet in Judith's palm. Sucking in a deep breath, she sprang like a cat and snatched up the bauble with a fierce gesture, like an animal wresting raw meat from a rival predator.

Suzanne slipped the bracelet on her left wrist and turned it slowly. Her face softened and her body relaxed visibly. "Thank you," she said in an almost humble voice.

A weary silence filled the room. Rain was running down the twin windows with their pale yellow voile curtains and daffodil-patterned valances. Usually, the room — like all of the guest quarters at Hillside Manor — seemed cheerful and comforting. But on this gloomy autumn afternoon Judith found the spring-like motif false, even mocking.

Self-consciously, Judith cleared her throat. "You know," she said, "I was in love with a man who belonged to someone else. Guess what? I still am — and after over twenty years of waiting, he belongs to me."

Suzanne frowned. "I don't understand."

"I think you do."

Suzanne turned to look at Judith. "No. *You* don't understand."

"I know love when I see it," Judith said softly.

"Oh, yes." Suzanne's mouth twisted, a bittersweet expression on her face. "But not the kind you think. Rudi is my brother."

Judith was flabbergasted. And embarrassed. "Oh, dear! I've made a fool of myself. I'm sorry."

"I'm not," Suzanne said doggedly. She seemed to have gotten control of her emotions, though Judith felt she was still in a fragile state. "Rudi's wonderful. He's so talented and so ambitious . . . he's everything I've never been."

Tactful questions eluded Judith. "I'm confused," she admitted. "Was Blake Farrow Rudi's father?"

"No." Suzanne couldn't look at Judith. "His father was Dolph Kluger. Dolph was already married, you see, when my mother met him and fell in love with him. I suppose the police may find all this out. Not that it matters."

"It matters to you," Judith said. "That is, I sense that your family situation has been . . . difficult."

"Define *difficult*," Suzanne said with a faint spark in her eyes. "Some people would say I had a wonderful family. We were well-off, respected." She bit her lip. "Still, I've always felt like a freak."

"You're not a freak," Judith asserted. "But I think you're lonely and unfulfilled in many ways."

Suzanne's gaze locked with Judith's. "You're very observant. That's why I was so glad to finally find Rudi, but it didn't happen until after Mom married Dolph."

"Did you know Rudi existed?"

"Not really." Suzanne sighed, and again looked at Judith. "I sensed there was something — or somebody — in her past that she was hiding. There were strange phone messages and letters and things like that. Then Rudi came back from Europe — he'd studied over there for a while under one of Dolph's colleagues — and I happened to meet him at a charity benefit for the New York Philharmonic. I looked into his eyes. They're so blue, you know. And I felt something come over me. Not physical attraction, but some sort of bond, as if I'd always known him."

"Of course," Judith murmured. "His eyes are very like your mother's."

"Yes." Suzanne turned the bracelet on her wrist. "Rudi *knew.* That is, Dolph had told him that he — Rudi — wasn't Dolph's only illegitimate child. In fact, Dolph bragged about it. I honestly think he felt he was doing the world a favor by begetting children who might inherit his musical abilities."

"But Dolph didn't play, did he?"

"Oh, he played several instruments," Suzanne said. "But he didn't have the talent to become a professional. Instead, he had the ear — and the ability to drive other people to become successful."

"That's a talent, too," Judith said. "I gather you and Rudi became close after your first meeting. How did your mother take that?"

"Mom was very upset," Suzanne replied. "I was twenty-five at the time. I wondered why they hadn't legally adopted Rudi after they got married, since he was Dolph's son. But Rudi was too old, and making a name for himself. He'd chosen Wittener because it was Dolph's mother's maiden name. Furthermore, Rudi didn't want that kind of publicity. People who serve on symphony boards can be very conservative."

"Did your father, Blake Farrow, know about Rudi?" Judith asked.

Suzanne looked sad. "No. Mom met Dolph in Europe when she was still a teenager. She came back to Connecticut, where she'd been raised, and went to live with an aunt who had a summer home in Maine. She had Rudi there and put him out for private adoption. Somehow, she erased him from her life. Even later, there was no bond between Mom and Rudi. Anyway, a couple named Brown had adopted him, but they died in a car accident when he was fifteen. Rudi had been a child prodigy, but the Browns weren't musical. Mom knew about the family, and contacted Dolph, who took over Rudi and his career. That was when Rudi changed his name. He felt Rudi Brown wouldn't cut much of a swath in musical circles. But Mom still kept her distance from Rudi. Maybe she considered him as excess baggage, a huge mistake from her past. Mom hated mistakes."

"Was your mother talented?" Judith asked.

Suzanne laughed sadly. "That was ironic. She was tone-deaf."

"Suzanne," Judith said as gently as possible, "what happened to your mother?"

Suzanne's face crumpled, but she didn't cry. "A broken heart. Truly. She couldn't live without Dolph. He was her only real love."

Judith knew of husbands and wives who had died within months, weeks, even days of each other. But they were usually elderly. Andrea Kluger had been no more than sixty. Still, she had loved Dolph since she was a teenager. First loves could be lasting loves.

"Was she in good health?" Judith inquired.

"I think so." Suzanne looked out toward the nearest window. "She wouldn't eat much and she had trouble sleeping after

Dolph died. But then Mom always was a poor sleeper. And she wasn't really into food."

A noise in the hall startled both Judith and Suzanne. "I'd better see what's going on. You stay here," Judith urged. "I'll be right back."

Renie was standing outside of Room Three. The door was open.

"Ambulance guys," Renie said. "They're taking Andrea away. How's Suzanne?"

"Talkative," Judith said in a low voice. "I'll tell you later."

"Arlene came back." Renie frowned. "Nobody was home at the Wittener house. Arlene did everything but break and enter."

"Where's Arlene now?" Judith asked, avoiding the morbid activity that was going on inside the guest room.

"She went home," Renie replied. "Carl told her some of their kids were coming for dinner."

"Let's move," Judith said. "I don't need to see another body wheeled out of here."

The cousins slipped into the narrow hallway that led to the smallest of the guest rooms, Room Two. Judith took the opportunity to tell Renie what Suzanne had disclosed.

"My poor brain!" Renie exclaimed. "I

can't keep track of this crazy crew! Rudi and Suzanne are half siblings? Andrea's second husband is really Rudi's father? That's nuts!"

Judith kept a straight face. "Is it?"

"Oops." Renie looked sheepish. "Sorry, coz. Frankly, I tend to forget Dan ever existed. It's like you were always married to Joe."

"Funny," Judith said in a musing tone, "I don't feel that way." She glanced around the corner toward the open hallway. The ambulance men were wheeling a covered gurney out of Room Three. Judith held her breath, hoping that Suzanne hadn't realized what was happening.

The gurney disappeared from view, presumably down the stairs. The cousins headed out through the narrow passageway.

To their surprise, Suzanne was in the hall by her room. "She's really dead, isn't she?" the young woman said in an awed voice.

"Yes," Judith said, puzzled. "I'm so sorry."

Suzanne's mouth curved into a wide smile. "I'm not. I'm free!" She twirled around in a circle. "Thank God Almighty, I'm free at last!"

# CHAPTER NINETEEN

Judith was astonished by Suzanne's jubilation. "Are you sure you're okay?" she asked as the young woman waved her fists in triumph.

"Yes!" Suzanne laughed out loud. "Yes! Yes!" Abruptly, she composed herself and looked at Renie. "Are you the one with the black Coach handbag?"

Renie stared. "I am," she said after a pause.

"Now I can pay you back," Suzanne said excitedly. "I apologize for any inconvenience."

Renie exploded, her hands shaped like claws that would rip out Suzanne's throat. "Where are my credit cards? Give me my money now!"

"Please!" Suzanne held her own hands in front of her face to ward off Renie. "I need time. I didn't spend that much. Your credit cards were no good. I tossed them all in a

Dumpster."

Renie's eyes had narrowed to slits. "I'll hound you every ten minutes until I get my money. Isn't there any cash in your mother's purse? She's dead, she won't care."

"Coz!" Judith cried as she saw Suzanne's face start to crumple. "Don't be so crass!"

"Crass, my —" Renie stopped. "Okay, okay. I can wait — but not for long. I'm really pissed."

"We've noticed," Judith said. "I don't blame you. But consider the situation."

"Yeah, right," Renie grumbled. "As they say in the army, 'SNAFU — Situation Normal, All F—' "

"Stop!" Judith's own temper was about to burst. "Hear Suzanne out."

Suzanne waited a moment until Renie unfurled her fingers and stepped back a pace or two. "You see," Suzanne said, her features becoming animated again and her eyes shining, "I inherit everything. Until now, my money was all tied up in a trust." She hugged herself. "Oh, happy day!" She twirled some more.

"For you," Renie muttered.

Estelle came pounding up the stairs. "What's this? What's this? Miss Suzanne!" The maid grabbed the younger woman by the upper arms and shook her. "Calm down! Do you hear me? Stop it!"

"No!" Suzanne wrenched free and pushed Estelle into the wall by one of the linen closets. "Go away! You're fired!"

"Holy Mother," Renie muttered. "Where's Rosemary? We need handcuffs!"

Suzanne danced off down the hallway, heading for the back stairs. "I'm going to New York! I'm going to buy a gym!"

Rubbing her shoulder, Estelle regained her balance. "What's wrong with that girl? She's lost her mind!"

"Maybe she's in shock," Judith said. "I'm going downstairs." She stopped, halfway down the hall. "Where *is* Rosemary?"

"The detective person?" Estelle had clambered to her feet and was straightening her tailored skirt. "She left with . . . the body."

"Oh." Judith continued down the hall.

Renie was right behind her. "What's Suzanne going to do? She can't try to use my maxed-out credit cards to make a plane reservation because she claims she tossed them."

"She must already have a return ticket," Judith said as they started down the back stairs. "The airline can make changes when there's a death in the family."

"How about two?" Renie said. "Why not go for three? Maybe the airlines give you bonus miles for that."

On the next to last step, Judith stopped, holding out a hand to keep Renie from bumping into her. "Listen," she whispered. "Suzanne's on the phone."

"Fritz!" she said excitedly. "It's me, Suzanne. Mom's dead. We can get married!"

"Ohmigod!" Renie exclaimed softly. *"Fritz?"*

Judith nudged her cousin to keep quiet.

"Here, back there," Suzanne said. "I don't care. We could get married in Syria, as long as we're together." She was silent for a moment, obviously listening to Fritz. "Then don't tell your mother," Suzanne urged, sounding faintly irritated. "Just because she's a failure doesn't mean you have to spend your life coddling her. Meet me at the airport. I'll let you know what time our flight will be when I find out."

The cousins stood motionless on the bottom two steps. A long silence ensued. Judith felt as if she didn't dare breathe.

"Why should Rudi care?" Suzanne finally said, graduating from irritation to anger. "He should be glad you'll be rich."

Another silence, though briefer.

"What does it matter? Dolph's dead, so he can't do any more damage than he did twenty-five years ago. Wake up, Fritz. This is your big chance. *Our* big chance. I'm going to buy a gym. You can run it."

An even shorter pause.

"But New York is where everything's happening. Who needs trees? Oh, stop arguing! I'll call you back in half an hour. Your mother will still be at the bookstore, right? . . . Okay." Suzanne hung up.

Judith decided to wait for Suzanne's next move. It sounded as if she was still in the kitchen, perhaps looking up the airline's number in the directory. But a moment later, the cousins heard her walk out of the kitchen — and close the front door.

"Where's she going?" Renie asked as she and Judith descended into the hallway.

"I don't know," Judith replied. "Let's go see."

In the entry hall they met Estelle, who was just coming down the main staircase. "Where's Miss Suzanne?" the maid demanded.

Judith looked out through the window in the door. "She's going over to the Wittener house, but I don't think they're home."

Estelle barged past the cousins and yanked open the front door. "Suzanne!" she called. "Come back here! Now!"

Suzanne kept going. Estelle hurried out of the house. Suzanne, who had cut across the cul-de-sac, reached the sidewalk in front of the Wittener rental. The maid started to follow the same route, but was suddenly cut off by the arrival of a large SUV. Rankers children, grandchildren, and a couple of dogs tumbled out of the vehicle, accompanied by various yelps, shouts, and whoops of hilarity. Estelle was ambushed by a barking Boston terrier, which seemed to find her thick ankles extremely attractive.

"Tulip!" Arlene shouted from around the hedge. "Don't bite the nice lady!"

Tulip, however, ignored the command. Estelle stumbled and fell against the front of the SUV. By the time Judith looked across the cul-de-sac, Suzanne had disappeared.

The herd of Rankerses went into the house. Arlene came to the rescue. The second dog — a cocker spaniel named Farky Two — followed the humans. But Tulip sat in the street by Estelle, barking his — or, Judith thought, maybe her — head off.

"Come, Tulip. Leave the nice lady alone. She won't hurt you. She only *looks* mean."

Estelle looked more furious than mean. Tulip didn't budge. Arlene scooped up the dog, which began to lick her face. "I love you, too, Tulip," she said. "Let's go inside so you can bite Carl."

Judith finally came out to the edge of the porch. "Are you okay, Ms. Pearson?"

Estelle shot her a dirty look. "What do you think? I'll be black-and-blue for a week," she declared, clinging to the SUV's radiator grille to get to her feet. "This is the most violent place I've ever visited! I was in Los Angeles during the Rodney King riots in 1992, and they were nothing compared to this neighborhood!"

Judith refrained from mentioning that the Kluger clan seemed to have brought the current violence upon themselves. "Do you need anything?" she asked as Estelle limped toward the house.

The maid examined her arms and legs. "I'm bruised, not broken," she muttered. "I'm going to lie down." Estelle made her laborious way inside.

Renie came out on the porch to join Judith. "Where's Suzanne?"

"Beats me," Judith replied. "Maybe Rudi or Taryn came home after Arlene was over there."

"Or they wouldn't come to the door when Arlene called on them," Renie suggested.

"There's a car in front of the Wittener place," Judith noted. "It's that blue Honda I've seen before. I think it belongs to Elsa Wittener."

"I thought Suzanne said on the phone that Elsa was working at the bookstore."

Judith glanced at her watch. It was going on four o'clock. The day had flown by. "Elsa seems to have a key to her ex's house. I wonder if she's on a break. I don't like this."

"You mean Suzanne and Elsa facing off while Rudi and Taryn are away?"

"Exactly." Judith looked up at the shifting gray clouds. The rain had dwindled to a drizzle. "But I don't think we should interfere."

"Excuse me," Renie said in an uncharacteristically humble voice, "are you back on the case or just being compassionate?"

Judith walked over to the porch swing and sat down. Typical for September in the Pacific Northwest, the weather was mild — if wet. "I don't know," she admitted. "I got so caught up in Suzanne's pathetic life story that I got sucked in again. The problem with these awful situations is that they always involve *people.* And I'm a chump when it comes to feeling sorry for them."

Renie sat next to Judith in the swing. "So . . . ?"

"So I feel compelled to help." Judith's expression was ironic. "Am I a sap?"

"No." Renie smiled fondly at her cousin. "You've got a huge heart. You're lucky, really. Mine's the size of a pea."

"Not really, coz," Judith said. "You simply don't like to show — oh, good grief! Look who just limped into the cul-de-sac!"

Renie looked. "Gregory Whoozits? Swell. What now?"

Gregory was coming straight toward Hillside Manor. He was wearing his long black raincoat and carried a black umbrella. Seeing the cousins, he pointed a finger in their direction.

"I'm back," he said as he reached the porch steps. "Where's Suzanne?"

"Not here," Judith replied. "Where've you been, Gregory?"

"With my aunt," he said, coming up onto the porch. "She made me lunch. We had egg-salad sandwiches."

"Does your aunt live around here?" Judith inquired.

"Just a block away," Gregory said, standing by the porch railing and surveying the cul-de-sac.

Judith nodded. "That would be your Aunt Olive, right?"

"What?" Gregory seemed distracted. "Oh — yes. My aunt raised me after my mother hanged herself." He pointed to the Honda on the other side of the cul-de-sac. "Who owns that car?"

"I'm not sure," Judith hedged. "Back up, if you don't mind, Gregory. You say your mother hanged herself?"

"I think so. She's dead, at any rate." He turned to look at Renie. "Can you tell me more about my past, present, and future?"

Renie seemed as startled as Judith felt. "I'm not sure," she said. "The muse isn't with me." She felt Judith nudge her with an elbow. "But I can try. Want to go inside? Maybe I left my muse on the hat rack in the entry hall." Leading the way, Renie was followed by Gregory, with Judith behind him.

"Let me get you some water, coz," Judith said. "Gregory? Is there anything you'd like?"

"No, thanks." He rubbed his stomach. "I'm still full. Aunt Olive and I ate a late lunch. She made lots of tea."

Gregory wandered into the living room while Judith and Renie went into the kitchen.

"What am I supposed to do?" Renie whispered. "Conjure up Frederica again?"

"Try it," Judith urged. "If not, go for Olive. Gregory is clearly off his rocker."

"Who isn't in this ménage?" Renie grumbled, accepting the ice water from Judith. "Okay, here goes Swami. Damn."

"I'll be lurking in the entry hall," Judith said.

Judith stood just out of sight by the threshold to the living room. She assumed Renie and Gregory were by the fireplace.

"I'm sorry I don't have my wand with me," Judith heard Renie say, referring to the cattle prod she'd used in her earlier session as a bogus seer. "But the ashes will serve almost as well. I'll use the poker to stir them up."

"Can I ask questions?" Gregory inquired.

"Sure, why not? I mean," Renie clarified, "the ashes may or may not respond."

A brief silence ensued. "Well," Renie said in an awestruck voice. "I see her again. Frederica. She's holding something."

"What is it?" Gregory asked eagerly.

"I can't tell. It's not very big. That is, it's sort of . . . medium."

"Aren't you the medium?"

"No. Mediums do séances. That's not my bag. Hmmm . . ."

"Is Frederica holding a baby?"

"Let me see . . . yes, you're right, it *is* a baby. Frederica seems puzzled."

"Yes, yes, she would be. Upset, confused, distraught."

"And frustrated," Renie added. "She's in a predicament. What to do, what to do."

"Do you see a noose?"

"A moose? No, but that could be an elk in —"

"A *noose*," Gregory repeated.

"Oh!" Renie cleared her throat. "Sorry. These twigs on the hearth look like antlers. But of course they're a rope. How stupid of me."

"I'm the baby," Gregory said.

Judith wished she were in Renie's place. Would her cousin ask the right questions? Could she guess the mother's name? Would Gregory volunteer it?

"The woman looks familiar," Renie said. "I've seen her before —"

"Frederica!" Gregory exclaimed. "That was my mother's name. You saw her when you did this earlier."

"Yes. Yes!" Renie exulted. "She loved Pink Floyd."

*Aha,* Judith thought. Renie was on the right track.

"It kept my father from marrying her," Gregory said in a sad voice. "He couldn't marry anyone who liked popular music. Instead, he married somebody else just after I was born." Gregory sighed so loudly that Judith could hear him. "Aunt Olive's been good to me," he said, his voice more normal.

*Or as normal as this guy gets,* Judith thought.

"I call my mother Frederica because she was Aunt Olive's sister, so we always use her given name. What else do you see?"

"Aluminum foil," Renie replied. "That won't burn. It should go in the garbage can."

"What?" Gregory sounded puzzled.

"I mean silver," Renie said quickly. "Not a silver spoon, as in born with one in your mouth. But a gift, a talent for music. You showed an interest in music from an early age."

"How true!" The excitement had returned to Gregory's voice.

Renie spoke a trifle louder. "Ah. I also see a small ape. He has glass eyes and is watching TV."

Judith gritted her teeth. *Oscar.* Why couldn't Renie stick to the point? She was mentioning that damned stuffed ape only to rile Judith.

"What's he watching?" Gregory asked, sounding puzzled.

"Girls in bikinis. He's drooling," Renie said. "Uh-oh. The TV picture has changed. There's a large man on the screen now. He's talking about Fritz Kreisler. Oscar — I mean, the little ape — just fell off the sofa."

"My father!" Gregory cried. "Is he talking about the violin bow?"

"I can't tell," Renie said, her voice returning to normal. "I gather the large man's no longer with us. He's with Frederica."

"Yes. And that's good." There was a pause. "Now," Gregory said, "tell me where my inheritance is."

"Your . . ." Renie hesitated. "Oh, yes, of course. That violin bow. Let me see . . . Ah! Part of it is here in this house."

"I knew it!" Gregory cried. "That's why I came here the first time! Where is it? Please!"

"Well . . . it's not exactly *all* here," Renie said haltingly. "Only the horsehair part."

Gregory exploded. *"What?"*

"Hey — back off! I don't have it," Renie said in an annoyed tone. "Oh, darn — everything has gone dark. I can't go on."

"I want to see the part that's left," Gregory said, still sounding shaken. "Why would anyone dismantle it?"

"Good question," Renie said. "All the better to hide it, I suppose. Do you know who stole it?"

"Rudi stole it the first time," Gregory replied. "I don't know who stole it from him — unless nobody did, and he's lying."

Judith strolled into the living room. "Are you finished?"

"Yes," Renie said. "The muse fled just

before I made a complete ash of myself."

"Any startling revelations?" Judith inquired in a casual tone.

"I'll let Gregory tell you," Renie replied. "I'm only the instrument."

Gregory, who had been kneeling on the floor by Renie in front of the hearth, stood up and wiped his hands on his raincoat. "You think I'm a fraud, don't you?" he said to Judith.

"I don't think anything," Judith said innocently. "I heard Suzanne's vilifications, but that doesn't mean I believe them."

Renie moved around the coffee table. "I'm going to wash up. I've wrecked this thousand-dollar suit. I should've changed clothes."

Judith nodded vaguely at her cousin. "So what did the seer see?" she asked, sitting down opposite Gregory on the matching sofas.

"She's good," Gregory said, rubbing his thin hands together. "She saw me when I was a baby. She saw Frederica — my mother. She saw Dolph, my father. She told me the horsehair part is here. Is that true?"

"Yes, it is," Judith said. "But that's not valuable, is it?"

"No," Gregory agreed. "I wish she could see the rest of it."

"Look," Judith said, trying to judge Gregory's mental stability, "you say that Rudi stole the bow from you. Yet Rudi claims it was stolen from him. Can you explain that to me?"

Gregory sighed. "It's really simple. When I was growing up, my father — Dolph — kept track of me. He sent money and wrote letters and even called me sometimes. I met him in Europe for the first time when I was nineteen. It wasn't his fault that my mother — Frederica — was kind of . . . neurotic. I mean, lots of women have babies when they're not married, especially these days. Gosh, she'd been to Woodstock! You'd think she'd have been liberated. And she loved music — but the wrong kind, as far as Dolph was concerned." He paused. "Have you got a banana? That ape made me hungry for one."

"Yes," Judith replied. "I have bananas. And some people I know have gone bananas."

Gregory frowned. "Who do you mean?"

"Never mind," Judith said.

"Oh." Gregory's expression lightened. "That Trennkost diet is getting me down. I don't think it's good for you in the long run. Aunt Olive doesn't think so, either. But she didn't have any fresh fruit."

Judith called to Renie, who was coming back into the room. "Can you get Gregory a banana? There are some in a bowl on the counter."

"Sure," Renie said. "I think I'll have one, too." She reversed her route and disappeared.

"The bow," Judith reminded Gregory.

"Oh, yes. The bow." Gregory frowned. "Anyway, Dolph told me that if I could master the violin, he'd give it to me. He'd gotten it from Fritz Kreisler. But I never learned to play well enough. Dolph said that he'd keep it for my inheritance because it'd be worth a ton of money someday. I don't care about the money. But I did want the bow. And then I found out that Rudi has it!" His face darkened and he tugged at his short beard. "I was furious. Why Rudi? Just because he plays in a symphony orchestra? That's no big deal. Rudi must have swiped it."

Renie came back with three bananas. She handed one to Gregory and offered another to Judith.

"Why not?" Judith murmured. "I could use the potassium. Unless you want to take it home to You Know Who."

"We have plenty of our own," Renie said. "But thanks for being so considerate."

Judith ignored the sarcasm. She accepted the banana and took a moment to collect her thoughts. Did Gregory know that Rudi was also Dolph's son? Was the young man aware that his father seemed to have considered himself responsible for populating the world with musical geniuses? *A serial impregnator,* Judith thought. "Why Rudi?" she finally asked. "That is, why might Dolph have given the violin bow to Rudi instead of someone else?"

"He shouldn't have," Gregory replied indignantly. "It's mine!"

Judith realized she couldn't argue the point. "I see," she said.

Gregory's mood shifted as he concentrated on peeling the banana. He worked very carefully, splitting the fruit with a fingernail and pulling down the skin segments one at a time. He studied the banana closely. "It looks unblemished," he declared.

"Oh, good," Renie said, having devoured a third of hers already. "How about some rhubarb?"

Gregory gave a start. "I hate rhubarb! It's bitter, like gall!"

"Aweed," Renie said, her mouth full of banana.

"It might as well be a weed," Gregory said. "It's not a fruit, it's not a vegetable —

it's nothing."

"My cousin," Judith clarified, "said she *agreed.*"

"Oh." Gregory shrugged. "Could I see the horsehair?"

Judith couldn't think of any reason why he shouldn't have a look. "I'll get it," she said.

Judith had reached the entry hall when the doorbell rang. One glance told her that Olive Oglethorpe was on the porch. "Ms. Oglethorpe," Judith said. "Come in. Are you looking for Gregory?"

"Yes!" Olive's smooth cheeks were pink. "He's here?"

"In the living room," Judith replied.

Olive marched past Judith. "Gregory!" she cried. "You shouldn't have left me. How often have I told you not to go wandering off?"

"I came to find the bow," Gregory responded, defensive. "You know I won't rest until it's mine."

"Well?" Fists on hips, Olive planted her sturdy little body in front of the coffee table. "Do you have it?"

"No," Gregory said in a mournful voice. "Only the horsehair part is here."

"Who told you that?" Olive retorted.

Gregory pointed to Renie. "She did."

"What?" Olive stared at Renie. "She's a retirement-home salesperson. How could she know about the bow?" She looked at Judith over her shoulder. "Are you buying a retirement home, too? I thought you were an innkeeper."

"Even innkeepers retire eventually," Judith said meekly, thinking it best to let Olive believe Renie's tall tale.

"I'm working the neighborhood," Renie said glibly. "Mrs. Flynn and her husband are thinking about retiring to a woodsy area. I've got just the place for them on the Stillasnowamish River."

Judith didn't flinch at the reference to the family cabin site. "So peaceful," she murmured. "So calm." She certainly wasn't going to admit that she'd almost been killed there not once but twice by cold-blooded murderers.

"Does it have a piano?" Olive asked.

"Piano!" Gregory exploded. "Who cares? What about my bow?"

"Come along, Gregory," Olive said in a quiet voice. "Maybe we can talk to Rudi about it. You really must go back to the . . . *your* home."

"I don't want to!" Gregory shouted. "I want to live with you, like I did in New Jersey and New York."

"You can't," Olive declared. "I'm moving. I'm retiring as of November first. I told you that while we were having lunch. Please come with me." She glanced at Renie. "We'll be in touch."

"Right," Renie said, watching Gregory, who was cringing on the sofa.

"Excuse me, Ms. Oglethorpe." Judith had moved into the middle of the living room. "Did you come here looking for Gregory?"

"What?" Olive seemed to tense. "No. Not specifically. But since he's here, I'd like him to leave with me."

"Then," Judith said, managing to block Olive's passage from the sofa area, "why did you come?"

Olive hesitated. "I . . . I wanted to apologize for being impolite the other day when you stopped by my apartment house. I was very busy. The start of the symphony season, you know."

"All you needed to do was pick up the phone and call me to say you were sorry," Judith pointed out.

"That's so impersonal," Olive said. "I'm very old-fashioned. Anyway, I ask you to forgive my abrupt manner."

"Fine." Judith smiled halfheartedly.

"Also," Olive went on, keeping an eye on Gregory, "I must inquire about my platter.

Has it been returned yet by the police?"

"No," Judith replied. "It takes time, but I'm sure they'll be very careful with it."

"I hope so," Olive murmured. "It's all I have left from my family's ancestral china collection. It dates back to the mideighteenth century, and was made in England." She shifted her gaze briefly from Gregory to Renie. "The platter belonged to a very distinguished ancestor."

Before anyone could speak again, the front door opened. Judith backpedaled just enough to see who was coming into the entry hall.

It was Suzanne. She looked as if she'd gone three rounds with a five-hundred-pound gorilla. Her clothes were torn, her face was scratched, and there was blood on the back of her hands.

Judith hurried to the young woman's side. "Suzanne! What happened? Did you have an accident?"

"An accident?" She was dazed, staggering by the foot of the stairs.

"Yes." Judith noticed that Suzanne looked as if she'd been hit in the right eye. It was half-closed, red, and swollen. "Who hurt you?"

Suzanne opened her mouth to speak, but no sound came out. Instead, she collapsed at Judith's feet.

*Not another body,* Judith thought.

But Suzanne had merely passed out. As Judith bent over her the young woman's lips moved. She uttered a single word.

"Elsa."

Suzanne plunged into unconsciousness.

# CHAPTER TWENTY

Judith was joined by Renie and Olive.

"What now?" Renie asked anxiously.

"Suzanne got into a fight with Elsa Wittener," Judith said, rubbing the young woman's wrists. "I think."

Olive bristled. "What did you say?"

Judith ignored her. "Get some water, coz. I think Suzanne's coming around."

"*Coz?*" Olive said sharply. She stared at Renie. "You're Mrs. Flynn's cousin?"

"Even retirement-home salespersons have cousins," Renie replied blithely, and rushed off to the kitchen.

Suzanne moaned and groaned, but didn't open her eyes. Judith wanted to avoid calling 911 — again — at all costs. As far as she could tell, the young woman's injuries were superficial.

Olive was peering at Suzanne. "I can't imagine Elsa fighting with anyone," she declared. "She has weak wrists. It's not like her."

"That's a moot point right now," Judith retorted as Renie came back from the kitchen with a glass of water. "Good. Suzanne's eyes are opening."

Renie offered the water while Judith helped Suzanne into a sitting position.

"I can't deal with this," Olive declared. "I'm leaving." She turned around and went back into the living room. "Gregory?"

Suzanne took two swallows of water. "Thank you," she whispered.

Judith nodded. "Are you seriously injured?"

"No," Suzanne replied, putting a hand over her damaged eye.

"Are you sure?" Judith asked.

"Yes. I know my body. Nothing's broken." She took several deep breaths. "I gave Elsa as good as I got. She's fast on her feet, though."

Judith became apprehensive. "Where *is* Elsa?"

"Where is Gregory?" Olive demanded, coming back into the entry hall. "He's disappeared. He couldn't have left without us seeing him come through here."

"The French doors," Judith said impatiently.

"Oh." Olive sounded dismayed. "I didn't notice them. Oh, dear!" She raced out of the house via the front door.

Suzanne scowled. "What did Olive want? Was she here to offer condolences about Mom's death?"

Judith and Renie exchanged quick glances. "I'm not sure she knows about it," Judith admitted. "She was looking for Gregory."

Suzanne rubbed her right shoulder. "He was here again?"

"Yes," Judith replied. "Please — where is Elsa?"

"I'm not sure," Suzanne said, twisting her neck this way and that. "I left her at Rudi's house."

Judith was losing patience as her fears for Elsa increased. "Is she badly hurt?"

"Not bad enough," Suzanne retorted, her voice much stronger. "That woman's evil."

"I'd better go over there," Judith said. "Is the door unlocked?"

"Maybe." Suzanne took another sip of water. "I'm not sure. Oh, I hurt!"

Judith looked at Renie. "Can you take over?"

"Sure," Renie said. "But be careful."

Despite the drizzle, Judith didn't need a jacket. She started out the front way, but stopped short of the Persian area rug in the entry hall. Suzanne's running shoes had left zigzag muddy tracks on the parquet flooring. That wasn't unusual with all the rain and all the guests. But what caught Judith's eye were some white flecks mixed in with the mud. She bent down as far as she dared, picking up one of the shards. Pottery or crockery, maybe. But the smooth surface could also indicate teeth. Judith shuddered. She must hurry to the scene of the latest debacle. Elsa Wittener might need medical attention.

Still, she paused on the Wittener house's small porch. Not that she ever enjoyed going inside. One gruesome murder had already occurred there years earlier. Then Herself had moved in. Now Rudi and his not-so-merry band of oddballs. The house seemed to attract strange — even dangerous — occupants.

The Honda was still parked at the curb. Judith couldn't bear to use the doorbell and hear the chime of Vivian Flynn's ode to booze. Instead, she knocked. And realized that the door was ajar.

"Ms. Wittener?" she called, stepping inside.

Judith hadn't entered the house since one of her rare visits to Vivian. Gone were all traces of Herself's pseudo–Italian Provincial decor. Instead, what little furniture she could see from an open arch off the small entryway seemed to be American antiques, covering at least two centuries. An eighteenth-century armoire, an early-nineteenth-century settle, and a Colonial rocker looked authentic.

Elsa Wittener was nowhere in sight. Nor was there any indication that a brawl had taken place in the living room. Judith called out again. No response. She went into the kitchen, then through the small hallway that led to the bathroom and two bedrooms. Again there was no Elsa and no sign of a struggle.

Fearing the worst, Judith went out the back door and down the short flight of concrete steps that led to the basement. She remembered that the area had been converted into a studio for Taryn's piano lessons. Maybe that's where the confrontation had taken place.

A small room had been created out of what Judith assumed had once been a coal bin. The door was open.

The piano bench was overturned; sheet music and lesson books were scattered around the floor; a metronome lay on its side on a brightly striped rug that looked as if it had come from Peru. But no Elsa.

Judith was about to upright the piano bench, but thought better of it. *This could be a crime scene,* she thought, shuddering. *I shouldn't touch anything.* Feeling helpless, she stood in the middle of the room and tried to think.

"Get out!"

The voice shot from behind her, only a few feet away. Judith turned on legs that suddenly wobbled.

"Elsa?" she said in a breathless voice.

"Mrs. Flynn?"

"Yes." Judith's mouth was suddenly dry.

Elsa leaned against the doorjamb. Like Suzanne, she sported evidence of a struggle: scratches, bruises, torn clothing, and red hair in wild disarray as if someone had tried to pull it out by the roots. A large Band-Aid covered her lower right arm.

"I was trying to find you," Judith said, not sounding like herself.

"I was in the downstairs bathroom treating this cut," Elsa replied, holding up her injured arm.

Judith licked her lips. "Do you need a doctor?"

"No." Elsa rubbed her wrists. "I've already spent time in the emergency room this week. I'm not going back."

"I don't blame you," Judith said, still

uneasy. "Can you drive?"

Elsa's mouth twisted into a sardonic smile. "Are you suggesting I leave?"

"Of course not," Judith replied, noting that Elsa still seemed to have all of her teeth. "I was wondering if you could get home by yourself. You seem to be in pain."

"That's none of your concern." Elsa, however, sounded as if she were running out of steam.

"But it is." Judith was bluffing. "I'm responsible for this house."

"What are you talking about?"

"Maybe you're not aware that the owner is a Ms. Flynn." Judith tried to ignore the sacrilege she was about to commit. "Vivian Flynn is my . . . sister-in-law. I look out for this rental when she's in Florida." Luckily, Herself had hired an agent to oversee the property. Neither Judith nor Joe had wanted to assume responsibility in his ex-wife's absence. "I have to check for damage that may have occurred as a result of your row with Ms. Farrow."

Elsa gestured at the studio mess. "See for yourself. We had our face-off right here. Everything belongs to Taryn Moss." She sneered. "You and your in-law needn't fret."

"Good," Judith said with a lift of her chin. Her nerves had settled and she was gaining confidence. "The rest of the house seems unharmed. However, there's always the liability of personal injury to either you or Ms. Farrow. How did this quarrel occur?"

"That's none of your business," Elsa snapped.

"True." Judith noticed that blood was oozing through the Band-Aid. "You'd better let me change that bandage. It's leaking. Let me get another Band-Aid."

Elsa glanced at her arm. "It's fine," she asserted.

"No, it's not," Judith countered. "You can't drive like that. You'd better sit." She righted the piano bench and indicated a rail-back chair that had somehow survived being tipped over. "Go ahead."

Elsa's eyes snapped angrily, but she obeyed. "I took a couple of extra Band-Aids from the medicine cabinet." She used her left hand to reach into the pocket of her gray slacks. "Here."

Judith carefully removed the original bandage. "It needs to be tighter," she said.

"I used my left hand," Elsa said, still hostile. "I'm right-handed. And I was shaking."

"Of course." Judith used a tissue she had in her pocket to wipe the wound, which looked relatively superficial despite the

419

blood loss. "Do you take aspirin regularly?" That, she knew, would account for excessive bleeding.

"Yes." Elsa paused. "I have some chronic pain."

"I understand," Judith said, tightly applying a fresh Band-Aid. "I suffer from a form of migraine. Not to mention I have an artificial hip." She sighed. "Life's tough as we get older. And being a single mother is hard, isn't it? I know, I was one for years."

"I beg your pardon?" Elsa was caught off guard.

Judith perched on the piano bench and shook her head. "An only son — that makes it harder. I lost my first husband when Mike was still in his teens. At least Fritz's father is still alive." *And so is Mike's,* Judith thought, *but Elsa doesn't need to know that.*

"Why are you telling me this?" Elsa demanded.

"Because I know what you're going through." Judith's expression was cloaked in sympathy. "You only want what's best for Fritz. It's not that he's so much younger than Suzanne, it's that she's unstable. In fact, for all I know, Fritz is more mature than she is. Suzanne has led a very sheltered life, like Rapunzel in the tower."

Elsa's eyes widened. "How do you know?

Did Suzanne tell you?"

"No, certainly not." Judith looked innocent. "But I understand people. I read them fairly well. If Dolph Kluger had what is called an 'ear,' maybe I have an 'eye.' " *And maybe I shouldn't brag. It doesn't sound like me. But Elsa won't know the difference.* "In any event, this is no time for Suzanne to make big decisions. Her mother hasn't been dead for more than a few hours."

"Did she expect me to care?" Elsa retorted bitterly.

"You mean Suzanne?"

Elsa nodded — and winced. "That hurts. My neck." She grasped the back of her head. "That silly little bitch!"

"Suzanne?" Judith's voice was calm.

"Yes! Suzanne! Who else? Why should I care what happens to her or her snooty mother? A broken heart indeed! Andrea probably overdosed! She's been a pill popper ever since I've known her."

"You've known her a long time, I take it?"

"Of course." Elsa sighed wearily. "Ever since she married Dolph. Andrea was always active in the social scene for music benefits, even if she couldn't tell a sharp from a flat. She was a regular do-gooder when it came to fund-raising. Though where those funds ever went, I don't know. Rudi didn't, either."

"Are you talking about embezzlement?" Judith inquired.

Elsa gave Judith a disparaging look. "I'm not talking about anything to you. I must go." She stood up, though her legs seemed unsteady. "I don't know where you got your information about Suzanne and Fritz. Keyholes, probably. But I'll thank you to mind your own business. I can handle Fritz. He's devoted to me."

"Wait." Judith couldn't stop herself. "You know perfectly well that Suzanne and Fritz can't marry. She's his aunt."

Elsa froze. "You don't know anything."

"I know what Suzanne told me," Judith declared.

"She's wrong. Fritz isn't Rudi's son." Elsa's lips curved into a wicked, triumphant smile. She wobbled out of the studio.

Wearily, Judith stood up. If Rudi hadn't been Fritz's father, who was? Dolph? He certainly was the obvious suspect. If that was the case, then Suzanne and Fritz weren't related.

Judith gazed at the chaotic remains of the quarrel between Elsa and Suzanne. Taryn could finish the cleanup. It was her studio.

Which made Judith wonder what Elsa had been doing downstairs when the fight must have started. And why she seemed to visit her ex-husband's house fairly often. Looking around the small room, she couldn't see anything that didn't pertain to music lessons and piano playing. The only thing that struck Judith as odd was that the keyboard lid was closed. Maybe that was to keep out dust. Judith never shut hers. She didn't want to discourage guests who might enjoy using the piano for their own entertainment.

She was still surveying the room when she heard Elsa calling to her. "Mrs. Flynn! Help me!"

Elsa didn't sound frantic, but frustrated. Judith left the studio and headed for the outside-stairs entrance. Sure enough, Elsa was leaning against the door, breathing hard.

"I can't turn the knob," she said. "I hurt my wrists."

"I'll do it." The knob on the inside was stiff, but Judith managed on the second try. "It needs oiling. Are you sure you can drive?"

"Yes, I'll be fine." Elsa flexed her fingers. "Thank you." Her tone was far from gracious.

Judith watched her climb up the stairs. Elsa clung to the rail and took her time. A moment later, she disappeared around the corner of the house, heading in the direction of the cul-de-sac.

For almost a full minute, Judith teetered on the brink of a decision. She should go back to Hillside Manor. But she was inside the Wittener house, and she was curious. If Rudi or Taryn should come home, she could always use the excuse that Vivian Flynn had called to ask her to check on the rental. Neither Rudi nor his live-in love could know that Joe and Judith had very little contact with Herself. Or, she thought, she could tell the truth. It wasn't her fault that Suzanne and Elsa had staged a knockdown brawl on the Wittener premises, and that Judith had felt an obligation to see if Elsa had survived.

She went back inside. Beyond the studio and at the end of a short hall she found the half bathroom. An open doorway led to the rest of the basement, which seemed quite ordinary: storage boxes, tools, garden equipment, and odd pieces of luggage were among the expected items. The boxes were labeled with black marker pen: music scores; lesson plans; tapes and CDs; books; photographs; directories: USA and Canada, Europe, Far East. For creative types, Rudi — or Taryn — seemed very organized. Nothing appeared to have been disturbed. Judith walked back out into the little hall.

For some reason, the studio beckoned to

her. She went back inside, feeling she had missed something. She lifted the piano bench's lid. There appeared to be nothing but music and lesson books. The brightly striped rug that covered most of the floor had gotten caught under one of the bench's legs after Judith had put it right side up. She used her foot to smooth the fabric and suddenly lost her balance.

"Damn!" she swore out loud, catching herself on the edge of the piano. Her other foot touched something next to the instrument. It was a smaller hammer. She hadn't noticed it before, probably because the bench had blocked her view. A hammer seemed like an odd thing to find in the studio. Had Elsa or Suzanne used it as a weapon? Or at least as a threat? That seemed plausible. Judith left the hammer on the floor and started to move away. But she couldn't. She walked back to the piano and raised the keyboard lid.

The white ivories had been smashed; so had some of the black keys. Particles fell onto the floor, some landing on Judith's shoes. Only then did she notice that there were other bits and pieces of the keys embedded in the various colors of the rug — the same kind of shards that Suzanne had tracked into Hillside Manor.

The attack had been savage. Who else but Elsa would — or could — have done such a thing? But why? Judith turned around and hurried out of the studio, into the hall, and outside to the cement stairs. At the top, she took a deep breath. The air smelled damp, with just a hint of autumn's decay. Judith looked around the enclosed garden. It had not been well tended since the original owners had lived there. Vivian was no gardener, and apparently Rudi and Taryn weren't, either. A few dahlias and chrysanthemums had prevailed, the flowers drooping on leggy stalks as if they'd given up hope of better days.

But someone had been working in one of the flower beds near the fence. Judith walked across the small patch of grass. There was a barren patch between dead tomato plants and lettuce that had gone to seed. Someone had gone to the trouble of digging up whatever was planted in the middle of what originally had been a vegetable garden. Judith could think of one possible reason.

Rhubarb.

# CHAPTER
## TWENTY-ONE

"I was about to call the cops," Renie said from the front porch when Judith returned to the B&B. "Again. What took you so long? I was getting worried."

Judith waited to respond until the cousins were inside. She flopped down on the sofa in the living room and related her adventures at the Wittener house. "Where's Suzanne?" she asked when she'd finished.

"Taken to her bed," Renie said, "or at least gone upstairs. If I'm going to spend the night, I have to go home and check on Clarence. I should see how Oscar's doing. He may want to watch TV for a while."

"Aaargh!" Judith exclaimed. "Don't start with Oscar. I'm in no mood for it."

"You're in no mood for much," groused Gertrude, who sailed into the living room in her wheelchair. "What happened to lunch? Now it's almost time for my supper."

427

"Oh my God!" Judith cried. "I . . . we had another tragedy here today." She dragged herself up off the sofa and went to her mother, who had stopped the wheelchair just short of the coffee table. "A guest died."

"So? Does that make me next — from starvation?" Gertrude looked unmoved by the latest disaster. "I'm lucky I had some pickles and candy in my prison cell." She turned her beady glare on Renie. "And where were you, my nitwit niece? Taking care of your martyred mother or out carousing with sailors? Either one would make me puke."

"How about a nice TV dinner?" Judith suggested. "I'll put it in the microwave so it'll be done in just a few minutes. Turkey? Fried chicken? Salisbury steak?"

"I want pig hocks and sauerkraut," Gertrude said. "Nefle, too. And make it right. Be quick when you cut the noodle dough into the boiling water. Oh, carrots sound good, too."

"I don't think I have any pig hocks —"

"Then get some," Gertrude ordered. "Make sure they're already boiled or it'll take too long to get 'em tender." She glared at her daughter and her niece. "What's wrong with you two? Sitting around the living room when it's going on five o'clock."

Renie, however, wasn't sitting. She had gone over to the phone on the cherrywood table and was making a call.

Gertrude paid no attention. "Well? Are you just going to stand there like a stick, dopey?" she demanded of her daughter. "Go to the butcher shop. Get some boiled pig hocks. At least I'm not going to ask you to make the sauerkraut from scratch. That takes days . . ."

Judith tuned out Gertrude and edged closer to Renie, whose back was turned.

"Mom," Renie was saying, "I've already called twice today. I told you I was staying with Judith while Bill was . . . No, Bill didn't drown . . . No, I haven't fallen down and skinned my knee . . . Listen, Mom, please . . . No, I don't need to drain my sinuses . . . Mom! Do you have any pig hocks?"

Gertrude was still ranting about the nefle. "The last time you made it, the noodles were hard as marbles. I broke a tooth, remember? And don't make spaetzle instead. You get that out of a stupid box, and the box would taste better than the noodles. I want . . ."

"Great," Renie said. "I'll bring her over." She hung up. "Hey, Aunt Gertrude, you have a dinner invitation. Mom has pig hocks that she cooked a couple of days ago. She'll make you exactly what you want for dinner. I'll drive you over to her apartment. Let's go."

Gertrude looked startled. "My sister-in-law has pig hocks?"

"Sure," Renie said. "She likes them, too."

"Do I have to listen to her gab?" Gertrude asked as Renie unlocked the brake on the wheelchair.

"You can listen or not," Renie replied. "In fact, how would you like an overnight with Mom? Maybe she could get a couple of your chums in to play bridge."

"Bridge, huh? Play for quarters?"

"Why not?"

"Because your mother doesn't like to gamble for money. She'd rather talk everybody's ears off. She doesn't pay attention to her cards. The last time she was my partner, she passed after I bid one no-trump. It turned out she had ten points in her hand and we could've made a . . ."

Judith sighed with relief as Renie accompanied Gertrude out the back door. She couldn't remember when she'd completely forgotten to feed her mother. Guilt overwhelmed her. She'd gotten so involved — and trying *not* to be involved — that she'd neglected Gertrude. Judith felt that her priorities had gotten out of whack.

But she still had to prepare dinner. Renie would be starving in another hour, too. Judith started for the kitchen just as Estelle limped down the main stairs.

"Mrs. Flynn," she said, sounding less curt than usual, "might I get something for Suzanne and me to eat? I could get along, but I worry about her. She rarely consumes what I consider hearty meals."

"Yogurt and fruit mostly?"

The maid nodded. "It's as if she were depriving herself for some reason. If she'd been a Catholic, I'd expect her to join a convent."

"Yes," Judith said slowly. "I understand. Suzanne's dedicated to keeping fit, but she's rather like an ascetic. It's an austere, disciplined lifestyle without the goal of spiritual improvement."

"I really think her mother's death has shattered her mind," Estelle said, and promptly put a fist to her lips. "I mustn't say such things," she added after an awkward moment had passed.

To Judith's surprise, Estelle seemed close to tears. "Are you referring to the quarrel with Elsa Wittener?"

"Partly." Estelle leaned on the newel post. "If only I'd stopped her from going over to the Wittener house. It's all so foolish."

"Come into the kitchen," Judith coaxed. "I'll make you some tea. Unless you'd like something stronger?"

Estelle sighed wearily. "Brandy, perhaps. I don't drink alcohol as a rule, but Mr. Kluger always swore that brandy was a great restorative."

"I have some in the dining-room liquor cabinet," Judith said. "It's not terribly expensive like the brand that Fritz brought for the party the other night, but —" She stopped just at the edge of the entry hall.

"Yes?" Estelle was right behind her.

"Uh . . . nothing. I'm just trying to remember what kind I actually have," she fibbed. "I'm pretty rattled about now."

Thinking hard, Judith went to the washstand that served as the guest liquor storage. She found an Ararat Five Star bottle of brandy that was almost full and poured an inch into one of the snifters she kept in Grandma Grover's breakfront.

"Here," she said, handing the drink to Estelle. "Sit in the kitchen while I figure out what to make for dinner. What sounds good to you?"

"Chicken," Estelle replied, lowering herself into a chair. "I always like chicken. And Suzanne will eat that. She avoids red meat."

Judith opened the refrigerator's freezer

compartment and removed a package of boneless chicken breasts. "Had you known about Suzanne's feelings for Fritz before this?"

Estelle took a sip of brandy and made a face. "Oooh! I don't really like the taste. It's very strong."

"I can still make tea."

"No." She sniffed at the liquor. "I'll pretend it's medicine."

Judith put the chicken breasts in the microwave while she waited for Estelle to answer the original question. But the maid remained silent. Judith tried another route. "How long has Suzanne known Fritz?"

"For some time," Estelle replied. "Off and on, over the years."

"What's the attraction?" Judith inquired, trying to sound casual. "They seem like an odd match."

Estelle frowned as she took another sip of brandy. "Not really."

Judith hit the defrost button on the microwave. "How so?"

"They don't fit into their families," the maid said. "They're not musical. They're oddities, as far as their parents are concerned."

"But Andrea isn't — wasn't — musical," Judith pointed out.

"Madam had no talent," Estelle clarified. "But she was keenly interested in classical music. She was always involved in money raising for various artists and organizations."

Judith recalled that Elsa had begrudgingly told her as much. "Tell me," she said, "who is Frederica?"

Burying her nose in the brandy snifter, Estelle hesitated. "Frederica?" She looked up. "I don't know anyone by that name."

Judith wasn't sure that Estelle was telling the truth. In fact, she thought Estelle was feeling the effects of the brandy. Her eyes looked unfocused and her pale cheeks were turning pink.

The microwave timer went off. Estelle jumped. "What was that?" she asked in alarm.

"The microwave," Judith replied. "I've been defrosting the chicken. I understand Frederica liked all kinds of music, popular and classical."

"Wouldn't know," Estelle mumbled. "I don' feel s'good. Musta been tha' tumble I took outside. Feel like I fell off m'horse." She closed her eyes and sucked in her breath. "Oh, no!"

Judith stared at the maid. "What horse?"

"Don't 'member that, either," she mumbled. "All a blur. Jus' as well. Gruesome sight." She bobbled the snifter as she used one hand to rub at her eyes. "Like Ichabod Crane. Oh, my!" She polished off the brandy in one gulp and started to cough.

Judith patted Estelle on the back. "What do you mean? Are you talking about Blake Farrow?"

Estelle's head bobbed up and down — and then from side to side. "Feel awful. Room's spinnin'. You're spinnin'. Oh, my, my, my!"

Judith's concern overcame her curiosity. "Do you want to lie down in the living room?"

The maid coughed a few more times, sputtered, and shook her head. "No," she gasped. "Gimme a minute."

Judith waited. Finally Estelle hauled herself to her feet. "G'bye," she muttered, shuffling out of the kitchen.

While she sautéed the chicken, put water for rice on to boil, and cooked broccoli, Judith wondered about Suzanne and Fritz, about Dolph's numerous progeny, about Elsa's invasion of the Wittener house, about Estelle's strange reference to the headless horseman, Ichabod Crane, and a myriad of other things associated with the two deaths. By six o'clock, dinner was almost ready. Renie still hadn't returned, but Judith wasn't surprised. Getting Gertrude organized and taking her to Aunt Deb's would require time at both ends of the trip. If Gertrude had agreed to spend the night — and might have, given the lure of a bridge game — then she would have made all sorts of demands on Renie before they even left the premises. And when Renie got to her mother's apartment, Aunt Deb would talk her daughter into a virtual comatose state. Furthermore, Renie had chores at home. Judith was turning everything down on the stove and in the oven when the phone rang.

"O'Grady here," Rosemary said cheerfully. "I'm keeping you informed, Murder Maven. We won't have an autopsy report on Mrs. Kluger until Monday. Everything slows down on weekends. But there were no outward signs of foul play."

"That's reassuring," Judith said. "Still, I'd think that this investigation would have top priority, even on a weekend. What about the results from those liquor bottles?"

"Uh . . . I don't know yet," Rosemary replied. "How's Suzanne?"

For some reason, Judith was reluctant to unload on the detective. Her pity for Suzanne, not to mention her confusion about the young woman's emotional state, favored discretion. There was also something about

Rosemary's attitude that bothered her, but she couldn't put her finger on it. Maybe Rosemary was waiting to confer with Morgenstern.

"Suzanne's doing as well as can be expected," Judith said.

"I see." Rosemary sounded less than convinced. "No hysterics?"

"No," Judith answered truthfully. "She's calmed down this afternoon." *Except for the punch-out with Elsa.* "I'm making her dinner."

"Oh. I'll let you go, then. Just checking in."

"Thanks."

"Of course," Rosemary said with a smile in her voice. "Honestly, it's such a comfort to know you're right there with those . . . people. Or what's left of them. I don't suppose you've learned anything new?"

"Nothing worth mentioning just now," Judith hedged, still feeling protective of Suzanne. She didn't know what to make of Gregory, except that maybe he was mentally unstable; she felt it unwise to report Elsa's claim that Fritz wasn't Rudi's son or that . . . *Too much information, too much of a muddle.* Judith had to sort it out for herself before passing anything on to Rosemary.

"I'll keep in touch," Rosemary promised.

Judith set the phone down on the counter. She might as well take trays up to Suzanne and Estelle. Renie could be gone for another half hour at least. Maybe the cousins would have a cocktail before dinner. Judith felt as if she could use one. Her physical and mental energies were depleted.

Room One was nearest to the head of the stairs, so Judith rapped first on Estelle's door. There was no response. The brandy might have put her to sleep. For once, Judith wasn't filled with dread. She left the tray with its covered dishes on the floor. The maid could eat it cold when she woke up or come downstairs and heat it up in the microwave.

Suzanne responded immediately. "Dinner?" she said, sounding as if the concept were novel. "What is it?"

Judith explained that it was chicken Divan, except that she'd used broccoli instead of asparagus, which was out of season.

Suzanne gingerly fingered her bruised chin. The black eye was becoming more apparent, but otherwise the young woman seemed improved. "I suppose I should eat something. Thanks." She took the tray from Judith.

"I'm glad," Judith said, "I found out that you and Fritz aren't related. That upset me."

Suzanne dropped the tray on the side table with such a clatter that Judith thought she might have broken some of the dishes. *"What?"*

Judith shrugged. "After what you told me about Rudi's parentage, I couldn't believe you'd marry his son, who had to be your nephew. But of course he isn't, is he?"

Suzanne's face became even more distorted. "How do you know?"

Judith shrugged again. "I couldn't help but overhear you talking to Fritz on the phone. It bothered me. The relationship seemed too close to be . . . legal. But I should have guessed Rudi wasn't Fritz's father even then. You referred to Elsa as his mother, but to Rudi by his first name, not as Fritz's father. That was inconsistent if Rudi really was —"

"Oh, stop!" Suzanne snarled her short hair with her fingers. "What difference does it make? Leave me alone. I'm fine."

"Good." Judith walked out of the room.

*They're all crazy,* she thought as she trudged downstairs. *How could so many people connected to one another all be nuts?*

Heredity, maybe, or so she asserted after Renie breezed through the back door a few minutes before seven.

"That's possible," Renie said, avoiding

Sweetums, who had followed her into the house. "People inherit insanity. Sometimes I think it's contagious. It looks like this bunch is driving you to drink."

Judith glanced at the scotch rocks she'd poured for herself just before Renie arrived. "You're right — they have. Bourbon for you?"

Renie shrugged as she sat down at the kitchen table. "That or Canadian. Explain why you've come to this latest conclusion."

"Explain first what you've done with my mother," Judith said, shooing Sweetums off of the counter as she reached for a bottle of Gibson's Canadian.

"Simple," Renie said. "Before we left the toolshed, I called a couple of the other old girls from the SOTS bridge group and asked if they wanted to come to my mother's place tonight. I promised them Chocolate Decadence. They were delighted. Mary Anne Colpecchia still drives, so she's picking up Theresa McCoy. I finally got your mother out of here, stopped at Falstaff's to get the party dessert — which set me back fifteen bucks, I might add — and we went on to Mom's. It only took me ten minutes to escape from her apartment. Happily, Mom and Aunt Gert got into an argument about whether Mary Anne was legally blind and if Theresa had booze in her cough-syrup bottle. I crept out while they were going at it. But Mom already had dinner cooking, so all should be well."

"Mother's spending the night?"

"Yes." Renie grinned. "They can torture each other instead of us."

Judith bodily removed Sweetums, who had jumped back on the counter. "I'm glad. Mother doesn't like to leave the toolshed, no matter how much she complains about it, but the change will do her good."

"No, it won't," Renie said, pouring some 7-Up into the whiskey Judith had handed her. "But we can pretend. Tell me what I've missed."

It didn't take Judith long to relate the conversations with Estelle and Suzanne. "The way Elsa stated that Rudi wasn't Fritz's father was like a victory cry."

Renie looked thoughtful. "The usual suspect, Dolph?"

Judith stood up to refill her drink. She poured out only half a measure of scotch, thinking she must be more upset than she realized. She'd certainly downed the first cocktail in record time.

"It'd fit, given Dolph's alleged track record," Judith said, trying to avoid Sweetums, who was weaving in and out between

441

her feet. "Maybe Suzanne feels she and Fritz belong together because they don't fit in with the rest of this crew. Both were raised in musical families. Blake Farrow's company made musical instruments, Andrea was always active in the social whirl of music, and then she married Dolph, a revered figure in that world. Rudi was one of Dolph's protégés and Elsa had been his student. Suzanne and Fritz don't seem to give a hoot about music."

Renie's expression was skeptical. "Suzanne couldn't find some other guy more her age who didn't care for music, either?"

"I wonder if she ever looked," Judith said. "Her life has been very narrow."

"True. Sad." After a pause, Renie changed the subject. "Do you think Elsa smashed up Taryn's piano?"

Judith had sat down again at the table, but she glanced at Sweetums, who was still weaving around the floor. "It had to be either Elsa or Suzanne," she responded. "Unless —" She stopped and shook her head. "I can't think why Rudi or Taryn would do it. Fritz, of course, is a possibility. But my point is that Suzanne and Fritz feel like outsiders. Estelle told me that. Somehow, Suzanne wants to create a family unit where she feels she belongs. Fritz is apparently the way she figures she can belong."

"I wonder if the feeling is mutual," Renie mused.

"He may be in it for the money," Judith said. She was still watching Sweetums, who continued to bob and weave, though more slowly, as if he were a toy running low on batteries. "What's wrong with that cat? Now *he's* acting odd."

"Did you feed him?"

"Yes, right after I took the tray upstairs to Estelle and Suzanne." She watched the cat's big orange-and-white body wobble and waver, as if the floor were greased. "That's all I need — a sick cat."

Sweetums collapsed on his side, a couple of feet from Renie's chair. "You're right — he's definitely not well," Renie said. "Stay put, I'll see if he's . . . uh . . . alive."

As Judith held her breath, Renie got down on the floor and gently touched the cat. Sweetums didn't move. His eyes were closed, though he was still breathing. She leaned closer. And gasped.

"Your cat's not sick, coz. He's drunk. I smell scotch on his breath."

Judith jumped out of the chair. "Oh, for . . . No wonder my drink disappeared so fast! He was guzzling it off of the counter!" She stared at the unconscious animal.

"What should we do?"

Renie shrugged. "Let him sleep it off. He'll probably have a hangover when he wakes up." She grimaced. "I don't want to be around when that happens. His disposition is terrible when he's sober."

Judith kept watching the cat. He certainly didn't appear to be in any distress. In fact, she could have sworn he was smiling in his sleep.

"Let him be," Renie said, sitting down again. "He couldn't have drunk very much. He's not puking."

Judith looked at her glass. "Gack! I've been drinking out of this! Cat germs! I'll probably be the one who throws up!" She grabbed the glass, reached around to the sink, and poured the contents down the drain. "I'm starting over."

"Clarence has never taken a drink in his life," Renie said as Judith got a fresh glass out of the cupboard. "Bunny lips that touch liquor will never touch mine."

"Double gack," said Judith. She was getting ice out of the refrigerator when she heard someone moving around upstairs. "Suzanne," she murmured. "I guess she recovered enough to exercise."

Renie gazed at the ceiling. "That doesn't

sound like a workout to me. It's got no rhythm."

Judith listened. The noise had stopped. "Damn," she swore under her breath. "I'd better go see what she's up to."

"I'll come with you," Renie volunteered.

The cousins trooped up the back stairs. Suzanne was nowhere in sight, but the door to her room was open. One glance told Judith that the young woman wasn't there. All the other guest-room doors were closed. Judith was about to check the bathroom between Room Four and Room Three when Renie stopped her.

"I think I heard something downstairs," she whispered.

Judith hurried out of the bedroom. "She must have gone down the front stairs while we were coming up the back way."

Renie led the way to the main floor. Judith was flagging. She had overdone it, sapping her strength and making her hip ache more than it had in months. She had only two guests, but they were too much. She felt like collapsing along with Sweetums.

The front door was open. Renie was already outside. Judith heard her voice — and Suzanne's.

"You can't stop me," the younger woman said. "I have a ten-thirty flight to New York.

My town car will be here any minute."

"What about your mother?" Renie was saying as Judith came outside. "You can't leave her here in the morgue."

"Why not? She often left me alone," Suzanne replied bitterly. "She was always busy with her charities and benefits — or she was sick."

Judith approached Suzanne warily, noticing that she had not only her own luggage, but her mother's as well. "I don't think leaving is a good idea," she said softly. "The police won't like it."

"The police!" Suzanne hooted with laughter. "They think I killed my mother? Or Dolph? That's crazy! Mom killed herself!"

"You mean," Judith said, "she overdosed on purpose? That's a terrible thought!"

"No, it's not." Suzanne looked at Judith as if she must be stupid. "She couldn't live without Dolph. Or her guilt."

"What guilt?" Judith asked.

Suzanne didn't answer. It was raining again, a steady drip that splashed in small puddles along the edge of the cul-de-sac. There was wind, too, blowing up from the bay. Judith was cold. She shivered and repeated the question: "What guilt, Suzanne?"

The young woman peered into the darkened night, apparently watching for head-lights. "Does it matter?"

"Yes," Judith said.

Suzanne shrugged. "I don't think it does now."

"You're wrong," Judith said, urgency in her voice.

"Mom's dead," Suzanne said flatly. "What difference does it make? Especially to you."

A car turned around the corner, headlights glowing in the rain as it slowly entered the cul-de-sac.

Judith put a hand on Suzanne's arm. "Then why can't you tell me about her guilt? Did she poison Dolph?"

Suzanne laughed. "Of course not!"

The car, which was indeed a black limo sedan, stopped at the curb in front of Hillside Manor. Suzanne hoisted the lug-gage strap of a fold-over onto her shoulder as the driver got out.

"Then what?" Judith urged, tightening her grip on Suzanne's arm.

"Ohhh . . ." Suzanne pulled away, not angrily, but firmly. "She didn't kill Dolph. But she did kill my father. Good-bye, Mrs. Flynn."

She walked down the front steps and headed toward the town car.

# Chapter
## Twenty-Two

Renie reported that Estelle was still alive and snoring. "I opened the door to Room One just enough so that I could see she was breathing."

"Thank goodness," Judith said, leaning against the newel post of the front stairs. "And thanks for saving me another trip up those stairs. I couldn't help but wonder if . . . well, you know."

Renie did know and gave her cousin a sympathetic look. "Too bad you can't put Sweetums in bed with Estelle. They could sleep it off together."

Judith's smile was weak. "I've got to call Rosemary," she declared. "The police can stop Suzanne at the airport."

"Aren't you glad to be rid of her?" Renie asked as the cousins went back into the kitchen. "And aren't you aware that I'm so hungry I could eat your drunken cat?"

Dialing Rosemary's cell number, Judith

told her cousin to warm up her dinner in the microwave. "It may be dried out by now," she cautioned. "Add water to the — Rosemary? This is Judith. I wanted to let you know that Suzanne just left for the airport." She gave the detective the flight time, adding that Suzanne might be accompanied by Fritz Wittener. "I assume," Judith added, "you don't want them leaving town."

"I'd prefer that they didn't," Rosemary allowed. "But legally, there's no reason she — and he — can't go. I'll see what I can do."

After she disconnected the call, Judith gazed down at Sweetums, who was still sleeping peacefully by the kitchen table. "When Estelle comes to she'll be furious to find out Suzanne has left."

Renie had dished up dinner for both cousins and was waiting for the microwave signal. "Give her some more brandy. Then she can pass out again."

"She's certainly not used to —" Judith snapped her fingers. "I almost forgot! It was the brandy." She sat down as Renie put the warmed-over plates on the table. "Remember when Elsa fainted?"

"Of course."

"She drank brandy as well as cognac," Judith said. "Fritz poured her the wrong stuff.

What if the rhubarb was in the brandy?"

"The poisonous distillation, you mean? Wouldn't the lab report have shown how the poison was ingested?"

"I'm not sure," Judith admitted. "It may be possible with modern toxicology to pinpoint the food or drink that contained the poison. But Rosemary says she doesn't have the tox report back yet. That's odd."

Renie stuffed her face with chicken and rice. "Yopoy?"

"My point is that Elsa didn't drink much brandy," Judith replied, "but Dolph gulped down quite a bit. Andrea mentioned at the time that it was his cure-all of choice. Gregory and Estelle said the same thing."

"Ah." Renie swallowed. "So you're saying that the creation of a crisis would force Dolph to gulp down the poisoned brandy."

Judith nodded. "Exactly. Elsa's collapse was sufficient to set him off. In fact, it may have been his second crisis of the day. He was upset after his first visit with Rudi. I'll bet that's when Dolph learned the violin bow had gone missing. But who set him up at the party?"

"Estelle and Gregory weren't around," Renie pointed out, "although they *might* have managed it."

"That's the problem," Judith said. "All

the liquor that was bought for the party and delivered by Fritz supposedly arrived here unopened. But we don't know that for sure."

Renie looked thoughtful. "Do you think Andrea overdosed — or poisoned herself with that same rhubarb stuff?"

"I don't know what to think," Judith said, "since the statement was made by Suzanne. What does she mean by saying that her mother killed her father, Blake Farrow?"

"Are we sure Blake was her father?"

"Are you kidding? With this bunch, we can't be sure of anything." Judith sighed. "I honestly think that Gregory may have escaped from the booby hatch. Remember that slip of the tongue by Olive?"

"About Gregory going back to *the* home?" Renie nodded. "That may be why you couldn't find him in the phone book or anywhere else."

"That makes sense," Judith said, "if any of this does."

"So who's Frederica?" Renie asked.

Judith waited until she'd finished eating some broccoli. "*You* saw her in the fireplace. According to goofy Gregory, she was his mother, who was Olive's sister."

"Maybe her name wasn't really Frederica," Renie remarked.

Judith looked up from her plate. "What

makes you say that?"

Renie grinned slyly. "You're not the only one who can have sudden insights and inspirations. Ever hear of Fort Frederica in Georgia?"

"No," Judith replied. "What is it?"

"A national park," Renie replied. "I came across it a couple of years ago when I was doing research for a travel brochure. Back when I had work." She grimaced. "Anyway, it was built in the 1730s to protect the southern boundary of the Georgia colony from Spain."

"So?"

"So I remember weird things," Renie said. "The name of the colony's founder was Oglethorpe. Just like Olive's last name."

Judith regarded Renie with interest. "Olive mentioned that her platter came from England and that her ancestors were distinguished. I wonder . . ."

Renie shrugged. "It may not mean much, though." She gobbled up more food.

For a few moments, the cousins ate in silence, broken only by Renie's customary slurping and chomping.

"I'm still curious," Judith finally said, "as to what Suzanne meant about Andrea killing Blake Farrow. I assume she didn't mean literally. You know how people make such remarks."

Renie nodded. "What they mean — like in this instance — is that Blake didn't really want to go on the foxhunt that day, but Andrea insisted. Or he never cared for foxhunting, but she enjoyed the prestige of belonging to an elite hunt club."

"Yes," Judith agreed. "It could even be that the foxhunt had nothing to do with it. That is, Andrea's spending habits or her pill popping or some other thing she did made him reckless. Anyway, Suzanne's unbalanced, so I'm not putting a great deal of stock into what she said about her parents."

"I suppose that's smart," Renie allowed. "I'm trying to remember the details from when I listened in on your conversation with Rosemary. The guy who was fiddling with Blake Farrow's books at the musical-instrument company went to prison and died there, right?"

Judith nodded. "I jotted down some notes. I think they're in the drawer by the phone base." She got up and went to the counter by the computer. "I only wrote down basic facts. Let me see . . . Gosh, my handwriting's deteriorating."

"We're deteriorating all over," Renie said drily as Judith sat down.

"Here's what I've got," Judith said, reading the fragments aloud. " 'Foxhunt, New Jersey, fall.' I assume that means the time of year, not what happened to Blake. 'B rides all' . . . No, that's 'off,' not 'all.' " She paused, trying to read the next words. "I think it says 'Andrea and MH' — that must be master of the hunt — 'ahead of B.' "

"So far so good," Renie put in. "I recall most of that."

Judith scanned the last of her notes. " 'Instruments,' 'cooked books,' 'Chandler,' 'C's knife' . . . no, that's 'wife' . . . 'died in prison,' 'old money,' 'German co.' " Judith shrugged. "That's it."

Renie frowned. "What does 'sees wife' mean? I don't remember."

"That's *cap* 'C's wife'," Judith corrected. "Blake was riding with Chandler's — the embezzler's — wife, whose name was . . . Laura? Lorene?"

Renie stood up, leaned across the table, and peered through the kitchen window. "No. It was . . . Laurel." She pointed outside. "Like Rankers's hedge."

"That's right," Judith agreed. "Laurel Chandler was lucky she couldn't keep up with Blake or she might have gotten killed, too. The crucial part is how Andrea and the hunt master could've ridden that same route and not been harmed. Of course I don't know much about foxhunting. Maybe the riders don't follow the exact same route."

"Maybe not," Renie acknowledged, leaning back in her chair. "The few times I went riding, I let the horse go wherever it wanted. I rarely argue with anybody or anything that's ten times bigger than I am."

"Back up," Judith said suddenly.

"My horse wouldn't do that, either," Renie said.

"No," Judith contradicted. "I mean to that Chandler woman's name. Laurel, right? What would be a good name for Laurel's sister?"

Renie made a face. "Coral?"

"No." Judith's smile was sly. "How about Olive?"

Renie considered. "Ah. Olive wreath, laurel wreath. Parents who were into Greco-Roman — or they just liked shrubs." She slapped the table. "You're onto something, coz."

"But where's it taking us?"

"Be like me on the horse — hang on and see where it goes."

Judith shook her head. "If Olive's sister was Laurel Chandler, what happened to her?"

"Didn't somebody say Olive's sister died?"

"That's right," Judith replied. "Should I call Rosemary to see if she can check it out?"

"How about calling Olive?"

"She won't tell me," Judith said. "Unless . . . hand me the directory."

"I've got her number." Renie reached around to grab her big handbag off of the counter. "Remember, I'm her retirement-home rep."

"Good," Judith said. "Then you can call her."

Renie scowled at Judith but agreed. "Why not? One more lie won't add much weight to the handcart in which I'm riding to hell."

Judith tidied up the dinner things while Renie placed the call.

"Hello, Ms. Oglethorpe, this is Serena Jones from D'Otage C'est Bon Retirement Châteaux. I need just a little more information to finish the paperwork on your form."

Judith looked up at the kitchen's high ceiling. Could Olive possibly be that gullible? Or did Judith just know Renie too well?

"Elementary school," Renie was saying. "Yes, I have it. And high school . . . yes, as well as the business courses. Parents' names . . . Charles and Martha. What were their middle names? . . . It's not vital, but . . . oh,

fine . . . yes . . . Henry and Rose, very nice
. . . Siblings' names? I don't have anyone
listed . . . Yes, you did say she'd died, but of
course your parents are deceased, too . . ."
Renie looked at Judith and gave her a
thumbs-up sign. "Laurel . . . Laurel what?
. . ." Renie frowned. "She never used it?
Why? . . . Oh, I see. But most women don't
drop their middle name when they marry.
What was her married name, by the way?
. . . Okay, got it." Another thumbs-up for
Judith. "That's very sad . . . I'm afraid the
good die young . . . Now, about nieces or
nephews — is Gregory your nephew? . . . I
see." Renie made a face. "Very kind of you.
Do you have his address and phone number
so we can list him as an emergency contact?
. . . Okay, when you find out, let me know.
Thank you, Ms. Oglethorpe. Oh — by the
way, I'm a history buff. By any chance, are
you descended from the Georgia Ogle-
thorpes? . . . How interesting! I find geneal-
ogy fascinating, too . . . Yes, in fact, Attila
the Hun on my father's side. Thanks. Good-
bye."

"Well?" Judith said, leaning against the
fridge. "Success?"

"About four for five," Renie answered,
"which means my batting average is pretty
high. Olive's sister was Laurel Oglethorpe

Chandler." She gave Judith a smug look. "Laurel didn't use her first name when she was young because she never liked it. As far as I can tell, Laurel died not long after her husband went to prison. Not dramatically by hanging herself from a Venetian chandelier, but a mundane car accident on the Jersey Turnpike. From then on, Olive took Gregory under her wing."

Judith was thoughtful. "Gregory would've been born long before Laurel went on the foxhunt with Blake and Andrea Farrow. If Gregory really is Dolph's son, maybe he was born before Laurel married the crooked Mr. Chandler. So where does Frederica come in?"

Renie finished the dregs of her drink, which had melted to mostly whiskey and 7-Up-flavored water. "I figure that was Laurel's middle name. Olive's is Georgia. And yes, Olive and Laurel descended from the Oglethorpe who founded the colony. Thus, I cleverly deduce that if Olive was given the name of the colony, Laurel ended up with the name of the fort — Frederica. Ta-da!"

Judith nodded. "Excellent logic, my good coz."

"As for Gregory's residence, Olive became

vague," Renie said. "She told me he's moving."

"More likely being moved from one institution to another," Judith remarked. "If Dolph was a musical genius — in terms of his so-called ear and ability to nurture talent — he may have been mentally unstable. Genius often borders on madness. At the very least, his idea of propagating the world with music talent makes him an egomaniac."

"Or a sex fiend," Renie said, grinning. "Men! Excuses, excuses."

Judith finished loading the dishwasher. "I must check on Estelle."

Renie lifted the sheep's head from the cookie jar. "Empty. Drat."

"I haven't had time to bake," Judith replied. "Are you coming?"

"I might as well," Renie said. "No cookies."

To Judith's relief, Estelle opened Room One's door after the first knock. "I just finished my dinner," she said, looking haggard but composed. "It was rather good. Thank you. I was about to put the tray out in the hall."

"How long have you been awake?" Judith inquired, taking the tray from the maid.

Estelle looked at her watch. "Half an hour or so. A noise in the hall woke me. I must have been more tired than I realized. How is Suzanne?"

"She's gone," Judith said.

"Gone?" The maid blanched. "Gone where?"

"To New York," Judith said, "but I don't think she'll get that far."

Estelle grew more agitated, her fingers frantically clutching at the open door. "No! How could she go without me?"

Judith explained that Suzanne had booked a ten-thirty flight. "The police may prevent her from going," Judith said. "She asked Fritz Wittener to go with her."

"Impossible!" Estelle retreated into her room and began flinging items into her suitcase. "I'm going to the airport! Call me a taxi!"

Renie couldn't resist. "You're a —"

"Shut up, coz," Judith said sharply, pinching Renie's arm.

"Ouch!" Renie gave Judith a dirty look. "Couldn't we use some comic relief?"

"No," Judith snapped. "Really, Ms. Pearson, I think it'd be better if you stayed . . ."

The maid whirled around and glared at Judith. "You don't understand! Suzanne is totally irresponsible! I must stop her! Please! Call a cab for me!"

Reasoning that if Rosemary decided to

force Suzanne to remain in the city, Estelle wouldn't be going anywhere either, Judith surrendered. "Okay, I'll use the phone in the hall."

After she'd ordered the taxi, Judith asked Renie to fetch Suzanne's tray from Room Four. "I don't think she touched it," Judith added. "When I looked in there earlier, it seemed just the way I'd seen it earlier."

Five minutes later, the cousins were in the entry hall, waiting with Estelle for her ride. The maid had calmed down a little, but still showed signs of anxiety.

Judith smiled kindly at her. "Isn't it time you leveled with us?"

Estelle looked puzzled. "I don't understand."

"I know you were in the city before your supposed arrival," Judith said, trying not to make the words sound like an accusation. "Why?"

Estelle gazed up at the small Tiffany-style chandelier that hung in the entry hall. "Madam asked me to come. I had planned on visiting relatives in the southwestern part of the state, but she begged me to change my itinerary. She was terribly worried about Suzanne and Fritz. I daresay she sensed what might happen when they saw each other again. Mr. Wittener made it possible

461

for me to stay with Olive Oglethorpe. Madam wanted me close by. She became alarmed after Mr. Kluger died, so she summoned me to your B&B. It seems her worst fears were realized."

"Does Fritz reciprocate Suzanne's feelings?" Judith asked.

"I don't know." Estelle shook her head sadly. "Fritz Wittener has no purpose in life, as far as I can tell. He drifts. Elsa Wittener has made him utterly dependent on her. It's so unwise."

"But Suzanne was equally dependent on *her* mother," Judith pointed out.

"Yes." Estelle gave a start as a horn honked outside. "That must be the cab. Good-bye. And thank you."

"Pathetic," Renie remarked as the cousins watched Estelle get into the taxi. "Will she — and Suzanne — be back?"

Judith shrugged. "Who knows?" Closing the front door, she sighed. "Saturday night — and an empty B&B."

"I'm here," Renie said.

Judith smiled at her cousin. "Thank goodness. I haven't been alone in this house . . . ever. Before I married Joe, before I started the B&B, while Mike was away at school, Mother was always here. Then it was guests and then Joe, and now . . ." She made a

462

helpless gesture with her hands. "I hope I can start accepting reservations this coming week. I could use a big dose of normal life about now."

"Me, too," Renie agreed as the cousins went into the living room. "We both need our work. I'm not ready to retire, and you obviously aren't, either."

"No," Judith agreed. "Frankly, even with Joe working part-time, we'd have trouble making ends meet on his pension and Social Security. I can't take mine and get the full benefits for over another year."

"I know," Renie said. "We're in the same boat, and it's leaking like a sieve right now. Speaking of retiring, I'm going to take my bath upstairs and change into my nightgown and robe. That's my schedule at home. Then we can watch TV. But please — no chefs. I love food, but I don't want to know where it's been."

"Okay," Judith said. "Let's watch it down here. The picture's bigger and better than the one in the family quarters. Besides," she added, "the so-called guests may return. They didn't take their keys, and I locked the front door after we came inside."

While Renie was upstairs Judith finished cleaning up the kitchen, emptied the dishwasher, and turned out all the lights except for a table lamp in the living room. She was checking the TV listings when she heard a noise from somewhere in the house. Renie, she guessed.

But Renie would have gone to the family quarters on the third floor, where her clothes were stashed in the spare bedroom. It was impossible to hear anything that far away in the solidly built house that was nearing the century mark. Maybe the sound had come from outside. The driveway, perhaps.

Judith got up from the sofa and went to the bay window that overlooked the drive. Heaven help her if kids were tampering with the Joneses' Camry — or "Cammy," as Renie and Bill affectionately called their car. Worse yet, she wouldn't want anything to happen to Joe's precious MG, though it was parked in the garage.

There was no moon in the ebony sky; there was no wind in the trees or shrubs next to the house. The rain was straight and steady, though only a trickle of water crept down the edge of the slightly sloping driveway. Judith couldn't see anyone outside. Kneeling on the window seat, she glanced at the grandfather clock, which had just chimed the quarter hour past nine. Looking outside again, she could see a light on in the upstairs window of the Ericsons' angular house. From her vantage point, that was the only other house she could see except for the roof of the Dooleys' Colonial behind the garage.

Judith went back to the sofa. She knew that Renie liked to soak in the tub. That was a luxury Judith had given up after hip surgery. Getting in and out was hazardous. She took showers in the morning, which helped her become fully alert and ready to face the day.

Another noise. Judith frowned, trying to figure out where it had come from. The basement, she thought. Maybe Sweetums was on the prowl. She realized that the cat hadn't been sleeping on the kitchen floor when she'd been tidying up.

Still, Judith worried about him. Like Estelle, he wasn't used to drinking liquor, and the aftereffects might harm him. Judith decided to go down to the basement and see if he was all right. Maybe he was lonesome for Gertrude. The two shared a bond, both being predictable only in that they could be more ornery than most of their respective species. She didn't bother turning on the main lights in the kitchen, but flipped the switch on the small overhead above the sink. It was sufficient to guide her through the familiar hallway.

But at the top of the stairs, Judith turned on the basement lights. She hadn't taken a step before she heard another noise. Pausing, she listened and heard the faintest of sounds.

"Sweetums?" she called. "Here, kitty. I'll get you some tuna."

She waited at the head of the stairs, then realized that the tuna cans were still in the carton Joe had bought at Gutbusters and stored in the basement. Wearily, she traipsed down the steps. "Here, Sweetums. I'm too tired to play hide-and-seek."

At the bottom of the stairs, Judith's gaze searched for the cat. Sometimes he napped in the basement, especially during the summer when it was the coolest place in the house. Usually, he curled up on top of the clothes dryer. But not this time.

Judith gave a start. The window above the washer and dryer was ajar. She'd closed it firmly after inspecting it with Rosemary O'Grady.

The cat couldn't open the window. He came and went through his small flap in the back door. Judith stood rooted to the spot. She should get out of the basement immediately. But she felt immobilized. Her ears were primed for any sound — including a human breath.

The only places a person could hide in the basement were behind the furnace or in the narrow space that allowed for the outside vent between the dryer and the wall.

She heard a faint noise. Not someone breathing, but a soft little sound, like weight shifting. Judith forced herself to move. And to speak.

"Okay, Sweetums, stay down here," she said loudly, hoping to sound normal. "No tuna for you."

With legs that felt like lead, she lurched toward the stairs. Gripping the handrail to steady herself, she started making the ascent. One, two, three, four . . .

At last, she reached the top. Judith felt as if she'd climbed Mount Everest. Closing her eyes and sucking in air, she turned the corner into the narrow hallway — and collided with something all too human.

Judith screamed.

So did Renie.

"What the hell are you doing?" Renie demanded, clutching at her bathrobe. "Are you in a daze?"

Judith leaned against the wall, pale and shaken. "Yes. No." She licked her dry lips. "The basement," she whispered. "Somebody there. Call 911."

Renie's eyes grew enormous. Her lips formed the word "Who?"

Judith shook her head, gesturing for her cousin to move.

"I can't see," Renie hissed. "Why aren't the lights on?" But she managed to find the phone in its cradle on the counter. "I'd like to report a prowler at . . . Hey, never mind the wiseass cracks! Just send some cops!" Ringing off, Renie turned on Judith, who had crept into the kitchen. "What's with this 911 operator? She started to give me guff."

Judith motioned frantically for Renie to be quiet. "It's okay. She'll send help. We need it. Come on, let's go outside."

"In my bathrobe?" Renie shook her head. "It's raining."

"You're a native," Judith said, still keeping her voice down. "I'm going." She started toward the back door, but detoured into the pantry to grab a heavy flashlight.

"Okay, okay," Renie whispered, right behind Judith as they quietly went out the back way. "You're lucky I'm wearing sturdy slippers."

"*You're* lucky," Judith retorted. "I'm not the one who's ready for bed."

Judith hadn't yet turned on the flashlight, but a faint glow from the toolshed's window enabled the cousins to see.

"Who's in the basement?" Renie asked as they ducked down behind the garbage cans and recycling bins at the corner of the house.

"Don't know," Judith replied, peeking over the top of a green recycling bin to watch the basement window. "Still open," she whispered. "Has he — or she — fled?"

"Let's hope so," Judith said. "You keep an eye on the back door. Our perp may try to leave that way."

"What about the front?" Renie asked.

"I doubt it. The back door's much closer to the basement."

The cousins waited in the cool, damp night. Judith was grateful that the house's eaves protected them from the rain, but she wished she'd paused to grab a jacket from the hallway.

Five minutes passed before the cousins saw the lights of the patrol car in the cul-de-sac. "Thank goodness," Judith said with relief.

Darnell and Mercedes got out, cautiously approaching the driveway. Judith turned on the flashlight, but didn't say a word. The uniforms quickened their step.

"Mrs. Flynn!" Darnell said softly as he

and Mercedes reached the cousins. "What's going on?"

Judith explained about someone hiding in the basement, adding that it could be the same person who might — or might not — have entered via the window earlier in the week.

"You think he's still there?" Mercedes asked.

"It's likely," Judith said. "I think we'd have heard some kind of noise if whoever it is tried to leave. It may even be a she."

"Right," Darnell said. "We're going in. You want to wait on the porch or inside?"

"Inside," Judith said. "That way we can watch the front door — just in case. And we can keep an eye on the other side of the house, although the windows there are sealed fairly tight."

"Okay. Go." Darnell waved a hand.

The cousins scooted back to the porch and into the house. They entered carefully, though, tiptoeing down the hallway.

"I'll take the door," Judith said to Renie. "You watch from the kitchen window."

"Aye, aye, Commander," Renie said, saluting Judith.

"Are you okay?" Judith asked suddenly.

"I am now," Renie answered. "But I'll be even better when Darnell and Mercedes find your mystery guest."

Judith's smile was a little awry. "Agreed. We got lucky this time. No face-off with somebody who might be a killer and probably is a thief."

"Lucky," Renie repeated. "Yes." But she didn't sound convinced.

Suddenly Judith wasn't, either.

# CHAPTER
# TWENTY-THREE

Standing by the front door, Judith couldn't hear any noise coming from the basement. After the first couple of minutes, she began to fret. Had the prowler already left? It was possible. Her ruse in pretending to talk to Sweetums might not have been convincing. Certainly the cousins' screams could have scared away whoever was hiding in the basement. The open window wasn't necessarily a sign that he or she hadn't made a hasty exit. Judith couldn't expect a person in flight to cover tracks.

Almost ten minutes passed before she heard the uniforms coming into the kitchen. Renie was asking what they'd found.

"Nothing," Mercedes said as Judith came through the dining room and pushed open the swinging half doors. "No sign of anybody." She saw Judith. "Are you certain someone was down there?"

Judith hesitated. "Well — yes. At first I

thought it was our cat. But I could swear I heard someone moving."

Mercedes shrugged. "Whoever it was isn't there now," she declared with a touch of apology. "There is some dirt — more like mud — on top of the clothes dryer. But your cat could have done that, right?"

"Cats don't open windows," Judith insisted.

"No," Mercedes allowed. "They don't. We can search the rest of the house and the yard."

"Thanks," Judith said, noticing that Darnell was taking a call on his cell.

"We got a big brawl at the civic center," he announced to his partner. "Kids, drugs, Saturday night," he said to the cousins. "We're backup. Sorry." He turned back to Mercedes. "Let's go."

The officers went.

"Drat," Judith said, turning on the kitchen lights. "I guess our crime session is over for the night."

"Then how about some microwave popcorn?" Renie suggested.

"Okay," Judith said, searching in the cupboard for popcorn with extra butter. "It'll take three minutes and seven seconds. I noticed Mother left a light on in the toolshed. I'll go turn it off while you do the popcorn." She tossed the packet to her cousin.

"I'll melt extra butter," Renie said.

"It's already buttered," Judith said from the hallway.

"There's no such thing as too much butter," Renie declared. "I consider butter a food group."

Shaking her head, Judith went outside. She glanced at the window in the basement. It had been closed, probably by Darnell or Mercedes. If someone had escaped through that window, it had to be a fairly slim and agile person. Suzanne. Fritz. Taryn. Gregory. Or someone Judith didn't even know.

Beaming the big flashlight on the walkway to the toolshed, Judith reached the ramp that led to the door. She stared. The door was open a scant inch. She could imagine Renie trying to hustle Gertrude to leave as fast as the stubborn, finicky old lady would allow.

The light inside suddenly went off. There had never been a second door in the small building, despite the city zoning codes that required two exits. Judith's hardheaded handyman, the aging but able Skjoval Tolvang, had managed to outwit — and outlast — the inspectors.

Pausing on the threshold, Judith played

the flashlight around the little sitting room. The card table was overturned; the floor was littered with magazines, playing cards, and candy. It was unlikely that Renie and Gertrude had made such a mess. And it was improbable that the light had burned out just as Judith entered the toolshed.

She backed out across the threshold and slammed the door behind her, realizing that she could lock it from the outside. The habit of carrying a master key in her pocket served her well. Swiftly, she locked the door, shooting the dead bolt. Like so much of Skjoval's work, it was tricky, and would take time for the prowler to figure it out.

Renie was just getting the popcorn out of the microwave.

"Coz!" Judith cried. "Call 911 again! We've got our perp trapped in the toolshed!"

"Oh, for . . ." Renie tossed the popcorn bag onto the counter and grabbed the phone. "No smart-ass stuff this time," she barked, recognizing the voice at the other end. "Prowler alert still in effect. Send cops quick." Renie clicked off and stared at Judith. "Hey — that twit didn't mouth off."

"When she sees our address and phone number come up, she ought to know we're never kidding," Judith said grimly as she headed for the back door. "Dare I go on the porch to keep an eye on the toolshed?"

"No!" Renie shouted, coming up behind Judith. "Watch through the window or the cat hole."

"I'll take the window," Judith said. "You get on the floor. I can't."

"Okay." Renie knelt down and opened the cat flap. "Yikes!"

Judith gave a start. "I don't see anything."

"I do." Renie retreated.

"What?"

"It's the cat."

Sweetums marched through the opening, huge plume of a tail swishing, malevolent yellow eyes fixed on Renie.

Judith barely took her own eyes away from the window in the door. "Only the bedroom window opens," she pointed out, "and I can watch it from here. Of course whoever it is could break the windows in the sitting room. I can't see the third one on the toolshed's far side."

"But our perp would have to run in front of the toolshed to escape," Renie noted. "Climbing the retaining wall between your place and Dooleys' would be tough, and that hike up the side hill below the condos isn't easy, either. I won't even mention the Rankerses' man-eating hedge."

Judith shifted her weight off of her artificial hip. "Where are those cops? Are you sure that operator took your call seriously?"

"There's a brawl that's probably turned into a riot at the civic center, remember? The police may be tied up," Renie said, again looking through the cat door. "It's only been five minutes since I called. Relax."

"Are you kidding?" Judith shot back. "I'm a wreck. *You* didn't go down in the basement. *You* didn't go out to the — ah! I hear a car!"

No headlights shone in the driveway, at least not that Judith could see. Maybe they had been dimmed to prevent alerting the prowler. Judith opened the door a tiny bit so that she could hear more clearly.

"Watch it," Renie growled from the floor. "Contrary to what Bill says, my head's not made of brick."

Judith gasped. "Someone's coming through the little window in the bedroom! Feet, legs first! I think it's a man!"

"I see him," Renie said. "Jeez, where're the cops? Maybe that wasn't them."

But a voice called out as soon as she finished speaking.

"Police! Stop where you are!"

"Rosemary!" Judith exclaimed. "Thank heavens!"

The prowler was stuck in the window. All

that the cousins could see were his legs and part of his rear end. Rosemary hurried toward the toolshed, gun drawn.

"I'm armed," she said in a more normal voice. "Can you get through that window?"

Judith could hear only a muffled, angry voice as the perp squirmed and wiggled but made no progress. "Skjoval never did get those windows quite right," she murmured.

"Can you put your hands behind you?" Rosemary asked.

Silence.

"Then you'll have to stay there until backup arrives," Rosemary said. "I'm not coming any closer."

A stream of unintelligible profanity erupted from the window. The feet kicked, the legs flailed, the rump bumped. With a mighty heave, the window shot up a couple of inches and the prowler slid unceremoniously into the small flower bed next to the toolshed.

"There go your zinnias," Renie remarked. "Who the hell is it? I can't see through this damned cat hole." She stood up.

Rosemary provided the answer. "Lie facedown and spread out. You're under arrest, Fritz Johann Wittener, for breaking and entering."

"Fritz!" Judith exclaimed. "Well, well."

Approaching the prone suspect, Rosemary was still talking. "You're also under arrest for suspicion of murdering Dolph Ludwig Kluger."

"No!" The word flew out of Fritz's mouth as he jerked his head up.

"Huh?" said Renie.

"Thief yes, murderer no," Judith declared, opening the door all the way as Rosemary cuffed Fritz.

"Then who?" Renie asked as they hurried from the porch.

Rosemary turned as soon as she heard the cousins. Fritz was still on the ground, protesting his innocence.

"I've got it all tied up with blue ribbons," Rosemary announced in her chipper voice. "Backup is on the way."

Judith saw two vehicles pulling into the cul-de-sac. One was a squad car. The other was a van that bore the KINE-TV logo.

"How did they get here so fast?" Judith asked.

"What?" Rosemary's innocence seemed feigned. "Oh! Goodness, I suppose they picked it up on the scanner."

Fritz's voice was pitiful. "Can I stand?"

"Not yet," Rosemary retorted, keeping a foot on the young man's leg. "My guys are just getting out of their car."

And, Judith noticed with chagrin, Mavis Lean-Brodie was emerging from the television van with her camera crew.

"Oh, no!" Judith cried, seeing her sometimes nemesis and occasional ally. "Mavis!" she called. "Quick!"

Rosemary was reading Fritz his rights. Judith pulled both Mavis and Renie over to the recycling bins.

"Rosemary O'Grady's arresting Fritz Wittener on suspicion of murdering Dolph Kluger — not to mention breaking and entering and perhaps grand larceny," Judith explained rapidly as Darnell Hicks and Mercedes Berger hauled the suspect off toward their squad car.

Mavis looked mildly interested. "So?"

"I think I know who really killed Kluger," Judith whispered.

"Thanks for telling me," Renie snapped.

"I said," Judith responded, "I only *think* I know, but here's who I've fingered." She was still whispering when she uttered the name.

"Ah," said Mavis.

"Well, well," said Renie.

Judith had one more bit for Mavis. She gave the anchorwoman a name and number. "Call as soon as you can."

Rosemary was coming toward them. "Did

your cameramen get that?" she asked, gesturing at the squad car.

"Sure," Mavis replied. "They started taping right away. We've got just under an hour before the eleven o'clock news. You want to make a statement?"

"You bet I do," Rosemary said, preening for the minicam. "This is my first homicide case, and I've cracked it."

Mavis, whose natural demeanor was skeptical, tipped her head to one side. The shoulder-length blond hair swayed gracefully on command. "You're sure?"

"Of course." Rosemary scowled at Mavis. "I'm a pro." She shot Judith a sidelong glance. "You think I rely on luck like some amateur? How about taking some footage of me by the official squad vehicle?" she said. "Unmarked city cars aren't dramatic."

Mavis shrugged. "Why not? Move over there. But I'll interview you at central booking." She shot Judith a knowing look. "I want this to be official before we air it."

Rosemary looked dubious, but agreed.

"Okay," Mavis said to her two-man crew, "that's a wrap. Let's head downtown for live coverage. We'll break into the regular newscast."

Judith was already heading into the house, using the front entrance. Renie took a detour to collect the popcorn and grab a Pepsi.

"Now what?" she asked, a handful of popcorn heading for her mouth.

"Now we wait," Judith said. "I'm not going to explain anything until I see the broadcast."

"Unfair," Renie said as a couple of popcorn pieces fell onto her bathrobe.

Judith turned on the TV. "Here. Watch *Heat.* Feel right at home."

"Of course," Renie responded, shoveling out more popcorn while butter dripped from her chin. "I've only seen De Niro and Pacino face off about two hundred times. It's one of Bill's favorites."

"Joe's, too," Judith said, scribbling on some Post-it notes. "I'm glad he was never like the cop Pacino plays."

"I wish Bill was like De Niro's bank robber," said Renie. "We could pay our bills." She spilled more kernels. "What are you writing?"

"Never mind," Judith said, reaching over to scoop out some popcorn. "Watch the movie."

Renie settled back on the sofa. Judith resumed writing.

The movie ended. The grandfather clock struck eleven. Judith clicked the remote, changing the station to KINE. The weekend anchors delivered the first three stories — none of which pertained to Dolph Kluger's murder — before going to a commercial break.

Renie had polished off the popcorn. "A grilled-cheese sandwich sounds good," she remarked.

"Shut up and watch the news," Judith said. "They must be about ready to show Mavis at headquarters."

They were, announcing breaking news as soon as the cameras came up again on the studio set. Mavis stood in the central booking area, every blond hair in place, Armani suit perfectly draped over her tall, slim body. "KINE-TV has just learned of an arrest in the poisoning case of world-famous music mentor and teacher Dolph Kluger who died earlier this week while visiting the city."

Rosemary had edged into the picture. Mavis turned slightly. "I have with me Detective Rosemary O'Grady, who arrested a suspect just an hour ago. Fritz Wittener, twenty-one, has been charged with second-degree homicide and is being interrogated even as we speak. Detective O'Grady, would you tell us how you broke this case?"

Rosemary had difficulty containing her glee. "It was my first homicide investigation. Naturally, I can't reveal all the evidence we have against the suspect. I checked birth records that showed that Fritz's real father was the late Dolph Kluger. Fritz hated Kluger for abandoning him. The murder was a simple matter of revenge. The solution was arrived at by solid detection and careful gathering of evidence, not only in the homicide case but the theft of a priceless violin bow. While the bow has not yet been recovered, I found evidence at the scene of the theft from a rental home near the site where I just made the Wittener arrest." Rosemary couldn't stop looking smug.

"Drat!" Judith exclaimed. "Rosemary never told us that! I figured the thief might have been Fritz because he could've taken his mother's key to Rudi's house. But he must have left some sort of evidence — footprints, fingerprints, whatever — that Rosemary found and kept to herself. The woman's a snake! To think I trusted her. At least until the past day or so. I had begun to wonder. She was acting differently."

"Thank you, Detective," Mavis said, turning around to look off to her right. "I also see that someone else is being brought in wearing handcuffs. Can you identify that person and the man I assume is a plain-clothes law officer?"

Rosemary also turned. Judith and Renie leaned closer for a better look. The prisoner was a stony-faced Elsa Wittener. The detective in charge of her was a solemn Levi Morgenstern.

"Aha!" Judith exclaimed. "Good for Levi! He's got the killer!"

Rosemary had gone pale. Mavis was trying to edge her out of the picture. Rosemary pushed back.

"Ooof!" Mavis grunted into the microphone before slamming an elbow into Rosemary's midsection. The detective fell out of camera range.

"It appears that there's some confusion," Mavis announced with total aplomb. "On the basis of a tip to this reporter earlier this evening, another person has been arrested and charged with Kluger's homicide. Elsa Wittener, Fritz Wittener's mother, is in custody and has confessed. We'll be standing by for more breaking news."

"Thank goodness," Renie said as Judith muted the volume, "Levi got to Elsa right away."

"I doubt that he had to go get her, even though I gave his name and number to Mavis," Judith said. "The first call Fritz was allowed to make undoubtedly went to his mother. She wouldn't let him take the rap for her crime. She probably walked right into the station before Levi could go after her. That ambitious little twit Rosemary withheld the information about Fritz breaking into the Wittener house and stealing the bow before he hid it — or part of it — in our basement."

"Why steal it in the first place?" Renie asked, bending down to retrieve a few stray popcorn pieces off the floor.

"Probably to get back at Rudi," Judith answered, "and sell it on the black market to make some money. That would've appealed to Fritz far more than marrying an unbalanced heiress like Suzanne. Anyway, he couldn't have known when he stole the bow that Suzanne was coming into big money." She stood up, walked over to Renie, and began sticking the Post-it notes on the sullied bathrobe.

"What the hell are you doing?" Renie demanded.

"Answering all of your damned questions," Judith retorted. "I'm sick of this case and these crazy, mixed-up people."

Renie started peeling the notes off her front. "This one says Fritz bought liquor, Elsa paid big bucks for it, knew Dolph liked brandy, 'more exotic the better.' Hey, this is like fortune cookies!"

"You don't need to read me what I wrote," Judith declared.

"Yes, I do," Renie argued. "Your handwriting is atrocious, especially when it's this small. Here — Rosemary concealed facts from you and Levi. 'Not sharing with partner — big no-no.' 'Elsa — poison book — easy.' Oh. Elsa swiped the poison guide. Easy because she worked there." Renie paused for Judith's nod of approval. "'Floorprints' — what the hell is that?"

"Foot- or fingerprint casts from Fritz," Judith said, "that Rosemary made at the Wittener house."

"Next is 'Where's the bow?' " She frowned at Judith. "And the answer is . . . ?"

Judith shrugged. "I don't know. If Fritz stole it, the priceless half disappeared. That's why he searched the basement and the toolshed."

" 'Rhubarb old rose.' Huh?"

*"Ruse."* Judith scowled at Renie. "The killer poisoning herself to divert suspicion."

"Got it." Renie peered at another note. "This says 'D's temper,' 'wrists,' 'ruined T's piano.' " She held up a hand. "Wait. I get it! Dolph taught Elsa, had a tantrum, smacked her on the wrists, and ruined any hope of a professional career for her."

"It must've been more than a smack," Judith said grimly. "Elsa still suffers from her disability. That kind of heartiness Dolph exhibited often coexists with a passionate person's darker side. That type is often an extremist. I can imagine how furious he could get with an unwilling or undisciplined student. Dolph would lash out savagely."

"Why did Elsa wreck Taryn's piano? Pure spite?"

"Probably," Judith said. "The piano — which both women played — may have been a symbol to Elsa. Not just for her failure to become a professional but maybe a symbol for Rudi. Taryn not only had undamaged wrists, but she also had Elsa's ex-husband."

Renie removed the last note, along with a burned popcorn kernel. "All this says is 'A' with a question mark."

"Andrea," Judith said. "The police will have to ask Estelle about that. I think she was at the foxhunt. When she first talked about it, it sounded as if she might have been an eyewitness — or at least have seen Blake's remains. I thought maybe I didn't understand her correctly. But later, when she got tipsy, she mentioned falling off her horse — as if it was something she actually had done on occasion. There was also her reference to Ichabod Crane, the headless horseman."

"Gack," said Renie.

"But most of all," Judith went on, looking sheepish, "I think Estelle was blackmailing Andrea. I found a checkbook in Estelle's belongings that showed monthly deposits of twenty-five grand. I'll bet she was milking Andrea ever since the so-called accident."

"Wow!" Renie tried to whistle, but, as usual, failed and made a whooshing noise instead. Then she scowled at her cousin. "Why didn't you mention that before — or to the cops?"

"Because it could have been an annuity or something innocent," Judith explained. "Estelle's father was the family chauffeur, remember? Maybe Blake's father or Blake himself had set up something for his faithful retainer's daughter. But I'll bet that Andrea somehow arranged that accident to Blake. How else can you dismiss the fact that Andrea and her riding partner avoided getting decapitated, too? As to whether Andrea's death was an overdose or suicide, I'm taking the latter. Maybe she wanted to get rid of Blake so that she could finally marry Dolph or at least get back together with him. Maybe she thought her husband's company was going down the drain and she wanted out before scandal struck. I don't know. But when Dolph was murdered,

Andrea must have felt it was retribution. She wasn't very stable, either. She decided to take the easy way out."

"Is that what sent Suzanne around the bend?" Renie asked. "She seemed a little odd, but not crazy until then."

"The bird in the gilded cage realized she could fly away," Judith replied. "It unhinged her. She was very fragile emotionally. Heredity, maybe."

"They were all a little nuts," Renie said, tossing the notes into the fireplace. "Maybe Gregory wasn't the only one who should have been kept in the loony bin."

"True." Judith grimaced. "And we're still stuck with Rudi and Taryn. I almost wish —"

"No, you don't," Renie interrupted.

"No," Judith agreed. "I can learn to love the violin easier than I can learn to love Herself."

Joe and Bill got home on a Sunday afternoon that boasted blue skies and clear autumn air. Their wives greeted them in the driveway.

"We both limited," Joe shouted before Judith and Renie could get off of the back porch. "Beauties, too. Bill got a thirty-pound and a twenty-two-pound King. Mine both came in right around twenty-four pounds. Who wants fish for dinner?"

"I do!" Renie cried, running over to her husband. "Kiss me, Fisher Fellow."

"You had a good time, then," Judith said, hugging Joe.

"Oh, man, did we! It was a little rough out on the ocean, but we didn't get seasick." Joe disengaged himself from his wife's embrace and opened a Styrofoam chest to show off their catch.

The wives oohed and aahed.

"Let's finish off this roll of film," Joe said. "We'll put the fish on this stick and hold them up."

"Good idea," Bill said as Joe picked a long, slim piece of wood out of the trunk.

Judith stared. Renie let out a yip.

"Stop!" Renie cried. "That's the bow!"

Joe eyed the wood curiously. "Why, so it is! Now, how did that get in with my fishing tackle?" He and Bill chuckled.

"Funny guys," Renie muttered.

"The reward," Judith said, her dark eyes huge. "Thirty-five grand!"

"Split two ways," Joe said. "Bill actually found it after I got my rod out."

Renie was jumping up and down. "Yay! We can pay off Saks! We can pay the plumber! We won't have to sell the house to Olive!"

"What?" said Bill, looking mystified.

"Never mind," Renie said.

Joe announced that he'd fire up the barbecue as soon as they unloaded the car. Judith decided not to mention the homicide case until later. By five o'clock, the alder chips were hot, the salmon steaks were basted with butter, and the two couples sat on the patio hearing the men recount their ocean adventures.

"A perfect day," Judith murmured as the phone rang.

Judith picked up the receiver from where she'd left it on the porch steps. The message was brief. She walked slowly back to the patio with a lame little smile on her face.

"What's wrong?" Renie asked in alarm.

Judith turned to Joe. "Give me my car keys. The mothers are coming to dinner."

Joe sighed. "There goes the perfect day."

# ABOUT THE AUTHOR

**Mary Richardson Daheim** is a Seattle native with a degree in communications from the University of Washington. Realizing at an early age that getting published in books with real covers might elude her for years, she worked on daily newspapers and in public relations to help avoid her own creditors. She is married to David Daheim, humanities professor emeritus, and lives in her hometown in a century-old house not unlike Hillside Manor, except for the body count. Daheim is also the author of the Alpine mystery series and the mother of three daughters.